Clare Connelly was raised in small-town Australia among a family of avid readers. She spent much of her childhood up a tree, Mills & Boon book in hand. Clare is married to her own real-life hero, and they live in a bungalow near the sea with their two children. She is frequently found staring into space—a surefire sign that she's in the world of her characters. She has a penchant for French food and ice-cold champagne, and Mills & Boon novels continue to be her favourite ever books. Writing for Modern is a long-held dream. Clare can be contacted via clareconnelly.com or at her Facebook page.

Joss Wood loves books and travelling—especially to the wild places of Southern Africa and, well… anywhere! She's a wife, mum to two teenagers, and slave to two cats. After a career in local economic development she now writes full-time. Joss is a member of Romance Writers of America and Romance Writers of South Africa.

D0540311

Discover more at millsandboon.co.uk.

DESERT KING'S FORBIDDEN TEMPTATION

CLARE CONNELLY

THE BABY BEHIND THEIR MARRIAGE MERGER

JOSS WOOD

MILLS & BOON

First published in Great Britain 2023
by Mills & Boon, an imprint of HarperCollins*Publishers* Ltd,
1 London Bridge Street, London, SE1 9GF

www.harpercollins.co.uk

HarperCollins*Publishers*, Macken House, 39/40 Mayor Street Upper,
Dublin 1, D01 C9W8, Ireland

Desert King's Forbidden Temptation © 2023 Clare Connelly

The Baby Behind Their Marriage Merger © 2023 Joss Wood

ISBN: 978-0-263-30677-4

05/23

This book is produced from independently certified FSC™ paper
to ensure responsible forest management.
For more information visit: www.harpercollins.co.uk/green.

Printed and Bound in the UK using 100% Renewable Electricity
at CPI Group (UK) Ltd, Croydon, CR0 4YY

DESERT KING'S FORBIDDEN TEMPTATION

CLARE CONNELLY

MILLS & BOON

PROLOGUE

THE WATER WAS always darkest near the surface, though that wasn't how it was meant to be. There, in the inches beneath atmosphere and air, there was supposed to be light, the sun's warmth permeating the thickness of the sea. Always, the water at the top shimmered. But this wasn't reality, it was a dream, a nightmare, and the laws of physics need not be obeyed.

He sucked inwards, seeking air, finding only water, drowning, reaching out, touching, feeling, remembering. Something foreign yet achingly familiar, close but always, always out of reach. The nearer he came to remembering, to catching the threads that danced on the periphery of his unconscious, the more they shimmied beyond his reach. A fleeting touch, soft and infinitely comforting, a fragrance—vanilla and persimmon—sunlight dancing on ancient timber floor boards, dust motes and laughter—his, and someone else's, a voice, a faraway, long-ago voice without a face.

Frustration gnawed and burst him from his dream; a young boy had been drowning, unable to find purchase in the darkness of the ocean's depths, but now a sheikh awoke, showing not a hint of the nightmare that had taunted him.

There were mysteries in his past, questions that dogged him when he allowed them to slip beyond his defences, but of one thing he was certain: the duty to rule Savisia was his and his alone, and Sheikh Tariq al Hassan would fulfil that destiny with his dying breath. Whatever was required of him, he would offer gladly. He owed this country that much, at least.

CHAPTER ONE

IT WASN'T SOMETHING she'd consciously sought, but nonetheless, it was an undeniable fact that Eloise Ashworth had become masterful at studying and understanding people. Like all skills, it had been borne of necessity, and her tumultuous young life, with parents who fought viciously nonstop, then her existence after their deaths, had sharpened already keen powers of observation.

Now, they were impossible to switch off, so she found her eyes lingering on the Sheikh's face for a moment too long. Where others might have simply glimpsed a look of benign disinterest, Eloise saw beyond it, to the small furrow of his brow, the slight narrowing of his eyes, the very barely noticeable clenching of his jaw, and she wondered—how could she not?—what had happened to frustrate him?

The obvious answer was that he wanted to avoid this marriage. That he didn't welcome it. Given that his palace had proposed it, three months earlier, that didn't make much sense. Unless someone else was pulling the strings? Her eyes swept the six men who flanked the powerful Sheikh of Savisia; she discounted the idea almost immediately. For no reason she could put her finger on, she didn't for a moment believe the powerful Sheikh was someone who could be made to do a thing he didn't want to. The marriage had been his idea, only he didn't like it, she was sure of it.

She leaned back a little farther in her seat, studying him quite openly. After all, no one was looking at her. Of the twelve people gathered to discuss the possibility of this match, she was the only woman, and the only attendee who didn't hold government office. She suspected her opinion and insights weren't of much value—even her seat was at the far end of the table, and not once had a single head turned in her direction, to ask for her thoughts. Ironic, really, given her best friend in the whole world, Crown Princess Elana of Ras Sarat, had sent Eloise with the sole purpose of determining if the marriage should go ahead. After all, the Sheikh had somewhat of a glittering reputation: he was heroic, intelligent, staunchly patriotic and adored by his people, but that didn't give any insight into what he was like as a man. In fact, his private life was incredibly well guarded, so repeated internet searches had brought up a heap of photographs at official events but nothing of interest beyond that.

And so, Eloise had been sent to evaluate the man, the potential of the marriage, and to go back to Ras Sarat ready to advise Elana.

It was Eloise alone that Elana would listen to; her counsel the only voice that would matter in determining if Elana would consent to the match. Oh, she wanted to marry Sheikh Tariq—or rather, Elana accepted the necessity of it. The truth, however, was that she didn't want to marry anyone, and if she'd been a private citizen, she would have grieved for her late fiancé for the rest of her life. Elana had loved deeply, and lost, and she wasn't likely to ever love again. But that wasn't what this prospective union was about: theirs would be a marriage of political expediency.

For all that Tariq's kingdom was large and fabulously wealthy, Ras Sarat was small, and decades of mismanagement had left it in a parlous financial and political state.

Marriage to a man like Tariq would shore up her government and provide a badly needed influx of money. It would also take an enormous burden off Elana's shoulders—a burden no one but Eloise understood she carried—and for this reason, Eloise desperately wanted to like the Sheikh. To believe he would be a good husband for her friend, that the marriage would work.

And so she watched him: as he spoke, but also, as he listened, and it was in these moments that she saw the most. The small flex of his jaw when he disagreed with something someone was saying, the inclining of his chin as he considered a point, the tightening around his mouth and eyes. His face remained quite expressionless for the most part, but she read beyond that. She saw the minute body language shifts that caused the air around him to reverberate, silent signals that she alone seemed aware of.

Papers were shuffled, chairs scraped back, and Eloise sat perfectly still, though now, it had less to do with the Sheikh's responses and more to do with a strange heaviness in her legs that made it impossible to move. She was staring at him to learn what she could of the man but somehow, something had shifted, and now her eyes lingered not for this purpose but rather, out of a selfish desire to see and study. Out of a hunger to look at him.

She was familiar with his appearance thanks to her internet snooping and the security file she and Elana had pored over. But there was something about him that didn't translate to two dimensional images. Where he was clearly handsome, there was a magnetism and charisma in real life that was impossible to ignore.

He was…spellbinding, and in that moment, for the briefest second, she felt the spell weave around her, ensnaring her exactly where she was.

As if he sensed her momentary weakness, in the flurry of activity as other advisors and diplomats pushed away from the table to take a short recess, his eyes sought the calm of the room, and landed with a thud on her.

They were beautiful eyes. Fascinating and shifting, compelling and magnetic, so that she couldn't do the wise thing and look away. Instead, her gaze locked to his, sparking something unfamiliar and unwanted in her bloodstream, making her conscious of every breath she took, of the way the hairs on her arms lifted.

He studied her with the same level of scrutiny she'd been regarding him with for the past hour, only this was far more pointed, more obvious. More entitled. He was a sheikh, and even if his personal bearing left anyone in any doubt of that, which it didn't, the room in which they sat would have served to underscore his incredible wealth and power. Enormous, with ceilings at least three times the normal height and a full wall of windows that overlooked a spectacular garden with pools of water and ancient date palms forming a spiky barrier, the walls were gold, the table a solid marble, and the Sheikh sat at a large chair, only slightly less dramatic than a throne—at its centre, commanding easily. He'd been raised to rule, his duty from birth had been to claim his birthright. With the death of his father, the beloved Sheikh Samir al Hassan, five months earlier, Tariq had taken on the role he'd been groomed for all of his life.

He was adored by his people—he always had been, ever since his parents had assumed the throne and he'd been catapulted into the role of heir apparent.

After that, his birthright had become an imperative—he embodied all the traits his people most admired. He was brave, honourable, strong, fearless. Not only was he

Sheikh—he became a teen idol, a heart throb, a celebrity feted and adored by all.

He regarded Eloise now with absolute impunity.

He studied without a hint of apology.

And when finally, Eloise gathered her wits sufficiently to push back her own chair, and reach for her folder with slightly trembling hands, he spoke in a voice that didn't invite a hint of dissent.

'You will remain a moment.'

She'd been listening to him speak all morning, so why did *these* words make her bones feel as though they were melting into puddles of nothing?

She lifted a hand and pressed it to her chest, between her breasts. 'Me?'

She cringed inwardly at the weakness the query showed, but his command had rattled her. Until that second, she hadn't realised how much she was looking forward to leaving the room and drawing in a deep breath. To looking at something *other* than this man.

He dipped his head once then gestured to the chair opposite him. 'Please.'

It was not said in the way 'please' usually was. This was no plea, no query of hopefulness. There was no expectation of a refusal. Suddenly, she was conscious of everything: the swish of her long, linen skirt as she moved around the table; the knocking of her knees; the shimmer of light streaming through the window and bouncing off the mahogany tabletop; the size of the room and the echo of his voice; the time it took—seconds that felt like years—to reach the chair opposite him; the feeling of the timber beneath her fingertips, cool and smooth, worn and ancient; his eyes on her with the same unashamed curiosity she'd exhibited all morning. She drew back the chair and sat into it. As a child, Eloise had studied dance. In fact, she'd lived for it, and though her great aunt hadn't approved of the lessons, the innate sense of grace and musicality hadn't left Eloise; it was evident even in the small motion of sitting down.

Only once seated did she drag her eyes to his, and the moment they connected, her bloodstream seemed to come to life for the very first time. She could *feel* it in her veins, rushing like a river, gushing through her, her arteries paper thin, almost unable to cope with the frantic deluge.

He was the Sheikh; this was his palace, his meeting, his request that she stay, and so Eloise sat perfectly still and silent even when her unending curiosity, combined with suddenly jangling nerves, had her wanting to blurt out the question: What do you want?

But she stayed as she was, hands clasped in her lap to disguise the telltale trembling, knees pressed hard together, body strangely energised and tingling all over.

'You were not introduced.'

Her lips pulled to the side in a wry acknowledgement of the fact. 'No, Your Highness, I wasn't.' What more could she say? That the Ras Sarat advisors didn't see the purpose for her being on this trip? That they'd fought her tooth and nail over every issue since her official appointment as one of Elana's advisors? If only they knew how vital her assessment would be in shaping this marriage. If Eloise reported back to Elana anything negative, then there would be no marriage, no union, and none of these negotiations would matter at all.

'Let's rectify that now.' Again, it was an order, rather than a suggestion, and this was no mere formality. There was a sharpness to his words, and she understood something else important about the man: he liked to be in possession of all the facts. He was wary and private. Negotiating this marriage was unpalatable to him, for some reason, but if he had to do it, it would be in front of trusted advisors only, not random women from foreign countries. 'Your name?'

'Eloise, Your Highness.' His eyes widened and then darkened, and her blood heated at the speculation she saw in his gaze. Her heartbeat kicked up a gear.

'Eloise?' he prompted, his voice rough and incredibly appealing. It was a shame that Elana had sworn she'd never like, much less love, her future husband. Eloise understood how badly heartbroken her friend was, but Sheikh Tariq would be quite easy to fancy.

Easy to fancy?

Easy to fantasise about, more like.

'Ashworth,' she added.

'English?'

She nodded.

'And yet you work for the royal family of Ras Sarat?'

'Yes, Your Highness.' 'Royal family' though, was a misnomer. There was only Elana and an old uncle related by marriage, who had ostensibly served as a regent for Elana in the years between her father's death and Elana's coming of age.

Again, his eyes flexed in that fascinating way, and something low in her abdomen stirred. She shifted a little in her seat, then wished she hadn't, because awareness was flooding her veins, and heating her most feminine parts, so she had to dig her fingernails into her palms to get a grip on the situation.

'For how long?'

She tilted her head to the side, torn between her duty as a representative of Ras Sarat and her confidence as a woman of the twenty-first century. The former won out—just. 'Three years.'

He frowned. 'You don't look old enough.'

Her smile was laced with a hint of amusement. 'I'm twenty-five, Your Highness.'

He rubbed a hand over his chin. 'The same age as the Princess.'

'Yes.'

'Do you know her well?'

'Yes.'

He leaned forward a little, eyes scanning her face. 'You're friends?'

Surprise at his perceptiveness held her silent a moment, but after a beat, she said, 'Yes.'

'Close friends?'

'You could say that.'

He lifted a brow and she had to remind herself that he was a powerful ruler of this wealthy country. For some reason, she found it easy to speak with him as an equal, but he wasn't, and their difference in rank needed to be observed.

'We're close, yes, Your Highness,' she murmured with deference.

His eyes narrowed once again. 'And she asked you to come to these negotiations and report back to her?'

Eloise hadn't expected the challenge, but it didn't bother her. She was used to being challenged, and if he wouldn't accept her presence, then the marriage would be in serious trouble. 'Is that a problem?'

'Not at all.' He surprised her by responding instantly. 'It's wise. The Princess and I met some years ago, but only briefly. I'd consider her a fool indeed to agree to this without a little more information.'

'Her advisors will assess the merits of the match,' she said after a moment, strangely pleased by his reasonable reply. 'But my job is…of a more personal nature.'

'I see.' And he *did* see, of that she was certain. If Eloise was an expert at reading people, then it was a skill she was certain she shared with this man. 'And if you don't approve?'

'The rest of the delegation is thrilled with your proposal,' she said instead.

'I am asking about your approval, though.'

She hedged the question again. 'Is there a reason you think I won't approve, Your Highness?'

His lips quirked in a quick sign of appreciation of her response. 'I don't know enough about you to say. After all, your own life experiences will colour your judgement, will they not?'

'I try to be impartial when advising Her Highness.'

'Even on matters such as this?'

She lifted her slender shoulders. 'This is the first marriage proposal I've considered on her behalf.'

Another quirk of his lips and her heart lifted. She liked seeing him smile. She really liked it. That scared her into straightening, the smile slipping from her face completely, her features assuming a mask of cool command.

'Does my presence bother you, Your Highness?'

'No.' His eyes homed in on hers. 'But your answers are illuminating.'

'Oh?' Her heart kicked up a gear.

'Am I right in presuming your input will matter most to the Princess?'

Her lips parted in surprise and his gaze dropped swiftly to her mouth, lingering for just long enough to scatter her thoughts in a billion directions, before his attention moved back to her eyes.

Eloise licked her lower lip, frowning a little.

'It is not a difficult question.'

'Isn't it?' she murmured, lips once more pulling to the side in an unconscious gesture of amusement.

'You tell me.'

'Well, Your Highness, while I hate to disagree...'

'Go on,' he invited, leaning forward.

'Well, then, if I answer in the affirmative, I'm essentially admitting to sidelining the members of her advisory cabinet who've travelled here to meet with you,' she pointed out sensibly. 'I would also be suggesting your time, which is, I'm sure, very valuable, has been wasted in these meetings about citizenship amnesties and debt forgiveness.'

'Because, despite the common-sense nature of those proposals, and the clear advantages to Ras Sarat in both of those arrangements, if you return to the Princess and tell her you don't like me, she won't go through with the wedding?'

Eloise pulled a face. 'It's not about whether or not I like you.' The last words were somewhat breathy. She cleared her throat. 'Your Highness.'

He ignored the addition of his title. 'Approve of me?'

'That's closer to the truth.'

'And what, pray tell, is your metric?'

'I'm sorry?'

'What tools are you using to assess my suitability?'

'I'm afraid it's not quite so scientific,' she said with another shrug. 'Ellie is my best friend in the whole world and has been for a long time. In truth, we're more like sisters; I know her better than anyone. I can't say what I'm looking for, but she deserves to be happy. And I don't know—I would like to know that you could make her happy, especially after all that she's been through.'

He ran a hand over his chin. 'I read about her fiancé.'

Eloise's face paled. It had been an awful time in Elana's life, which meant it had also been awful for Eloise. She swallowed, searching for what to say in response and decided there was nothing she could offer.

'She took his death hard?'

Eloise frowned. 'Of course, Your Highness.'

'They loved one another.'

She nodded, a small smile of nostalgia touching her lips. 'Madly.'

'I imagine she has mixed feelings about my proposal then.'

Eloise's eyes widened. 'I—' Damn it. She'd said too much. 'If Elana had decided against your offer, she would never have sent me.'

He was quiet, evaluating those words, and finally, he nodded once. 'And you also want this marriage to go ahead?'

How could she answer that without giving away the precarious circumstances the nation of Ras Sarat was in? The dire state of their economy and political system was something Eloise had no intention of revealing to this man. 'I make it a point to keep an open mind at all times.'

The flex of his brows intrigued her. A new reaction, one she hadn't witnessed yet.

'Besides being a loyal friend to the Princess, do you have any qualifications that makes you suitable for this role of trusted advisor?'

'The most important qualification is that she trusts me,' Eloise said softly. And that was saying something: Elana had frequently found herself surrounded by piranhas until Eloise had come to Ras Sarat. 'But I have other qualifications that she relies on, beyond this.'

'Such as?'

'Is it relevant, Your Highness?' Her eyes widened and cheeks glowed warm as she realised how she'd just spoken to him. 'I'm so sorry. That was unforgivably rude of me.'

'Direct, not necessarily rude. And in case you hadn't realised, I prefer frank conversations.'

'Nonetheless—'

'I'm not interested in your apology.'

He crossed his arms, drawing—and holding—her attention on his broad pectoral muscles. He wore the traditional thobes of his country, loose and crisp, but now, they showed a hint of the definition she'd observed in photographs online, pictures of him at events overseas, when he'd worn western clothes and his body had been more discernible. Her mouth went dry. She reached for a water glass before realising it belonged to the previous occupant of her chair.

The Sheikh stood and now it was his height that had her mouth drying out, and her eyes widening. He was easily six and a half feet, his frame and physique things of great beauty, of rare, fascinating proportions, so she felt as though she were in the presence of an ancient god. He moved to an ornately carved table at the end of the room and poured a fresh glass of water. Little pieces of lemon and pomegranate bobbed on the surface, and when he placed it in front of her, she caught a hint of the fragrance.

'Thank you,' she murmured.

He dipped his head once, but rather than returning to his own seat, he perched his bottom on the edge of the boardroom table, close enough that the fabric of his thobe draped a little over the arm of her chair. Surreptitiously, she moved both hands towards the water, out of the way of temptation. Temptation? A fine bead of perspiration dampened the back of her neck and she looked away hurriedly, focusing on the exquisite view she had through the palace window, of a grove of fig trees, planted in perfect lines, hundreds of years old so they were each enormous enough to provide a significant canopy.

'Your qualifications,' he prompted, voice silky and mesmerising and so close she could almost imagine it wrapping around her, filling the spaces inside her chest.

She swallowed hard then replaced the water glass to the table, keeping one hand on it as though it were an anchor to reality and her obligations to Elana. It would be an easy thing to narrate her resume to this man, but something held her back.

'Why do you think I have any, besides my friendship with Ellie?'

'Your presence here would not be tolerated if it were friendship alone.'

Her brows lifted up. 'My presence here is *barely* tolerated,' she muttered, before realising how revealing that comment was. Heat flooded her cheeks and she hoped like heck she wasn't blushing.

'You weren't here yesterday; no one seemed to expect you today.'

He was very, very perceptive.

'Yes, Your Highness. I didn't travel with the contingent.'

'Why not?'

There were two answers to that, both valid: she hadn't been wanted by the negotiators, and they'd gleefully done everything in their power to come without her. But more importantly, she never flew anywhere if she could avoid it. Even the thought of it had her breaking out in a cold sweat. 'I drove,' she said after a beat.

'From Ras Sarat?'

'It's not so far.'

'It must have taken days.'

'Yes.' She rushed to fill the silence before he could push her further. For some reason, her fear of flying wasn't something she intended to share with this man. It was too personal, made her feel too vulnerable and raw. 'I like to take the scenic route whenever I can.'

His frown showed that he wasn't convinced, but he didn't push the matter further.

'As for my qualifications,' she said, 'I obtained a law degree from Oxford, and an economics degree from the London School of Economics.'

If he was surprised, he didn't show it. If anything, he appeared validated, as though he'd suspected her credentials.

'You studied with the Princess?'

'At high school and Oxford, yes.'

He mulled on that a moment and finally moved to the door, opening it. 'We will resume now.'

As if they'd all been waiting just on the other side for this exact moment, a line of delegates began to file back into the boardroom, and Eloise stood, moving quickly back to her own seat at the end of the table.

Their interaction had been strange and unfulfilling, and his rapid closing of their conversation had left her dejected and disappointed. Deflated. She'd been enjoying sparing with him and having his undivided attention. It was hard not to feel resentful now that he was addressing a room filled with others.

But then, he spoke, and the entire world seemed to tip completely off its axis. 'These negotiations should resume in a week's time. There is no purpose continuing at this stage.'

The chief diplomat from Ras Sarat spluttered and Eloise felt her pulse skyrocket for a whole other reason now. Had she said something wrong? Had she frightened him off? She'd come here to appraise his suitability, not ruin any hope of the marriage. Though Elana would never love him, she desperately needed this to work out.

'But, Your Highness, with all due respect, this is a very

worthy match. While the finer details require some attention, surely you cannot intend to abandon the idea altogether?'

'Did I say that was my intention?' he asked coolly, addressing the portly man who'd responded.

'Well, no, but I cannot understand what other reason you could have for postponing—'

'Only that the Princess is yet to make up her mind. If she does not wish to marry me, arguing over import tariffs is a waste of all our time.'

'If Her Highness was not serious about the marriage, she would not have dispatched us so swiftly.'

'She would also not have sent an emissary to appraise my suitability as her husband,' Tariq said, and now Eloise *knew* her cheeks were as pink as they felt hot. All eyes in the room pivoted to her. 'A marriage is about more than trade arrangements and governmental cooperation. My own parents were an excellent example of the value of true partnership and cooperation.' Did anyone else in the room hear the underlying tension that accompanied that last statement? Eloise was conscious only of the Sheikh now, aware of every nuance and inflection in his voice. 'Her Highness has demonstrated great judgement in exercising caution despite the incentives for this wedding. But until Miss Ashworth is prepared to recommend the union to the Princess, it would be a waste of time to negotiate further.' He turned to Eloise with the full force of his attention now and all the air left her lungs in one crazy, wild whoosh.

'Therefore, Miss Ashworth and I will spend a week getting to know one another. I will make myself available to answer any of her questions. As the Princess will reside in Savisia, Miss Ashworth will also tour the palaces and familiarise herself with the culture of our country. At the end of that time, she will be better placed to offer her opinion to the Princess and, if suitable, we can resume negotiations then. Until that time, please, enjoy the hospitality of my palace, gentlemen.'

CHAPTER TWO

THE DIPLOMAT FROM Ras Sarat opened his mouth to reply but a man to the Sheikh's right beat him to it. 'His Highness has spoken.'

It was all that was needed to silence the rest of the room and move them towards the door. Eloise felt the barbed looks aimed in her direction as they filtered from the boardroom but she kept her back straight and pretended not to notice—ironic when she was such a keen student of human nature and expression. When they were almost all gone, she collected her folder and began to move towards the door herself, needing that fresh air and breathing space even more now.

'Not you, Miss Ashworth.'

Miss Ashworth. Hearing him address her in that way made her body tingle all over. 'Your Highness—'

'Yes, Miss Ashworth?'

Again? She dug her fingernails into her palms.

'Really, Your Highness, I don't think this is at all necessary.'

'Did I say anything you disagree with?'

He brow furrowed. 'Not exactly, but—'

'But?' He moved closer, his voice deep and mesmerising.

She swallowed, wondering if he felt the air crackling around them too. It was deeply inappropriate to reprimand a sheikh, particularly when acting as a representative for Elana, and yet she heard herself say, stiffly, before she could stop herself, 'I suppose a little notice of your intention wouldn't have gone astray.'

'I'm not in the habit of consulting anyone about my decisions.'

'Evidently.'

'Is that a mark against me already?'

Her lips quirked and again, despite the fact she knew she should be exhibiting purely deferential behaviour, she said, 'Let's just say I'm not a fan of autocracy.'

His laugh was as unexpected as it was delicious. She stared at him, open-mouthed, the sound rich and raw and virile and mesmerising. She gripped the back of a chair for support, and it was just about the only thing holding her upright.

'Let me see if I understand you, Miss Ashworth.'

She couldn't bear it any longer. It was so seductive to hear what his voice and accent did to her very prim surname. 'Eloise, please,' she insisted, allowing the informality on the basis that this man was very likely going to marry her very dearest friend, which would make them...friendly. It was okay for him to use her first name, surely!

'Eloise.'

Uh-oh. Hearing him say her name was like falling into a warm lagoon—even more dangerously seductive than the way he'd rolled his tongue around 'Ashworth'. She tried to tamp down on the butterflies in her tummy, but they beat their wings frantically regardless.

'You have come here uninvited—'

'I was sent here by the Crown Princess of Ras Sarat,' she interjected sharply, before she could stop herself.

His eyes narrowed. It was obvious that he wasn't interrupted by anyone, ever, and Eloise was almost as shocked as he! She had had three years of being spoken down to, denigrated, disrespected, and yet she held her course with calmness and dignity—always.

'Unexpected even by your own delegation,' he continued as though she hadn't spoken, and she was glad he didn't react, because her interruption was a misstep she didn't intend to make again. 'Your purpose in being here is to appraise me as a suitable husband. To ascertain the likelihood of your princess's happiness if this marriage were to proceed. I have signalled that I will work with you to make your job easier, and yet you think I'm somehow being…autocratic?'

He was right. This was above and beyond, and it would indeed make it easier for her to advise Elana. Nonetheless, Eloise couldn't help ticking her head to the side and studying him a moment.

'Say whatever it is you are thinking, Eloise.' Was he doing this on purpose? That time, he almost seemed to slow down as he said her name, like he could taste it, like it was the most delicious thing he'd ever tried.

'Only that we were speaking for several minutes, and there was ample opportunity for you to perhaps discuss your intention with me so it didn't come as quite a surprise when you announced it to the room.'

'Would you have agreed?'

'Elana is relying on me. Trusting me.'

'So you would have agreed?'

'We'll never know, as you didn't ask me.'

'I'm asking you now.' His arms crossed over his chest and the room seemed to shrink, so she was aware of him, her, and the volume of air between them, every little cubic centimetre of atmosphere. Her ears popped as though she were ascending a hill far too fast.

'Isn't that a little like shutting the gate after the horse has bolted?'

His eyes widened at her colloquial expression, and she wondered if she'd gone too far. 'You're doing everything you can to avoid agreeing with me, but you know that I am right.'

Her jaw dropped. He *was* right, damn it. 'I don't think a week is necessary,' she muttered. 'Your Highness,' she forced herself to add.

'We're talking about a lifetime commitment.' He waved a hand through the air. 'Take a week. Once Her Highness agrees to this, there is no turning back, for either of us.' Again, there was that look in his face of apprehension, of doubt. She leaned forward, breath held, fascinated by him, by his mind, his thoughts. Far too fascinated than was wise. 'I'm sure you'd prefer to know, beyond a shadow of a doubt, that your advice to her has merit.'

He had her cornered. There was no way she could refuse his suggestion now.

'Fine,' she said with a small nod, and then, because she worried she might seem churlish, she forced a smile to her lips. 'Thank you.'

His own smile showed; he saw through the polite acceptance, but she barely noticed his cynicism. Her eyes were transfixed by the curve of his mouth, and the beauty it gave his chiselled, symmetrical face.

'My chief of staff will have your things moved to the palace.'

'The palace?' She gaped. 'That won't be necessary. I have a perfectly adequate hotel room in the city.'

'You are here to appraise your princess's future life, are you not?'

She bit down on her lower lip, nodding slowly.

'Then you'll come and stay at the palace. Live as she would live. It will be the best way to give qualified advice.'

Another excellent point, but she wanted to buck against it. But the room...the man...everywhere she looked, she was reminded of his power and importance, his political prestige. It was in his air, his manner, his assessing gaze. He was not a man to be argued with—not over details that barely mattered. 'If you're sure, Your Highness.'

His chuckle was softer this time, and slower, so it wrapped around her like tentacles of smoke, pulling her towards him even when she stayed perfectly still.

'I'm sure, Eloise. Come, my chief of staff will take you to a guest suite.' He moved towards the door, big and strong, his thobe billowing behind him. She could only watch, frowning, as he drew near the door then pulled it inwards. He turned to face her, their eyes locked, and the floor seemed to give way.

'Do not look as though I am about to feed you to a pack of wolves. I assure you, it's not necessary.'

'What was that all about?'

'Showing my future wife the kindness of respecting her decision-making process? Do you think I erred?' Tariq pushed his own best friend and trusted advisor, studying the man carefully. A view of the Savisian gulf glistened in the distance, the sun bouncing off the surface as it often did by day. Though never, Tariq remembered with a shiver, in his nightmares.

'Of course not. I did wonder, however, if you were having second thoughts?'

'No,' he denied sharply. After all, Tariq didn't have the luxury of second thoughts. Not after what he'd learned. His lips tightened at the memory of the conversation he'd endured five months earlier, a day after burying his beloved father. It was the kind of conversation one could never forget, words that had shaken him to the foundation of his core, changing every single thing he knew about life and his place in it. The indefinable sense of rightness to his position in Savisia, to his role as ruler, was suddenly awash, adrift on the very same turbulent ocean that had swollen and rocked his sleep for years.

'Your father never wanted you to learn the truth, my darling. He was adamant I could not tell you.'

Tariq had considered that. For as intrigued as he'd been by his mother's pronouncement, he was also unfailingly faithful to his father, and trusted his wishes implicitly.

'If this secret mattered so much to him to keep, perhaps you should hold it for a little longer?'

'I can't. His death changes things.'

Her worry had been obvious and Tariq, ever the protector, had hated seeing her upset. He'd crouched beside her, bracing for whatever was to come.

'What things?'

She'd pleated the fabric of her pale skirt, fingers working meticulously to form line after line after line. He'd watched the gesture, waiting, every cell in his body locked.

A sob had bubbled from his mother. Such a shocking sound, he'd been a child once more, afraid of the dark, of small spaces, afraid even of his own shadow at times. Those were irrational fears he'd overcome many years earlier, fears his father had helped him face and rise above. Now, he feared nothing, not even the march of time itself.

But his mother's sadness…

It was too much.

'Your burden is heavy. Tell me, what is it? I promise, it will change nothing, Mother. Nothing of importance.'

What a fool he'd been then! So arrogant, so self-assured. He hadn't understood that he was standing on a shifting piece of earth, that his place in Savisia was subject to any force that might exert itself, at any point. He'd crouched beside his mother as she relayed the truth of his birth to an unknown mother, in a foreign country. There'd been an accident when he was just a baby; he'd been badly hurt, his family—two parents and a brother—had died, leaving him alone in the world.

The Sheikh and his Sheikha had found him on a routine tour of the hospital. His father had not been the ruling Sheikh, but only the younger brother. There was no plan for him to inherit the throne and what they did in their private life was exactly that—private. Years of infertility had meant his mother had suffered miscarriage after miscarriage. She was broken-hearted, facing a childless life, and yet here was a baby, all alone in the world, who needed her, desperately.

'I loved you from the moment I saw you, darling, and I knew, somehow, that the woman who'd given birth to you would have been grateful, would have wanted me to take you, because I would always love you.'

Tariq's father had fought it. It went against his customs, his beliefs, and while within their country, adoption was legal and practiced in circumstances such as this—when it was merciful to take a child into your home and raise them, when there was no blood relative left who could take custody—it was not commonplace enough to believe that it was a path open to them, members of the royal family. Even second brothers had constant scrutiny to deal with.

But Tariq's mother had refused to leave him.

She'd insisted. And fought. And cried. And on the tenth day of their tour, the Sheikh had relented. They would care for him for one month, he'd suggested. Just a month, while he got back to good health and an alternative was found.

Of course, one month turned into three, and then a year, as the little boy from Spain smiled and laughed and hugged them when he cried, so they both fell completely in love and realised he was their son in every way that mattered. Their intent had been to move to a small village and live a quiet life, just the three of them, but fate had other ideas...

He was so like them, with his dark skin and black eyes, dimpled cheeks and intelligent, inquisitive nature. It was impossible not to feel that in all the way that matters, Tariq truly was theirs.

They could never have known that by bringing him home and passing him off as their son, they would one day foist an outsider onto the throne, that they were asking the country to accept someone originally of a wholly different nationality as their ruler. The bloodline, an ancient pride of all Savisians, had ended with his parents.

Tariq was an imposter.

But there was salvation: an idea that had come to him in the middle of the night, when he recalled something he'd learned in grade school. His country and Ras Sarat had, hundreds of years earlier, been one and the same. Lands and borders had shifted over time, alliances had ended, but the bloodline remained intact. The Crown Princess Elana was royal, and in her body flowed the ancient royal lines that mattered so much to his people. By marrying her, he could redeem himself and ward off any possible claim another party might make to the throne.

For though he was not, as it turned out, born to rule, he had been bred for it, and little else. He knew he was an excellent sheikh, and that was all that mattered.

His marriage to Elana must go ahead at any cost: even if

that meant hand-holding Eloise around the kingdom for the next seven days to ensure his generous and common-sense proposal was accepted.

'I have no second thoughts,' Tariq reiterated with the will of iron for which he was renowned. 'The wedding makes sense. It has to happen.'

'Yes. And it doesn't hurt that your intended bride is utterly stunning, I suppose.'

Tariq considered that, trying to conjure a mental image of the Crown Princess. Only there was another pair of eyes that flooded his brain, wide-set and the creamiest, almond butter–brown with flecks of gold and thick dark lashes. A heart-shaped face with a dainty ski jump nose and a swan-like neck that was perfectly in proportion to her fine-boned, dainty body. Unlike his swarthy complexion, her skin was obviously creamy pale, though slightly tanned courtesy of her life in sun-drenched Ras Sarat. Her fingers had been so fascinating, her nails short and sensible but somehow… beautiful.

Eloise.

Even just her name had an effect on him, so he ground his teeth together, forcing his legendary focus onto the matter at hand.

He hadn't been with a woman since his father fell ill. His body was craving what he could not have—and it was abundantly clear that the very best friend of his future wife was not a suitable partner. Any and all fantasies from this point on were strictly forbidden.

Even if her Cupid's bow lips had drawn his attention as she'd gulped back water, and made him imagine them cupped with just as much enthusiasm around another, worthier vessel…

He bit back a curse and gripped the railing more tightly.

'Beautiful or not, she is royal, and she is available. Having met her once or twice, I know she's sensible and conversant in the ways of royal life.' He shrugged. 'That's the beginning and end of my wish list.'

Jamil considered his friend a moment and then nodded. 'Then you should do everything you can to win over Miss Ashworth.'

Tariq didn't think about the fun he could have if he truly wanted to win her over. After all, he'd sworn he couldn't have her, so there was no purpose wondering just exactly what she'd sound like when he kissed her.

There was only a little over an hour between being shown to the most sumptuous suite of rooms she could possibly imagine, and a servant appearing at her door, asking her to come to meet with Tariq. She wasn't sure what she'd expected, but at the servant's arrival, her heart had leaped into her throat. She thought of the brief text message exchange she'd shared with Elana, and her friend's gratitude.

This is perfect, Lissie. You're such a good judge of character and a week gives you long enough to really come to understand him. I owe you so much for this.

Of course, that wasn't accurate. Elana had saved Eloise, and they both knew it. In high school, she'd been utterly miserable, and Elana had sensed that, had made her smile again, had helped her through the darkness of grief and displacement. They were true best friends in every way, always looking out for each other.

I could never let you marry a man I didn't approve of. I'm glad to have the opportunity to appraise him.

She added a 'fingers crossed' emoji, then slipped her phone into the deep pocket of her dress, falling into step behind the staffer. This was about Elana, and what was right for her, nothing else. Certainly not the buzzing in her belly at the thought of seeing the Sheikh again.

She turned her concentration to the building, forcing herself to admire the enormously high ceilings, carved from marble and stone, with gold leaf detailing at the top of each pillar, and then the sparkling white tiles beneath them, marble as well, with a vein running through them that looked like silver. She ached to stop walking and take a closer look, to chase a vein with a fingertip and feel it pulse beneath her skin.

She adored history, and the ancient buildings of this part of the world were quite beyond compare. It wasn't just the grandiose furnishings and architecture she admired, but the older relics, too, like the tapestries that were hung with details of life millennia ago. She looked at them wistfully as they passed, making a mental note to come back another time and pore over them one by one, to understand this ancient, beautiful land.

The Royal Guard of Savisia was evident here, with armed guards in traditional uniforms standing sentry at each doorway. She passed twelve before the staff member leading her turned into another corridor, this one lined on one side with windows that framed a distant view of the sparkling ocean. Here, there were vases on either side of the corridor, with enormous arrangements of flowers that were native to this region. She breathed in the fragrance as they passed and was strangely homesick for Ras Sarat.

When had that country come to feel like home? When had she stopped craving the rolling fields of the Cotswolds, the sound of bees buzzing over the blackberry vines in spring, the feel of milky sun on her skin and late-afternoon rain, drizzling all around? She couldn't say, only that while she still loved England, it was very firmly a part of her past now, rather than where she felt she belonged.

Perhaps that old adage was right: home is where the heart is, and to all intents and purposes, her heart was with Elana. She had no family left of her own. Her parents had died, her great aunt had passed. There was no one else. Just Eloise. She and Elana were kindred spirits in that way.

Which was why she had to get this right.

It was a huge responsibility, but she knew Elana, and she knew what she wanted in a partner—what she deserved. Not love, because that wasn't what Elana wanted, but respect, happiness and similar life outlooks that would make sharing the rule of both countries easy. She also knew the dire straits of the Ras Sarat economy, and how much pressure was on Elana's young shoulders, so if there was any way of making this work, Eloise was determined to see that happen.

With renewed purpose, she followed the servant all the way to an enormous pair of doors, framed on either side by floral arrangements at least as tall as she was.

The servant knocked, and Eloise waited, trying to ignore the way her stomach was somersaulting.

It was no use.

As soon as the doors opened inwards, and she saw the stunning room, with Sheikh Tariq in the centre, her heart slammed into her rib cage and her knees felt weak. It was an effort just to smile at him, and she was sure the result was a travesty of tight-lippedness.

'Eloise.' She was half tempted to ask him to revert to calling her *Miss Ashworth*. Anything to stem the strange sensation overtaking her body.

'Your Highness.' She dipped into a curtsey out of habit, then straightened.

'How is your accommodation?'

Her lips twisted. 'Beautiful, thank you.'

'Good.' He nodded, and there was something in his eyes that made her feel as though he genuinely cared for her comfort. She ignored that—it was all about Elana. As it should be.

'Are those the rooms Elana would occupy, as your wife?'

His eyes were loaded with speculation when they met hers. 'My wife will share my apartment,' he corrected. 'It's more than big enough for two, or more.'

She was so conscious of the thundering of her pulse, she wondered how he didn't hear it. The noise was loud enough to flood her ears.

Reminding herself she was here to find out as much as she could about this man, she forced herself to put aside her own peculiar reactions and do what this position required of her. 'More?' she prompted easily.

'Well, yes. Naturally children will be required.'

'Children, plural?' she prompted, something wistful twisting in her gut. Flashes of desires she'd pushed to the back of her mind a long time ago suddenly danced right in the centre of her vision, so for a moment, all she could remember was her fervent hope for a large family. As an only child, she'd had a quiet childhood and hers had been particularly lonely. She'd craved noise and love and fun, all the idyllic notions she'd conjured as she'd sat solitary, reading or colouring. But then, her parents' vicious fighting had overshadowed that, and Eloise had come to crave solitude and silence—a life lived alone, without the risk of pain her parents had seemed to delight in inflicting on one another, and splashing back onto Eloise, on a daily basis.

'That would be my preference. I grew up without a sibling,' he said, after a brief pause. 'It is a large burden to place on a child's shoulders.'

'What burden is that?'

'Inheriting the throne.'

She nodded thoughtfully. She'd heard Elana make a similar remark often enough. She didn't doubt it was the truth. But hearing it from this man intrigued her—far more than it should have. Frustrated by her ever-present curiosity, she told herself she was only acting as an agent for her friend. 'Do you resent it?'

'Not at all.' His response was swift.

'And yet, you feel it to be a burden?'

'It's a precarious position,' he said after a beat. 'Your friend and I are in the same scenario. There is no spare, for either of us. Marriage, and children, is a sensible precaution.'

'So you'd want children quickly?'

'I wouldn't see any point in delay,' he said with a shrug, as though it barely mattered.

That gave her a moment's pause, and she couldn't say why.

'Is that a problem?'

'I can't speak for Ellie.'

'Isn't that why you're here?'

'To see for her,' she corrected with an involuntary smile. 'There's a difference, Your Highness.'

'Indeed.' He gestured to a banquet style table behind them. 'I presume you haven't eaten lunch?'

'In fact, I haven't had breakfast,' she said. 'I was late to the meeting this morning and didn't get a chance.'

'Then let's eat while we talk.'

Right on cue, her stomach gave an almost audible growl. She fell into step beside him, and at the table, he put his hands on a chair, pulling it back, dark eyes watching her intently, indicating she should take a seat.

Her heart had lodged firmly in her throat. She stared at him for a few seconds too long then moved to the chair, consternation rioting inside her at his gesture. The last thing she wanted was to move anywhere near that close to him. Steeling herself for the inevitable, she approached the chair warily, eyeing it, before sliding into it quickly, her breath rushed as he eased the seat into the table. As he went to move to his side, his hand brushed her shoulder and a thousand sparks ignited through her bloodstream, so her eyes flew to his face, wondering if he'd felt the same searing connection, the electric shock of awareness.

He gave nothing away, and she felt like a fool for such an obvious response.

He took the seat opposite, and despite the size of the table, it felt far too intimate. It was absurd. They were in a state dining room, and yet, the fact they were alone made her all too aware of him as a man, rather than a sheikh. Suddenly, she wished, more than anything, that she had more experience with men! A few dates in college, one semi-serious boyfriend a couple of years ago, didn't exactly leave her with the sort of blasé attitude she suspected would come in handy right about now.

It was simply the novelty of this, that was all.

'Do you think the Princess would prefer to wait before starting a family?'

It was surreal to lurch from fantasising about him one minute to imagining him married to her best friend the next. She almost had whiplash at the conflicting notions.

'With respect, I've told you, Your Highness, it would be indiscreet of me to speculate.'

'Shouldn't this go both ways?'

'Meaning?'

'You're here to learn what you can, but it occurs to me you can provide information about my prospective bride that I don't currently possess.'

'Wouldn't you prefer to get to know her in person?'

He shrugged nonchalantly. 'That will come.'

A shiver ran down her spine and she looked at the food, simply for something to do, as a distraction. Tariq changed gears, gesturing to the dishes and explaining each delicacy carefully, before easing back in his chair and watching her through hooded eyes.

She took a few scoops of various meals, then a sip of her drink, before she felt brave enough to meet his eyes again.

'Does it make you uncomfortable?'

Feeling utterly transparent, her eyes widened. 'Does *what* make me uncomfortable?'

'Talking about Elana.'

'Oh.' Relief rushed through her. 'Not talking about her, *per se.* But sharing her personal details and wishes, yes.'

'And yet, you expect me to bear my soul—'

'I expect no such thing, Your Highness,' she promised, instinctively shying away from the idea of that. This man's soul, she suspected, would be every bit as dangerously fascinating as his body and face.

'Then how can you advise your friend properly?'

'I don't need to understand all your inner secrets to know if you're capable of making her happy. It's enough to see that you're decent and kind.'

'These are the traits you value most?'

'What I value is beside the point. I'm only thinking of Elana.'

'Of course,' was his whip smart response. 'And this is what she's looking for in her marriage?'

'Isn't everybody?'

He pulled a face. 'That's quaint.'

'You're making fun of me?'

'Perhaps I am.'

'Why?'

'People get married for many reasons, some considerably more mercenary and cynical than you're suggesting.'

Her lips parted. 'You take a dim view of marriage?'

'I proposed to the Princess, didn't I?'

'Why did you?' she asked, the question one she posed to satisfy her own curiosity.

'As I said, with no siblings, the lineage is imperilled. Until my father died, that didn't seem so urgent. Now, I'm the last remaining Sheikh. A situation I intend to rectify.'

'I see.' She dug her fork into a chickpea and prune curry, the fragrances making her stomach clench. She tasted it, then moaned, as delightful flavours assailed her. 'This is wonderful,' she said quickly.

'You seem fixated on the issue of children,' he said, ignoring her rapturous praise for the food. 'Is there a reason for that?'

Her heart went into overdrive. 'Such as?'

'A reason you think this might be a problem for your friend?'

'A problem? No, nothing like that.' In truth, she knew Elana understood the necessity of children. But it would break her friend's heart to bear those children to a man other than her late fiancé. It was a grief Eloise hated knowing Elana would need to go through. 'We haven't discussed it in years,' she murmured. 'But Elana has, as you pointed out, the same motivation as you. I'm sure she'll be amenable to your schedule.' She took another bite of food, then a sip of water, before hastily adding, 'But I'm not committing her to that. Obviously, that's a conversation the two of you will have to have, if you decide—'

'I have decided,' he said, quickly. 'I want to marry her. The only remaining choice is hers.'

Something strange panged in Eloise's side. She felt as though she were being pressed into with the sharp blade of a knife.

'Why Elana?'

'Why not?'

She pulled a face. 'You can just tell me if you don't want to answer a question, Your Highness.'

His smile was perfunctory. 'Our cultures have a long, entwined history. It makes sense.'

'Yes,' she said, wondering at the emptiness in her gut. 'It does.'

'But you are English. Do you find the idea of an arranged marriage strange? Unpalatable?'

'If you and Elana are in agreement, it hardly matters what I think.'

'Nonetheless, I'm interested.'

She pressed a finger into the rounded tip of her fork, steadying her nerves. 'What if you don't like my opinion?'

'It will change nothing about mine,' he said. 'Your opinion is exactly that—your thoughts.'

'Well, then, Your Highness, seeing as you asked, I find the idea of any marriage off-putting.' She lifted her glass from the table without drinking from it.

'Why?'

'I'm not sure. Probably because my parents' marriage was such a red-hot mess.'

'In what way?'

They were straying into territory that really didn't matter, and yet she didn't point that out to him. 'They were miserable together. They fought all the time.' She smiled to hide the pain of those memories. 'They only stayed together because of me. I can't tell you how many times I found myself wishing they'd just put each other out of their misery and divorce. I must be one of the only children who's felt that way,' she said with a shake of her head.

'What did they fight over?'

'The air they breathed,' she responded sharply. 'Absolutely, unfailingly everything. They were so different; I can't believe they ever thought it would work out between them. My mother was a control freak—a lawyer, in fact—and incredibly unyielding about everything in her life. She was neat and fastidious and anxious. My father was a total hippy who couldn't hold a job for longer than a week. He was messy and drank alcohol until he was loud and silly—not that I realised that at the time. He would forget to do the jobs she'd asked him to take care of.' She tried to get control of her emotions, to push the heavy memories away. 'Anyway, they died a long time ago.'

'I'm sorry.'

She lifted her shoulders. 'I was sad, of course, but in some ways, I was also quite numb. Every day of my life felt like such a roller-coaster, their deaths was just another drop off the side. Does that make sense?'

He nodded once. 'I imagine you got in the habit of carefully guarding your emotions around them, so that you had some defence mechanism already in place when they passed away.'

Her eyes were saucer-like in her face when they lifted to his. It was the most succinct way of describing exactly what she'd felt. 'Yes,' was all she could say, though it was completely inadequate.

'And so you've decided to avoid marriage in case it turns out like theirs?'

The question brought her closer to what they'd been discussing, but she was off kilter, feeling raw and exposed by the things she'd just shared with him, memories she usually kept far from the surface washing over her now.

'I...haven't made any firm decision,' she said with a slightly haunted expression. 'But it's a moot point, anyway.'

'Oh?'

'I'm not seeing anyone,' she said, wondering if he heard the brittle tone to her voice.

'Why not?'

She lifted her brows. 'Is it a prerequisite?'

'I'm just curious.'

'Why?'

'Because you're here.'

She laughed softly. 'Gee, thanks.'

'That's not intended as an insult.'

She sighed. 'I work long hours,' she said after a pause.

'As an advisor to the Crown Princess?'

'Yes.'

'What other matters do you advise her on?'

She hesitated. The state of the Ras Sarat economy wasn't a secret, but Eloise felt disloyal to go into too much detail. 'A broad range,' she hedged carefully.

'And if she chooses to marry, will you accompany her here?'

The question was far more loaded than it should have been. Something inside her chest lurched and she found the vision of that future strangely barbed. 'I...couldn't say,' she said after a beat. 'It would depend on Elana's wishes.'

'It sounds to me like she relies on you a great deal. Will that end when she marries?'

'She'd have your advisors, Your Highness. And you.'

'And yet she'd also have her hands full, adapting to life

here, and as my Sheikha. Your support would no doubt be invaluable.'

'If she felt that way, of course I would accompany her,' Eloise agreed finally, wondering why it felt like she was inking a deal with the devil. Something was warning her that she should keep her distance from this scenario, that for all she wanted to serve and help Elana, her own needs might come into conflict with those goals.

She didn't like that feeling.

For as long as she could remember, she and Elana had been on parallel tracks. She didn't like the idea of coming to a point where she could no longer serve her friend. And why shouldn't she come to Savisia? What difference would it make where she lived? It was a question she couldn't answer, but she knew, on some intuitive level that it *did* make a difference, and she suspected the man opposite was the beginning and end of that reason.

CHAPTER THREE

'IT'S SO MUCH bigger than I realised,' Eloise said, staring down the hallway at the palace and then, at the man beside her. 'Are you sure you have time for this?'

'This wedding is of the utmost importance to me. You have my full and undivided attention for the next seven days. Starting with a tour of the palace.'

Her eyes flared wide, as they often did, and he felt a strange rush inside him. Desire. He'd stopped pretending he didn't recognise the feeling around the time she first tasted the chickpea curry. Her eyes had fluttered shut, her lips had swollen and parted, and she'd made a noise that was, oh, so similar to what he'd envisaged she might sound like if he were to kiss her. He'd found it almost impossible to think straight from that moment on. He'd stumbled through the rest of the meal, giving far too much attention to the full sweep of her lips, the curve of her breasts, the gentle movements of her hands, so he'd been as hard as a rock when their coffee had been cleared away. Grateful for his generous thobe, he'd suggested a tour in the hope the historical detail of the palace would take the edge off his physical awareness.

The only problem was that Eloise Ashworth was clearly a history buff. Every room they entered enticed such a delighted, cooing response that if anything, his awareness of her was growing by the minute.

It was…unexpected.

Reminding himself he'd had months of abstinence, he assured himself that he could slake his needs with another woman and return to the status quo tomorrow. Only…the idea left him cold. There was no woman he could think of in that moment that he wanted in his bed as he did Eloise.

And she was one woman he absolutely, definitely couldn't touch. His marriage to Princess Elana was the insurance policy he desperately needed. Through her legitimate place on the throne of Ras Sarat could he stave off any future challenges to his own rule. Such a challenge would not be based in law—technically, the fact that Tariq had been legally adopted meant he was conferred with the same rights as a biological child, in this instance that made him the heir to the throne. But something theoretical was not necessarily the case in reality and he couldn't imagine the people of Savisia happily accepting a foreigner as their Sheikh—not without an added legitimisation of his place on the throne, such as marriage to the Crown Princess of Ras Sarat.

Desiring his future wife's best friend was a recipe for disaster. Grinding his teeth together, he nonetheless allowed himself to move closer under the guise of gesturing to one of the tapestries that adorned the walls in the morning room.

'My mother uses this space to entertain,' he said. 'She likes the decorations.'

'So do I,' Eloise murmured. 'These tapestries are stunning. How old are they?' She spun around, perhaps not realising how close they were now standing, and she very nearly bumped into him.

Her lips parted and warm breath pressed to his cheek, courtesy of the face that was tilted to his. 'I—'

He knew he should say something to take the awkwardness out of their situation, but he didn't want to. He liked watching the expressions flitting across her face, showing that her own awareness of him was distracting her, making her contemplate something that they should both assiduously avoid.

'You?' he prompted, and with the spirit of the devil stirring, he leaned forward, ever so slightly, so her eyes fluttered shut quickly. He stared at her face with surprise, as if just realising how beautiful she was.

He'd been attracted to her immediately, but in Tariq's experience, desire was never hung on one thing or another—he was just as likely to be drawn to a woman who made him laugh as he was a woman he found physically appealing. But Eloise was like a finely crafted doll, her features exquisite and somehow hauntingly fragile, so they stirred something quite protective and defensive in his chest.

Her throat shifted as she swallowed and before he could stop himself, he lifted a hand, his finger pressing to the base of her jaw, so her eyes skittled open and lanced his. But hers were heavy with her own needs, as though she were wading through desire just to be able to look at him. 'This is—'

He said nothing this time, only stared. Her pulse was racing beneath his fingertips. Whatever she might say, her body's response to his was obvious.

Which was, as a point of fact, an enormous problem. If his desire was one-sided, then he'd never dream of acting on it. It would have been easier to ignore her. Knowing she felt as he did made him want to rip the long, elegant dress from her body and take her right there on the ancient rug at their feet, to hell with who might interrupt them, to hell with anything.

Not since he was a teenager, and perhaps not even then,

had he felt so overcome by his physical needs. Even with his monumental control at play, Tariq wasn't sure he could keep this situation in check. Nor that he even wanted to.

'Your Highness.' Her breathy words were a plea and God help him, hearing her call him by his title made his already rock-hard arousal strain painfully against his pants. 'I think…'

He waited, staring at her, heat buzzing between them, the air thick with their breaths and awareness, with a mutual, desperate need. 'You are very beautiful.'

It was not something he'd intended to say.

Her eyes fluttered shut but she stayed where she was, dangerously, tantalisingly close. And then, of its own volition, his hand lifted, finding a stray clump of dark hair and tucking it behind her ear.

'Your Highness.' Now her voice shook a little. 'Stop.' But she whispered the last word, and if anything, swayed forward, so their bodies touched and electricity arced frantically around the room, lightning striking in response to the physical contact. 'We can't—'

'No,' he agreed, not moving. 'We can't.' His hand dropped to her chin. He'd meant to pull his hand away, but it sought her flesh, desperate to touch, to feel her skin for himself, and it was every bit as soft as he'd predicted. Like a rose petal on a dewy morning. He bit back a curse.

She lifted her face to his, and his hand moved, not down, as he'd intended, but higher, so he could trace the outline of her lower lip. Her breath released in a shuddering exhalation, and then her teeth pressed to her lip, her eyes clinging to his, swirling with a need he well understood—it was the same need rocking him to his foundations.

'It's crazy,' she whispered, eyes huge, but still she stayed where she was.

She was exactly right. He felt temporarily insane, made so by the depth of physical desire flushing his system.

'I intend to marry her,' he said, as if to agree with Eloise.

The colour drained from her cheeks and she blinked at him, as if the words didn't make sense.

'And yet,' he muttered, hating himself, hating her too, just because something about her was capable of making him want things he absolutely shouldn't.

'Your Highness,' she whispered plaintively.

'Perhaps you should call me Tariq.'

She shook her head, dislodging his thumb. His hand dropped to their sides, and captured hers, fingers weaving together.

'I can't. That's too…real.'

He understood. They were in an alternate reality, or at least one adjacent to the real world, but boundaries still mattered.

'I've never met anyone like you,' she said, and something ancient and primal soared in his chest. 'I don't usually feel…'

'What do you feel?' he asked, frustrated, when she trailed off into nothing.

'Isn't it obvious?'

His pulse slammed through his body. 'I want to kiss you.'

She groaned, shook her head slightly, but then, she was lifting up onto the tips of her toes, her mouth a mere inch from his. 'This is so wrong.'

She was right. It was crazy and wrong and also utterly unavoidable. Being alone with her made this inevitable—perhaps they should have realised that before now and avoided a situation like this. But they were here, and it was impossible to think they'd be interrupted. Not here, not now.

'Do you want me to stop this?'

Her smile was sardonic. 'Do you think you can?'

His eyes flared at her acknowledgement. She too felt the inevitability of this. 'No.' And he dropped his mouth then, closing the distance and kissing her as though his life depended on it. She tasted like coffee and almond essence, and he plundered her mouth desperately, seeking more of her, all of her. His hand lifted to the back of her head, cradling her, so he could steady her for his thorough inspection, his tongue flicking hers at first before taking complete control of her mouth, revealing every part of her for his delight. His body was so much bigger than hers, he felt he practically enveloped her as they stood like that, her own slight curves moulded to his frame, her breasts softly crushed to his torso, so he growled into her mouth, his free hand lifting to stroke the side of her stomach before moving higher, his fingers finding the underside of her breast and running over it possessively, hungrily. There was nothing languorous about his touch; he needed her with a ferocity that could have terrified him, and his kiss was a signal of that.

She kissed him back with the same fervent need though, her breathing frantic, her body writhing against his, as if trying to *feel* more of him than their clothes allowed.

He swore, desperate for more, reaching down and finding the expansive fabric of her skirt, pulling it up, and up and up, over her legs, until he held it bunched in his hands and he could reach around and cup the silk of her underpants, pushing her against his rock-hard arousal.

She whimpered into his mouth as she rolled her hips, and he took her lead, pushing himself against her, thrusting as if he could somehow miraculously be inside her moist warmth. He swore once more, and the hand that was cupping her buttocks moved between her legs, pushing aside her underpants so he could press a finger to her sex before striking inside of her.

She cried out, breaking their kiss only so she could drop her head backwards, her face scrunched with pleasure as her tight, moist muscles spasmed around him, gripping him so tight it was impossible for a little seed not to spill from him in response to these sensations.

'I want you,' he growled, stating the obvious, moving his mouth to her throat and sucking the flesh there, while his fingers moved between her legs and her voice grew higher in pitch and far more urgent. 'I know this is wrong and we will both regret it, but I cannot tell you how much I don't care right now. Say you want me too.'

He didn't need her to say it. He could *feel* it. He knew it with every cell in his body, and yet he wanted her to admit as much, to speak the words. Too much was at stake for both of them, for him to follow his instincts alone.

Her crescendo was building, fiercely wrapping around them, so he rode the wave with her, sucking her neck as he drove her over the edge of pleasure, her orgasm fierce and intense, her muscles convulsing around his fingers, her voice heavy in the air. He held her tight, his arousal desperately seeking entrance, needing her, needing to get this out of his system so he could return from the brink of insanity. He pulled his hand away purely so he could remove his clothes but in doing so, something between them shifted and she lifted her hands to her mouth, staring at him as though seeing him for the first time.

'Oh, my God,' she whispered, eyes clenched shut, not on a wave of pleasure now but one of comprehension. 'Your Highness, that was—' She turned her back on him, her slim shoulders shaking. 'I'm so sorry.' Her soft apology tore at something inside him.

'What for?' He moved to her, so they were toe to toe once more. His own desire had not abated.

'For letting that happen. For wanting it to happen. For standing here and basically begging you to make love to me.' She grimaced, her face paler than paper. 'That was a terrible, terrible mistake.'

It was the very last thing he wanted to hear. 'A mistake? Hardly.'

'You think not?'

'It's…inconvenient,' he said, choosing his words with care.

'Elana is my best friend,' she groaned. 'And I'm here to see if you're a good match for her. What am I meant to say? That you're a very smart, handsome guy who hits on any woman in his proximity?'

'That's not what this was,' he said quickly.

'Oh? Then what was it?' she demanded.

'I haven't been with a woman in months,' he clarified.

'That's even worse! So you would have had sex with me just because it's "been a while"?' All formality was, for the moment, lost. 'Even though my best friend is your future wife?'

His eyes narrowed, and just like that, his desire faded, leaving something hollow in its place. Tariq was known for many things, his black-and-white morality amongst them. 'She is not yet my future wife,' he reminded her, aware it was really only a technicality. 'Neither of us has officially agreed to the marriage.'

'But you *intend* to marry her,' Eloise muttered. 'If she'll have you, which she will, if I recommend it. Don't you understand? She trusts me! She's relying on me. I can't—I can't go back and tell her to marry someone that I've—if we've—'

He understood perfectly. Everything she was saying made perfect sense, he just didn't particularly like hearing it.

'Fine, it was a mistake,' he agreed with her first summation. 'It won't happen again.'

Disappointment that dulled her eyes. 'Good,' she whispered, running her hands down her dress, straightening it, pulling away from him. 'It *can't* happen again, Your Highness.'

'Then please, call me Tariq,' he said after a pause. 'You keep using my title and I have to tell you it leads me to want to rip every shred of fabric from your body and make you shout it from the rooftops.'

Her gasp was loud enough to split the room in two, the imagery as evocative to Tariq as it was to Eloise.

'Duly warned,' she said quietly. 'That can never happen again... Tariq.'

It was impossible not to envy him, and to marvel at his prowess, for not ten minutes after making her see stars, she was watching the Sheikh of Savisia speak to his mother as though nothing earth-shattering had taken place, whatsoever.

'I've always loved Ras Sarat,' the Sheikha murmured, her greying hair pulled up into a loose bun, intelligent eyes focused on Eloise, so it took all of her concentration not to blush. Surely her face showed exactly what had just happened? Damn it, she wished they hadn't met like this, but it had been unavoidable.

Tariq had insisted on walking Eloise back to her suite, where she'd intended to hide out for at least the next century, only the older regent had been sitting in a dappled courtyard they happened to cross through, and when she offered tea, Eloise knew it would have been very poor form to demur.

Despite the fact tea was the last thing she wanted. Despite the fact she could barely think straight. Despite the fact her knees were wobbling and her breath rushing and her breasts tingling and her stomach in knots.

She plastered a smile to her face, forcing herself to sit demurely, to remember all of the etiquette lessons she and Elana had joked about over the years. Hands clasped in her lap, shoulders relaxed, feet crossed at the ankles.

'Do you travel there often?'

'Yes, in fact. It's where we took our honeymoon.' Something wistful crossed the older woman's expression and belatedly, Eloise recalled the recent passing of the Sheikh.

'I was sorry to hear about His Highness,' she murmured, aware of Tariq's eyes on her. Aware of them? Hyper-aware, more like. They burned her, lingering on her skin, tantalising her, mocking her, reminding her of what they could be doing, if only she hadn't panicked.

'It was a great loss.'

'I'm sure.'

'Did you ever meet him?' the Sheikha prompted.

'No, Your Highness. I didn't have that good fortune.'

'He was there quite recently.'

'He met with the Crown Princess, in fact,' Eloise said, with a nod. 'She always praised him.'

'My husband was an excellent man.' The older woman's eyes moved to Tariq, love obvious in their depths. 'And my son made him very proud.'

Eloise's heart skipped a beat. 'I'm sure.' The words, to her own ears, were slightly wooden, and she saw in the answering flicker of Tariq's lips that he heard and understood.

'Have you lived in Ras Sarat for long, dear?'

'A few years.'

'And what brought you to this part of the world?'

'Friendship, and occupation.' She wrinkled her nose. 'And a need for change, and perhaps the *umm ali*.'

The Sheikha smiled. 'One of my personal favourites.'

'I didn't have a sweet tooth until I tried it.'

'Our chef makes the best you've ever tasted.' She turned to Tariq. 'Will you have some made for Eloise?'

'Would you like some, Eloise?' he asked, his voice hinting at a double entendre, so her stomach twisted and she sent him a furious glance. How could he make light of this? She ground her teeth together, offering a saccharine smile.

'I shouldn't. I know it's not good for me.'

'Sometimes it's good to be bad.'

'But the consequences,' she added, flicking a tight smile at the Sheikha, who was oblivious to the undercurrent of tension.

'It's your choice,' he said with a lift of his shoulders, his eyes sparking with hers to the point she couldn't bear it.

She stood abruptly, her trademark grace nowhere in sight as she quickly came behind her chair and gripped the back.

'Excuse me, Your Highness,' she said, ignoring the Sheikh. 'I promised the Princess I'd check in with her, and I'm overdue. Do you mind?'

'Of course not, dear. Thank you for taking the time to speak with me. I enjoyed meeting you.'

Her heart gave a strange clutch. 'And I you.'

She turned without another glance in Tariq's direction. She couldn't look at him. She had the strangest feeling that she would cry if she wasn't very, very careful.

'Eloise.' His voice arrested her as she passed through the doors that led to the inside of the palace.

She dug her fingernails into her palms and stood perfectly still, without turning to face him.

'You forgot this.'

Now she tilted her face, just enough to see him holding her handbag.

Inwardly, she groaned, forcing herself to nod her thanks. But when he was close enough that only she could hear him, he murmured, softly, 'You're running away from me.'

Her eyes flared wide and she made her escape while she still could, legs trembling all the way back to her suite of rooms.

CHAPTER FOUR

'TARIQ!' SHE STARED at him, heart kicking into overdrive, mind racing at his sudden appearance at her suite. 'It's almost nine o'clock.'

'Yes, it's late. I had a meeting. But as you haven't eaten, I've come to collect you.'

'How do you know I haven't eaten?'

He lifted his brows. 'I asked.'

'Why?'

'I'm not in the habit of explaining myself to anyone in Savisia.'

It was so arrogant she almost laughed. 'Why don't you give it a shot?'

He didn't react, but she felt the amusement humming through him and delighted in that. She liked making him smile. She liked… Danger sirens blared, and she heeded them, gripping the door more tightly.

'You're my special guest. I made plans for our dinner.'

'Together?' she squeaked.

'Unless you are afraid to be alone with me?'

'I'm not afraid.'

'Then you are a fool,' he muttered, a rueful expression on his face. 'We're playing with fire, you know.'

'I'm not playing with anything.'

'We'll see.'

'And even if that were true, isn't it all the more reason for us to keep our distance?'

'I can't do that.'

'Why not?'

'I've announced to my cabinet and yours that I am spending the next week with you. I intend to see that through.'

'But surely this afternoon—'

'Changes nothing,' he said flatly. 'It can't.'

'I know, but—'

'You still want to get to know me, don't you? To see if you should recommend this marriage to Elana or not?'

She closed her eyes, caught between a rock and a hard place. 'Yes,' she admitted, finally, grudgingly.

'Then come and share a meal with me.'

'You make it sound so simple.'

'Isn't it?'

It should have been. After all, what they'd shared was meaningless, in the scheme of things. He wasn't to know that her experience with men was so limited. Clearly, his knowledge of female anatomy was first rate, undoubtedly garnered through extensive experimenting. So why couldn't they just forget the kiss, and everything else, and focus on the reason she'd come to Savisia in the first place?

'Fine,' she said with a huff. 'But don't even think about touching me.'

'I can't promise that,' he murmured. 'But I won't act on those thoughts unless you ask me to.'

Her lips parted and she groaned. 'Why are you doing this?'

'What am I doing, Eloise?'

'Flirting with me.'

'I'm simply being honest.'

'Well, don't do that either,' she snapped. 'At least, not

about…us. I can't even think about this,' she said, pointing from his chest to hers, 'right now.'

'Then I envy you.'

She growled. 'I'm serious. You might be master of all you survey, but don't think I won't stomp on your foot if you keep saying things like that.'

'Stomp on my foot?'

'Sure. Or knee you somewhere significantly more painful.'

He laughed, a deep, husky sound that made her blood bubble and overheat. 'But then, I'd have to defend myself.'

She shouldn't ask. She really shouldn't ask. 'And how would you do that?'

'I suspect it would involve your wrists being pinned to a wall, for a start.'

Just the suggestion made her bones melt. 'Damn you,' she snapped, but the words were breathy, lacking any true sense of outrage.

'Relax. I won't touch you. I won't flirt with you. Tonight, I will be on my best behaviour.'

She tried to ignore the shearing sense of disappointment, but it was impossible. She bit into her lip and finally nodded. 'Okay. Dinner. And only because I'm starving.'

'I'm flattered.'

She scowled. 'Somehow, I think your ego's probably sufficiently supersized to survive a few home truths from me.'

He laughed and again, her body reacted with a sharp ping of desire. She forced herself not to reveal it.

'You know, your reaction makes me think you don't get kissed anywhere nearly often enough.'

She gaped. 'I'm not having this conversation with you.'

'Why not?' he asked, gesturing for her to step out into the corridor. Begrudgingly, she did so, eyes firing to his.

'How about, because it's none of your business?'

'Is it a big deal?'

She rolled her eyes. 'No.'

'A state secret of some sort?'

'No.'

'So?'

'You really want my kissing resume?'

'Not a full resume,' he said with a tilt of his head. 'More of an overview.'

'And do I get the same information about you in return?'

'Are you sure you'd like it?'

'I think I'd be neglectful not to ask,' she said after a pause. 'After all, you're hoping to marry my very best friend.'

'Does my sex life impact on my suitability as a spouse?'

'It might.'

'Fascinating. How so?'

'I don't know. Just how active is your sex life?'

'Currently? Until this afternoon, I'd say it was non-existent.'

She stopped walking, lips parted, floundering. 'That's not fair.'

He lifted his hands in a gesture of surrender. 'You asked for the truth, though.'

'Yes, well, could you try to speak it in a less inflammatory fashion, please?'

He dipped his head. 'Your wish is my command.'

Something twisted in her gut. She was having *fun*. Despite the forbidden nature of what they'd shared, despite the lurching feeling that she'd taken a serious misstep and was letting down the one person on earth she thought of as family, she couldn't deny that sparing with Tariq was a highly enjoyable activity.

He stopped walking, and two servants opened a pair of

doors. She stepped inside, looking around in a cursory manner until it became apparent that he'd brought her to a courtyard, though not the same one she'd seen that afternoon, with his mother. This one had a very beautiful fountain on the edge and a sunken seating area with a fire pit at the centre. Though the day had been warm, the evenings were cool, thanks to the desert air, and she moved towards the fire on autopilot.

'My father's death changed things for me,' he said quietly, close behind her, so with her back to him, she allowed herself the indulgence of closing her eyes, of listening to him, hearing his words, allowing them to weave through her soul. 'I haven't been with a woman since we buried him.'

Five months. All the breath left her lungs as she began to understand why he'd found it so hard to control himself around her. She was probably the first woman he'd been alone with since then. No wonder he'd struggled to keep a distance. After all, his libido was somewhat legendary. What exactly was her excuse?

'You must have loved him very deeply.'

'Yes.'

'And before he died?' she whispered, afraid that he was right: that she didn't want to know.

'Why do I think you already have the answer to that?'

'Because you're a smart man.'

'Yet you want to hear it from me?'

'Yes.'

'I enjoy the company of women, and it is not something I've ever been short of.'

She forced herself to turn then, to face him, and caught him in a moment of reflection, his eyes on the flickering flames.

'Have you ever been in love?'

The question had his eyes flickering to hers, then away again. 'No.'

She frowned. 'Why not?'

He hesitated, and she felt a weight in that silence, a consideration that spoke of thoughts he was choosing not to express. 'I can't answer that.'

'Because you don't know?'

'Because it's too personal.'

She compressed her lips, trying not to show how much that hurt. But it did, and even Eloise was surprised. After all, why should she care so much?

'So these women you enjoy the company of are what?'

His lips curled. 'Surely you're familiar with the concept of lovers?'

She gasped, his raw honesty startling and confronting, hateful and…so deliciously seductive. She turned her back on him, lifting her hands to the flames and pretending to warm herself.

'You're deliberately baiting me.'

'Am I?'

'I meant to ask if you dated them, or simply took them to bed…but on reflection, I don't think I need to know. Just tell me that when you marry Elana, you'll be faithful to her.'

The silence that hung between them was heavy and she wondered if he could hear the rushing of her blood, the throbbing of her strangely erratic heart.

'I take vows of any kind very seriously.'

'I'm glad.'

He came to stand beside her. 'Your turn.'

'What for?' She blinked up at him with wide-eyed innocence.

'Your, what did you call it? Kissing resume?' His eyes fell to her lips and she knew that if she were being completely honest with him, she'd tell him there'd only ever been one kiss that mattered, one kiss that had the power to reshape the entirety of reality and gravity and cosmic power.

But instead, she lifted her shoulders in what she hoped would pass for nonchalance and pursed her lips. 'I don't keep an exact count.'

There was no humour on his face now, and the intensity of his gaze made her breath shallow. 'Have you ever been in love?'

She reached for a blasé answer, but something about his intelligent, assessing eyes and the stars that shone so brightly overhead, and the crackling of the flames in the pit in front of them, made her feel that their conversation was taking place out of time and space. She shook her head almost without realising it.

His eyes skimmed hers, reading her. 'Is that so?'

'You think I'm lying?'

'I'm simply surprised.'

'Why?'

'You're beautiful and fascinating. Surely you have men beating a path to your door.'

'Even if that were true,' she said with a small shake of her head, 'attracting the interest of men is not quite the same thing as welcoming it. Or being in love.'

He was too shrewd, too seeing. 'And you don't welcome male attention.'

She turned away from him. 'I think I'll take a leaf out of your book. That's too personal.'

'Is it?'

She dipped her head. 'This whole conversation is absurd,' she said, after a beat. 'I told myself I wouldn't let this happen again, but here you are, weaving the same spell around me as you did this afternoon. I can't do this.'

She turned to walk away but he caught her hand, pulling gently, drawing her back to him, and now the tears she'd been fighting all afternoon felt dangerously close to the surface.

'She's my best friend,' Eloise whispered, lifting her free hand and pressing it to his chest. 'She's more than that. Elana is the only family I have. I would never do anything that would hurt her. Please, you have to respect that.'

His eyes bore into hers and she held her breath, waiting, needing, wishing, but their souls were speaking now, making a pact that went beyond her plea and his promise.

'You're right,' he said quietly, releasing her hand and taking a step back. 'I'm sorry.'

His apology was the last thing she'd expected. It pulled at something inside of her. Emotions that she had no experience with were zipping out of control now.

'Your loyalty is a quality I greatly admire. It was wrong of me to ask you to betray her.'

'To be fair, I was pretty complicit,' she couldn't resist saying, the words brittle, laced with shame.

'I shouldn't have let things go this far. If you were not her friend, then things would be different, but you are. I understand.' He lifted her hand to his lips and kissed it, but quickly, chastely, with no promise of anything further. Her heart developed a fissure right down the centre, but she told herself it was with relief and gladness.

'Okay,' she forced a smile to her mouth but it felt wooden and heavy. 'Thank you.'

His eyes glowed when they met hers. 'Let's eat.'

For three days, the Sheikh was on his best behaviour and Eloise told herself she was glad. Glad he was being businesslike and professional, glad he delegated some of the sightseeing to minions, glad that he kept a respectful distance from her at all times.

Glad that he didn't touch her or kiss her or even look at her as though he wanted to.

Glad that her evenings were kept free, except for one thing: when she was alone, he was in her thoughts, her mind, his phantom touch on her body, his lips on her lips, his taste in her mouth, his touch in her body, so she was almost mindless with exhaustion and distraction by her fourth morning in Savisia.

Eloise had been so sure that she wasn't interested in a relationship with anyone—what were the chances of the first man who got under her skin and made her question everything being a man who'd proposed marriage to her best friend?

A hysterical laugh bubbled inside of her, so she reached for her cup of tea, still piping hot, and sipped it, glad for the way it scalded her throat a little. His marriage with Elana would be purely one of convenience. For Elana, it was essential to boost her country's flagging economic and political position in the region. But what about Tariq? Why had he chosen Elana? She frowned, contemplating that.

Why did he need children so desperately *now*? He was young and virile, and while he was the last of this line of the Savisian royal family, at thirty, and in good health, it was hard not to think he had at least a few years. Years in which to find a bride and marry for love. To marry someone he cared about, not just another princess.

But that wasn't why she'd come here.

Eloise's job was to see if she could recommend the marriage. She thought now of everything she knew about Tariq, everything she'd known before arriving and everything she'd heard and seen since, and her heart gave a funny little pang.

His reputation had preceded him. He was well-regarded by absolutely everyone. Not a single person could fault him. He was respected, liked, admired, but in person, it was impossible not to recognise his many personal charms, not to be overwhelmed by them. Elana would not likely love him—her heart had been lost when her fiancé had died—but she would like him. She would really like him, and she'd enjoy being married to him. They were definitely compatible.

Eloise felt a tick in the centre of her chest. She ignored it. She had to focus on Elana now, not her own stupid, selfish desires and wants. Not the little fantasy she'd developed in which Tariq was a normal man and she was not the best friend of the woman he'd sought to propose marriage to.

With a groan, she banged her palm against her forehead, wanting to push all thoughts from her mind that weren't relevant, but they pursued her, rushing through her, pulling at her, so eventually, she gave up, deciding on a walk to clear her mind instead.

The palace was incredibly beautiful. Beyond anything she'd ever seen before, in fact. It wasn't simply the grandiose nature of the architecture—and it *was* impossibly grand—but also the way the palace had been designed, at some long ago point in time, to make the most of nature's bounty. In one direction, large curved windows framed striking views of the desert, the vastness making one feel inconsequential and vital at the same time. In the other direction, the ocean shimmered, the capital city a testament to modernity with glass-and-steel monoliths cutting like blades through the crisp blue sky. The palace was surrounded by lush, green gardens—a testament to genius aquaculture, the diversion of a nearby river offered year-round irrigation, making for dense, immaculate lawns. The trees were mostly natives to this region or those with similar temperatures, and prospered in the climate: junipers, date palms, figs. Strong and sturdy, reminding her, quite suddenly, of the Sheikh of Savisia. She stopped walking abruptly, staring at one of the trees as her breath quickened in her throat.

He was so completely of this land, it was a part of him, and he of it. He'd proposed marriage because it was his duty to marry, and he would marry for that same reason. He would marry Elana because it made sense.

She forced her feet to move, taking her step by step towards the wide doors that led to one of the many courtyards surrounding the palace. She'd explored extensively in the last few days and knew this was one of the ways she could access the gardens. The sky was turning, fading from the brightness of the afternoon to the magical light of the dusk, the stars beginning to peep down on Savisia, the desert birds issuing their lilting night cries. She inhaled, the fragrance familiar yet different, so like Ras Sarat, and yet so unique, quite unlike anything she'd ever known before.

Her hands trailed a nearby rose bush and an errant spike caught her finger. She lifted it to her face for closer inspection, noting the perfect droplet of blood that seeped out. With a grimace, she kept walking, past the rose bushes, to a large field of citrus trees that reminded Eloise of an army— each tree stood strong and proud, heavy with leaves and blossoms, preparing for the winter when fruit would burst on these limbs, weighing them down, dragging them closer to the earth. She imagined the delight of a sun-kissed orange eaten here. She imagined peeling the skin and lifting the quadrants to her lips, tasting the sweet flesh as juices ran down her fingers. She imagined Tariq taking her by the wrist and drawing her sticky, citrus scented fingers to his mouth, licking each one, eyes locked to hers, mesmerising, heavenly.

She gasped, pushing the errant thought from her mind.

But that wasn't enough. The strength of her thoughts had conjured him—or so it seemed to Eloise, who was startled from her X-rated thoughts by the sound of hooves thudding across the ground, and a moment later, the sight of Tariq astride a magnificent stallion, black with rippling muscles and a mane that had been expertly braided.

She could only stare as he made his way across the field beyond the citrus trees. He sat straight on the horse's back, his frame impossible to mistake for any other man's, his expert command of the beast never in question. He rode as though he and the horse were one, their thoughts shared, their purpose unified. She lifted a hand to her lips, knowing this image would be burned into her brain for life. The perfection of it, the rightness, the fascinating, undeniable sensuality.

A low groan formed in the base of her throat. It was silent. A thought, more than anything, but he responded as though she'd shouted his name, his head turning, eyes pinpointing her precisely, exactly, so she froze to the spot, fingers pressed to her lips, as she'd been fantasising about only moments earlier.

Everything shimmered. The horizon, the sky, the horse's mane, every cell in her body seemed to tremble and glisten. Without hesitation, he tugged on the horse's rein, and the beast responded instantly, changing course, tacking away from the open field, feet kicking up, moving faster, with an urgency that matched the fast flowing of her blood, until Tariq was riding through the citrus grove, cutting a path directly to her.

CHAPTER FIVE

SHE COULDN'T MOVE. Her legs were divorced from her body. She stayed where she was, trying desperately to rally her thoughts, to remember that she was there to serve her friend, not her own selfish, and terrifying, desires.

It was just that she hadn't seen him properly in days. It heightened everything, making her awareness of him as much a fundamental property as light and air.

'Eloise,' he said with a dip of his head, the words coated with something gruff and raw.

The horse expelled a breath, then studied her with un-disguised curiosity, so she smiled because the beast really was a mirror of its owner.

'Your Highness.'

His eyes narrowed and belatedly she recalled his warning about the use of that title. More precisely, she remembered what he'd said it made him want to do, and her pulse tripped into a chaotic rhythm.

'I was just exploring the garden,' she murmured, gesturing to the trees. 'It's such a beautiful evening, I wanted to get out of the palace for a while.'

She was babbling. The silence stretching between them made her need to fill it—an uncharacteristic gesture for someone who was usually self-possessed.

'Your horse is beautiful,' she added.

'I don't think Bahira would appreciate that adjective.'

'He's too alpha for beauty?' she asked, a smile tickling the corners of her lips.

'Oh, absolutely.'

'Handsome? Buff? Striking?'

'Tough,' he corrected, amusement in his tone.

'Well, he's lovely.'

This time, Tariq lifted a single, thick brow, then grinned, so her heart stammered.

'Anyway,' she took a step backwards, 'I won't keep you.'

'You're not.'

Her expression was laced with irony, yet she didn't move. 'Do you…ride often?' She cringed as soon as she'd asked the question. She sounded like a love-struck teenager.

'Yes.'

She took a step backwards. She really needed to leave.

'Does the Princess ride?'

Eloise told herself she was glad he'd brought up Elana. Every time she could remember why she was here, the better. 'She knows how to, but it's not her favourite pastime.'

'Oh?'

'She was thrown, as a child. She's never got over it. She was made to continue riding, after that, but it was a pretty traumatic experience for her.'

His eyes roamed her face. 'And you?'

She swallowed, her throat thick and dry. 'I… No. I've never learned.'

'Have you ever been on a horse?'

She shook her head.

'Why not?'

She pulled a face. 'I grew up in England.'

'Last I checked, horses existed there too.'

She laughed. 'Sure, but not for people like me.'

'Meaning?'

'My parents didn't have much money. They were aristocratic, but like so many in their position, death taxes and the high cost of maintaining big country homes drove them into debt, Your High—Tariq.' But now, his name felt like a caress. All she could remember was how she'd whispered it into his mouth, begging him to hold her closer, tighter, begging him to take her. It pushed all thoughts from her mind for a moment, so she had to concentrate to grab hold of what she'd been saying. 'And horse riding is an expensive hobby.'

'You went to an excellent school.'

She glanced up at him. 'How do you know—?'

'You met the Princess at school,' he reminded her. 'And I know where she attended. The fees are not cheap.'

'No,' she agreed. 'After my parents died, I went to live with a great aunt. She wasn't wealthy, for the same reasons as my parents, but I earned a partial scholarship, and she was able to cover the rest.' She lifted a hand tentatively, wondering if Bahira would allow her to pat his nose, and as she did so, Tariq's hands tightened around the reins, ensuring the stallion would remain still. 'Sadly, there wasn't enough left over for the upkeep of a horse,' she joked. 'Besides, when I learned of Elana's mistreatment at the hands—hooves—of one of these animals, I must say, I swore off the idea for life.'

'Is that so?'

She nodded. 'I can't say I've ever regretted that decision.'

'Are you still afraid, Eloise?'

Her lips parted at the direct challenge. He was manipulating her. She understood that, and yet she couldn't quite stop herself from taking the bait. 'I still have a desire to live,' she said, stepping back.

'Do you trust me?'

Something stuck in her throat. She lifted a hand, pulling

her hair back from her face. She stared at him, her heart galloping faster than any speed this steed could ever accomplish. 'I don't trust anyone.'

'Do you trust *me*?'

The distinction was like the throwing down of a gauntlet. They both heard it. 'Why?'

His eyes narrowed. 'That's not an answer.'

'What do you want me to say?' she muttered. 'I'm not riding any stupid horse.'

'What about this beautiful, lovely horse?' he asked with a lift of his brow, so her heart turned over in her chest and her eyes jerked to his face.

'He's enormous,' she said with a shake of her head. 'And while he seems perfectly content with you on his back, I don't think the same could be said for me.'

'I didn't say you'd be riding alone.'

She sucked in a sharp breath, shaking her head. 'I can't ride your horse with you.'

'Why not?'

'Come on, don't be so obtuse.'

'It's a horse ride. I'm not asking you to make love to me in the shade of the orange trees.'

Her gut twisted at the immediate, evocative imagery.

'There is something I have learned about fears,' he murmured, stepping off the horse in one swift, easy motion, coming to stand closer to her. 'The feeling of overcoming them is like nothing else.'

She stared up at him, his powerful, confident face, and something shifted inside of her. Did she trust him? Yes. And did she trust herself? She wasn't sure. Only, she knew one thing for sure—while this man would marry her best friend, they had these few days. Days she could spend time with him, be near to him, without crossing any lines of propriety again, but could stockpile memories of the ways he made her feel, something to nourish her in future years.

Elana had sworn off a love match. She didn't want to care about her future husband, it wasn't as though Eloise would be getting close to a man Elana hoped to fall madly in love for. In fact, if Elana was here, she'd be the first one to tell Eloise to let herself go, just a little.

If she turned him down now, she'd always regret it. She knew that.

Torn between loyalty for Elana and a desperate, heart-breaking need to take this one small pleasure, just for herself, she could only stare at him.

'I promise, nothing bad will come of this.'

She let out a shuddering laugh. 'It's not just the horse.'

'Nothing will happen between us.' He was close enough that his breath fanned her forehead and her body lifted in goosebumps. 'You have my word.'

It had to be enough. 'Okay.' Her voice was throaty, the two syllables a commitment to something that terrified and excited her in equal measure. 'But…erm…how exactly do I…?' She gestured to the horse. Where Tariq had made it look easy to dismount from the beast's back, she had no idea how to climb up. She noted there was no saddle nor stirrups.

'May I?'

She tilted her face to his, seeing the way he was looking at her, gesturing to her waist.

She had his word that nothing would happen between them. She had to trust that. She jerked her head in agreement.

She'd *agreed*, but she wasn't *prepared* for the feeling of his hands—broad, strong, capable and confident—wrapping around her sides, holding her steady, lifting her easily, as though she weighed nothing, onto the back of the magnificent beast. And there was no other way to describe the horse, who stood strong and steady as she was placed at the base of his neck. Her hands instinctively sought his neck, patting him, and a moment later, the powerful frame of Sheikh Tariq was at her back, his arms wrapped around her to secure the reins, his face so close to the back of her head that when he spoke it was as though the words were caressing her.

'Are you ready?'

No. She was terrified, as though she were stepping into the fires of hell. How much she wanted him made her want to throw all caution to the wind, to turn around and kiss him, to plunder his mouth as he had hers, to allow her body to answer the siren call of longing that had overtaken her almost from the first moment they'd met. But Elana was at the forefront of her mind, and what she owed her friend, and so she nodded curtly, keeping her gaze focused on the horizon.

'Then let's go.' He kicked the horse's side and the beast responded immediately. There was no opportunity to speak then. Though the horse moved more slowly than he had earlier, when only Tariq was on his back, it was still fast, the hooves cutting over grass first and then, the open field beyond the structured gardens of the palace. It took several minutes before Eloise properly exhaled. She wasn't afraid. She was exhilarated, but she was also intimately aware of every single movement Tariq made, even the subtle way he pulled on the reins to control his horse, or the way his legs moved at her sides, and the way his chest was at her back, framing her, keeping her safe. Protecting her.

She'd never been protected by a single soul in her life. Even her parents hadn't taken care of her. It was impossible not to feel a little in awe of this man, and the way he held her close, ensuring no harm would befall her.

Impossible not to feel a little addicted to that, even when she accepted this couldn't last.

Before she knew it, the grass gave way to sand, crisp and white and she imagined warm underfoot from the full day's sunshine, but the horse rode on, faster now, as if he had a destination in mind and wanted to get there as quickly as possible.

She shivered and perhaps Tariq felt it, or mistook it for fear, because one hand left the reins to clamp around her middle, pinning her back against him, offering extra protection and safety. Only it wasn't safer. Being held by him like this only made her aware of him in a far more visceral way, bringing memories back to mind of the way they'd kissed, of how good it had felt to be held by him.

She bit down on her lip, focusing straight ahead, trying to keep her brain occupied rather than allowing it to slide into a full-blown reflection of that kiss. That mistake.

The desert sands stretched so far ahead that she wondered when the horse was going to turn around. She couldn't say how long they rode in one direction before a rocky outcrop loomed in front of them. It was very nearly night now, the stars brighter overhead, the sky a translucent grey, and the rocks were imposing and unmistakable. When the horse slowed, her ears adjusted to the lack of noise, only to recognise another sound. Running water.

'Where are we?'

He released his grip on her stomach and jumped off the horse, before reaching up and lifting her down. 'I used to come here often as a child.'

'On your own?'

'Not at first,' he said, eyes shifting to hers. 'My father would bring me.' There was another heavy silence, and she knew there was something he wasn't telling her, something he was weighing in his mind, and so she stayed quiet, curious, but determined not to push him.

'As a young boy, I had night terrors. Vivid, terrifying dreams that would wake me in a cold sweat. I'd scream until my lungs burned. Coming here was the only thing that could calm me.'

She looked up at him, surprised. 'I can't imagine you being afraid of anything.'

'Everyone has fears,' he said, gesturing to the rocks in front of them. She recalled what he'd said, just minutes earlier. *There is something I have learned about fears. The feeling of overcoming them is like nothing else.*

She glanced to the horse. 'Do you need to tether him?'

'He will wait for me here.'

'So confident?'

He lifted his shoulders. 'Of course.'

'Because we're quite far away from the palace, Your Highness. If he bolts, I don't particularly want to stay here all night.'

'It is actually a very pleasant place to sleep.'

'You camp here too?'

'On occasion.'

It only cemented the impression she had of this man: that he was so thoroughly of this land, born of it, destined to rule it. 'How does that work?'

His expression showed bemusement. 'There's a swag on the ground...'

She rolled her eyes in an exaggerated gesture of impatience. 'I mean, how do you leave the palace without guards?'

He arched a brow.

'Elana has security with her, always.'

He nodded thoughtfully. 'As she would here.'

'But you don't,' Eloise pointed out.

'I expect our ability to defend ourselves is not equal.'

'You think she's weak?'

'No. More vulnerable to attack though. Besides, as my wife, it would be my duty to ensure her safety—that's a task I take seriously.'

She ignored the *frisson* that ran the length of her spine. 'And you don't need protection?'

He pulled a face and she laughed because it was so absurd.

'I came to an arrangement with the chief of palace security many years ago.'

'Which is?'

'That I inform them of my location. If I'm going to come out here to camp, I bring this.' He lifted a small beacon from his pocket. 'If I press the button, security scrambles to come to me. When I leave the country, it is always with protection. That's our compromise.'

She pulled her lips to the side.

'You don't approve?'

'I don't know, Your Highness. But I can't imagine how unpleasant it would be to have a constant shadow.'

'Does your friend complain?'

Eloise's smile was wistful. 'Elana? Never. She is the most forbearing and sweetest person you'll ever meet. I don't think complaining is in her repertoire.'

Tariq's eyes bore into hers for so long that Eloise jerked her eyes away, looking up at the sparkling constellations overhead instead. 'It must be so peaceful here,' she observed wistfully.

'Don't tell me—you've never slept under the stars before either?'

She shook her head. 'Just on school camps, and that was in dormitories. Not tents.'

'No tents here either. This is all the roof I need.' He gestured to the sky.

It was a magical, romantic notion, and it buried itself deep under her skin, letting her imagine, dream, wonder about this wild, free side of his life.

'What were your nightmares about?'

He tilted his face to hers, scanning her features, and she looked away, not wanting him to see the temptation that must be written there so clearly.

'Nothing discernible,' he said after a pause, so she didn't know if he was gathering his thoughts or keeping something from her. 'It was more an impression than anything firm.'

'An impression of what?'

'Drowning or being burned alive. And not being able to save myself.'

She shivered. 'That's awful.'

He dipped his head in silent agreement. 'Do you still...' She wasn't sure why, but she left the rest of the question unspoken.

'From time to time. Not often now.'

'Are they...' She searched for the right words. 'The result of a specific trauma?'

She could sense him pulling away, closing down the line of questioning, so it was no surprise when he lifted a hand and gestured to something. 'Look.'

With a small sigh of frustration—because she wanted to learn more about him—she followed the direction of his finger and startled. Something was glowing just a hundred or so metres from them. As fluorescent as any light she'd ever seen, but the most striking turquoise colour. 'What is it?' she asked, spellbound.

'A form of algae,' he said softly.

She wrinkled her nose. 'Well, now, I've always thought algae was a little bit gross.'

He laughed, a deep, gruff sound that made her pulse fire. 'It's stunning.'

They moved towards the water's edge.

'Some algal blooms are harmful, even toxic, but this is a natural reaction that takes place here every year. It lasts around a month.'

'I can't believe it's real. It looks like something out of a fairy tale.'

'It's remarkable,' he agreed.

'Everything about this country feels somewhat magical.' She regretted the admission as soon as she'd made it, but it earned Tariq's full attention.

'Oh? What else have you seen that you find magical, little one?'

Little one. The words punctured something dangerously close to her heart. She tilted her chin in defiance, silently reminding herself, and hopefully him, of all the reasons they couldn't give into the temptation that swirled around them.

'The palace. The gardens. The weather. The smell of flowers in the air. The birds.' Right on cue, a night bird made a whipping sound, so light and ethereal the stars almost seemed to titter in response. 'You're very lucky to have grown up here.'

Silence met the pronouncement.

'You don't agree?' she prompted after a moment.

'I love this country,' he said.

She frowned, wondering at the strange distinction. She didn't like secrets at the best of times but feeling that this man was keeping something from her weighed heavily on her mind. And why should it? Because he wanted to marry her best friend? Or because she felt as if something had formed between them that demanded total honesty and transparency?

'There is so much more for you to see,' he said, voice distracted.

She drew her gaze back to his face.

'The palace is one thing, and yes, I agree, it is beautiful, but there is much, much more.'

'And one day, I'll enjoy experiencing that,' she said, somewhat wistfully. 'If the marriage goes ahead.'

The air between them crackled.

'Does that mean you've decided to recommend the match?' His voice held a low, assessing quality.

'Perhaps it's better if you return to the negotiations with her cabinet,' she said with a tightening in her spine. 'While Elana will listen to me, I must listen to them. Only when all considerations have been met can I offer my own opinion.'

'You think the terms of our financial agreements as important as your friend's happiness as my compatibility with her?'

'My friend is very like you,' she said after a pause. 'While I want her to be happy and adored, she wants only what is best for her country. The pressure of being on the throne is great—she wants to make the right decisions for her people.'

'And the marriage is a powerful bargaining chip,' he said. 'After all, I've approached her, she must know I'm motivated to make this succeed. Therefore, she can leverage my interest to better her country's circumstances.'

She was quiet, but her heart was not. It thumped and flipped and groaned at the painful, necessary conversation.

'But perhaps she has miscalculated,' he said after a beat. 'Or perhaps you have. I know that your economy is almost bankrupt. By every metric, Ras Sarat is in a worsening position. It is not Elana's fault—her advisors have failed her—but she has to shoulder the weight of that. She knows that, in contrast, Savisia is wealthy, powerful and prosperous. Our marriage would benefit Ras Sarat. Is that what she's thinking?'

Eloise stared at him, lips parted. She shouldn't have been surprised by his summation of matters—he was intelligent and his advisors were thorough. Of course he knew how bad things were in Ras Sarat. But somehow it felt as though the rug was being pulled from under her.

She chose her next words with care. 'You seem to have pieced together Elana's motivations, but what of yours?'

He was silent now, his chest moving with each breath he drew.

'You want children, but surely these could be had by any woman of your acquaintance. Why seek out Elana?'

'She is suitable.'

'Suitable? What does that even mean?'

'Born to this life.'

'Why is that essential? Your mother was not a princess when she married your father.'

His eyes narrowed.

'You're not the only one who's done their research.'

'My mother was not royal, you're right.'

'And yet you feel you have to marry a princess?'

'Are you trying to urge me to reconsider?'

'I—' She floundered, caught off guard by his question. After all, that's exactly what she'd been inadvertently doing.

'Is it because you doubt I can make your friend happy? Or because my marriage to her will make *you* unhappy?'

It was far, far too close to home. She blinked, feeling as though the earth was tipping under her feet. 'Don't be ridiculous. This is nothing to do with me.'

She wasn't sure if he believed her, but he didn't speak for a long time, only looked at her, and in that fragment of time, Eloise felt as if her entire soul was laid bare.

She didn't like the feeling; her eyes flickered away.

'We should go back to the palace.'

'Why?'

'Because it's late.'

'Or is it that you don't want to have this conversation?'

Damn it. Damn him. She crossed her arms, her breath ragged. 'I want my friend to be happy. I want this to be simple. I want…' She stopped there. Too many things were on the tip of her tongue and none of them helpful to admit.

But even without speaking the words, they hummed in the air between them, flashes of need, imagery, memories, like little blades floating through the sky. She flinched as one impaled her, the feeling of his mouth on hers, a memory so clear and real that it could have been happening right then and there.

'You're right,' he said, abruptly. 'We should go back.'

It was like being tumbled off a cliff with no warning. She stared at him a long time, wondering what had changed, why he wasn't standing his ground, but then he turned to move, and she had no choice but to follow him.

They walked to Bahira in silence, and when he lifted her onto the horse's back, she almost sobbed at how desperate she was for his hands to hold her longer, to draw her against him in a proper embrace. He didn't.

Do you trust me?

He was showing his trustworthiness, showing that no matter how much they wanted to act on these feelings, they wouldn't, they couldn't. It was forbidden.

'Hold on, little one,' he murmured into her ear, clamping a hand around her waist. 'We'll fly back.'

And he pushed the horse to ride faster, to eat up the distance between them and the palace, to end this delightful, delicious torment more quickly.

* * *

He'd wanted to return them back to the palace as quickly as possible. Once the flame had ignited between them, he'd known it would be only a matter of time before one of them acted on it, and he'd been afraid of being the person to weaken first. He'd been concerned that despite having given her an assurance that he could be trusted, perhaps he couldn't be. That his desires would eclipse every other thought and feeling.

But the rapid race back to the palace did nothing to extinguish the flames. The horse jolted beneath them, throwing her back against him. In order to keep Eloise safe, he held her tight, so that every inch of her body was moulded to his, and his arm around her waist couldn't help but feel the soft underside of her breasts, his fingers splayed wide commanded the entire side of her body. How easy it would have been to let his hand slip between her legs, to pleasure her as they rode, to remind her that there was no escaping the delirium of desire they could share.

How wrong it would be, though.

He needed, more than anything, to get her off this horse and safely back into the palace.

His first instinct—to give her space—had been correct. He couldn't be this close and rely on himself to resist her. Every moment was a form of torture. He needed to be free of her and this. Legendary control be damned; he was starting to wonder if he'd ever truly come face-to-face with temptation before.

Finally, the sand gave way to grass and his horse was back on familiar ground, moving toward the stables without needing to be guided. But before they could approach them, he pulled Bahira to a stop.

Though he was Sheikh, and no one would dare gossip

about him, the same could not be said for the very beautiful foreigner in their midst. In order to save her from becoming the centrepiece of harmful chatter, he hopped off the horse, but before he could reach up and catch her, she moved one leg over, clearly intending to jump down herself.

He couldn't make a noise fast enough—she was determined, her face pinched, her eyes flashing to his with that same defiance he'd seen out in the desert and then she was sliding down the side. But she'd miscalculated. His beast was far too high for this, for a person of her stature, to dismount without help. He was easily a foot taller than her and used to riding.

He moved forward—too late to warn her, but not to catch her. She hit the ground and immediately fell sideways. She would have landed with a thud if he hadn't intercepted her body's trajectory, catching her and holding her weight in his arms.

'Let me go,' she said, panic in her words. Panic he understood, because despite what they'd said, something was exploding out of their hands.

'You should have waited for me,' he snapped, anger stirred by worry. For a moment, he'd seen her falling, seen her head cracking against the rock wall to their side, seen her blood stain the grass, and he'd *felt* a wave of nausea, of fear. It shook him.

'I'm okay,' she said, but the words trembled a little. She wasn't okay. But because of her near-fall, or because of the passion stirring between them?

'Are you?'

The question landed at her feet with a thud. She lifted her gaze to his and something seemed to strangle his torso.

This couldn't happen. He couldn't give in to this.

He conjured every iota of decency he possessed, focusing on the reasons he needed to marry Elana, the importance of that union, on the fact that Eloise was Elana's best friend, on the indecency of lusting after her, despite the fact he barely knew his intended bride. It was Eloise he had to protect, Eloise who would be put in a difficult position if anything more happened between them.

So why did he stay there, staring down at her, eyes locked as if he dared not look away?

'I'm glad you showed me that,' she said softly. 'Elana will love to see it for herself one day.'

The reference to Elana sparked anger in his gut. Honour be damned—he wanted to kiss the idea of anyone else from Eloise's mouth. He wanted to lift them up, far away from the palace, from this life, from his duties and needs as a monarch and place them in some tiny corner of the world where he was a man and she a woman, free to explore this hypnotic need.

It was just desire.

Strong, overpowering desire, but a physical need, nothing more. They could explore it, release the urgency and temptation, and then go on with their normal lives. Maybe that's what they both needed, in order to be able to function?

But for Eloise, how could that work? How could she return to Ras Sarat and counsel her friend to this marriage, knowing that she'd slept with him?

And what would it be like for Tariq? He didn't think he'd still be pining over Eloise in a year's time, but he intended to give himself fully to this marriage. How would that work if Eloise was there, in the background, advising Elana? How could it work if he'd slept with his wife's best friend? While both he and Elana seemed in agreement on the practical nature of their marriage, it would still be a legally binding partnership, and he would never allow himself to cheat on her. Eloise would be out of reach forever.

There were myriad reasons to run as fast as the blazes from this, but all he could think about was the beating of a drum, drawing him to her with urgency and all-consuming passion.

Which meant he needed to put as much space between them as humanly possible, and immediately. 'Go inside, Eloise. For God's sake, go now.'

The sound of a small sob pierced something vital in his chest, but then she turned and ran, all the way back to the palace, out of his line of sight but not, regrettably, from his mind.

CHAPTER SIX

IT WAS SOME time later that night, when he should have been fast asleep, that he found an idea spinning around and around until it took a shape he couldn't shake. An idea he should have known better than to indulge, that somehow went from preposterous and wrong to plausible and possible to finally, imperative.

He would take Eloise to see Ala Shathi. The city in the east was, to borrow her word, magical, but it was the mountains surrounding it he more particularly wanted her to see. Mountains that flowed with pristine water were covered with vegetation that offered privacy and seclusion and had long been a port in the storm for Tariq. Even before the business with his father, and the truth of his birth, he'd been drawn to the wildness of Ala Shathi. It was there that he felt most like a man, most unshackled from his royal duties and obligations, from the sense that he carried upon his shoulders the expectations of a country.

Where better to take this woman who couldn't fit into his world in any way, who he couldn't get from his mind?

It was not to seduce her, but to show her the beauty of the east, and to be alone with her, without the fear of being seen, judged, of things being complicated by outside appearances.

He simply wanted to be alone with her. Just for a while. Not to touch her, just to speak to her. To listen to her. To unravel more of what made her tick, to understand her, to lose himself in her.

It was a fantasy; she was forbidden, and he wouldn't forget that. But just for a night or two, he wanted to be selfish. After that, he'd resume his life. He'd get back on track, focusing on the marriage first, and then the business of begetting an heir.

His lips pulled downward grimly. He couldn't turn his mind to that yet. It was across a ravine, with no bridge in sight. He would swim there, or claw his way there, because it was essential to his country and his father's legacy, but he wasn't quite ready yet.

There was something he had to get out of his system first.

'I'm sorry. What did you say?'

'His Highness has the itinerary planned.' The woman spoke more slowly, as though Eloise might be hard of hearing. 'Please, come with me.'

'But where did you say we were going?'

'To tour the eastern provinces.'

'But, why?'

The servant's smile was cool. 'I'm not aware, madam. Would you come this way, please?'

Arguing was clearly pointless. She'd simply have to ask Tariq when she saw him.

She grabbed her handbag on the way out of her suite, keeping pace with the staffer. They emerged onto a driveway about five minutes later and a light breeze rustled past, so Eloise caught at her skirts right as Tariq stepped out of a black four-wheel drive with darkly tinted windows.

Something about it made her mouth dry.

Like his horse, Bahira, it was a car that was so perfectly suited to him. Powerful, enigmatic, thrilling.

'Your Highness,' she murmured, desperate to put them on a more formal footing.

His eyes flashed to hers though and a distillation of memories made her cheeks flush warm.

'Miss Ashworth.' Something twisted in her belly. 'This way, please.' He gestured to the car, at the same time a man in a military uniform opened the back passenger door, making her want to form a joke about being off to execution. Only the intensity of Tariq's expression stalled another word from leaving her mouth.

She stepped up into the seat, aware of Tariq's eyes on her the whole time, so she was reminded of the way he'd helped her on and off the horse the night before and her pulse quickened.

She clipped her seatbelt in place quickly, mind zipping, and when he slid into the backseat beside her, the air in the car zapped with awareness.

Two men took the front seats: a driver and, going by the size and build of the second, a security guard.

Eloise told herself she was glad for the company, glad they weren't alone, but a moment later, Tariq pressed a button and a screen came up, separating them from the front of the car.

She did her best to assume an air of businesslike authority. 'Where are we going, Your Highness?'

'Weren't you informed?'

'Just that we were going "to the east".' She waved a hand in the air, panic threatening to creep into her voice.

His eyes narrowed speculatively. 'It's a beautiful part of the country. I thought you'd like to see it.'

'Tariq,' she murmured, as the engine of the car throbbed beneath them. 'This is—'

He tilted his face to hers, skimming her features with an expression she couldn't read.

'Relax. I have a meeting out that way and thought you would enjoy accompanying me. It's a beautiful part of the country, you'll enjoy it. Plus, you can get to know me some more. It's why you came to Savisia, is it not?'

It all sounded so logical. And yet... 'It's not that simple. Surely you can see that?'

'Why?'

'Because there's danger here,' she said with hushed urgency.

His lips pressed together, but at least he didn't downplay her assessment. 'I see risk, not danger, and risk we can guard against. We both know nothing more can happen between us, and so it won't.'

Eloise could only wish she shared his confidence.

'Hold on a second. What are we doing here?'

He tilted a glance at her. 'What do you mean?'

She pointed a finger towards his Gulf Stream jet. 'Exactly how far are we going?'

A flicker of amusement warred with frustration and impatience. Not with Eloise, so much as with an indefinable force. 'To the east, I told you.'

'But, I mean, that could be an hour's drive away.'

'More like a two-hour flight.'

The colour drained from her skin.

'Relax,' he muttered, his ego smarting from her clear panic. 'I've promised you nothing will happen. I'm not dragging you across the country to have my way with you.'

That jolted her eyes to his and the look in them had something new shimmering in his gut. Shame. Confusion. He stared back, careful not to reveal a thing.

'I know that.' She held his gaze a moment then turned away, eyeing the plane once more with obvious trepidation. Was she that terrified of being alone with him? Did she trust him so little? 'Then let's go.'

Every step she took was accompanied by a frantic voice in her mind, telling her to confess the truth to him.

Tell him about your fear of flying. That you haven't been on a plane in forever and you don't intend to start now. Tell him you can't bear the thought of being in that tin can, high up above the earth.

But she was embarrassed by her childish phobia and how much it revealed about her, embarrassed to admit such a vulnerability to him, and so she ground her teeth together and took the stairs with a sense of purpose, telling herself all the things the therapist had drummed into her, years ago.

Planes fly every day. They're meticulously maintained. Driving is far more dangerous than flying. That the lack of control she'd felt growing up with two parents who fought so constantly had translated into an anxiety in any circumstance where Eloise wasn't in control, and flying was a perfect example of that. It was too much of a leap of faith, and Eloise didn't trust anyone except Elana.

She was shaking as she stepped onto the plane, but Tariq occupied himself, talking first to the pilot and then taking a call, so Eloise found her own seat and snuggled into it, closing her eyes as if she could blot out her location if she tried hard enough.

The door closed with a bang and she startled, eyes immediately landing on Tariq, who wasn't looking at her. Good. She still didn't want him to know what a chicken she was. It usually helped people overcome their anxiety when they understood the root cause of it, but for Eloise, that hadn't been the case. She dreaded relinquishing control, and there was nothing that would ever make her feel better about that.

The engine began to rumble and she dug her fingers into the armrests as the sound built and built to a deafening crescendo. She focused on the action outside the window, the men in military uniforms moving away from the aircraft, the airport in the distance, loaded with other planes. The emptiness of the skies—clearly a wide berth had been given to the Sheikh's aircraft.

She was so overwrought she barely noticed the extravagant luxury of the plane. She couldn't take in the details, like the plush leather seats, crystal chandeliers, cinema-sized screen at the back of the plane, oak dining table. Any other time, she might have been overwhelmed by the details, but she couldn't notice anything beyond her paralysing fear.

Her heart was firmly lodged in her throat.

She needed to get off the plane.

She flicked another glance to Tariq. He was off the call now, his eyes focused on the view beyond his window, a frown on his face. He was so handsome. Her gut twisted for a whole other reason now, making her blood spin and bubble.

How on earth could she navigate this?

If he married Elana—and he would, he must—then Eloise would have to take a step back. From her best friend. From her life. There was no way she could continue to live as sisters with Elana, while her best friend made a life with herself as Tariq's wife. She loved Elana and wanted only the best for her, but it would be painful beyond bearing to sit on the sidelines and watch that. Eloise would have to leave Ras Sarat, Savisia, the whole area.

She would be cast adrift, again.

Alone.

Friendless.

A lump formed in her throat and she blinked away, right before Tariq turned and looked at her. She couldn't possibly continue to be near him. It was hard enough now, knowing that the chemistry they felt was technically a mistake. But if he was married to Elana, it would be strictly forbidden, and neither of them could ever betray Elana. Seeing him every day would be a torment.

And not seeing him?

She dipped her head forward, almost glad for the resurgence of her fear as the plane lifted and wobbled a little from side to side as the air currents buffeted the beast of a thing. She made a soft gasping noise, but kept her head down as panic filled her mouth with the taste of metal and she gripped the armrests so hard her fingernails stung.

Two hours?

It wasn't long. She could do it. She had to.

Something was wrong. He'd heard her exclamation shortly after take-off, but then she'd kept doing whatever she was doing, and he'd presumed it was a reaction to something she was reading or watching.

But now, as the jet passed through some mild turbulence, Eloise looked as though she were about to pass out. Her skin had lost all colour, her eyes were huge in her face and her lips were smacking together like she was trying to speak but couldn't.

He stood abruptly and crossed to her, ignoring the now familiar lurching in his gut as he drew near. He crouched down at her side, his pants straining over his haunches as he studied her more closely.

She turned to face him, almost catatonic; she was unrecognisable. He swore. 'What the hell is it?'

She was trembling all over, her hands the worst of all.

'I'm—' But she couldn't speak. Her lips opened and closed without issuing any further noise.

The plane made another little jump and she screamed, pressed a hand to her mouth, then turned away from him, hiding herself. But he'd seen enough; he understood.

She'd driven to Savisia, rather than flying, and at the first sign of the jet, she'd balked. He'd thought it was because it meant being alone with him, but what if it had to do with something more basic, like a fear of flying?

It was the only thing that made sense.

'It's okay,' he murmured, moving past her to the seat opposite, at the window, lifting the armrest between them so he could draw her against his chest. 'It's okay,' he said again, quietly, the words rumbling between them. It didn't help. She was shaking uncontrollably.

He began to worry.

'You're afraid,' he said, needing to know that his suspicions were correct, to rule out anything more sinister.

He felt her sharp nod against him.

'Okay.' Relief washed over him. A fear of flying was something he could manage. He stroked her arm softly, gently, rhythmically, holding her tight, offering security in his grip, and wishing that his altruistic gesture of comfort wasn't making him far too aware of her soft curves and femininity.

'This plane is very safe,' he said. 'The turbulence is normal as we cross the mountains. You will be fine, little one. I promise you.'

Her teeth chattered together. 'How d-do you know?'

'Because I fly all the time.'

'But this time—'

'Will also be safe.'

The trembling didn't subside. All he could do was hold her, and so he did. He held her tight through the turbulence but even once it subsided, he kept her clasped to his chest. At some point, it stopped being because she needed it, and started being because he wanted her there, because he liked feeling her against him, because her breath was warm and her body soft, because his fingers liked trailing over her arms, because she fit so perfectly right where she was. He held her tight and refused to think about how he was breaking the promise he'd made.

He was crossing an invisible line every moment he kept her pressed to him. He knew it, she knew it, yet neither of them did a thing about it.

It was a stolen moment of illicit pleasure, innocent but still wrong.

He didn't fight it.

Something had shifted inside of Eloise. On the flight, she'd been breaking apart, and he'd held her together. They'd shared something, and for Eloise, it had been meaningful. It had also forced her to stop pretending.

There was a force at work between them, something she couldn't keep fighting. It was inconvenient and wrong, and she knew she couldn't act on it how she wanted to, but wasn't she entitled to experience these feelings, just a little? It wasn't a betrayal of Elana to spend time with Tariq, was it? To talk to him and share things with him, to explain a little about her life, including her phobia of flying?

After all, Elana had sent her here to get to know the man. Wasn't that what she was doing?

The city passed in a blur, ancient buildings mingling with modern high-rises, designer shops showing the affluence of the area, giving way to wide boulevards lined with restaurants. Another time, she'd have liked to stop and enjoy it more fully, to immerse herself in the area and discover little laneways and avenues all on her own.

'Do you come out here often?' she asked, turning to face him in the back of yet another limousine, this one accompanied on either side by shiny black motorbikes. He'd served as her protector during the flight. The way he'd held her so tightly, pushing fear from her body, had made it impossible not to be grateful, not to appreciate his size and strength anew.

'Every couple of weeks.'

She lifted her brows. 'But you're based in the capital.'

'I learned as a young boy the importance of remaining visible and informed of each province. In the past, there have been sheikhs who were deemed to be out of touch. I do not want this to be said of me.'

'You are hero-worshipped by your people.'

His eyes found hers and she blushed to the roots of her hair.

'I am fortunately respected,' he agreed after a slight pause.

'As your father was.'

He dipped his head. 'He was an excellent ruler.'

'You've known all your life that this would be your responsibility one day. Have you always welcomed that?'

There was a hesitation in his features, a look of consternation she didn't understand and then his trademark arrogance was back. 'I was raised for it.'

She frowned. It wasn't quite an answer. She tried again. 'Was there ever a time when you found yourself wishing you had a sibling? Someone who could share the burden with you?'

'My parents couldn't have other children. They tried,' he

said, looking towards his window a moment. His Adam's apple bobbed, though, and she knew he was grappling with the confession. She could understand why.

'They tried for years before conceiving me, and then,' he hesitated a moment, 'my mother kept me out of the public eye for the first couple of years of my life. She told me, as a boy, that she hadn't wanted to tempt fate.'

'That's a very natural way to feel,' Eloise sympathised.

'My father was not the heir to the throne and his life then was simply not of much interest to the media or people of Savisia. He lived, more or less, freely.'

She considered that. Much was revealed by his description of his parents' lives. 'And then the Sheikh died in that fire?'

'Yes. My uncle and his wife died before they could have children and the throne passed to my father overnight. We returned to Savisia at once.'

'And ever since, you've known this would be your life.'

'Yes.'

'Did it change things for your father?'

His smile was laced with nostalgia. 'Of course. We went from living as a family to being royal, to having servants and an enormous palace. I could no longer attend school, but rather had long lessons with tutors. I hated being indoors so much. While I enjoyed learning, I always wished to be running, or climbing trees—'

'Or riding a horse,' she posited.

His eyes bore into hers. 'Exactly. Or sleeping under the stars.'

'You must have found a balance at some point in your childhood? After all, it sounds like you were given a fair amount of freedom.'

'I suppose. My father, perhaps because he never thought

he would become Sheikh, was determined for me to enjoy a relatively normal childhood. It had to be balanced with the responsibilities and duties of ruling, but I know I enjoyed more freedom than my uncle did, for example.'

'And your children?' she asked quietly, aware that the pain in the centre of her chest was motivated by the knowledge that his children would be of Elana's body. That Eloise would watch her best friend grow round with his seed, would watch Tariq fall in love with a baby he shared with Elana. She tried to ignore the ice-cold tendrils spreading through her veins, and the sense of disloyalty that made Eloise despise herself. 'How will you raise them?'

'I haven't considered it.'

'The main reason for getting married is to beget an heir, yes?'

'Yes.' His hands tightened into fists in his lap before relaxing again.

'So you must have put some thought into this.'

'Why?'

She frowned. 'Isn't it obvious?'

'I presume my wife will want some say in how our children are raised.'

'And if she says they must be sent away to boarding school almost as soon as they can walk?'

'Is that likely?'

Despite the ache in the centre of her chest, she smiled, a sweetly nostalgic smile. 'No. Ellie will be a wonderful and hands-on mother.'

'You've discussed this with her?'

Eloise nodded softly. 'Many times. She's always known she wanted to be a mother. Her own life—' She stopped abruptly, aware that she was speaking about her best friend, perhaps revealing things she would prefer to be kept secret.

'Go on,' he urged.

She searched for how to explain what she meant without revealing more of her friend's innermost thoughts. 'We're very similar,' she said eventually. 'Neither of us grew up with a brother or sister—I think it's why we're so close, that we both recognised that absence, and moved to fill it—and from almost as soon as I've known her, she's spoken openly of her desire to have children. I suppose it was always going to be an expectation on her. To marry, have children, to secure the lineage of her kingdom. When she got engaged before, there was such a sense of relief—for everyone. And then, he died, and it took Elana a long time to...' Her voice trailed off, and she took a breath, searching for the right words. 'She took it very hard. She loved him, a lot, and just learning to put one foot in front of the other again took months. It was at least a year before I saw her laugh again. And all the while, her government has been pressuring her to move on, to marry quickly, to have children. The idea of which has been, until recently, anathema to her.'

'But now?'

Eloise gnawed on her lower lip, then stopped when his eyes fell to the gesture, his own expression far too fascinated to be able to ignore. She straightened her spine and stared beyond him, to the palace they were approaching.

'Time has passed. It's helped. She's ready.'

He hesitated a moment. 'I'm glad. This marriage makes sense. For both of us.' His voice was dark though, the words tinged with heaviness.

The car turned towards two dark black, wrought-iron gates. They were heavily guarded. She watched as a soldier approached the car and then bowed low towards the darkly tinted windows.

'And what about you, little one?'

She startled at the use of the term, somehow so intimate and personal, here, on the footsteps of his grandiose royal home.

'What about me?' Her voice was thick, hoarse.

'Do you intend to marry and have children? To live happily ever after?'

'I think,' she said on a rushed breath. 'That "happily ever after" can take many shapes.'

'Yours doesn't include children of your own?'

She toyed with her fingers in her lap. 'I don't think so.'

'Why not?'

Up until a few days ago, she would have given her standard answer: that she liked being on her own. Inwardly, she would have admitted that she hated the idea of being part of a family, given what her experience of family was like. Seeing the way her father was with her mother had given her a unique prism through which to view promises of love. She was naturally suspicious of the whole idea. But then she'd met Tariq and a different kind of resistance had stitched its way into her soul. How could she ever think of marrying and having children with anyone else?

It terrified her to realise how completely he'd taken over her soul in such a short period of time. When had that happened? And why hadn't she stopped it? Because she couldn't? Because she hadn't realised it was happening until it was too late? It was immaterial. The damage was done and she'd have to live with the consequences.

'Eloise?'

She flinched a little, then forced a tight smile. 'It doesn't matter, does it?'

Because that was true. They needed to remember why she was there, and it certainly wasn't to discuss her own future plans. They were, in any event, in such disarray, she couldn't have elaborated on them for a million pounds.

'For some reason, it does. Humour me.'

The car drew to a halt but Tariq put down his window and, with a single hand gesture, stopped the four armed men from approaching the car. His place within the kingdom was formidable, but it wasn't simply a birthright. This man had a power that came from within, a way of speaking and being that spoke of true authority with every part of him.

'I've never been able to picture myself playing happy families.'

'Because your family was so far from that?'

Her eyes widened at his perceptive comment. Ordinarily, she might have obfuscated but with Tariq, a need to be completely honest drove through her. She nodded quickly, not meeting his eyes.

'Was he physical with her?'

She didn't look at him but nodded again.

His breath hissed from between his teeth.

'She was just as bad,' she muttered. 'It was an incredibly volatile relationship, swinging from over-the-top love one moment to deep, vitriolic rage and hatred the next. Some people might have, romantically, described it as "passionate", but it wasn't. It was madness. Utter, overpowering, lunatic behaviour. They should have ended it years earlier, but they were too addicted—to each other and the drama. Watching it from the sideline was hard enough, but then, more often than not, I was right in the middle of it.'

He reached out, pressing a finger to her chin, lifting her face to his, and the compassion she saw in his eyes made her want to weep.

'Please, don't look at me like that,' she asked, trying to rally her features into a mask of courage.

'How am I looking at you?'

'Like I might fall apart if you let go.'

His eyes shuttered closed for a few moments, his lips parting as he inhaled. 'That's not what I think.'

'No?'

'I think you are strong,' he said quietly, moving closer by degrees, so their mouths were only an inch apart. 'I think your life has made you strong, as mine has me. I think we share a lot, Eloise.'

It wasn't a declaration of love, and she couldn't have accepted that anyway, but his words sent her heart soaring into the stratosphere, and the smile that lifted the corner of her lips was genuine and immediate. She hated herself for feeling this way around him, but she couldn't stop it. All she could do was hold herself back from acting on it, and that she intended to do with every last fibre of her body.

She pulled away from him until her back was against the seat and her eyes were on the building beyond them, and when she could trust herself to speak, she said, 'What is this place?'

She wasn't sure if his rough expulsion of breath denoted frustration or something else, but she didn't look at him, and when he spoke, his voice was bland, all the emotion carefully flattened out of it. 'One of my palaces. My favourite, in fact. It's where I thought my family might live.'

That pulled at her. She whipped her face to his, lips parted. He'd brought her here to assess it for Elana. It was a relief, on some level, but also, a pain.

'When I finished school, I joined the army. I was stationed out of the city here. They were some of the best years of my life; I have an affinity with the east.'

A thousand questions blew through her. 'I remember reading that you'd served in the army,' she said quietly. It was one of the many things his people adored about him—his genuine love of service.

His lips flattened a little. With disapproval? 'I wish that you did not know so much about me.'

Her eyes widened. 'I didn't research you for the fun of it. My job demanded that I come to Savisia prepared.'

'I know. Of course. It's only—' She waited, watching him carefully. 'There are things about me that *I* would like to tell you. Because I like speaking with you, Eloise.'

Her heart trembled. Danger felt imminent. 'You can speak to me,' she said, trying desperately to keep her voice casual. 'That's also part of my job, remember? Now, why don't you show me this palace so I can tell you if Elana will like it.'

CHAPTER SEVEN

THERE WAS NOTHING about the palace *not* to like. While it was grand and beautiful and very old, it was also smaller than the palace in the capital city, and somehow felt more conducive to family living. There were gardens and swimming pools and the view of the city was quite stunning, so she could easily imagine the joy of living in such a home, of taking children out into the ancient city for ice cream and treats, to exploring the markets they'd driven past, with the enormous spice towers. Of course, it wouldn't be her experiencing any of that, but Eloise knew her best friend well enough to know that Elana would love living here as much as Eloise would have.

The day progressed, and Eloise, left to her own devices for much of it, felt a strange tiredness overtaking her. The heat, she imagined. She stifled a yawn and then, when half an hour later there was still no sign of Tariq, asked one of the women who'd been assigned to guide her if there was a sitting room she could use, to have some iced tea and take a break.

She was immediately shown to a delightful parlour with sumptuous furnishings and large windows with golden shutters that showed a view all the way into the city. She sat herself down and inhaled, spice and history filling her soul.

Sometime after enjoying a tray of refreshments, with Tariq still not in evidence, she kicked off her shoes then lifted her feet onto the sofa, and pressed her head to the armrest, intending only to close her eyes for a moment. Except her dreams had been so tormented of late, sleep such a difficult commodity to come by, that she fell into slumber, a dreamless, heavy repose, that lasted until the sun was low in the sky and the night birds began to sing.

Tariq found her fast asleep. He dismissed his servants immediately, stepping into the room and clicking the door shut silently, staring at her from across the room with a growing sense of unease in his gut.

Their situation was precarious and they both knew that.

Asleep like this though, it was easy to fantasise about waking her with a kiss, about pulling back the threads of her dreams with his body. His nostrils flared and he crossed his arms, needing to dismiss those thoughts. Too much was riding on his marriage to Elana to engage these fantasies.

She was just a woman, like any woman he'd met.

That wasn't true and he knew it, even as he forced the rhetoric down his throat. But she couldn't be more special to him than that. He had to marry Elana of Ras Sarat. He needed her royal bloodline to legitimise his right to rule Savisia. It was a pre-emptive strike against any future claim to the throne. And it was apparent that *any* claim would hold more merit than his own, despite the legal rights adoption conferred on him. Were he an ordinary citizen that would be credible, but belonging to the royal family was different. In a country like Savisia, which prided itself on its royal family's connection to the ancient bloodline of sheikhs, his presence would be an insult. He wasn't even born of Savisian parents! Were there a worthy contender to replace him, he would have relinquished the role he wasn't sure he deserved, but those who might seck power for themselves were hardly the sort who should possess it, and in this case, there was only a distant cousin, a man who was of questionable enough character for Tariq to know that abdicating wasn't the right option for the people of Savisia.

He had to do what was right. He owed his father that much, his mother too, and his people. He would continue to do his duty, to marry a princess, so that his own children would grow up free from this sense of illegitimacy.

Hardening his resolve, ignoring a burning need for Eloise that was overtaking him, he walked to the sofa and pressed a hand to her shoulder, intending only to wake her.

But she shifted, and his hand slipped, moving from her shoulder to the top of her breast, and he froze. His limb was no longer within his control. His fingers sat there, lightly against her flesh but feeling the gentle swell of her and almost igniting.

She blinked her eyes open, confused at first and then smiling, welcoming him with that look she had, so he ground his teeth, wanting her and knowing he couldn't have her, his body completely at war with his mind.

'Hello, Your Highness,' she murmured, and her voice was so lightly flirtatious, without the heaviness that accompanied them always, as both worked to deny their instincts, that he knew she'd forgotten all the reasons they couldn't act on these feelings. She'd been dreaming, perhaps even dreaming of him.

He was at a crossroads. Honour pulled him in one direction, clearly dictating that he should step back and speak firmly, but desire drew him in another, skittering all of his very best intentions… Curiosity pushed his finger higher, to the pulse point at the base of her neck. He held his fingers there a moment, eyes on hers, watching for a signal, no matter how small, that she didn't want him to touch her.

She blinked languidly and stretched a little. Was she fully awake? Or did she believe this too was a dream?

'How did you sleep?' Her pulse thundered beneath his touch.

'I was tired.' She stretched again and then, as his fingers trailed along her collarbone, towards the lower part of her neck, she startled and sat up, knocking his hand free in the motion, face pale.

He dropped his hand to his side, staring down at her, waiting for her to say something next.

'I didn't mean to sleep,' she said quietly, eyes fixed on the carpet at their feet. 'It's the heat, I think.'

'It's been a long day. My meetings were not as easily concluded as I thought. I hope you weren't bored?'

'Not at all.' They were being so polite; it infuriated him. She moved to stand, carefully keeping at least a metre of space between them. 'I've enjoyed touring the palace. It's beautiful.' She paused, eyes washing over him a moment then landing on the carpet again. 'Elana would love it here.'

He wanted to tell her Elana could go to hell, but the truth was, that wasn't the case. He needed this marriage to the Princess. Besides, he suspected Elana's best friend wouldn't exactly appreciate the sentiment, no matter how much they desired one another.

'Are you ready to leave?'

Her gaze lifted to his again. 'Already?' She squeezed her eyes shut, as if regretting the word.

He understood her sentiment, and an idea he'd already dismissed as ill-conceived latched in his mind, demanding his indulgence. 'Not back to the palace,' he said quietly. 'There's something else I'd like to show you first.'

There was wariness in her features. 'For Elana?'

He dipped his head once, when the truth was, this was

his own personal place, somewhere he wanted to show El-oise, because he wanted *her* to see it. This was nothing to do with the Princess he knew he had to marry.

'Okay,' she agreed softly. He fought an urge to reach for her hand and hold her close to his side as he guided her from the room.

'Are you sure you know where you're going?' It was the first either of them had spoken in over an hour. The streets of the city had given way to rural stretches of road and then, finally, to mountains narrow roads barely illuminated by the dusk light, but sufficiently enough that she could see an increasingly steep drop out of her window, with thick veg-etation on his. Tariq drove these roads as though he knew them well, and just the sight of him behind the powerful car, was doing funny things to her pulse. Behind them, an-other car followed—a four-wheel drive packed with four security guards.

'They establish a perimeter when I'm in the woods,' he'd said carelessly, as they'd set off from the palace, and she'd tried to tamp down on the idea of this rugged mountain of a man out in nature.

'Do you seriously doubt me?'

She found herself grinning despite the tension that had been coiling in her belly since that afternoon. 'We seem to be in the middle of nowhere is all.'

'Not quite.'

'Nearly the middle of nowhere?'

'About ten clicks west of it.'

She lifted her brows. 'It will be dark soon.'

'That tends to happen at night.'

Her lips parted. 'Tariq…'

'Relax. We're not staying out here.'

She expelled a shaky breath. It wasn't that she hated the idea…quite the opposite. But she knew they had to get back to reality, sooner rather than later. Even if that meant taking another ride on his private jet.

He continued to drive, navigating the turns in the road expertly, leaving Eloise free to look over the edge into the ravine below, or to chase the golden orb of the sun as it continued to drop low and finally disappear into the horizon. At some point, the four-wheel drive that had been following them, peeled off, presumably to establish the perimeter he'd mentioned.

'I like privacy,' he explained, as if somehow intuiting her thoughts.

'Where will they be?'

'They set up a checkpoint on this road—the only way to reach the cabin.'

She nodded slowly, her heart in her throat.

When he brought the car to a stop, half an hour later, the sky was still glowing with the last hints of purple and gold, the clouds silver-fringed pewter. She looked around, her gaze landing on a cabin made of stone in the middle of a dense woodlands.

'What is this place?' she murmured, craning forward to see it better.

'Somewhere I like to come when I want to get away.'

She turned in her seat to face him fully. 'This is yours?'

'All this land belongs to the palace,' he said, gesturing to the mountains they were on.

She let out a low whistle. 'And your guards, how close are they?'

His eyes locked to hers for a moment too long and her stomach tightened into knots. 'Close enough.'

'As in…?'

'You don't have to worry, Eloise. I gave you my word I wouldn't touch you, and I won't. I just wanted to show you this place.'

She shivered, but it was not a shiver of fear so much as anticipation. She ignored it, her eyes roaming the cottage with undisguised curiosity. 'Okay.'

'Come on.'

He stepped out of the car and a moment later was at her door, opening it before she could, holding it for her to step out. Her heart skidded into her ribs. 'Thank you,' she murmured, careful to step around him, careful that they didn't touch. It didn't matter though. The air between them seemed filled with electrical pulses, so whether she touched him or not, she was conscious of a zapping just beneath her skin.

He gestured towards the cabin and she walked beside him, several feet away—still getting used to the idea of being completely alone with him. There was a crude path, paved with gravel; he left it for her to walk on. They approached the cabin and he lifted a hand, running it over the stone. 'My father and I built this, many summers ago.'

She was filled with awe. 'Really?'

'He believed we were men first, sheikhs second. The royal life threatens to disconnect one from reality; he wanted to avoid that.'

She echoed his movement, tracing the building with her palm, feeling the roughness of the materials and shivering as she pictured Tariq in the act of constructing it, laying stone by stone until the work was completed. 'You must have been very proud of yourself.'

'There was a great sense of achievement.'

'Why did you choose to build it here?'

'This was one of my father's favourite places, before it was mine.'

'You'd come out here together?'

He nodded once.

'And you still like to escape here, whenever you can,' she murmured, as he went to the door and moved something aside to reveal a pin code. He entered a succession of six digits and the door clicked open.

'Yes.' He stood back to allow her to enter first, then flicked on a light switch. She stepped into the cabin, looking around and smiling, because it was basic but also, absolutely charming. The layout was simple enough: a living area with a kitchen, wooden table and chairs and a single sofa. Two doors came off the space, both were open. One revealed a double bed, the other a bathroom.

'Very rustic,' she said, flicking a quick glance at him.

'It's for camping,' he said with a shrug. 'And hunting.'

'Hunting?'

'A national pastime.'

She shivered.

'Not to your liking?'

'Not particularly,' she said, pulling her lips to the side. 'I've never been a fan of the idea.'

He moved closer almost unconsciously. 'Then you don't have to hunt.'

'I'm glad. I'd hate to think there was some royal decree demanding I take arms against innocent animals.'

'Not on this occasion,' he responded in kind, lightly teasing. Goosebumps lifted over her skin.

It was too easy to flirt with him, to tease him, to joke with him. Too easy to slip into a conversational groove. She had to keep things focused on Elana. That was the reason she was here.

'Her Highness is an avid outdoors person,' she said after a beat, and she knew she wasn't imagining the way his eyes darkened.

'Is she?'

'She's the only reason I was able to survive the school camp experience, in fact.'

'You didn't enjoy it?'

She shook her head quickly.

'You said it was dormitories, though? That's not exactly roughing it.'

She hesitated a moment, the truth something she'd only ever told Elana. And yet, here, with this man, she felt it slipping through her like a river she couldn't dam, no matter how hard she tried. Slowly, she moved towards the kitchen, simply to have something to do with her hands.

'When I was younger, and my parents would fight, my mother would lock me in a closet. Ostensibly, it was to protect me. I don't know, maybe she thought sound couldn't travel through the flimsy walls,' she muttered, so caught up in her admission that she didn't see the way his body had grown tense. 'I hated it. I was scared of the dark. Scared of their fighting. Even more scared of the silence that followed. Sometimes she would forget me—'

He swore, and she looked at him, pain in her eyes.

'I'd be too scared to bang on the walls, in case they got angry with me, so I'd sit there and wait.'

He moved closer and it didn't occur to her to mind.

'I've hated small rooms ever since. Any enclosed spaces, in fact.'

'Airplanes?' he prompted gently.

'I think that's more about a loss of control,' she said with a lift of her shoulders. 'I get…anxious…when I have to rely on others.'

His eyes narrowed perceptively.

'I saw a therapist for a while, but it didn't help. I find I just avoid cramped rooms as much as possible, and I'm okay.'

'How's this?' He gestured to the cabin surrounding them.

'Actually,' she frowned, 'it's not so bad. It's bigger than the camp dorms,' she said with a tight smile.

'I'm glad. I wanted you to see it.'

Her heart tripped over itself. It wasn't the first time he'd said it, but she didn't for one second think he meant he wanted her to see it as Elana's advisor. This was personal. 'Why?'

His expression was hard to read. 'I don't know,' he admitted, finally. 'But it felt important.'

She toyed with her fingers. It felt important to her, too.

'Are you hungry?'

She looked around the kitchen. 'Why? Are you hiding some gourmet snacks in here somewhere?'

'Not quite gourmet.' He grinned. 'But the freezer should have something, and the stove works.'

It was, oh, so very tempting, but the idea of staying with him for dinner was fraught with possibilities, and danger.

'I think we should go back,' she said, without meeting his eyes.

'Is that what you want?'

Frustration bubbled over inside her chest. Frustration at the way he was pushing her, tempting her, deliberately showing her a place like this that meant so much to him, even when they knew how close they were moving to an invisible line they couldn't step over.

'Damn it, this isn't about what I *want*, Your Highness.'

A muscle clenched at the base of his jaw. 'You need to call me Tariq.'

'You are the Sheikh of Savisia—'

'I'm aware of that.' He crossed his arms over his broad chest and a thousand sparks ignited in her bloodstream. 'But when I am alone with you, I am simply a man.'

She stared at him, angry and frustrated and lost. How could she argue with that? When they were together, that's exactly how it felt to her, too. There was no longer a question of rank between them, they were simply a man and a woman with the kind of chemistry that was rare and unique.

'Tariq,' she said on a soft sigh, lifting a hand and tucking her hair behind her ear. His eyes latched to hers and the world seemed to stop spinning. Everything grew very still, and despite the fact she knew his guards were out there, somewhere, she felt as though they were the last two people on the planet.

'Let's stay here for dinner,' he said gruffly.

Oh, she wanted that. Here, on the edge of the earth, where nothing else seemed to matter. 'We shouldn't.'

His eyes sparked. 'Why not?'

She bit down on her lower lip. 'You know the answer to that.'

'I'm asking you to join me for dinner, not a night in my bed.'

Her cheeks flushed red, heat overwhelming her body as the idea of that sent her senses into overdrive.

'I—' Her heart was in her throat, her breath constricted as she tried to form two coherent thoughts, to put into her words how she felt and what she wanted. In the end, all she could do was nod.

'Good.' His answering nod of approval skittered her nerves further and a moment later, he was stepping into the kitchen, so close to her that Eloise's tummy twisted into a tangle she'd never felt before. He turned his back, giving her an opportunity to relax, and also to regard him. The two were incompatible; she settled on staring.

He moved with a natural athleticism; a lithe strength contained in even the simplest of movements. He pulled a container from the freezer, placing it on the bench, then crouched down to remove a pan from the cupboard. She watched, fascinated, as he opened the Tupperware then emptied it into the pot, placing it on the stove. A moment later, he turned to face her, his expression lightly amused, as though he recognised she'd been staring at him completely unreservedly.

Chastened, she stood straighter, a defensive tilt to her chin.

'Will you be offended if I remove my thobe?'

She furrowed her brow.

'It's easier to cook,' he explained, and when she didn't immediately refuse, he turned his back and carefully undid the button that held it in place, unwrapping it from his body and laying it with care across the back of a chair.

Her mouth went dry. It wasn't as though he'd stripped naked—he wore traditional cuffed trousers and a loose-fitting cotton shirt—but there was something so intimate about him undressing in front of her, even if just down to clothes. She looked away quickly, cheeks heated.

'How old were you when your parents died?'

It was a direct question, asked as if he had a right to the information, and strangely, she didn't resent that.

'Eleven.'

He nodded thoughtfully, moving to the fridge and removing a bottle of mineral water. 'How did it happen?'

Another direct question. She focused on the deft movements of his hands, shucking the lid off the bottle, then pouring it into two thick glasses.

'A car accident.' His hand shifted, slightly, so the top of the bottle knocked a glass. It was a strange, jarring movement from a man who was in such possession of himself. 'They'd been at a party.'

'You weren't with them?' His voice sounded normal, though. Nothing untoward. She frowned, remembering that night with a heavy heart, as always.

'No. They left me home.'

'Alone?'

She lifted her shoulders. 'I liked to be home alone.'

Sympathy softened the corners of his eyes. She blinked away, self-conscious.

'I read a lot,' she elaborated.

'Because it helped you escape?'

'Exactly.' Her heart expanded with how quickly he'd understood. Their eyes met and the world seemed to contract and expand rapidly, so she wondered how everyone didn't feel the gigantic fault lines forming. 'Somewhere in the early hours of the morning, a policeman came to the house. My mother had survived long enough to tell them about me.'

'How did you feel?'

She took a gulp of mineral water. 'My parents had just died. How do you think I felt?'

'Conflicted,' he responded, without missing a beat. Her lips parted in surprise.

It was like he had a direct tunnel into her thoughts.

'I was devastated. I loved my parents very much,' she insisted defensively, cupping the glass with both hands. 'But yes,' she admitted slowly, reluctantly, and yet, also gladly, because she'd never spoken to another soul about this— even Elana. It was impossible to admit without feeling that it made her a terrible person, and yet with Tariq, that didn't seem important.

'For a moment, I was relieved. Their fighting was so awful, Tariq.' Her eyes swept closed. 'So soul-destroying. For a brief moment, when I realised it would stop, that I would no longer have to live with it, I felt…at peace.' She winced. 'I know that's awful.'

He reached over, pressing his hand to hers. It was a gesture of comfort, and it did comfort her. She felt warm, and complete. 'Life is complicated.' His voice was deep. 'Love even more so.'

'I thought you'd never been in love?' she prompted, the words catching in her throat.

'Romantic love,' he said with a shrug, not removing his hand from hers. 'But I have parents. I know that things are not always simple.'

'In what way?'

His features tightened but his eyes were kind. Her heart was mush. 'Relationship dynamics, expectations. Children have to live with the consequences of their parents' decisions. It's not always easy.'

'Why do I feel like there's something you're not telling me?'

His grin was dismissive, but a sixth sense, an innate understanding of this man, told her he was hiding something from her. She hated that. She wanted to peer deep into his soul and see all of his secret recesses as she knew he could hers. 'Because I am the Sheikh of Savisia: there are a great many state secrets I must take to the grave with me.'

She expelled a soft sigh, letting him get away with it. 'Is what we're eating one of those things?'

His smile deepened and now her heart skipped so many beats she wondered if it had stopped working. 'Be patient; soon, you'll see.'

CHAPTER EIGHT

SHE SLEPT SOUNDLY at his side, so beautifully peaceful that he found his eyes straying to her far more times than was wise, given he was navigating the tight corners of the mountain roads and it was almost pitch black.

He hadn't intended for them to stay at the cabin so long. Hell, he hadn't *intended* for any of it to happen. Bringing her here had been a spur of the moment decision, a desire to share something with her that had made no logical sense. Whatever form his marriage took, he wasn't foreseeing a relationship in which he brought his bride out here. This was *his* space. His bolt hole, and haven.

So why Eloise? Why now?

A loud noise demanded his attention and he immediately pressed his foot to the brake, assessing the situation, all senses on alert. Ears heard the rumble, eyes registered the dust first, plumes silhouetted against the night sky, the falling trees next, and then the smell of clay, finally, the rumble of their car. He swore harshly, loud enough to wake her, so she sat bolt upright.

'What is it?'

'An earthquake,' he said with confidence—they were not uncommon in this region, though not usually of this magnitude. 'And a landslide.'

A tree fell, right in front of them, blocking their path.

Eloise's breath was loud, but she sat perfectly still, her

eyes staring through the windscreen, as though her powers of concentration could somehow supercharge his to ensure their safe departure.

'It's blocked the road. We'll have to go back to the cabin,' he added, without looking at Eloise.

'Oh.' A tiny sound in the void of the car.

He heard it, and he understood.

They'd both been very careful to skirt around their attraction, but the cabin was quicksand. He closed his window, staring straight ahead while waiting for his heart to stop racing so hard.

'It will be all right,' he assured her, and the statement was a blanket reassurance, covering their present state of emergency, as well as the future possibility of carelessness. It was also a promise to himself, one he badly needed.

His fingers tightened on the wheel and he undertook a five-point turn, so he could drive forward and reach the cabin as quickly as was possible.

It looked different now. Ridiculous, given they'd only left here an hour or so earlier. But that had been after a quick bite to eat, polite conversation about the state of politics in the region—a conversation in which she'd been pleased to more than hold her own, to show her knowledge of the various issues facing both Ras Sarat and Savisia. After all, she advised Elana on a plethora of subjects. As the evening had progressed, she'd felt his attention narrowing, his questions growing more specific, as though he was testing her. But to what end?

'Go inside,' he said. 'I will just call my guards and inform them of our situation.'

'Maybe they'll send someone tonight,' she said, hopefully.

'I will make sure they don't,' he responded quickly. 'It

would imperil their lives, and I do not subscribe to the ridiculous notion that my life holds more value than any of theirs. First light will have to do.'

She turned back to the cabin, butterflies exploded in her belly.

He stalked to the door and pressed in his code again, pushing the thing open. 'I'll only be a moment.'

She nodded, excitement and anxiety at war within her. Stepping into the cabin, she reached for the light switch, flicked it, then frowned when it didn't do anything. She flicked it again.

'Uh-oh.' She pulled her phone from her pocket, turning on the torch function, moving into the kitchen and rooting around for candles and matches. She presumed both would be available, given there was a fireplace in the corner. In the third drawer down, she found what she was looking for, and busied herself arranging candlesticks in glasses, bunching them together.

The result, a few minutes later, was more light, but far, far too much ambience. Her veins felt sticky. He stepped into the cabin, and even in the dim light of the candles, she saw the look on his face as he scanned the room.

'The lights aren't working.'

He moved to the switch and tried it himself. Nothing.

'The generator should still be powering things. I'll go and inspect it.'

He departed quickly, evidently as keen to avoid a night in a candlelit cabin with her, as she was him. She paced the floor as she waited, listening to the sound of the night now—birds, the breeze in the trees, and nothing else. It was so quiet up here. So peaceful.

She stopped walking and closed her eyes, inhaling deeply. It was easy to understand why he and his father would come here.

'It's fried,' he said with a shake of his head, striding back into the cabin.

'Fried?'

'A casualty of the earthquake. It will have to wait until tomorrow.'

'Candles it is then,' she said, aiming for a lighthearted tone and failing.

He looked around, and she almost laughed, because for the first time since meeting him, he looked lost.

She understood.

They were fighting this thing so hard, and yet here they were, stranded in a beautiful cabin on the edge of the world, as stripped away from the concerns of royalty and nationhood as it was possible to be. But none of it was real—their isolation was just an illusion. In the morning, he'd still be the Sheikh of Savisia, destined to marry her best friend.

She crossed her arms over her torso and moved to the sofa, weaving around him carefully, sitting right on the edge.

'I'll check the bed,' he said stiffly. She heard the tone of his voice and understood. He was holding on to his control carefully, but it was taking effort.

This was insufferable.

'What for?'

'So you can sleep in it.'

She furrowed her brow. 'You can't be meaning to sleep on this?' she said, her hand slicing through the air. 'It's far too small.'

'I'll sleep on the floor.'

'You'll do no such thing,' she responded with a shake of her head. 'I'll take the sofa; you have the bed.'

'Absolutely not.'

'Why? It's logical.'

'You are a woman and the bed is more comfortable. Naturally you should sleep there.'

She didn't know how to tell him she wouldn't be doing much sleeping, knowing he was within a couple of metres of her. 'That's ridiculously old-fashioned. I'm fine with the sofa.'

'But I'm not.'

'Yeah, well, what are you going to do about it?'

'Need I remind you I'm the Sheikh of Savisia?'

'Believe me, I'm well aware of that.'

The air crackled between them.

'I'm not going to have this argument with you,' he said, all regal hauteur.

'Good. We don't need to argue.' To emphasise her point, she snuggled down on the sofa. It was small enough that her legs were bent up, but she closed her eyes and pretended contentment.

The swishing of his thobes told of his departure, and she celebrated the micro-victory, until a moment later he returned. 'The bed's fine. No spiders. You can go in there now.'

She sat up, staring at him and then she burst out laughing. 'This is ridiculous,' she said with a shake of her head, and then, he was laughing too, hands on his hips, eyes resting on her face. 'I'm not even tired right now.'

'You were asleep in the car.'

'What can I tell you? I guess an earthquake and a landslide shake you right back awake.'

'A fair point.'

She looked around the cabin. 'Do you have anything to do here?'

He lifted a brow. 'Perhaps you should be more specific.'

'A board game? Cards?' she rushed to clarify.

He moved to a small bookshelf and withdrew a silver

box, carrying it towards her. He hesitated, gesturing to the other side of the sofa. 'May I?'

Her heart in her throat, she nodded. It was, after all, his cabin.

As soon as he sat down, she felt the error of her decision. They were so close. The sofa wasn't large enough for them to sit side by side without touching. She went to move, to jerk to stand, but his hand on her knee stilled her.

'It's okay,' he said, gruffly. His smile was slow. Gentle. 'It's just cards.'

It didn't feel like 'just cards'. Not then, and not when he began to speak slowly, his accent heavy, recounting the rules of the game his father had taught him—the subtle gathering of houses to form a suite—patiently explaining for the first few hands then setting about ruthlessly demolishing her until she learned enough lessons to hold her own.

It didn't feel like 'just cards' as they laughed in unison at a poor twist of fortune, nor when he commended her for beating him, his eyes glowing with something suspiciously like pride.

It felt like *so much more*.

'I…' The word hung between them. She pulled back a little. 'I should go to bed.'

'You're tired now?'

'Not really,' she responded. 'But I should go to bed anyway.' If she stayed there any longer, she wasn't sure what would happen. His promise that everything would be fine felt as shaky as the earth outside the cabin.

'If you wish.' He stood, his ingrained manners fluttering something in the region of her heart. 'There are spare toothbrushes in the bottom drawer of the bathroom. Soap in the shower. Make yourself at home.'

She nodded without a word. She didn't trust her voice to speak.

There was no hot water so she shunned the idea of a shower, but she brushed her teeth gratefully, then stared at her reflection in the simple mirror above the sink. Slowly, she pulled her hair from its neat chignon, letting it fall down her back. She splashed her face with water then towelled it dry, aware she looked younger without the light make-up she habitually wore. There wasn't much she could do about her clothes—she didn't dare remove a single item—but when she stepped out, it was to find Tariq hadn't shared her reservations. He'd stripped down to his cuffed pants. His torso was bare, the pants slung low on his waist.

The breath exploded from her lungs and she could only stand there and stare at him, everything inside of her burning at fever pitch.

'I've put a spare tunic of mine on the bed, in case you'd prefer to sleep in it.'

Her lips were parted and refused to come back together. Her eyes wouldn't cooperate. They feasted on him even when she knew she needed to look away.

He made no effort to conceal himself, but rather, submitted to her inspection, standing like a very desirable statue. Something tilted inside of her.

'You have to understand,' she said, quickly, even when he hadn't asked. 'That Elana is very special to me. I don't have any family, but I have her, and I would never do anything to hurt her. Ever. I would never betray her.'

He stood very still. 'Am I asking you to?'

Her brow furrowed and then, gradually, her gaze lifted higher, so their eyes met. 'If I asked you to kiss me, would you?'

His eyes flared and heat simmered between them.

'I can't ask you to. That's my point.'

'I am not engaged to her, you know.'

'But you intend to be.'

He dipped his head. 'Perhaps.'

Her heart raced with a shameful degree of hope and she despised herself for that.

'But that is in the future. We're here, now.'

She shook her head. 'You know that's just a technicality.'

'Then answer me this,' he said quietly. 'If our wedding plans become official, the date will be set some months in the future, at least. Six months, let us say? To allow everyone time to organise the essentials. Do you think I will stay here, celibate and alone for half a year or more?'

She gasped, his words far more hurtful than surely he intended.

'You said you'd be faithful to her.'

'And from the moment I say my vows, I will be. Until then, I consider myself a free agent.'

'Well, I don't,' she muttered. 'And even if I thought that of you, I'm not…not free to do anything with you, I mean. So if you want to "free agent" yourself around town, you just have to get through tonight and then you can go and find someone else to take to bed tomorrow night. Okay?'

'I don't want someone else. I want you.'

The bold statement hung between them. A moment later, he dragged a hand through his hair and she felt her heart lurch crazily.

'I want you.' The words were said with even more determination. 'I wish I didn't. I hate that I do. I have tried to fight it, to control it, to ignore it, but it's here, inside of me.' He pressed a hand to his chest. 'I don't know what you did to me. Some form of voodoo or magic. I can't get you out of my head. You are in my thoughts, my dreams, my mind, all the time. I want to be with you, Eloise.'

These were words she desperately wanted to hear, but they were also words that pulled her apart, so she took a step backwards, searching for her indignation.

'You want to be with me because you're a free agent,' she said with a shake of her head. 'But you don't care about me. You don't care about the bomb you'd be throwing into my life. How could I look at Elana again? How could I advise her to marry you? And if I did, and she became your wife, how could my friendship with her endure? Can't you see what you're asking me to do? To betray? To give up?'

'But what would you get in return?'

'What are you offering?' she spat angrily, waving a hand through the air. 'A night with you? Two? A secret, shameful affair that neither of us could ever speak of? And for that, you'd expect me to betray my dearest friend?'

He made a dark sound of irritation. 'I'm asking you—' He shook his head. 'This isn't going away,' he said firmly. 'I thought spending time together would help. It hasn't. The more I see of you, the more I need. I am on fire, little one, and only you can help me.'

She wanted to absorb the words. To allow them to soak in and become a part of her, but she was terrified of the consequences, terrified of the fissures that would form in her world.

'You're a free agent,' she said with a shake of her head. 'Choose someone else.'

'You're being deliberately argumentative now.'

'I'm arguing with you, yes, but not because I want to. Because what you're suggesting is so preposterous, so wrong...'

He closed the space between them, his hands capturing

her upper arms, bringing her to him, so their bodies melded and their faces were just inches apart. 'Does this feel preposterous and wrong, *habibi*?'

Her legs trembled with enough intensity to make standing difficult.

'Do you want me to let you go?'

Say yes. Tell him to stop.

'Tariq,' she groaned, because it felt *so* good to be held by him, so good to be this close. Her heart was rabbiting in her chest, threatening to pull her apart. 'I can't do this.'

His nostrils flared and his jaw remained clenched. Despite what she'd said, she moved slightly, her body soft against his hardness, needing to feel every inch of him, then shivering when she succeeded. His arousal was unmistakable, and it called to her, so she bit back a sob.

'I know,' he said, finally, dropping his head so their foreheads were touching and breath mingling. 'And that makes me want you all the more.'

She closed her eyes, inhaling his intoxicatingly masculine fragrance, before he dropped his hands and stepped back.

'Go to bed, little one. I will not disturb you. You have my word.'

It wasn't just the noise that broke her sleep, but the immediate recollection of Tariq saying that he and his father would come to the mountains to hunt. The question occurred to her far too late: to hunt what?

The sound outside the window of her bedroom was unmistakable though. An animal. Large enough to crack tree limbs.

She sat bolt upright, staring at the window first, and then towards the door, heart in her throat as she threw back the covers. She had no thought for her state of dress—she wore only the tunic Tariq had provided, but it was swimming on her smaller frame, so kept falling down one shoulder, revealing an expanse of creamy skin, her arm and the top of her breast. She rushed to the door and pulled it open.

Tariq was awake, moving towards the window of the kitchen.

'What is it?' she whispered, eyes huge in her face.

He cast a glance over his shoulder then turned back to the window. He concentrated on the darkness beyond the cabin and then signalled for her to join him. Belatedly, she recognised the gun at his side, a rifle, and she wondered how the sight of something she actively despised could somehow seem so distractingly erotic when paired with a man like Tariq.

'Come and see.'

Her fear had evaporated at the sight of the Sheikh. Not because of the gun, because he looked like someone who could tackle a bear, or a tiger, or whatever the heck was outside with his bare hands.

She looked through the window, beyond their reflections. Only one candle was lit, but it was enough to cast a distracting amount of light. 'Do you mind if I blow this out?' she asked, leaning closer to him.

He lifted the candle and extinguished it, plunging them into darkness. With that, came a rush of awareness of all of her other senses. She could *feel* his blood pumping. She could hear it. His breath was like a marching band. She tilted her face towards him, and even though it was now almost pitch-black in the cabin, she could *see* him as clearly as if the sun was right in the middle of the room.

'Look,' he said, but his voice had changed, gone lower, deeper, his tone gruff. 'Out there.' He moved behind her, lifting a hand to guide her attention, but now all she could focus on was the feeling of his body wrapped around hers. It was mesmerising and perfect.

She tried to control her breathing, but everything was rushing out of her, tumbling with panic and excitement and raw, undeniable need.

'What am I looking for?' she whispered.

'Over there.' He bent his head down to her level, so it pressed to her shoulder, and now she forced herself to concentrate, to look where he was looking, until she saw something shining in the clearing just beyond the car. Two gemstones, at hip height.

'Eyes!' She said, gasping.

'Tiger's eyes,' he said quietly.

'A real tiger? Here?'

He nodded, the gesture moving his face closer, so their cheeks brushed, and she closed her eyes a moment, savouring the feeling.

'An Arabian tiger. They're endangered in these parts. We use these mountains as a sanctuary, a breeding ground for them.'

'So there are lots here?'

'Not as many as there should be, but the population is growing year on year.'

'And you didn't think to warn me?'

'What for? You were never in danger.'

She shivered. 'Says the man with the gun.'

'He can't come into the cabin,' Tariq pointed out. 'You're perfectly safe.'

'And if he's still there in the morning?'

'He won't be.'

'You sound way more confident than I would be.'

'It's not my first night in the cabin.'

She turned a little, but it was a mistake, because their

faces were so close, and this brought them closer. It almost brushed their lips together. She sprung back a little, jabbing her hip on the kitchen bench in the process. 'Did the tiger wake you?'

'I wasn't asleep.'

'It's two in the morning.' She'd checked the time before scrambling into the lounge room.

'I wasn't tired.'

Eloise tried not to read into that statement. She tried not to hope he might have been thinking about her.

'And now I'm wide awake.'

They stared at each other across the small space between them. Every breath was painful. Every moment she resisted him was an agony.

A moment later, there was a familiar sound—the striking of a match—and the candle was relit. His eyes lifted to hers, boring into her, his face set in tense lines as he studied her as if looking for an answer.

She stared back, confounded and confused.

He stepped forward, and she held her breath. He reached out, slowly, eyes on hers, until his fingers connected with her bare shoulder, then ran lower, catching the fabric of the caftan and pulling it higher, back into place. She swallowed past a lump in her throat.

'It's too big,' she explained unnecessarily.

He dipped his head, agreeing, but also, moving closer. 'Just a little.'

The thing swum on her.

'If you were not working for Elana, what would you be doing?'

'I don't know,' she whispered, wondering why the question hurt so badly.

'There must have been something you wanted to do, before coming to Ras Sarat.'

She contemplated that. 'As a child, I wanted to be a dancer.'

'You are very graceful.'

She smiled softly. 'I loved it. I would dance for hours and hours. I think it was a form of escapism. My ballet teacher used to let me stay and help her, even after my lesson had finished. Mum and Dad frequently forgot to pick me up anyway, so Miss Melanie would drop me home afterwards. I could dance for hours and hours and never get tired of it.'

'You didn't pursue it professionally?'

'It's not an easy job to get,' she pointed out. 'But in any event, once my parents died, my great aunt raised me, and she didn't approve.'

'Of dancing *or* horses? The philistine,' he said lightly, but his body was so close, and she saw the disapproval on his face. He was trying to make her feel better, but he was angry.

'I know. What a neglected childhood.'

He lifted a hand to her shoulder again, touching her through the fabric of the caftan, a frown on his face. 'You should have been able to keep dancing.'

'I did dance. In my room, when no one was looking.'

'I would like to see.'

Her throat felt strangled. 'I don't dance anymore.'

'Why not?'

'I grew up.'

'You deserve to dance.'

She shook her head and emotions bundled through her, making her eyes sting with salty tears. 'Don't, Tariq.'

'Don't what? Tell you the truth?'

'It's *not* the truth. Those were childish dreams. I grew

out of them. I studied law and economics. I graduated with honours. I moved on. This is my life now.'

His hand dropped to her waist, holding her there, and she couldn't help but contemplate how *right* his touch felt. How perfect and simple and true.

'Working for the Crown Princess of Ras Sarat, advising her, strategising her marriage. These are noble pursuits, but what of your life and dreams?'

'Why can't this be my dream?'

'Because you're more than this.'

'Don't. Don't belittle who I am and what I do. I like my life.' She lifted her shoulders and the caftan slipped down again, revealing her creamy skin.

He was quiet a moment and then, slowly, oh, so slowly, he dropped his head. 'I'm glad.' His lips brushed her bare skin and she felt as though she'd been electrocuted. A thousand blades of lightning flashed inside her veins. She lifted a hand and clutched his shirt, holding on for dear life.

'For some reason I cannot explain, your happiness has come to mean a lot to me. I like to think of you having everything you want in life.'

She couldn't tell him, she didn't dare, that she would *never* have everything she wanted in life. She couldn't. Her best friend would marry the man she'd fallen head over heels in love with, and there was nothing Eloise could do about that.

CHAPTER NINE

WHEN EVENTUALLY TARIQ fell asleep, he had the nightmare. The same nightmare that had tormented him for years. He was drowning, unable to draw breath, but this time it was worse, because he'd now seen Eloise in the distance, and she was struggling to breathe as well. She was drowning, just out of his reach, and no matter how hard he kicked through the water, he couldn't get to her. His lungs were burning with the effort, and his legs might as well have been weighted with cement, for all the use they were to him.

He swam harder, but the water churned, and then, she disappeared, so he ducked beneath the surface, reaching for her, looking for her, aching for her; she was nowhere.

He woke in a cold sweat, looking around disorientated and confused, until the events of the prior evening came rushing back to him: the landslide, their being trapped here, playing cards, his desire to kiss her, the boundaries she kept erecting, that he was forced to respect. The tiger, her shoulder, the feel of her flesh beneath his mouth, her responsive body curving towards his, her trembles and shivers, her warmth and softness.

How forbidden she was to him when all he wanted was to make her his, utterly and completely.

Would that cure his fixation?

Even as he thought that, he dismissed it. This wasn't just lust. It wasn't just desire. There was that, too, but he was

CLARE CONNELLY 135

fascinated by *her*. By everything about her. The childhood she described so carefully, omitting, he was sure, the worst details. Her school life, her professional choices, her hopes and dreams. He could listen to her talk all day, and yet, even that felt like a betrayal.

He could live with that.

He could sin and then spend a lifetime paying penance, if that was what was needed, but he had seen the angst in her face, when she'd pleaded with him to understand that she could not betray her friend in that manner. He couldn't ask her to weaken, no matter how spectacular it would be.

If he cared about Eloise at all, he had to protect her from those feelings. He had to be strong even in the face of the biggest temptation he'd ever faced. He had to control this.

And he would. First and foremost, he was Sheikh Tariq al Hassan, exalted leader of Savisia; he could control anything. This would be no different.

She had dressed carefully before leaving the bedroom, neatly folding the caftan and replacing it on the bed. Memories of the way he'd kissed her shoulder had haunted her dreams; the skin still tickled there.

She needed the armour of her own clothes.

Her hair she'd pulled into a loose ponytail, and on her feet, she wore a pair of dark socks of Tariq's. He was awake when she emerged, and the kitchen smelled like coffee and pastry.

'Good morning.' He too was dressed, the thobe he'd carefully removed and stored the night before wrapped around his body, but it didn't matter. Last night, she'd seen him without a shirt, and that imagery would be with her always.

He lifted his gaze to her and offered a tight smile. 'There's coffee in the pot by the stove, and pistachio buns too. My security detail will arrive in around ten minutes.'

Disappointment was like a rock, dropping to her toes. 'Ten minutes?' She fairly groaned the words and had to force herself to take a breath and calm her fluttering nerves. 'I'm surprised they were able to clear the road so quickly.'

'Apparently, the idea of their Sheikh being stranded in a cabin is a powerful motivator.'

Something occurred to her, something unpleasant and tricky to bring up. 'Tariq, when they arrive and see me here, won't they think—'

'No.' The word was uttered with confidence. 'They know I am a man of honour. No one will think anything.'

Her smile was ambivalent. 'And yet, it could have.'

'It didn't. Neither of us would have let it.'

Her eyes held his and then she looked away, not wanting to admit how close she'd come to creeping out again, to crouching beside the sofa and asking him, begging him, to kiss her.

'But what if they think—'

'They will think nothing,' he said more firmly. 'And even if they were to think it, they would certainly not say it. My security guard is made up of experienced servicemen. Their discretion is expected.'

She pulled her lips to the side, hoping he was right. She didn't want Elana to hear of anything like this. It would be too hard to explain, and the last thing she wanted was to hurt her friend.

'Are we going back to the capital today?'

'I am. My flight will leave as soon as I get to the airport. Someone from my guard will drive you across country. It should take most of the day.'

She stared at him, her heart strangling in pain. 'I see.'

'I presume this is what you'd prefer?'

How tragic was she? Even given her fear of flying, she'd prefer that to driving, if it meant an extra hour with him.

'I suppose it makes sense,' she admitted begrudgingly, not holding his eyes.

'That was my thought.' He sipped his coffee, eyes lingering on her face a moment. 'I've given instruction that marriage negotiations will resume tomorrow.'

He wasn't being deliberately cruel, she was sure of it, but Eloise felt as though she'd been punched in the gut, and badly winded. All the warmth drained from her face and unconsciously, she took a step forward, her fingers pressing to the edge of the kitchen bench for support. Everything between them had changed. He was walling himself off from her, pushing back any intimacy they shared, treating her like…a stranger. It was courteous but so cold, and it almost killed her to feel that from him.

'Tariq, what's happened?'

His eyes met hers, something stirring in their depths. 'What do you mean?'

'You're being so…'

She stared at him, searching for words, for how to finish her sentence, but everything was shifting and she could no longer tell what was real and what was fantasy. What if she'd misunderstood everything? What if he'd been flirting with her for fun? To entertain himself on an otherwise boring evening? What if he did this sort of thing all the time? What if it had all been a lie?

And so the walls he was erecting somehow extended extra bricks and reached out to wrap around her as well, offering her protection she badly needed. She straightened, squaring her shoulders and staring at him with a carefully controlled expression.

'You're right,' she said, instead. 'This is for the best.'

Oh, so briefly, surprise shimmered in his eyes and then he nodded. 'Help yourself to some refreshments.'

She ground her teeth together, hurt and smarting. But to hide those feelings, she stalked into the kitchen and poured herself a coffee, heart bruised and aching.

She only had a chance to take two sips before a large four-wheel drive trekked through the woods, covered in dust. Six men in military uniforms jumped out, and a moment later, another four-wheel drive pulled up.

'The cavalry's here,' she murmured, casting a glance over her shoulder. But Tariq was already gone, moving towards the door, without a backwards glance.

The next day, still tired and a little stiff from the drive, she took her seat at the foot of the negotiation table, watching as Tariq, in the centre, listened to the advisors on both sides, nutting out details that had more to do with trade and financial agreements than it did marriage.

She looked at him more often than she should, willing him to look at her, willing him to *see her*, but always, she was disappointed.

It was as though they'd never met.

As though she was any other member of the Ras Sarat delegation, and his treatment of her hurt like the devil.

The meeting stretched into the afternoon, and she sat through it all, switching off her mind and heart and forcing herself to take an almost out of body perspective on this, to act purely in Elana's interests even when her heart was slamming into her and her stomach was in knots.

At one point, around four o'clock, she lifted a hand and absentmindedly kneaded the sore flesh at the back of her neck. Only then did Tariq turn to her swiftly, eyes narrowed, assessing the gesture, missing, as it turned out, nothing. Her hand dropped away quickly, her eyes fell to the table and her skin lifted in goosebumps. Blood flushed her body and her cheeks went a vibrant pink. For the rest of the meeting, she sat perfectly still, as though a magic wand had been waved, turning her to stone.

It had been a long day and Tariq was at the end of his patience.

He was doing the only thing he could, but ignoring her was a form of hell on earth. She hadn't spoken. Not once. Not even when he'd craved the sound of her voice or wanted her input badly. She'd stayed resolutely silent, occasionally making notes or frowning as if she disagreed with an opinion that was being put forth, but not venturing a counter viewpoint of her own.

He'd felt hatred then. Not for Eloise, but for his family and his role in Savisia and the duty that was on him to marry someone royal, to have royal children quickly. Hatred for her loyalty to a friend he barely knew, hatred that she wouldn't lower her scruples and enter into a short, wonderful, affair.

They both knew he would marry Elana, but why did that mean they couldn't be together in the interim?

He knew the answer, of course he did, but his ego, his libido, weren't satisfied by it. Nor was something else, something indefinable and urgent, a part of him that he couldn't comprehend but was jumping up inside of him, telling him to hell with the expectations and obligations on him, to hell with what his father would expect him to do: Eloise was right there, he could reach out and grab her, keep her here in Savisia with him, kiss her until she saw sense, until she begged him to make love to her.

And then what?

Have her wake up and hate him?

For all that he could use their physical connection to overcome her defences, he'd never do that. It was beneath him.

She had to come to him willingly.

She had to want him more than she wanted to fight this. Or it would always be something he regretted.

And she'd made it abundantly clear she was going to fight temptation with her dying breath.

However, resuming wedding negotiations and forcing her to sit through them had been a low move. He felt that with every single minute of the day. She was so strong, so determined not to show any emotion, yet he felt it resonating off her, and more importantly, he felt it within his core. He judged himself, and yet he didn't call off the meetings again. He couldn't. This was the path of his future, he'd committed to it, and there was nothing that could stop it now. He would marry the Crown Princess of Ras Sarat, no matter how badly he wanted a completely different future.

The next morning, Tariq was preparing for the meetings when he received a call from his private secretary.

'Go ahead,' he muttered, taking a sip of scalding hot coffee.

'I'm aware your day is already scheduled, Your Highness, but I've had an interesting request. Something I wanted to run by you before responding.'

That was, in and of itself, unusual. 'Yes?'

'Have you heard of Graciano Cortéz?'

'Of course. The property developer.'

'In fact, he is also an investor in many industries but primarily, he is known for his development work.'

'What about him?'

'He intends to buy a large amount of land in the city and convert it to hotel accommodation. He's asked to meet with you.'

'I hadn't heard anything about this.'

'It's all happened in the last two days.'

He closed his eyes, trying not to think about where he was two days ago, and how much he'd give to be back in the cabin with Eloise and her delicious, soft, creamy skin. His gut rolled and something in the middle of his chest ached.

'Why does he want to meet?'

'I suppose because of the scale of the development. I can make up an excuse, of course.'

'No, I'd be interested to hear his plans. I'll make the time. Schedule it in for today.'

'Thank you, Sheikh. Good luck with the negotiations.'

Tariq hung up the call, then swept from the room with determination and blinkered vision. He wouldn't think about Eloise today. Only Elana, and the necessity of this future.

'Are you deliberately using the blandest words you can think of?' Elana pestered, so Eloise cringed. Bland was not how she could ever describe Tariq.

'Not at all. I just don't want to colour your thoughts on him. You'll meet him soon enough and you'll know how you feel.'

'Okay, fine, but what do you feel?'

Eloise almost choked on her pomegranate juice. 'I feel nothing,' she said quickly, the words strange in her throat.

'So I'm going to marry a guy and you have no idea if he seems nice or has three heads or kills cats in his spare time?'

'Actually, he does hunt,' she said, relieved when Elana laughed.

'I'd be surprised if he didn't. What else?'

'Ellie, I can't,' she whispered, looking down the hall at the increased action. 'He's coming now.'

'Call me later. Promise?'

'Yeah, I promise.' She disconnected the call, feeling like the worst friend in the world. The feeling only intensified as Tariq approached and her eyes seemed incapable of tear-ing themselves away from him. He walked with such confidence, flanked on either side by members of his cabinet. As he drew near the boardroom, his gaze travelled to her, met hers, then briefly flashed over her body, so a thousand arrows launched through her veins, but then he looked away, and moved beyond her.

Ice filled her body; she hated him then. How could he turn off from these feelings?

It just proved that she'd been right to resist him.

He hadn't really wanted her. He hadn't really cared for her. He'd wanted to sleep with her but when she'd refused, he'd accepted it and had obviously already moved on.

She hoped her heart would do the same thing.

'We've made good progress this morning.' His eyes encompassed the group, lingering, perhaps, a moment longer on Eloise than anyone else, but barely, so she was sure she was the only one who noticed it. Her shoulder tingled, as if he were kissing her there again; she looked away.

'I have another matter I must attend to. Please carry on without me. I'll check in this afternoon.'

Everyone stood respectfully, bowing as he walked from the room. Eloise stared at him in consternation. Ever since that morning in the cabin, she'd felt as if a part of her was being dragged from her body, a limb, an organ, something vital and essential.

That feeling compounded as he left the room.

She took her seat again and tried to focus, but her mind was, from that moment on, split in two directions.

Graciano Cortéz was a man whose reputation well and truly preceded him. He was one of the wealthiest men in the world, his developments known for their flair and appeal.

He was environmentally conscious, culturally respectful, and made a point of employing local workforces as much as possible, meaning an investment by him in Savisia was a tantalising prospect.

Therefore, Tariq knew he should bring more of his focus to the meeting but unfortunately, he was no longer capable of doing any such thing. A part of him was always with Eloise, studying her, thinking about her, wondering about her, missing her. Fortunately, Tariq al Hassan on a bad day was still incisive and intelligent.

He strode into the ornately formal sitting room, eyes taking in the guards first and then, the man at the centre of the room.

'Graciano Cortéz?' he queried, moving close enough to extend his hand.

The Spaniard stared at it, and then lifted his eyes to Tariq's, causing the Sheikh a moment of confusion. Had they met before? There was something in the other man's eyes that was completely familiar.

'Your Highness,' Graciano said with a curt nod, belatedly reaching out and taking his hand. 'Thank you for meeting with me.'

'I was interested to hear of your development. I'd like to know more.'

'I have all the information over there, but that's not why I requested this meeting.'

Curiosity moved through Tariq. 'Isn't it?' He moved away a little, giving him some space to observe the other man's body language. 'Then why don't you enlighten me.'

Something was bothering Cortéz. He paced the room from one side to the other, then stopped abruptly, dragging a hand through his hair in a gesture Tariq found strangely familiar, before turning to Tariq with a look of uncertainty.

'You don't remember me.'

Tariq was careful to give nothing away. 'Should I?'

The other man's features shifted, disappointment obvious. 'No. You were too young...'

Something like adrenaline prickled along the back of his neck.

'Have we met?'

'You could say that.'

'I meet a lot of people,' Tariq said after a pause.

'I'm sure you do.'

'Is it important that I remember?'

Graciano's laugh lacked humour. 'I was hopeful.'

'I'm sorry to disappoint. Now, your development—'

Graciano's eyes flared, irritation obvious now. 'I came to talk to you about your family.'

It was like being speared by a bolt of lightning. The sensational words seemed to ricochet off the walls, making Tariq's heart feel as though it were breaking into pieces.

'That will be all,' he dismissed his guards with a curt nod, waiting until the room was empty save for the two men, then turning back to Graciano with the full force of his attention.

It was possible Graciano meant the Sheikha and late Sheikh.

Possible that Tariq was jumping to the wrong conclusions.

'What exactly did you want to discuss?' Tariq said, his voice emerging cool and level.

'What do you know of your parents?'

He stiffened. 'My parents are—'

'Dead,' Graciano interrupted, but gently, sympathy in his features. 'They died when you were a baby. It was a car accident. You are aware of this?'

Tariq was careful not to betray his feelings but inside, a

part of him was crying out, tortured by what Graciano was saying, tortured and hurting.

'I think you should do the talking,' he said eventually, careful not to betray his feelings.

'If you wish.' Graciano dipped his head in a nod. 'Your parents were killed. You were taken to a hospital, badly injured. It's a miracle you survived, in fact. I believe your adopted parents saw you, took pity on you, and brought you home with them, where you were nurtured back to health, cared for by the best doctors in the world, and raised as their own son. Of course, it was never intended that you would assume the throne. They simply fell in love with you and wanted to give you a better life. Am I right?'

Tariq's lips compressed in a grim line. So far as he knew, only four people on earth were aware of this: his mother, the doctor in Spain, Tariq and the prime minister of Savisia.

'Are you attempting to blackmail me in some fashion?' he asked, surprised, because everything he knew of Graciano Cortéz spoke of a man of integrity and honour.

'To blackmail you? Do you seriously think... To what end?' He looked bemused. 'Do you think I need the money?'

'I couldn't say. Why have you come here?'

'Because you were not the sole survivor of that crash. Are you aware of that?'

He was drowning again, a voice, a laugh, so familiar, so achingly familiar, a voice with no face. His dreams were all around him, memories haunting him, taunting him with their opaque, impossible to reach hold of quality.

'Who are you?'

'Graciano Cortéz,' he said quietly, moving closer. 'I am your brother.'

It wasn't true. It couldn't be. 'I have no brother,' Tariq said angrily, lying, because as Graciano spoke, fragments were piercing him, shocking him with their strength. 'My mother told me—she was told by the hospital—I was orphaned.'

'Orphaned, yes, but not alone.'

Tariq crossed his arms over his broad chest. 'Then why were we separated?'

'I cannot say, for certain. An accident? Or perhaps because of the donation your parents made to the hospital—it was very generous. I cannot speak for the motives of anyone else, but I am your brother. That much is fact.'

Brother. He groaned, dropping his head forward. He had been so young when the accident happened. He didn't remember his brother, and yet, he did. There was a sense enveloping him. A feeling of familiarity and comfort and, overwhelmingly, of love.

'My brother,' he said with a shake of his head.

'Look,' Graciano said, reaching into his wallet and pulling out an old photo, handing it to Tariq. He took it, but the force of recollection was so strong he almost blacked out. He gripped it harder, forced his eyes to focus. A man and a woman stared back at him, and two boys—one tall and gangly and the other just a chubby, dimply boy on his father's knee. He saw his own face, unmistakably, and the eyes that had been just out of reach all this time, those of Graciano Cortéz.

'Oh, my God,' he muttered, dropping his head. He was almost identical to the man in the photo, their features so similar, their skin darker than the other two, their hair thick and black. 'This is me.'

'That's us,' Graciano said. 'I have looked for you, from as soon as I had the means to do so. I have searched for you. But it was only recently that the truth was found—'

It brought Tariq back to the present, to his country, his people, his duties. 'How? How was the truth found?'

'I hired an investigator.'

'The adoption was a secret—everyone involved went to great lengths to ensure that it remained so.'

'You knew about this?'

'Not about you, but after my father passed away five months ago my mother told me the truth. I always felt that a part of me was missing. I always felt that there was something, someone, a part of me I couldn't make sense of,' he said with a shake of his head. 'It was all a lie. My parents were grieving in Spain—my mother had endured another miscarriage. They saw me, and they wanted to help me. That was all, at first. But days passed, with my mother coming to sit by my bed, and each day that went by without family coming to check on me made her certain she had to bring me home.' Tariq's eyes narrowed. 'My mother didn't mention you. I can't believe she knew about you—'

'Probably not,' Graciano responded with a small shrug. 'There was a lot of money involved. It would have been in the hospital's best interests to keep me out of the picture. I came to see you once, in hospital, but after that, I was forbidden. I thought I'd done something wrong, but it turns out, they just wanted to keep us apart.'

Tariq swore, handing the photo back, his eyes lingering on the faces. They looked happy. Warm. A family.

'Our father always said to me, "he's your responsibility. You must take care of him".' Graciano smiled wistfully. 'I adored you almost as much as they did. You were such a happy child—you smiled whenever we entered the room—but for me, it was different. You'd hold out your hands, wanting me to lift you up.' He laughed on a quiet exhalation and Tariq was jealous then, jealous of his brother's memories and knowledge of their family before this life. 'When I saw you in hospital, all broken and bruised, I wanted to take care of you with everything I was. But I wasn't allowed. I was too young to fight it, but I never stopped thinking about you, wanting to find you.'

'I have had nightmares,' Tariq said quietly. 'There was a voice. Your voice, I now realise. I couldn't see you, but you were there. I have had these nightmares for years, since I was a little boy. I thought it was because of the accident, but now I realise, it was my mind trying to make me remember. To look for you.'

Graciano moved closer, and they stared at each other for several moments before they embraced; two big, strong men wrapping their arms around each other, making the past disappear, so there was only this moment.

Emotion swamped Tariq.

There was love and anger and frustration and a total lack of comprehension. There was loyalty—to his birth parents and his adoptive parents, to his brother, to his people and kingdom, to his late, beloved father and the promise he'd made him, to care for Savisia with his dying breath. There was the realisation of how this news threatened that, because if Graciano knew, if an investigator knew, it was only a matter of time before this became more widely understood, and the threat to his reign was tantamount.

There was the crystallising of resolve, and an underscoring of the need of his marriage to Elana, and with that came despair, because he didn't want to marry her. He didn't want to be with anyone if it made it impossible for him to be with Eloise.

Everything swirled in a vortex. His past, present and the all-important future. The weight was immense.

He pulled away, keeping a hand curled around his brother's arm.

'The situation is complicated.'

Graciano's grin took his breath away because it was *his* smile. The same smile he'd known all of his life. He shook his head, wading through the mess of his life to admit that in this moment, there was good. The discovery of a sibling was a blessing.

'I anticipated you'd say that.'

'Can I rely on your discretion?'

'Do I seem like a man who shares his private life with the world?'

'Nonetheless, this is particularly sensitive.'

'I'm aware.'

'I'm not saying I won't speak publicly on this matter—I think that will be inevitable—but I need a little time to reflect, to speak to my mother and government first.'

'Naturally. I didn't come here to pressure you. Only, as soon as I knew where you were, I had to see you. I've looked for years…'

'I'm glad you came,' he said quietly, and it was the truth. It might have thrown a grenade into his life, but Tariq wouldn't have it any other way. 'Will you stay in Savisia awhile?'

'I'm here another week, for the development.'

'And then?'

'I'm based in London. But I can come back often.'

'London.' He nodded. 'There's so much I don't know about you. So much I want to know.'

'It's mutual.'

Tariq straightened, pulling away a little, needing to get his head around this. 'I'll have to take a couple of days to manage things here.'

'I can wait.'

CHAPTER TEN

SHOCK MORPHED INTO something else, something darker, as the day went on, and he tried to understand all the pieces of his life, all of the decisions and actions that had led him to this place in space and time.

He had been raised as a Savisian. The country was in his blood and bones, he would die for this place. And yet, he'd been born a Spaniard. He considered himself an only child and yet he had a brother, a brother he felt an immediate connection to, a brother he'd been denied for too long.

He had a future that was no longer in his hands. He had to marry Elana. Any hope of being able to find a way around it disappeared with the certainty that this news would soon be public—how could it not? If one person knew, it was only a matter of time.

Announcement of his engagement to the Crown Princess of Ras Sarat would calm most of the ruffled feathers and would placate those traditionalists who wanted to see a true royal baby on the throne of Savisia.

It would avert a possible civil war, or an uprising at least.

What would his father say if he were here?

He couldn't even seek comfort from that because his father had laid the groundwork for this. His parents should have made sure there were no other survivors before taking him. They should have thought before acting.

He stared around the boardroom, eyes landing on Eloise and lingering with a lack of control that bothered him almost as much as the rest of the day's revelations.

Her eyes lifted, straying to his, then jerking away, her lips parted.

Anger coursed his veins.

He was bobbing on a turbulent ocean, no anchor, no boat, no help in sight. Control was a faraway illusion. He needed to get away from this, from them. He needed to get far away.

Abruptly, he stood, scraping back his chair.

'That's enough.'

The room fell silent.

'We'll resume tomorrow morning. We're done for the day.'

The rest of the chairs pushed back, and one by one, the occupants bowed and left the room. Eloise was last. She lingered by the door, turning to face him, but in that moment, his anger was aimed even at her, because he needed her, and she was holding herself back from him.

He ground his teeth together, staring at her with ice in his veins.

'Are you okay?' she whispered.

Was he okay? Hell, he wasn't okay. How could he be?

He stared down his nose at her, eyes glittering in his face, focusing all of his anger at her because she was there and she'd let him down. She'd put Elana above him. He knew it wasn't a reasonable feeling to have, that she had shown loyalty and bravery in treating her friendship with so much respect, but what about her feelings for him, and his for her? What about what they owed each other?

'Why wouldn't I be?'

'You seem—'

'You are not here to psychoanalyse me, Miss Ashworth.

I suggest you go back to your rooms and check in with your friend.'

She flinched and he felt his gut twist in response. Her eyes clearly showed her hurt. He'd done that to her, and none of this was her fault. His anger was totally unreasonable. But damn it, if they couldn't make love, they could make war—it was better to spark with her in anger than not at all.

But not if it made her feel like this. Not if he hurt her.

'Very well, Your Highness.' She curtseyed with that beautiful dancer's grace, and the moment she left the room he braced his hands on the edge of the table and dropped his head, feeling that he'd hit the low point, in that moment.

He'd pushed her away.

He'd sought to hurt her.

Why?

What had that achieved?

Why, when he wanted her with every cell in his body, had he thrown more barriers between them?

Something dark churned inside of him and suddenly, he was no longer thinking, but acting on instinct alone. He burst into the corridor, deserted except for a few members of the national guard, and looked left and right, searching for her familiar figure. He chose to walk left, striding the corridors with purpose until he rounded the corner and found her, walking with a frown on her face, eyes skimming the walls and barely registering the art that hung there.

He reached her easily but didn't touch her. He didn't dare.

'Would you come with me?'

She hesitated a moment. Wisely. Control was a long way back in his rear vision mirror.

'Come where?' It was hearing her voice that pushed him firmly over the edge, the sadness and resignation. The admission that she would go anywhere with him, no matter the cost. How he wished he could be the bigger person and release her from this hell of their creation, but his needs overpowered everything else.

'Into the desert,' he said, leaning down, his face just an inch from hers. 'But I should warn you, *habibi*, I am no longer able to honour the promise I made. If you come, I cannot tell you what will happen between us.'

She startled, eyes wide, face pale. 'Tariq, what is it?'

'Are you coming?'

Her lips parted, she swayed a little; still, he didn't touch her.

She stared up at him and he waited, nerves stretching, then finally, he turned, calling her bluff. He stalked away from her, not looking back, but hoping, hoping with all of himself, that she would follow.

She found him at the stables. Her lungs hurt from running, her heart was in tatters, and her knees were weak. Mostly, she was bursting with curiosity and concern. It was obvious that he'd reached a breaking point, and she couldn't fathom why.

'Tariq, wait,' she said, uncaring for the servants that were there, that heard her address him as a man, not as Sheikh. She couldn't.

His nostrils flared and with a short nod, the staff left the stables, giving her an interested look as they filed out.

'What's happened?'

He flicked a latch, opening a door for his stallion, who stepped out and made a guttural noise, tilting back his head.

'Are you coming?'

'This is madness.'

'I'm leaving now.'

'Wait,' she muttered. 'This isn't fair.'

'No, it's not. Ten seconds, Eloise. What's it going to be?'

'You can't do this to me.'

'Do this to you? Do this to *you*? What the hell do you think it's doing to *me*?'

She flinched and again, he felt like a total bastard, but he didn't care.

'I really hope you know what you're doing,' she said, eyeing the horse warily.

He crossed his arms. 'What does that mean?'

'Well? I can't get up there on my own.'

His eyes raked her and then he moved, fast and powerful, determined and in control, lifting her easily onto the horse. A second later, he was at her back and kicking the sides of Bahira, spiriting the beast out of the stables and away from the palace. He rode hard and fast, so she held on to the reins for dear life, but there was never any danger. Not with Tariq's strong arm around her waist, pinning her back against him, holding her there, needing her. She didn't know how she knew that, but she did.

He needed her, as much as he needed the desert and his freedom and some space from the palace and wedding negotiations.

Wedding negotiations. Her heart skidded and ached for Elana, for their friendship, for the decision she'd just made. As if he sensed it, he leaned closer, and doubt disappeared. Something more was between them, something that demanded *this*, whatever this was. She was at the whim of fate now, not thought, and it was a relief to let go and see what happened.

He rode like the wind. Sand whipped their faces; neither cared. He rode until they reached the rocky outcrop with the stream, he rode with the afternoon sun on their backs, warming them, and then, only once they were near the water, did he bring the horse to a halt and let himself breathe. But not think. Thinking would lead him to doubt and he refused to do that.

There was only one thing that would make this better. Not for good, but just for now, and that was enough.

He jumped off the horse and a moment later was grabbing her, drawing her with him away from Bahira to the large, ancient rocks that were flat and gently sloped. He moved quickly, sure footed on their surface after years of exploration. Around the corner, they levelled out and it was there that he stopped, turning to face her with nostrils flaring, thobe blowing in the gentle breeze.

She stared up at him, so trusting, face so calm, and then he groaned, passion almost eating him alive.

'Damn you,' he said, shaking his head because of all the women he could want with this passion, why did it have to be her? Why now? Perhaps if they'd met years ago, if his father had been alive and the truth of his adoption not remotely on his radar...but fate was cruel, and this was how things were.

'Damn *you*,' she responded, lifting her hands and pushing at his chest. 'Damn you.'

He caught her wrists, holding them there, and it was like being stung by a swarm of bees. Every cell in his body reverberated. Her breath was ragged, and he understood, he knew what she was feeling because it was burning him alive as well.

'I have to marry her,' he said, the fact something he couldn't ignore. 'I have to marry her.'

A tear glistened on her lash line and then fell down her cheek, rolling slowly before splashing to the ground. He stared at the silvery line it left on her face and honestly thought he could have punched something then. Her grief would be with him always.

'I know,' she whispered, though she didn't. How could she understand the new imperative that was at his back?

'But this is… If we don't… I will always regret…'

She sobbed then and nodded, the palm that was pressed to his chest curling in his clothes. 'I know.' She trembled. 'Me too.'

It was all he needed. They both understood what this was. A one-off. One chance, one time, so that they wouldn't look back and wonder and wish.

'No regrets,' he said emphatically.

'No.' But her tears were falling and it was more than he could bear. He kissed her then, hard and passionate, filled with all the dark emotions that were swirling through him, with the feelings that were rioting in his gut, with his need for her and his feelings for her, feelings that went beyond lust, that were knitted into stranger, heavier parts of his soul.

He kissed her like she was a delicate vase at first and then he kissed her as an equal, ancient and primal sensual desire controlling his every impulse. He tasted the salt of her tears and did everything he could to drive them from her heart and mind, so that only pleasure sustained her. They stripped their clothes in unison, a frantic tangle of hands and fingers and limbs moving, shucking fabric from skin until they were naked, their bodies wrapped together, his pulling her to the stone, careful to place her on his discarded robe, to save from the cold hard edges of rock, but she didn't notice, didn't complain, only lifted onto her elbows to seek his mouth, to kiss him back, hungrily, needing, with the same abandon of sense and logic that had corrupted him completely.

His life had fundamentally changed and yet this, with

Eloise, was the only thing that made sense. 'Damn you,' he groaned, but it wasn't her he was angry with, so much as everyone else. None of it mattered though. Not when her body writhed beneath his and her legs parted, silently inviting him to take her, to be with her. How could he refuse? How could he doubt the perfection of this? The hunger he'd felt since that first day had grown and grown so he thrust into her and almost exploded with the pleasure of that fulfilment. It took a monumental effort to bring himself back from the edge, to stop from coming right there, as her muscles tightened around him and welcomed him in euphoric completion.

She scraped her nails down his back and cried his name, filling the afternoon sky with the proof of her madness, of their madness, and he kissed her harder, tasting that pleasure, hearing it in his soul, aching for her even as he moved within her. It wasn't just her body he wanted but her total surrender to him, her admission that she was all his, and always would be. What an ass. Even in that moment of abandon he recognised what an awful thing that was to want—he would be married to another woman, sleeping with her, making her pregnant, yet he wanted Eloise to put her life on hold and pine for him always?

It was cruel and unfair but it was also human instinct—his instinct.

It was what he might have done if their positions were reversed.

He pushed the thought aside, terrified by it, by everything that was happening between them, even as he knew the experience was building him up, making him a different man, a stronger man, the man he was born to be.

'Tariq, I'm—I need—' He knew what she needed though. He understood her on some soul-deep level. He moved them in their own unique dance, his body anticipating and delivering, until she was trembling and falling apart and then he dragged his mouth all over her skin, flicking her, tasting her, tormenting her, bringing her back to the brink again, and then again, until the fourth time when she exploded and he went with her, wrapping an arm behind her back and lifting her up, so they were melded completely, not a hint of space between them as they shared the richness of that moment, as they found the fulfilment of release as if they were one person, not two, on very different paths.

'What happened, Tariq?' She shifted beneath him, ever so slightly, pinned as she was between him and the hardness of the rock.

'Is it not self-evident?'

She pushed aside his flippant response. This was not a flippant moment. 'What happened to upset you?'

His lips compressed and a muscle throbbed at the base of his jaw. She lifted a finger to it, touching him gently, then shifting her touch sideways, to lips she'd wanted to reach for since she'd first laid eyes on them. Doing so now was crazy and liberating. She refused to reflect on how temporary this state of freedom was.

He wasn't hers, and having slept with him, every single anchor point in her life had shifted.

She was adrift, but for right now, there was Tariq, and she would make the most of it, just for a little longer.

He expelled a sigh, pulling away from her so her body thundered with a silent complaint, but he only rolled onto his back then brought her to his chest, reaching for his discarded shirt to cover them a little. She smiled against his skin despite the heaviness that was dragging at her.

This moment was one of the few in life that was absolutely perfect. She closed her eyes and breathed in, waiting for him to speak, her fingers tracing idle, hungry paths over his chest.

'When I was just a baby, I was in a bad car accident.'

She lifted up, propping her chin on his chest so she could see him better.

'My body was broken—doctors thought I would die.'

She frowned, the hand that had been tracing lines over his chest coming to rest against his heart, feeling the sturdy beating with gratitude now. She didn't want to contemplate what could have happened.

'My recovery was slow. It wasn't certain that I would ever have full mobility or strength, but the doctors were wrong. I learned to walk, and then to run. To run fast and hard. My father was determined that I would be strong, much stronger than anyone else. He wanted me to be unbreakable.'

She felt his heart and knew that it was the case. Tariq al Hassan had been rebuilt, and he was everything he'd just said.

'He taught me to ride horses, to swim miles, to walk this desert as though it were the greenest grass in the world. He taught me to climb mountains, to move rocks with my bare hands, to fish and to hunt. He taught me to ignore pain, to endure just about anything.'

She made a soft noise because it was all so evident. When she looked at him, that strength was exactly what she saw.

'There is a legend about the sheikhs of this land, about the iron that fills our blood that makes us more than mere mortals. Borne of warriors, destined to take our place on the throne, to rule with the kind of compassion that can only come from an unbreakable commitment to what's right. I'm simply one in a long line of men like me.' He tilted his face to hers, eyes boring into hers. 'Only I'm not.'

She frowned. 'I don't understand.'

'After my father died, I learned the truth—he hadn't wanted me to know, but my mother wasn't comfortable with that.'

'What truth?' she pressed urgently.

He was still a moment, contemplative and then nodded, as if committing this to himself. 'I'm adopted, Eloise.' He waited for those words to filter through to her. 'My biological parents died in the accident that injured me so badly. Until today, I believed I was alone, that the accident left me an orphan. No parents, no siblings, just me.'

She pulled up closer to his face, urgency drawing her eyes together. 'What happened this afternoon?'

'My biological brother came to see me.'

She gasped, lifting a hand to her mouth. 'You have a brother?'

'I don't remember him.' He frowned. 'And yet somehow, I do. I felt a link to him immediately.'

'But…you're angry about this?'

He expelled a breath. 'No, not about discovering a brother. Eloise, don't you realise what it means?'

She furrowed her brow.

'I'm not royal. My place in this country, on the throne, it's all predicated on a lie.'

She shook her head, rejecting that outright. 'You might not be the biological son of the late sheikh but you were born to this. You are strong and powerful, smart, wise, kind, all the things that are necessary for a role like yours, all the qualities you just listed as being required by your customs.'

'But I am not royal,' he stressed adamantly, and finally, the penny dropped.

'And Elana is,' she said with a soft gasp. 'That's why you proposed this marriage.'

'Not only is she royal, many generations ago, our blood-lines were of the same royal lineage. Her heir would sit on the throne of Savisia, and this would negate any discontent. It would avert a civil crisis—most importantly, it would right the wrong of my parents' decision.'

'What your parents did was save a boy who needed saving.'

He shook his head. 'They should have told me the truth.' He closed his eyes, features showing anger.

'For years, I have had this single nightmare,' he said quietly. 'I didn't realise it, but when my mother told me the truth, I realised immediately. It is a strange memory, not of anything specific, just a familiarity I have with someone, something else, somewhere else. I was only nine months old, but somehow, a part of that life is imprinted on me, a part of me; it's as though I've always known I was different, that something was wrong. All my life this nightmare has tormented me. Now I believe it is my past, trying to be known. I just didn't realise there was something I needed to reach out and grab.'

She felt sympathy for him, not just that his parents had concealed the truth from him, but also because his world had been rocked to the foundations. Because he'd lived with this for five months, worrying about the political fallout from a deeply personal situation.

'How do you know there'd be a crisis?' she asked gently. 'Even if anyone found out...'

'People will find out. My brother's appearance changes everything. Too many people know. The only way to handle this is to get ahead of the information with an announcement of my own.'

'And what? Forfeit your right to rule?'

'It should not be mine, by right,' he said sharply. 'If there were anyone else—'

'But there's not. You were born for this, raised for it, at least.'

'Yes. I was raised for it,' he agreed gruffly.

'And you're good at it. How can you even think of walking away—'

'I'm not. Don't you see? Everything we've been doing here has been to secure my place on the throne, not to abandon it. However I might personally feel about this, I owe the people of Savisia a great debt of gratitude. I cannot desert them—'

'You don't owe anyone anything,' she interrupted.

'There is no one else. A distant cousin has a claim on the throne, but he is far from a suitable fit. He would drive the economy into the ground within a decade,' he said with a shake of his head. 'If there were someone, anyone, else I would abdicate, but I can't. Don't you see? I was raised to fulfil this role and I cannot walk away from that.'

Eloise's eyes were awash with sympathy.

He continued with gruff determination. 'Marriage to Elana is politically necessary for me, and also, for her. The kingdom of Ras Sarat hangs by a thread, but Savisia is rich, powerful, with strong alliances and trading partnerships. Everything about this makes sense.'

'I know,' she whispered, because it did, and it was Elana's hope that the marriage would come to pass. 'That's why you have to marry her.'

'But then, there's you,' he said quietly. 'Can't you see how this complicates things?'

'No,' she groaned, heart breaking. 'We both know it can't.' The two people she loved most in the world had everything to lose if the marriage fell through—Eloise wouldn't be responsible for that.

Silence fell. It was too early for the sweet chorus of night birds. The sun was still high, the sky blue; the warmth of the day surrounding them, even when her heart was cold.

He reached for her fingers, lacing them through his. 'What if you were to stay in Savisia?'

Her heart stammered. 'How would that work?'

'Stay for me,' he said, his voice rumbling. She felt like she was in free fall.

'And your marriage to Elana?'

'Purely for the sake of a royal heir,' he said. 'That would be unavoidable. But beyond that, she would be nothing to me.'

Eloise's heart splintered. 'She's my best friend. You can't think I'd ever want that for her?'

'And what about you? What do you want for yourself?'

'This,' she pressed a hand lightly to his heart, 'is a poisoned chalice. The thing I want, the thing I want with all my heart, would ultimately destroy me because of what that selfish choice had cost my friend. I could never do it, and I think you know that.'

He swore softly. 'And you said *I* was running away?'

'I'm not,' she said quietly. 'I'll continue to serve Elana's interests from Ras Sarat. It's my home.'

'Stay here, Eloise,' he said with urgency. 'As a friend, if that's all you can offer.'

'That would never work,' she said thickly. 'Please don't ruin this moment by asking me to do something I cannot even contemplate.'

His features were etched with determination. 'You can do whatever you want. You're afraid.'

'Yes,' she agreed without hesitation. 'I'm deathly scared of hurting the friend who's been with me through thick and through thin, who would give her life for mine. And yet I'm here with you, doing exactly that. Don't ask for more.'

It was what she'd said in the cabin. She felt it as strongly now as she had then.

'You won't even think about it?'

It was anathema to her. Every cell in her body rejected the idea of an ongoing betrayal of Elana, and she knew that the marriage had to proceed. But she nodded slowly, because she was greedy for just a few more moments of beauty with Tariq, the last few moments she'd spend with him, ever. She wanted to drink this in, to nourish her soul, so that when she left—and she would leave—she would have something to sustain her through the long years ahead.

He alone would have her heart, for as long as it beat in her body, it would beat solely, always, for him.

CHAPTER ELEVEN

DUSK BREATHED ACROSS the desert, gentle and iridescent at the same time, electrifying the atmosphere. The stars began to twinkle and it was like the falling of a hammer. They both knew it was time to leave.

Eloise shifted first, moving her head from his chest, trying not to think about the future, about how much she'd miss him. She had to be able to live with herself, and only by leaving him could she achieve that.

A poisoned chalice indeed.

'Have dinner with me tonight.' His command curled around her, tempting her, making her doubt her firm resolution to end this now, before things could go further. Before she could weaken.

'I think that would attract the wrong kind of attention.'

His eyes flared. 'We've eaten together before.'

'It's different now,' she chided gently. 'Everything's different.'

His jaw shifted as he ground his teeth together.

'Tell me about your brother,' she said, changing the subject, as she reached for her clothes and began to dress. 'What's he like?'

Tariq's gaze faltered, shifting to the palace. 'Familiar.'

'Like you?'

'Like someone I've known all my life,' he corrected. 'His voice, his eyes, his smile, they're all pieces of me.'

'It must have felt…a thousand things, actually, when you met him.'

'It was surprising.'

Her lips twisted, and her eyes feasted, as he too stood, stretching first then bending, picking up his loose cotton shirt, cuffed pants, and finally, his thobe. Before he could replace it, he came to stand right opposite her, toe to toe, his eyes scanning her face. 'No regrets?'

Her heart shimmied like the sky overhead. She regretted much about their situation but strangely, not what they'd just done. 'No. None.'

His nod was one of approval and it warmed her heart.

They rode back to the palace slowly, and he stopped where he had the last time, away from the stables and the curious eyes of his staff.

'Wait here for me.'

She was tempted to fight that, to leave immediately, but she wasn't yet ready. Her heart was still hungry for him. Hungry for more.

She watched as he rode away, his back straight, achingly strong, and only then did she let a small sob break from her lips, a tear drop from her eyes. She lifted a hand and pressed it to her cheek, then spun her back, focusing on the desert sky behind the palace.

Minutes later, she couldn't say how many, his hands came around her waist, pulling her back to him, so she closed her eyes and inhaled, the familiar presence of his body now a part of her.

'I can come to you tonight. Later. I can rely on my palace staff for discretion.'

She turned in his arms and pressed a finger to his lips. 'Let's not argue about this, Tariq.' She dropped her finger away. 'You can't come to me, and I won't come to you. What just happened was a beautiful piece of unreality.'

His eyes flashed with something dark but he contained it quickly. 'Let's not argue,' he agreed. 'We can discuss this further another time.'

'Tomorrow,' she said with a small nod, knowing that tomorrow, she'd be long gone.

'Do you have a moment?' His tone really didn't invite argument, and he knew the woman sitting across the room could sense, even from that distance, that her son was angry.

She nodded towards her companions, smiling softly. 'Thank you, ladies, that will be all.'

Four elegant Savisian women filed from the room, and with another curt nod, the two remaining servants, leaving the Sheikh alone with his mother.

'Darling, have you eaten? There are some leftovers...'

'I'm not hungry.'

His anger was palpable and new. Though he was a man who felt strongly, he couldn't recall the last time he'd been angry like this. Not since he was a child. It wasn't his way. He was a problem solver, and always had been. When he saw something that needed fixing, he simply worked out how to fix it. Anger, he'd always said, was a futile emotion.

'Then come and sit. Tell me what's happened.'

He paced towards her but didn't sit. He crossed his arms over his chest and stared out of the window behind her.

'Did you know about him?'

'About whom, dear?'

'Did you know, when you took me, that I had a brother?'

Tariq did nothing at first to ease her discomfort, but rather, stared at her, reading her face like an open book. It was abundantly clear he'd just floored his mother.

'It's not possible,' she said after a long moment. 'We were assured you were the sole survivor. It's why we brought you with us. I couldn't bear the thought of you alone. We were assured everyone else had died, told that there was no one available for foster care—you were going to be placed in a home once you left hospital. *If* you left hospital. How could I have left you there, Tariq?'

A muscle jerked in his jaw; even his name was a wrenching discomfort to him. It was not *his* name, not the name he'd been given at birth, and yet it was who he was now. 'You were lied to.'

'It can't be.' Her downward lips showed how perplexed she was. 'Why would anyone do that?'

'You were prepared to donate a considerable amount in exchange for my quick adoption, were you not?'

Her eyes swept shut, all the colour drained from her face. 'The hospital was underfunded. Your father and I wanted to help.'

He could well believe their altruism.

She stood, agitated, fidgeting her hands. 'And naturally, given your father's place in the royal family, we wanted things to happen quickly and quietly.' She groaned, shaking her head in obvious distress. 'But if I'd known about your brother, I would never have—no, that's not right. I would have brought both of you. I would have wrapped him in my arms and carried him here, caring for you both.' She moved closer to Tariq. 'When I saw your little body in the hospital bed, all I could think of was your mother.' Her voice grew thick with tears. 'They say the pain of losing a child is the worst thing in the world.' She pressed her fingers to her chest. 'But the pain of a mother leaving a child, of not knowing how their child will be cared for, of missing all the milestones, of not being able to tuck her little one into bed at night, to laugh with you…' Tears fell down her face. 'The moment I saw you, I made your mother a promise in my mind. I would love you. I would care for you. I would make sure you lived a good, rich, wonderful life. I would give you everything their deaths had put in jeopardy. You were mine, Tariq, from that moment.'

It was impossible not to feel the truth of that sentiment, not to acknowledge that she had acted from a place of love.

'But in your haste to care for me, he was left behind. We were separated.'

She pressed her palm to her mouth. 'I had no idea.' She hesitated. 'I know it must be hard to believe me. We kept this truth from you for a long time.' A hint of anger coloured the words, anger, Tariq imagined that was aimed at his father, who'd been determined Tariq should not know about his birth. 'It was a decision we made out of love— we wanted to spare you the pain of feeling *different*. Then you'd have those nightmares, and I knew you were, somehow, remembering the accident, that your little heart had watched your parents die in the most gruesome way, that you'd been trapped and unable to help them. Then, I wanted to save you from having to relive that. You were happy with us. We loved you so much, and you us. What good was there in stirring up the past by telling you about Spain?'

'Apart from the fact I had a fundamental right to know who I am?'

'Yes,' she whispered. 'Something I came to accept as you aged. For the most part, you are so like your father, but every now and again, I'd see a gesture or an expression, one I wouldn't recognise, and I'd wonder about the people who'd given you life. But never once did it occur to me that you might have family that survived.'

'Well, my brother did.'

'How do you know?'

'Because this afternoon, I met him.'

She gasped. 'He's here? In Savisia?'

He dipped his head.

'Oh, my darling.' Her hand cupped his cheek, but she said nothing more.

'This will come out,' he said, gently, as if to warn her. 'Too many people know the truth now.'

She flinched. 'How do you feel about that?'

His nostrils flared. 'I would rather live with the fallout than walk through any more lies. I'm ready for it, Mother. Are you?'

Dawn broke across the desert, the sky reassuringly familiar, even when all the major compass points of his world had shifted overnight.

He had replayed his conversation with Eloise over and over, analysing it from every angle, studying her facial expressions and the tone of her voice, trying to make sense of what she wanted and needed, trying to find an answer beyond the impossible to contemplate: that she wouldn't see him again.

There was one point on which he felt he could persuade her.

The prospect of her living in Savisia if he promised they wouldn't touch each other again. It was better to have her in his life in any capacity, as his own advisor, as a friend, than to lose her completely. While it was difficult to imagine that life, to imagine being near her and not wanting to have her, it would simply require discipline.

He was determined not to lose her, particularly not now, when his life was in such a state of flux. He needed her.

He dressed quickly, opting for a dark thobe without realising it—perhaps subconsciously he feared the worst?—then strode through the halls of his palace, until he reached his office. As soon as he arrived, he lifted the phone.

'Please have Miss Ashworth of the Ras Sarat delegation brought to me here as a matter of importance. We have business to discuss.'

He disconnected the call and began to wait, eyes practically burning a hole in the door in anticipation of her arrival.

Ten minutes later, there was a knock on his door and he braced for this moment, this conversation—one of the most important in his life.

'Come.'

He stood, aware of every limb and cell in his body. He grew hard with anticipation but schooled himself to calm down. After all, a lifetime of denial was about to begin. He hoped.

It was not, however, Eloise Ashworth who strode through the doors, but rather Jamil, his good friend and advisor.

'You,' Tariq grunted, crossing his arms.

'Good morning to you as well, Your Highness,' Jamil said with a hint of humour. 'You're up early.'

'I've been up all night, in fact.'

'Marriage negotiations?'

He flinched. The words felt like a betrayal. 'What are you doing here?'

'You asked for that woman from the Ras Sarat delegation to join you?'

'And you are not her,' Tariq pointed out.

'Not last time I looked.' Jamil grinned, clearly not reading the Sheikh's mood.

'Where is she?' It was early, Tariq reasoned. Perhaps she

was still asleep and the servants didn't want to wake her. Even at his command? That seemed unlikely.

'She left last night.'

Tariq's heart ceased to beat. The world stopped spinning. Everything was frozen solid. Only his breath punctuated the room in harsh little spurts.

'That's not possible.' There had to be some mistake. Jamil didn't even know her name, he simply referred to her as 'that woman from Ras Sarat'. How much could he know about her?

'I helped arrange her transportation myself,' Jamil said casually, with no idea of the rage that was building inside Tariq. Rage without focus, just all-consuming, devastating rage. 'Apparently there was a conflict in her schedule. She was quite adamant she couldn't wait until this morning.'

She'd run away from him.

She'd fled.

She'd never had any intention of discussing their situation further. She'd left, without saying goodbye. He pressed his palms to the desk.

'The other delegates have remained. This shouldn't affect today's meetings.'

Tariq dropped his head, staring at the desk.

'Your Highness?'

Tariq didn't respond.

'Tariq?' Jamil was closer now, directly opposite the Sheikh. 'What's going on?'

But something occurred to Tariq, and he grabbed hold of it. 'Who was driving her?'

'I don't know. One of the royal guards. Why?'

'Find out who, and where they are. It's been what, ten hours of driving? That might have taken them close to the Savisian border, but probably not. And ready a helicopter.'

'Tariq, you're not making any sense.'

'No, I'm probably not.'

'The car drove her to the airport, where she had a seat booked on a commercial airline, to take her home.'

Tariq jerked his face up, eyes piercing Jamil. 'She *flew*?'

A thousand feelings erupted inside of him. Foremost, the realisation that she must have been absolutely desperate to escape to even contemplate flying, given the depth of her fear. And then, the thought of her up in the air, afraid, with no one to hold her, no one to tell her it would be okay, no one to care for her.

He groaned softly, spinning away from Jamil's penetrating gaze, focusing on the lightening sky, the dawn of a day that would not include Eloise.

He found himself in her suite shortly after that. No one had cleaned it yet, and the air retained a hint of her fragrance, so his gut twisted and hurt as though he'd been punched hard.

He moved to her bed, and ran his fingers over it, imagining her here, sleeping, turning, dreaming of him. To her bathroom, where there was no sign of occupation, no toiletries remaining, everything perfectly neat and tidy, to the lounge room, and a little desk that overlooked the citrus grove. His eyes fell to approximately the spot they'd stood in the first day he'd met her on his horse and his gut jumped.

Slowly, he tore his eyes away, focusing on the desk, where a single white, sealed envelope was laid out, with his name written neatly on the front.

Not his name, but rather his title, to give, he presumed, the impression of the note containing official business. He lifted and opened it in one motion, fingers moving deftly.

T,

*To stay in Savisia and be anything other than what
we were in the desert would be a pain too intense to
bear. To share you, to see you live your life publicly
with anyone else, to have a family with them—these
are things I want for you, but that I cannot stand by
and witness. If I only loved you less.*

*You will be a wonderful husband. Please, take care
of her.*

Best wishes always

E

He scrunched up the note, keeping it balled in his fist,
and stormed through the palace, face darker than a storm
cloud, eyes flashing lightning.

'But it's so far away,' Elana decried, and with good reason.
The two had always promised they'd stay together, remaining inseparable until they were little old grannies.

'It's only a year,' Eloise said. 'The opportunity came
up while I was away and I knew you'd be happy for me,'
she added a teasing tone to her voice, even though she was
dying inside. The flight out of Savisia had been traumatic
enough, let alone that she was leaving Tariq and any idea
of seeing him again. And now? Hours later, she was telling
her best friend that she was returning to London to take up
a fictional dream job, simply because she couldn't bear to
live with the guilt of what she'd done.

'I am, of course,' Elana said quickly, frowning. 'But—'

'You will have more than enough to occupy you in the
coming months, Your Highness.'

Elana's face paled. 'Of course. My marriage.'

'Yes,' Eloise busied herself pouring tea rather than showing how the mention of such a marriage affected her. 'Your marriage, that's right. You'll be Crown Princess of Ras Sarat and Sheikha of Savisia. Your time will be well and truly taken up.'

'But how will I navigate all that without you?'

'You'll have His Highness,' Eloise said, and for a moment, she was glad for her friend, because Tariq was truly a wonderful person and he would be a good husband. She tamped down her own feelings, relegating them to the back of her mind.

'And you really think this is what I should do?'

'I think it's important for your kingdom,' she said quietly. 'And for his.'

'Will you at least stay until the wedding?'

'I'm so sorry...' Her voice faltered. 'They've asked for me to start as soon as possible. I was planning to leave today.'

'But you just got back!'

'I know. It sucks.'

'You're just too in demand, my dear friend. Do you have time to finish breakfast at least?'

She wasn't hungry, but she nodded anyway, reluctant to leave Ras Sarat and Elana, even when she knew she must.

He flew himself to the east, and drove to the cabin, noting the landslide had been largely cleared as he went. He needed to think. Space and time. He needed to be away from people, to get clarity and work out how to proceed. He had to pull emotion from the situation and see the facts as they stood. He needed answers.

In the cabin, he set to analysing all of the circumstances at play. His brother, Tariq's potential lack of suitability to sit on the throne of Savisia, civil uprising, Ras Sarat's finances, and finally Eloise. It was the last consideration that made the others seem irrelevant, but that wasn't so.

And he knew Eloise wouldn't see it that way.

She wanted him to marry Elana, for the sake of the kingdom of Ras Sarat. Any solution had to include a way to help that country.

And his own predicament?

How much was he prepared to sacrifice? How much could he gain?

He stayed in the cabin for two nights, and on the third morning, clarity shifted inside of him, as he began to see a better way forward. It would require the moving of many parts. The good will of almost everyone. But if he could succeed? He'd be king of the world.

He spoke to Mother first. 'I'm going to make a statement. This could be a bumpy time. I cannot say that there will not be civil unrest as a result, or perhaps another claim on the throne.'

Her lips pulled into a serene smile. 'You'll manage.'

That pulled him up short. 'Why are you so sure of that?'

She shifted in her seat a little. 'When we found you in that hospital bed, you were utterly destroyed. The accident had scrambled you all up. The doctors thought you wouldn't survive the first twenty-four hours, but you did. Then they thought you wouldn't last the week. They thought you might never walk and look at you now. You're a fighter, Tariq. You always have been. You have the strength of a thousand warriors at your back. And you'll always have me there, too.'

Graciano was next. Their second meeting was of a different nature, for the simple reason that he brought his family—a wife, Alicia, an eleven-year-old daughter and a toddler. Tariq suddenly felt his heart expanding to include this family, *his* family, his niece so like the mother Graciano had shown him in that photograph. It was only natural to include the Sheikha in the meeting, and she took such a shine to both Graciano and Alicia, the latter of whom was quite overcome at one point. Tariq saw tears glistening on her eyes and enquired if she was okay.

'Graciano and I were both alone a long time before finding each other,' she said quietly. 'Your mother is so welcoming, so loving. It's…been a lovely afternoon.'

Tariq had nodded softly. 'Would you mind sitting with her a moment longer? There is business I must discuss with your husband.'

'Your brother,' she said with a warm smile, then put an arm around him. Such a casual, unexpected gesture of affection, he found it quite natural to return it.

But when he looked at Graciano and Alicia, and saw their easy, obvious love, all he could think of was Eloise, and the desperate, aching yearn he felt to see her again.

The last visit he had to make was to Ras Sarat. Not to Eloise, though it almost killed him to fly into the country without planning to meet with her—yet. But there was no hope of a future with Eloise—to undo the poisoned chalice—without first speaking to the Crown Princess.

Knowing how much this woman meant to Eloise had him viewing her differently, as he entered the pretty sunroom a servant led him to.

Her Highness stood waiting, wearing an elegant green silk dress, hair pulled back in a low bun. Jamil was right, he realised. She was very beautiful, but nothing within Tariq stirred.

He bowed low. 'Thank you for seeing me.'

'Of course.'

Tariq was a man of his word, a man of honour, which was why the next conversation was one of the hardest he'd ever had to have. 'Your Highness, it is no longer possible for us to marry.'

Surprise etched itself on her features, but there was no disappointment. She stood right where she was, pretty features calm, head tilted, inviting him to continue.

'When you were still a child, this country was being driven into the ground by corruption and greed. The current state of affairs is not your fault.'

Now, she did gasp, and her cheeks coloured pale pink. 'Not my fault, perhaps,' she said with a small nod, 'but my responsibility.'

He admired her character greatly, then. She wasn't looking to avoid this: she wanted a solution. 'And marriage to me is indeed one way to help, but I have another.'

Urgency had her moving forward. 'What? I don't mean to sound offensive, but marrying you was not something I would have considered if there were any other way. And believe me, I've looked.'

He laughed gruffly at her frank admission. Perhaps it was because she was so close to Eloise, but he liked her instantly.

'Have you heard of Graciano Cortéz?'

'Of course.'

'He had been looking to build an enormous investment—a series of hotels and five-star retail precincts—in the capital of Savisia. What if his plans changed, and instead, he built them here, in Ras Sarat?'

Her lips parted. 'But why would he do that?'

'Your country is beautiful,' he said with a shrug. 'Investment from someone like him will employ tens of thousands of people and generate billions of dollars in revenue. Most importantly, it will begin a rejuvenation, bringing renewed investment, tourism and attention. You will need to turn your attention to overhauling your country's financial regulation system, to be sure political operatives don't siphon off the profits—'

'That's already underway,' she said with a nod. 'Eloise, my friend—I believe you've met her?—she has been working with the parliament for the last two years on legislative reforms to prevent the corruption of the past.'

Of *course* she had been. A smile touched his lips as he imagined her wading through the laws, tweaking them, scrapping them completely where necessary, her unquestionable sense of rightness leading her to fight for what was right. And her loyalty to Elana.

'There are other ways my country can help yours,' he said gently. 'I regret that it's taken me so long to realise your plight. You shouldn't have to shoulder this worry alone. Savisia and Ras Sarat were always friends, and we can be again.'

She sat down, looking overwhelmed by the offer.

He continued, needing to reassure her, perhaps to salve his guilt. 'For example, we currently only get ten per cent of our imports from Ras Sarat. That could be made higher, closer to twenty-five per cent.'

'We'd need to scale up to that over the next two years, and I'd need a firm commitment from your government in order to begin that process.'

'Consider it done.'

She nodded, but slowly, her eyes roaming his face. 'What's happened, Your Highness?'

He didn't pretend to misunderstand her, but nor did he rush into explanations. He wasn't sure if it was his place.

'Eloise gave me the distinct impression that you and your

people were determined for this marriage to happen. That it was best for everyone. The last thing I expected was to see you, only a few days later, urging the opposite.'

'Eloise was instrumental in bringing me to this point,' he said quietly. That was indeed the truth. 'Is she available to discuss some of these details?' He cursed how weak he sounded, but he'd been wrong to think he could come here and not see her. It was a marvel he'd made it through the last ten minutes.

'I'm sorry, no. But someone else from my delegation can step in, of course.'

He was trapped there. He stared at Elana, totally lost, caught between a rock and a hard place, wondering how to broach this without hurting the Princess's feelings, but needing to see Eloise more than anything else in the world.

'Your Highness.' She moved even closer, eyes scanning his face in a way that was unnervingly similar to Eloise. 'Something happened in Savisia, didn't it?'

He was very still, and utterly silent.

'Eloise came back ahead of the delegation. And she *flew*, which is shocking in and of itself, but then, she left almost immediately, once again, *flying* back to England. You have no idea how long it took her to get here originally because she refused to board anything that lifted off the ground.'

He would have smiled if he weren't battling the revelation that Eloise was no longer on the same continent as him.

'She values your friendship above all else,' he said, quietly, thinking, searching for the right words. 'She wanted you to marry me because she thought, as I did at the time, that it was the best way to serve your kingdom, and also meet my needs.'

'The marriage had some practical points in its favour, but I'm glad you suggested an alternative. I'm...not sure I could have lived with myself for making such a practical marriage.'

He lifted his brows. 'I didn't realise you were reluctant.'

'You weren't supposed to. Even Eloise didn't know the depth of my misgivings. If she had, she would have found a way to put a stop to it,' Elana said, and Tariq smiled, because her loyalty was fierce and strong.

'I spent a lot of time with Eloise while she was in Savisia. I determined early that she would be the person whose advice you would listen to, therefore, she was the only one I had to convince.'

'A wise interpretation of the situation.'

He dipped his head. 'However, there was a problem.'

She waited, silently encouraging him to continue.

'In spending time with Eloise, I found it impossible not to—' He stared at the princess, hating himself for having to have this conversation, worried he was doing something Eloise would never forgive him for. But everything he'd manoeuvred in the last few days had been to bring him to this point. 'I came to feel—' How could he explain it? What words would do justice to what Eloise had come to mean to him? 'I came to realise that I couldn't imagine my life without her in it. I fell in love with her.'

Elana stared at him and then, broke out into a smile. 'You love Eloise!' she said, clicking her fingers. 'Of *course* you do. How could you not? And she loves you! Why else would she have scampered away like that?'

He stood very still.

'She knew—or thought—that this marriage was my salvation. Perhaps she thought it was yours too. She wanted it enough for both of us that she was prepared to sacrifice her own happiness, to take herself completely out of the picture, rather than risk ruining it for us. That's so like her.' Elana's smile was watery. 'She is the most thoughtful, kind-hearted person in the world.'

'Yes,' he agreed without hesitation, feeling instantly bonded to Elana now that they were both on the same page: in complete adoration of Eloise. 'Tell me where I can find her?'

Elana grinned. 'But of course.' She moved to a desk and scrawled something out, then handed the paper to him. 'My home in London. I suggested she stay there while she found her feet with the new job, halfway hoping she'd hate it and come home before she'd signed a lease anywhere else.'

'She'll come home,' he promised, gripping the paper tight between his fingers. 'I'll make sure of it. Thank you, Your Highness.' He bowed.

'Please, let's not be so formal. We're like family now.'

Family. More family. He grinned as he left the room, on a quest to lock the last piece of the puzzle in place. There were still a lot of unknowns, but with Eloise, he knew he could stare each and every one of them down.

CHAPTER TWELVE

SHE READ THE Savisian newspapers each morning, looking for the announcement. For any *hint* of an announcement, telling herself that when she saw it in black and white, she'd exhale.

Then, it would be a *fait accompli* and she could stop questioning her decisions, looking for another angle, hoping for some way to have her cake and eat it too.

But the truth was, she could never do that to Elana. She couldn't do it to Tariq, either, nor the children they would have.

She wouldn't be a woman in the shadows, always on the periphery of their family. It was beneath her and so far beneath the loyalty Elana deserved.

Days passed, and still no announcement came. Texts with Elana revealed nothing new. Eloise grew restless. She knew she had to find work, something to occupy herself with, but she was suffering from a lack of energy.

She barely left the house. She went from the bed to the sofa to the kitchen to make a tea, then back to the sofa, and always, the events of her days in Savisia played in her mind like a film. Every interaction, smile, touch, closeness… They played over and over, so her heart throbbed and twisted and she ached for him, desperately needed him, in a way that was making it impossible to breathe. But this was now the rest of her life.

She had to learn to live with this.

On the fifth day, she dressed in jeans and a sweater, determined to *do* something. She ate a small breakfast, had a strong, black coffee then began to brush her hair, staring at her reflection with a frown. Already her skin looked to have paled. She missed the sunshine. She missed the heat.

She missed…everything.

A knock sounded at the front door, and she moved to it slowly. When Elana stayed here, there was a security presence, but for Eloise, a lock was enough. She unclicked it and opened the door a crack. Then froze.

'Tariq.' His name burst from her lips, shock, confusion, anger, love and need tangling inside of her, filling her mouth with longing. He wore full Savisian dress, and he looked quite impossibly handsome. Her heart stammered.

'Eloise.' His eyes glittered when they met hers. 'Do you have a moment?'

As if she had anything else to do! But this was an impossible conversation. 'I thought I explained in my note,' she said quietly. Then, softer still, 'Did you get the note?'

'Yes, little one, I got the note. Now,' his voice was gruff, 'let me come in or I will bang this door down.'

She didn't doubt him, but even without the threat, she would have opened the door. It had taken all of her courage and strength to walk away from him once; she couldn't do it again, not just yet.

Strangely, her first thought was that she was self-conscious. She'd only worn long, flowing dresses around him before. And the caftan in the cabin. And of course, nothing at all on their last afternoon together. But this was different. Today, she wore western clothes, and somehow it felt as though it delineated an invisible line between them, emphasising how far apart they were, in reality.

Only Tariq wasn't looking at her clothes. As he swept into the entrance foyer, he only had eyes for her. Her face, her eyes, her lips, her hair. He stared at her until her heart almost burst from her body.

'Has it really only been five days?' he demanded, lifting his hands and cupping her face, holding her steady for his inspection, staring down at her until she was trembling.

'Tariq, stop,' she whispered, with barely any strength, because being held by him, touched by him, was so, so good, so powerful, she could barely breathe. 'You can't be here.'

'Why not?'

'You know why not,' she responded quickly, the words breathy. 'You're going to marry my best friend. We can't do this. I won't.'

He moved his finger to her lips, pressing it there. 'How do you think I found you?' he asked gently, light reprobation in the words.

Fear twisted her heart. 'Oh, my God. You told her.'

'Yes,' he agreed.

She closed her eyes, stomach twisting. 'You had no right…'

'I had every right. Not only that, it was essential.'

She trembled for a different reason now, the betrayal eating away at her. 'Why?'

'Because she deserved to know.'

Eloise gasped. 'That's not your decision to make.'

His eyes narrowed. 'She deserved to know that we'd fallen in love,' he said quietly, and she sucked in an uneven breath, the admission that his heart was hers like a bolt of lightning. She basked in its light and warmth a moment before reality returned and she faced the original predicament head on.

'To what end?' she muttered. 'You're marrying her. Now you've just destroyed my friendship—'

'I am *not* marrying her, little one. How could I?'

She blinked up at him, her heart twisting. 'You *must*.'

'Why?'

'Because of your brother and your parents and because Ras Sarat *needs* you.'

'Ras Sarat needs an ally, and I will be that for them. But I can offer financial and trade support, and strategic regional assistance, without forcing Elana into a marriage she'd clearly prefer to avoid.'

Eloise's heart exploded. 'You'd do that?'

'Our countries have a history that goes back a long way. Of course I'd do that.'

'But what about you?' she asked, dropping a hand to his chest. 'You *need* a royal heir.'

'I need an heir,' he agreed. 'But the idea of making any other woman pregnant is anathema to me, so I think we should turn to a new plan. One in which you come back to Savisia as my fiancée. We'll arrange a quick wedding— after these past five days, I'd prefer not to wait at all, if I'm honest.'

Her head was spinning. It was all too much. She could barely keep up.

'But how could that possibly work? You're Spanish and I'm English. It's impossible to believe that I would ever be accepted by your people.'

'I am not Spanish,' he said with a shake of his head. 'I was born there, but my memories are of Savisia. I was reborn when my parents brought me home. Over time, I will work out how to marry the two distinct parts of me—the boy I was, and the man I've become. But either path leads me to the inescapable conclusion: I was raised to rule, just like you said. I enjoy the support of the people. If there is a civil uprising in response to my parentage, then we'll deal with that then, together.'

Her eyes swept shut. 'But marriage to Elana—'

'Cannot happen.' His nostrils flared, his eyes fired with determination. 'There are many things I would give up for my country, *habibi*, but a life with you is not one of them. Not you.' He dropped a hand, caught hers and lifted it to his lips, pressing a gentle kiss across each knuckle. 'I love you,' he said simply. 'And I need you in my life. Will you come home with me?'

She blinked up at him, her heart soaring, every part of her exploding. She tilted her head to the side, looking up at him for several beats, and she felt his worry, his doubt, and knew she had to put him out of his misery.

'I suppose I can risk one more flight, Tariq. For you, and the life we'll share together.'

'Actually,' he said, dropping his head and brushing their lips. 'I thought we could take the scenic route.' He kissed her slowly. 'What's the rush?'

They travelled across the channel by train, and then, once in Europe, Tariq drove them, through the vine-covered fields of France and the mountainous Alps, through ancient Croatian villages and into Greece, then they travelled in the Sheikh's magnificent yacht, across the Mediterranean until they landed at a port near the capital of Savisia. From there, things changed. She was no longer an advisor to the Crown Princess of Ras Sarat, but the fiancée of the Sheikh, and their relationship had to observe some more formalities. The yacht was met by a fleet of servants, fifteen of which were assigned to her, and several of which arrived with suitcases of clothes and jewels, so that when she stepped out into Savisia, she looked every inch the future Sheikha.

Her heart raced but then, she looked at Tariq and she knew there was no need to be nervous. Everything in her life felt as though it had been leading her to this point. Fate had always had this plan for her, she was sure of it.

Much to Eloise's delight, Elana was waiting at the palace, and Eloise cried when she saw her.

'You should have told me,' Elana chided gently, but hugged her best friend tight.

'I thought I'd ruined everything.'

'Instead, you made it a thousand times better,' Elana promised, reaching down and squeezing her hand. Eloise was then taken to the Sheikha, whom she had afternoon tea with, and after that, she met Graciano, Alicia and their children. By the end of the day, her head was spinning, and as happy as she was to be back in Savisia, she found herself longing for the sense of freedom their drawn-out trip through Europe had provided.

When she remarked as much to Tariq, he agreed. 'You know,' he said, leaning closer, 'I was thinking of taking a ride into the desert. I don't suppose you feel like joining me?'

She grinned up at him. 'I thought you'd never ask.'

The water still glowed with its beautiful phosphorescent algal bloom, but it was nothing to the brightness of their love and hope. Their future now secured, they had only to sit back and enjoy the ride.

Tariq had worried about how news of his parentage would affect the country, but in the end the focus was all on his marriage, his beautiful bride, and then, shortly afterwards, the announcement of her pregnancy. Far from any outcry over the lineage, there was universal adoration for the newest descendant of the royal family—and of course, that was how this child was viewed. The emphasis Tariq had placed on bloodline was, as it turned out, a far bigger deal to him than anyone else. Nonetheless, to avoid any future problems for his children, he had the Prime Minister introduce a referendum. The vote was overwhelmingly in favour of Tariq being acknowledged as the official and rightful heir to the Savisian throne. No challenge eventuated.

Years passed. Good, prosperous years for Savisia and, in time, Ras Sarat. Years of peace and fortune, years in which he felt grateful every day for the chance meeting with his wife, and the way they'd fallen in love.

They had four beautiful children, and when Annie, the oldest daughter of Alicia and Graciano, was finished with high school, their family relocated to Savisia, to be close to Tariq. Having missed so much of each other's lives, the brothers wanted to be as close as possible, and one of Tariq's favourite pastimes was hearing Graciano talk about their parents. His mother enjoyed this too, and had more or less become a de facto mother to Graciano and Alicia, whom she loved almost as much as she did Eloise.

Most importantly, Tariq came to understand over the years that family was about so much more than blood. Family was a choice one made, each day, to love and respect, to support and cherish, and with Graciano and Alicia, his mother, Elana and most of all, Eloise and their children, he felt the richness of his own beautiful, blended family.

He had been blessed, indeed.

* * * * *

THE BABY BEHIND THEIR MARRIAGE MERGER

JOSS WOOD

MILLS & BOON

CHAPTER ONE

STANDING ON THE balcony that ran the length of the Vane's ballroom, Addi Fields smoothed her hand over the slinky material of her satin slip-dress, conscious of the cool breeze blowing across her bare back. The dress, a deep navy-blue, drifted over her lanky body and, with its halter neck, looked demure from the front. It was anything but modest from the back, dropping exceptionally low to skim the top of her butt. Underwear had required a lot of thought.

Addi took a glass of champagne from a waiter and thought about the award she'd been handed earlier in the evening. One of the properties within the portfolio she managed for the hotel division of Thorpe Industries had won the award for small lodge of the year and she was comprehensively delighted. As there were rumours that Thorpe Industries was up for sale, she wasn't sure how long she'd get to enjoy the kudos that came along with the recognition.

Addi looked through the French doors into the busy ballroom. The room was packed with the hospitality sector's bigwigs: men and women who owned the most spectacular hotels, lodges and leisure operations on the continent. She was only there because Thorpe Industries was in a state of flux—Cole Thorpe had recently been gifted the company by his brother—and the hospitality division wasn't on his list of priorities. She'd asked for permission to represent

Thorpe Industries, realising it was a great chance to network. Someone here might give her a job if she lost hers when Cole Thorpe sold up.

Her new boss was due in the country within the next few weeks, and Lex, her half-sister and best friend, would be driving him around Cape Town in her role as Thorpe Industries' part-time chauffeur. Maybe he'd let something slip; maybe Lex would overhear his plans, something that would give her an edge.

Addi could only hope.

Besides, she hadn't been prepared to pass up the opportunity to stay two nights in one of the best hotels in the country and eat five-star meals. It was a pity she didn't have the time, or money, to visit the hotel's award-winning spa.

Normally, her days consisted of leaving early to avoid the hellish Cape Town traffic, working ten hours straight and driving home, to be greeted by her energetic, noisy half-sisters. After the younger girls went to bed, she and Lex enjoyed a glass of wine and curled up on either end of their old sofa.

Most evenings they discussed their finances, with Lex telling her the girls needed money for a school trip, or new school shoes, or that a toilet was leaking, or that the gutters needed cleaning. She earned a good salary but, with three half-sisters to support, money never went far. It never had. And she'd never had the luxury of taking her salary and spending it on herself. She'd started working part-time at the age of fourteen, and initially most of her wages had been given to Joelle, her oh-so-irresponsible mother. Later, any money she'd earned had been given to Aunt Kate to help with the costs of housing and feeding Lex and her.

Addi rested the award on the balcony and lifted her face to look at the sky. She wondered when she could leave, at what point her escape wouldn't raise eyebrows—assuming, of course, that anyone would notice. She was a seriously small minnow in a tank full of sharks. She felt out of place and uncomfortable, but the chance to network and be seen by potential employers was worth any discomfort.

But in her slinky, barely there dress, she felt exposed and just a little naked. She far preferred her men's style white shirts, pencil skirts that hit her knee and her sensible pumps. Her ultra-short bright blonde hair looked trendy, but she kept it short because it saved time in the morning and, being naturally blonde, only required a touch-up every four or five months. She didn't have the time or money to spend on her appearance.

While she knew she should work the room, Addi simply didn't have the energy. She'd had a long day, culminating in attending a talk by Jude Fisher, owner and CEO of Fisher International. In his personal capacity, he owned several off-the-grid hotels and lodges. He and his grandfather before him—Bartholomew Fisher—were legends in the industry, owning some of the oldest and finest establishments in Africa. His hotel in the Seychelles was rated one of the best in the world, and their safari operation adjacent to the Etosha Game Reserve in Namibia had a waiting list of four years. *Four years.*

Addi had sat in the back of the room, her notepad on her lap, and listened to him expound on how hotels could become greener and more eco-friendly. Like her, he had a passion for sustainability, and his talk that afternoon had been well attended. She hadn't written anything down for the first ten minutes or hadn't taken anything in... She'd simply stared at him, drinking him in.

She wasn't normally so easily distracted but, thanks to Fisher's charisma, masculinity and the way he'd taken command of the room, she'd completely missed his opening greeting and introduction. Unlike the majority of the speakers at the conference, he'd elected to forgo a designer suit and had been dressed in navy chinos, a soft leather belt and an open-collared button-down white shirt, the sleeves rolled up to show muscled forearms.

Under the casual clothes was a body designed to make angels weep. He was tall, six-foot-three or so, and broad with it, his shoulders wide. Addi had been able to see the outline of a bold tattoo on his right pec through the cotton shirt and another tattoo on his left bicep. His hands and forearms showed the raised veins of someone who took his fitness seriously.

He also had a ridiculously sexy face topped with curly hair, styled off his face, keeping the sides and back short. Black stubble dotted his cheeks and jaw, hiding what she thought was a sensual mouth. His nose was long and a little off-centre, as if he'd broken it once and hadn't bothered to have it reset.

But it was his eyes that had caught and held her attention. They were a deep, dark green, the colour of ancient forests, framed by spiky lashes. His voice was deep and rich, hot chocolate on a cold winter's day. He'd worn leather bracelets and a trendy watch on his wrist, and he'd been utterly at ease in front of his audience.

When Addi had pulled her attention off his body and face and started paying attention to his words, she'd quickly realised he knew his stuff. She'd expected him to know the sector inside out, as the CEO of one of the most famous leisure groups in the world, but she hadn't expected him to do a deep-dive into the intricacies of sustainability and eco-friendly options for the leisure industry. Neither had she expected him to be so passionate about the impact their industry had on the environment. He'd spoken with assurance and knowledge, occasionally interjecting his speech with flashes of humour. He'd had all of the women and a good portion of the men eating out of his hand by the end of the ninety-minute presentation.

Thank goodness it had been recorded because Addi knew she hadn't taken in as much as she should've... Or anything much at all. He'd had some brilliant low-cost and effective ideas, but she couldn't remember one of them.

'It's a lovely night.'

She turned and watched as he lifted his shoulder off the wall and stepped out of the shadows. Her heart banged against her chest and she tightened her grip on her glass, the moisture in her mouth disappearing.

Talk of the devil and there he was...

Good grief, he smelled fantastic. She didn't recognise his cologne, but it made her think of a fresh maritime breeze or swimming in a blue-green, cliff-lined bay—fresh and fantastic.

Stop staring at him and think, Fields. You are in the company of one of the most influential men in the industry and, since there's a chance you'll be out of a job soon, this is an opportunity to make a good impression, to network.

But talking shop was the last thing on her mind. And it didn't look like one of the country's—the continent's!—most eligible bachelors was interested in networking either.

In fact, he was looking at her with interest in his eyes.

A *lot* of interest...

Ugh. What was happening here? She was cool and prickly, tall and lanky, and she wasn't the type to attract the interest of David Gandy lookalikes at social events. In fairness, she didn't go to balls or parties, clubs or bars, so she had no idea whether she was anyone's type any more.

That was what had happened when at the age of twenty-six, and after a lifetime of disappointments, she'd undergone a monumental life shift. Not only had she been handed two half-sisters to co-raise and financially support, but her fiancé's promises to love her through good times and bad, to stick by her side through thick and thin, had evaporated as quickly as water on a hot stove.

'I'm Jude Fisher.'

Yes, she knew who he was.

'You were at my presentation this afternoon,' Jude said, coming to stand next to her on the balcony.

He'd noticed her—really? She'd sat in the second-to-back row behind a large man and a woman with big hair. Addi swallowed and nodded. 'I was,' she replied, cursing her croaky voice. 'It was interesting.'

He winced, humour flashing in his eyes. '"Interesting" good, or "interesting" boring?'

She raised one eyebrow at his comment. 'I wouldn't have taken you as someone who indulges in false modesty, Mr Fisher.'

He grinned at her sharp comment. 'I guess that'll teach me to go looking for compliments.'

'The room was packed, the attendees hung off your every word and you were mobbed afterwards,' Addi pointed out, trying to keep her smile from blooming.

'I noticed you slipped out as soon as I was done talking,' Jude said.

'Unlike the others, I didn't need anything clarified or any concepts explained.' Green energy was a passion, but she wasn't brave enough to tell him that she'd introduced measures to improve energy efficiency, reduce waste and recycle at all the accommodation establishments under her control.

She wasn't brave at all.

Jude gestured to her dress. 'You look lovely,' he said.

He didn't need to add that she'd looked very different that afternoon. She'd been wearing her corporate Thorpe Industries uniform of a white shirt, black skirt, pale-green jacket and low heels. Her uniform wasn't sexy or stylish, but it was free, and saved her from having to spend any money on work clothes. For that she was grateful.

'Thank you,' Addi said, catching the heat in his eyes. She'd been out of the man-woman 'I think you're hot' game for so long and she couldn't tell if he was interested or whether her imagination was running away with her. She gestured to his suit and lifted her eyebrows. 'That's a nice suit. Designer?'

Jude spread his arms and shrugged. 'I have no damn idea,' he admitted. He narrowed his eyes. 'Does it matter?'

'Not to me. Though it's a bold move, not wearing a bow-tie, or even a tie, when everyone else is wearing a tuxedo,' she commented, gesturing to his open-neck shirt under his black jacket.

'I forgot to pack a tie.' He shrugged, unconcerned. 'What are they going to do—toss me out?'

No, of course, they wouldn't. Frankly, the organisers would be grateful he'd chosen to attend the dinner and awards ceremony, because having him attend their conference had been a coup.

'Do you always do whatever you want to?' she asked, curious and not a little envious.

He lifted one shoulder in a careless shrug. 'Is there any point in doing anything else?'

Spoken like a man who'd never had to please anyone but himself. He had no idea what it felt like to be confined, to be forced into a situation over which you had no control.

'Don't you?'

'Don't I what?' she asked,

'Always do what you like, when you want to?'

She almost laughed but managed to swallow it, knowing that her chuckle would hold no mirth. No, she didn't. She worked, counted pennies, worked some more, drank wine with her sister and worked. Had she mentioned that? Before she could answer, he ran his thumb down her arm, his touch sending lightning bolting through her body.

She caught his hot gaze, saw desire flash within it and this time she had no doubt he was attracted to her. Heat flooded her system and goose bumps erupted on her skin. This was so strange, and she was miles out of her comfort zone. In some ways, she was standing outside of herself watching a movie, and she was in the starring role.

But tonight she didn't want to be normal Addi, the Addi who was super-responsible, who worked too hard and played too little. She wanted to be the woman who belonged in this dress, confident and cool, sophisticated and stylish.

Just for tonight, she wanted to be the type of woman Jude dated.

'As much as I can,' she finally answered. Her statement wasn't a lie. If she could have lived for herself, and been a little selfish, she would have. But at this point in her life she didn't have the bandwidth, emotionally or financially, to be self-centred.

Addi glanced down at his hand resting on the balcony, wondering how it would feel to have those big hands skim her body and explore her bare skin. She felt her nipples tighten and her heart rate picked up as heat bloomed between her legs. This was sexual attraction, hot and hard. It had been so long that she barely recognised it.

His eyes moved from her mouth and back up to her face. 'What is your name?' he demanded, his voice lower than it was before. It now reminded her of smoky whisky, of late nights and out-of-control sex.

'Addi,' she whispered.

'Addi.' He tested her name out on his tongue, his eyes not leaving her face. He touched her with nothing more than his thumb on the inside of her wrist and she felt as though she'd been plugged into an electricity substation. This was madness—the best type of madness, but still...

Madness.

Jude turned his head, and it was only when he stepped back that she realised how close she was to him, and wondered when one of them would make the move to close the gap between them. Jude took two glasses of champagne from the tray of a previously unnoticed waiter—honestly, an asteroid could strike in front of her but as long as Jude was within thirty feet she wouldn't notice!

He handed one to her, their fingers brushing. Addi lifted the glass to her lips and tipped it back, sighing when the dry champagne rolled over her tongue and down her parched throat. She turned to look out onto the gardens of the hotel, inhaling the combination of the smell of fynbos drifting down from Table Mountain and roses in the extraordinary rose garden below them. It was a sultry night, heavy with promise, the full moon peeking out from behind a thin cloud. It was the end of summer and, day by day, the sun would lose its heat and the night its sultriness.

She tipped her head up and looked at the night sky, wishing she could identify the individual constellations through the city haze. When she'd been a kid, star-gazing had made her feel connected to something bigger and better—what, she didn't know—and when she felt off-balance she still tipped her head up to the sky.

It didn't help much tonight; she was too conscious of the big, bold man standing next to her.

His arm brushed hers and he pointed up. 'You can just see the Southern Cross,' he told her.

Nope, the Southern Cross was to his right and down. She thought about keeping quiet, about letting him have his moment, but shook her head. She wasn't the type to play the dumb girl. 'You are about thirty degrees off,' she told him.

She expected him to pout—men never liked to be corrected—but he smiled, and she saw that famous double dimple appear on the left side of his mouth. His grin was wide and white, and his straight teeth flashed. 'Well, damn. I've been telling girls that's the Southern Cross for more than twenty years now.'

She smiled at him, enjoying his ability to laugh at himself. 'From now on, if I were you, I'd stay away from any star-knowledge seduction, Fisher.'

'Good to know,' he replied. He hesitated a beat before sighing. 'Damn, it was all I had. I'm never going to get a date again.'

She laughed and then rolled her eyes. 'Yeah, you're doomed,' she teased him. She did not doubt that the man had no problems picking up women.

That being said, while she didn't have the time to read the entertainment sections of online news outlets—she barely managed to keep up with the headlines—she'd never seen anything about Jude's personal life in the papers. There were no stories about him dating ballerinas, sportswomen, socialites and celebrities. As a journalist had recently noted, he either had super-ninja skills at keeping his love life private or he was a monk.

Standing here with him, she knew he wasn't a monk.

'Do you often do this?' she asked. 'Approach strange woman on hotel balconies?'

'You're the first. I tend to keep my...' he hesitated '...romantic interests low-key. I think that what I do in my free time is my business and no one else's.'

Fair enough.

He leaned his forearms on the balcony and linked his hands together. When he spoke, his voice was more serious than she'd expected. 'And what has been written is exaggerated.'

She examined his face and saw that his mouth was drawn into a thin line, and a muscle ticked in his jaw. 'Somehow the press always manages to get it wrong, or construct sand castles from a single grain of sand.'

He didn't like press reporters, that much was obvious.

'Why are you telling me this?' she asked, curious.

'I have no idea,' he replied. He lifted his champagne glass, tipped it up and drained the contents. 'When your eyes connect with mine, I feel like I need to tell the truth.'

'My eyes are just a very normal blue,' she informed him, a little confused. Sure, she was a blue-eyed blonde, but she wasn't anything special. In fact, she frequently wished she could have her sister Lex's exotic looks. She was a bold redhead with a freckle-covered face. People looked twice at Lex because she was interesting. Addi, on good days, was merely pretty. Unlike her fickle mother Joelle, she didn't have the Marylin Monroe sex-on-a-stick thing going on.

'Normal?' He scoffed. 'They are the colour of the sea at midnight, deep and dark and intensely mysterious.' He released a half-laugh and shoved his hand through his hair. 'Jeez, now I'm sounding like a greetings card.'

His words were smooth, but his delivery wasn't, and that was what kept Addi in place. She heard authenticity in his voice, seemingly caught off-guard by his attraction to her. She glanced down at the hand gripping the stem of his champagne glass and noticed the fine tremble in his fingers. Her eyes moved up and she noticed the tension in those broad shoulders, his bobbing Adam's apple and a hint of red on his cheekbones.

This man wanted *her*. The thought smacked her with all the force of a bullet train. And he was trying hard not to show it, was attempting to be the man about town the world thought him to be. She lifted her hand and touched his jaw with the tips of her fingers. The pads of her fingers skimmed his stubble, and she dragged her thumb across his bottom lip, her eyes locked on his.

She could see them, naked on a big bed, her skin pale in comparison to his tanned body. She could imagine the feel of the muscles of his back under her hands, his long legs tangled with hers, his dark head dipping to kiss her. She could feel the night air wafting in over their bodies from an open window and hear the sound of the party-goers in the ballroom below. They would be good together. He'd make her feel like a woman, strong and powerful. He'd make her scream, then sob, with pleasure.

She wasn't someone who jumped into a stranger's bed—one-night stands weren't her thing—but she knew she needed this night with Jude. She needed to feel like a woman, to feel like herself, to be anything but the stressed-out worker bee, the responsible older sister, the one who spent her nights trying to stretch a budget that had no give.

She needed to feel, to be body to body, mouth to mouth, and enjoy an intimate, physical connection. She had one more night away from her sisters, one night to be someone other than the woman she normally was, and she knew she'd be regretful for ever if she didn't take this time, take this man…

Didn't allow him to take her.

Jude turned his mouth into her hand and kissed her palm, his tongue coming out to touch her skin. She tensed and closed her eyes, and the intensity of his touch reached her newly painted, pretty toes. If he could make her feel so much with one small kiss, what would happen if he kissed her properly, if she allowed him access to every part of her?

Jude held her head in his hand and his eyes held hers as he lowered his head, bending his knees a little so that he could touch her mouth with his lips. She'd expected hard and fast, but she got gentle and slow, a 'hello, I'd like to know more' kiss. She held his strong wrists as his lips explored hers, nibbling here, sliding there. She sighed and his tongue slipped into the small opening. Her tongue met his and two universes collided and merged.

Suddenly there was only the air he could give her, his tongue feeding her hot, dark kisses. Pleasure spun her away, and she sighed when his hand came to rest on her bare lower back, his fingers flirting with the top of her butt. He pulled her into him, and her breasts pushed against his chest, her stomach resting against a fantastically long and hard erection.

Heat, desire, need and want ripped through her, as fast and unexpected as a hidden current in a sluggish river.

He groaned, palmed her breast and found her nipple with his thumb, eliciting another moan from her. He wrenched his mouth off hers and dropped hot kisses on her jaw and down her throat, sucking gently on the ball of her bare shoulder.

'I want you,' he muttered, his voice low and guttural. 'I wanted you when I saw you this afternoon. I want you now. Let me take you to bed.'

This was *her* time; this was *her* night. The night where she could be Addi, where she could be free. Free from responsibility, free to be herself. To feel, experience…

She stood on her tiptoes and dragged her mouth across Jude's. 'Yes, please.'

CHAPTER TWO

ADDI STARED AT the small window showing two blue lines and felt her heart go into freefall. Unable to believe what she was seeing, she picked up another test from the top of the toilet's cistern and peered down into that window. A flashing 'pregnant' pulsed in it. The third test also showed two blue lines.

There was no doubt that she was pregnant.

Addi sat down abruptly on the closed toilet seat and dropped her head between her legs, trying to get air into her suddenly too-small lungs. *Pregnant?* How? What? Well, the how she knew: she and Jude Fisher had made love twice—three times—eight weeks ago and somehow, despite her having been on the pill and he having worn a condom, one of his boys had met one of her girls.

She could explain the pill failing; she'd had a dose of antibiotics that week, and it was said that they could impair the efficacy of the contraceptive. But Jude had used condoms. They'd done everything right, everything they could to prevent a pregnancy, but here she was, a mummy-to-be.

How had that happened? And why had it happened to *her?*

Addi felt her stomach knot and her throat constrict. Standing up, she whirled around and flipped up the seat. She dropped to her knees in front of the toilet and heaved.

After rinsing out her mouth and splashing her face with water, Addi lifted her eyes to look at her reflection in the mirror. Two blue stripes ran under her eyes and her face looked blotchy, her lips chapped. Her eyes were bloodshot from spending too many hours looking at her computer screen and she'd lost weight, something she couldn't afford to do.

Addi gripped the sides of the basin and stared down at the plug, panic rolling over her in an insidious tide. She couldn't be pregnant, she didn't want to be pregnant—it wasn't in her five-or ten-year plan. It wasn't in her life plan at all.

And, God, how was she going to explain to Lex that she was pregnant via a one-night stand? They'd promised each other, promised themselves, they'd take precautions not to bring any unwanted children into their lives. They would *not* follow in their mother's five-kids-by-five-different-men footsteps. They'd be responsible, they'd be clever.

She'd failed on all counts.

And failure wasn't something she did, wasn't something she tolerated.

This was *so* Joelle, Addi thought, cursing herself—falling pregnant by a sexy guy who'd rocked her world, taking pleasure in a random encounter, was something her feckless mother would have done. Addi hated herself for giving in to temptation and sleeping with Fisher. Her mother was the sensual, impetuous one, prepared to put her pleasure over common sense, but Addi was not. She was the one who trailed behind her mother and picked up the messes she made. She was the one who'd rolled up her sleeves and gone to work, despite her broken heart, when Joelle had left two half-sisters for them to raise.

Addi stared at her shoes, fighting the tidal wave of anger threatening to consume her. Hadn't she been handed enough, forced to deal with more than most? She'd been born to the most irresponsible woman on the planet and she and her half-sister Lex had been lugged from house to house, room to room, depending on whom Joelle could seduce enough for them to take her two kids and her in. They'd missed meals and school, and their childhoods had been tumultuous. When Addi had been five or six, Joelle had married Tom and given birth to Storm, another half-sister. The years spent with Tom had been the happiest of her life, secure and stable.

Although she'd been so young, she understood that, easily bored, Joelle wasn't cut out for monogamy. When her mother told them they'd be moving on without Storm, who would stay with Tom, Addi had felt devastated but she hadn't been surprised.

Nothing good lasted for ever…sometimes it didn't even last three years.

The next years had been a blur, with too many faces and too many houses, and life had only made sense again when Joelle left them with her aunt Kate when Addi had been seventeen. The irascible old lady had given them their second dose of stability and, when she'd died, she'd left her house to Lex and her and a small insurance policy, enough for one of them to go to university. She and Lex had come up with a plan: Addi would go to university and get her degree in as short a time as possible. Lex would go out to work and her income, with the rooms they let to other female students, would pay for their living expenses. When Addi got a job, she would pay for Lex to attend uni.

She'd landed a fantastic job, Lex had enrolled at university and Addi had started planning her wedding to the love of her life, the man she'd met during her first year at university. Dean had been educated, successful and ambitious, and when she'd moved out of their house and into his luxury Camps Bay flat, the plan had been that Lex would rent the additional room in the cottage to provide her with an income while she studied for her degree.

Addi had had everything under control, planned and perfect. The wedding reception was to have been smaller than Dean had liked, but Lex and Storm were to have been her bridesmaids and Tom, her ex-stepfather, was to give her away. Believing that nothing could go wrong, she'd even sent a Save The Date card to Joelle and asked her whether she thought she might attend the wedding.

Ten days after Addi had sent the email invitation, Joelle had flown back to Cape Town from Thailand, accompanied by two half-sisters she and Lex hadn't known they had. Joelle had asked Lex and her to look after them for the weekend and that was the last time any of Joelle's girls had seen their mother.

She'd gained two half-sisters and lost her fiancé. Despite Dean having tried to make it work—she had to give him that—Nixi and Snow weren't what he had signed up for and he hadn't wanted to share her, his home, or his life with two little girls. She'd asked him to postpone their wedding for a year, maybe two, to give them time to wrap their heads around her life changes—love couldn't fade that quickly, could it?—but he'd called it quits, blithely informing her he didn't love her enough...

That he probably didn't love her at all.

And, at that moment, Addi had finally grasped the lesson that life had been trying to teach her: that people would always let her down, normally at a time when she needed them the most. It was always, always, better to rely on oneself. And she would never put her faith in anyone other than her sisters again. She'd vowed that Joelle's girls would be smart, responsible, independent and *better* than their irresponsible mother.

But she, responsibility personified, was the one who was pregnant. Addi was embarrassed and furious, but she was also scared. After Dean had absconded, she'd imagined that, since she had no intention of marrying ever again, having children wasn't on the cards for her. And maybe that was a good thing because, unlike Lex, she'd never managed to fully connect with her half-sisters. While she'd gone to work and tried to keep their financial heads above water, Lex had scooped them up, dispensed hugs and kisses, dried their tears and listened to their rambling stories.

Okay, sure, she wasn't around them as much as Lex, but when she got home they didn't rush to hug her as they did Lex, didn't curl up into her lap as they did Lex. Hers wasn't the bed they ran to when they had bad dreams, hers wasn't the opinion or reassurance they sought.

Lex was warm and she wasn't. While she had Joelle's features, her blonde hair and blue eyes, she came across as being haughty rather than sensual. Being naturally shy and very guarded, she disappeared behind a cool mask and talked in a clipped, no-nonsense style, fast and sharp.

She knew her work colleagues considered her stuck up, and she was never invited to join the younger staff members for a drink after work or go to their houses for a barbeque at the weekend. They didn't understand that she had all the responsibilities her older colleagues did, children to raise, a salary to stretch.

And now she had a baby on the way. How was she going to work, have a baby, raise Nixi and Snow and support Lex so that she could finish her degree? And, with Thorpe Industries being put up for sale, she'd be out of a job in a few months. The thought of going through the stressful interview process, trying to impress and convince owners or managers that she was worth taking a chance on, pregnant or not, made her throat close.

Panic filled her. She needed to work; she couldn't be without an income. She had three and a half people relying on her—what was she going to do? What plan could be made? All she could do was send out her CV and look for a new job. But was that enough? She didn't think so.

As Addi stepped back into the stall to get her tests and bag, she heard the door to the bathroom open and a few seconds later she heard a familiar deep voice bouncing off the walls. 'Addi, are you in here?'

She could easily imagine Greg, her assistant, stepping into the ladies'. He didn't have a reticent bone in his body.

'I'll be out in a minute, Greg.' Jeez, couldn't a girl take half an hour to do three pregnancy tests and have a mini panic attack without someone hunting her down?

'Cole Thorpe is looking for you. He's tried to video-call you twice.'

Her head shot up and she swept the pregnancy tests into her bag. She walked over to the basin and flipped the tap to wash her hands.

'Did he say what the urgency is?' she asked Greg. Why did the big boss and owner want to talk to her? What was she missing? What hadn't she done?

'No, but he told me to find you and that he will be calling back in fifteen minutes.' He drew a circle in the air, gesturing to her gaunt face. 'You need to put on some lipstick and blusher, and I'll make you a cup of coffee.'

Her stomach rebelled at the thought. 'Make it a cup of rooibos tea and you're on.'

Greg stared at her. 'You hate rooibos tea,' he pointed out, frowning.

Yeah, but she'd hate throwing up in front of her boss more.

* * *

'So, it's settled, then? Addi will be your liaison between you and Thorpe Industries. Nobody understands the division better.'

Jude looked at the two squares on his screen, the smaller one containing the face of his friend Cole Thorpe, the larger one reflecting the very lovely face of his one-night stand from two months ago. Jude rubbed his hand over his jaw, dropping his eyes briefly to look at the small block showing his reflection. He looked reasonably impassive. Unlike Addi, he wasn't wearing a *what is happening here?* expression.

Cole's eyebrows pulled down into a frown and impatience flickered in his eyes. 'Guys? Has my sound cut out?'

Jude nodded and managed a thin smile. 'Sure, that's fine. Let me have a look at all your hospitality assets and I'll let you know what properties I am interested in.'

'I'll give you a better price if you take all of them,' Cole shot back. Jude sighed. He knew Cole wanted to rid himself of an inheritance he hadn't wanted or expected but, old friend or not, Jude wasn't going to buy hotels, lodges or camps that didn't suit his, or Fisher International's, needs.

But to make an offer, or even look at what his friend owned, he'd have to work with Addi. It made sense on a business level. Her title was Operations Manager, and she was, per Cole, the hospitality division's trouble-shooter. Judging by the wealth of documents he'd already received from Cole, she had spreadsheets to keep track of her spreadsheets, and every entity was broken down to the smallest cup, blanket and spare part. The woman was scarily efficient.

She also, Jude noticed, looked exhausted. With her hair slicked off her face and red lips, the woman on his screen looked cool and composed on the surface. But her eyes were dull with fatigue, and she'd lost weight since he'd last seen her. Yet his heart still kicked up and the fabric of his pants suddenly felt one size smaller. There was something about her that heated his blood, that made his heart stutter, that closed his throat. And, whatever it was, he had to get over it before he met up with her again.

Talking of… 'I suppose we'd better check our diaries, Ms Fields.'

'Mr Thorpe has instructed me to make sure I'm available to you,' Addi replied in a cool voice. 'So I am completely at your disposal, Mr Fisher.'

His eyes met hers in cyberspace and he saw hers darken and flicker with want, or need. But an instant later they returned to being a murky blue. The woman on the balcony had fizzled and sparked; she had been sassy and confident, at ease in her skin. This Addi looked and sounded like a faded version of herself. In a very vague way, she reminded him of the way his mum had looked shortly before she'd died—worn down, exhausted, emotionally battered. He'd been young when she'd died from an ectopic pregnancy, just eight, but he'd had to grow up super-fast, becoming self-reliant almost immediately. That was what happened when one parent died and the other checked out. Then checked out permanently by dying.

'I'll leave you to it,' Cole said, and with a tap on his keyboard disappeared from the screen. Jude made sure he was gone before resting his forearms on his desk.

'I didn't know you worked for Cole,' he said, picking up a pen and tapping the end on his desk. He was working out of his study at his vineyard in Franschhoek, just an hour from the city. He glanced to his right, enjoying the view of vineyards rolling up to the edge of the sawtooth ragged peaks of the Franschhoek Mountains. This was the first day he'd seen the sun for a long time, and when the next cold front rolled in they would be having weeks, possibly months, of cold and wild weather.

'How would you?' Addi asked, shrugging. 'We didn't spend that much time talking.'

He couldn't dispute her words. After that brief conversation on the balcony, he'd kissed her, she'd kissed him back and then they'd both been eager to find the nearest bed. His suite happened to be closest, and they'd spent the rest of the night, and half of the next morning, making love. He'd only left the room because he'd had a brunch meeting and when he returned two hours later she had gone.

He'd been disappointed but, when that faded, also grateful. Thanks to the call he'd received from Cole just before his presentation, enquiring if he would be interested in purchasing the hospitality division of Thorpe Industries Africa, he hadn't had the time for an affair, however brief. Cole's newly acquired company owned some amazing hotels, a few of which he'd be happy to add to Fisher International's portfolio. There were also a couple he wanted for his personal chain of eco-friendly accommodation. It would be a next-level deal and he had been working sixteen-hour days for the last two months.

That was what it had taken to persuade the Council of Three to agree to him even investigating the potential deal.

Addi turned at the sound of a knock on her door and asked him to excuse her for a minute. On his computer screen he watched her walking away. She had a spectacular butt and incredible legs, and he rubbed his hands up and down his face. He didn't need to be distracted by a woman—not now.

Acquiring the hotels and lodges for Fisher International would be tricky. It would be the first major acquisition he'd done since he'd taken over from his grandfather and, he estimated, would cost over two hundred million pounds. That sort of expenditure—*any* unexpected expenditure—needed his three-person board of trustees' approval.

Jude felt the familiar swell of frustration and annoyance. He owned Fisher International outright but, because his grandfather hadn't trusted his judgement, for ten years following inheriting the company Jude had to seek approval from three men his grandfather had appointed. He clenched his fist and leaned back in his chair, looking over the vines and out onto the mountains. Nine years had passed and he just had to deal with them for one more year. Then he'd have full control of Fisher International. He could take it public, sell it, even run it into the ground, and nobody could say or do a thing.

He. Could. Not. Wait.

Addi slid back into her seat and lifted her eyes to the camera. 'I'm sorry about that, I needed to take an urgent call from the hotel in Zanzibar.'

He had an idea of her role but asked her to clarify what she did for Thorpe Industries.

'I see myself as a back-up system for all the managers. I help with budgets and staffing issues. I source people and commodities. I authorise bulk-buying orders for all the hotels, like linen and toiletries. I don't do any direct marketing, but I keep an eye on marketing to make sure they are not going off-brand.'

It sounded like a lot for one person to do. No wonder she looked exhausted. Jude tapped his pen against the side of his desk. They needed to meet, as soon as possible. Partly because he needed to get a better, more personal handle on what he was looking at in terms of Cole's assets, and partly because he wanted to see her again.

She'd been on the edge of his mind for the last eight

weeks, images of her—long legs, pale skin, him running his hands through her short hair, her elegant feet and the sexy moan she made when he'd slid inside her—ambushing him at entirely inappropriate moments. She'd burrowed under his skin, but he knew that working with her, the long hours spent poring over spreadsheets and figures, would cure him of any lingering sentiment. There was nothing that killed attraction quicker than spending long hours in front of a computer screen and arguing figures.

'When can we meet?' he demanded. 'This afternoon?'

'Where are your offices?'

'We are in the process of moving the company headquarters to a new building on the Waterfront, and while that happens I am working out of my home office in Franschhoek.'

Addi wrinkled her pretty nose. 'And when are you coming into the city again?' she asked, looking off-screen. He heard the tap of her fingers against her keyboard and assumed she was looking at her diary, trying to work out when she could fit him in.

Maybe she needed reminding that he was her first priority. 'I want to meet this afternoon,' he stated, his voice taking on an edge that suggested she not argue. He was being demanding but he needed to see her again, to look into those blue eyes, to inhale her sexy scent. Why? Why her?

Why hadn't he been able to get her off his mind?

Once he saw her again, he'd be able to move on, stop thinking about her and concentrate fully on his business and his career. That was what was important. His brief flings? Not so much.

'I'm free from two. I want an overview of the offerings, their unique selling points and their turnover and profit margins,' Jude stated.

Addi raised her eyebrows and, even though they were

meeting in cyberspace, he felt the impact of her hard, blue-eyed stare. 'You're joking, right?'

When it came to business, he was always deadly serious. 'Do I look like I'm joking?'

'You want me to pull all that information together in, what…?' She glanced at the functional watch on her left arm, and Jude couldn't help thinking that something delicate and pretty would suit her better. 'In five hours? And that's including the hour travelling time to Franschhoek? Are you mad?'

'Are you telling me you can't?' Jude suspected that, while she might not be able to give him nuts and bolts figures, she had most of what he needed in that big brain of hers.

Her eyes narrowed and her mouth flattened. 'I could give you an overview by this afternoon—'

'Good. Give me your phone number and I will send you a GPS pin.'

Addi held up her hand. 'Will you let me finish, please?'

He leaned back in his chair, impressed that he didn't intimidate her. That could be because he'd been charming Jude when they'd met, or it could be because she'd seen him naked, but he suspected that Addi wasn't a pushover in general. He liked that. He far preferred people who pushed back than suck-ups and sycophants. He lifted his head in a gesture for her to continue.

'I can't meet you at two; I have a lawyer's appointment.'

Why was she meeting with a lawyer? Was there a lawsuit against one of the hotels he wasn't aware of? If he was going to be pulled into a legal fight, he'd pull out right now. 'What's the problem?' he demanded.

'It's a personal matter, Jude, nothing to do with Fisher International,' Addi said, and he heard exhaustion in her voice.

He caught the wariness in her eyes, and his curiosity peaked. 'Why do you need a lawyer?'

'Are you normally this nosy?'

No, he wasn't, not by a long shot. In reality, he frequently had to cut women off when they shared personal information. He wasn't interested in the minutiae of people's lives; he kept his interactions with the opposite sex as shallow as he could—movies, books, current events...bed. Women couldn't be trusted with his thoughts, feelings, memories or his heart. And, if they didn't know anything about him or his business, they couldn't pass anything on to the press. For the past ten years or so, that strategy had worked well for him, and he'd rarely made the news for anything other than his business successes.

When he didn't answer, Addi spoke again. 'I can be with you around four,' she told him. 'But I can only give you a couple of hours because I need to be back in town by seven.'

'Do you have a date?'

Where had that come from and why did he care? He cursed himself, wondering whether some idiot had hijacked his brain. She was now a work colleague, and he had no call to question her about her personal life. But the thought of her sitting across the table from another guy, laughing with him, talking to him—going to bed with him—set the lining of his stomach alight.

Addi looked down her nose at him and he had to admire her sangfroid. 'That has nothing to do with you, Jude,' she told him, her voice colder than an Arctic wind. She placed her elbow on the desk and massaged her forehead with the tips of her fingers, as if trying to rub away a headache. When she spoke again, her voice was low and a little haunted. 'I don't know if I can do this...'

Do what—meet with the lawyers? Work with him? Drive out to Franschhoek? *What?*

Before he could ask, Addi lifted her head, straightened her shoulders and inhaled deeply. 'Four o'clock today? Or would you like to suggest another time?' she asked, her fingers drumming the desk next to her keyboard.

He couldn't wait. He wanted to see her...see those spreadsheets, get working on acquiring those hotels, he quickly corrected himself. Acquiring Thorpe Industries' assets at a good price was an opportunity not to be missed, provided he could get the proposal past the trustees. He'd made two massive errors of misjudgement—both involving women he'd cared for—and they'd led to huge unintended consequences. And he was still paying the price.

Not even Addi could tempt him to wade in more than toe-deep. He was immune to any commitment that lasted beyond breakfast the next morning. He'd learned his lesson...

Women, people in general, couldn't be trusted.

CHAPTER THREE

THIS COULD NOT be happening to her, not on top of everything else! Addi gripped the steering wheel of her company car, her eyes blurring with tears, which wasn't a good thing when trying to navigate a busy highway. She blinked furiously and swallowed down a sob threatening to escape. She hit the button on the electric window and icy air instantly dried her wet eyes. She left the window open a crack, thinking that red-from-cold eyes had to be better than scarlet-from-panic-and-distress eyes.

Seeing her speed creeping up, she eased off the accelerator and glanced at the clock. She was going to be twenty minutes late for her appointment with Jude but that couldn't be helped. After leaving the lawyer's office, she'd stumbled to her car and sat there for forty-five minutes, trying to make sense of what she'd heard…

Addi felt another tide of panic rise up her throat and sucked in a series of harsh gulps. She couldn't think about what she'd heard earlier; she could barely make sense of it. If she allowed herself to get caught up in that, she'd lose concentration and would find herself intimately connected with the back of a passenger bus or a heavy-duty truck.

No, she had to park it…just for a little while.

Her navigation system directed her to take the next exit and Addi moved across the motorway, weaving her car between a truck and an overloaded bus to scoot off. It had been ages since she'd been in Franschhoek, but she had too much on her mind to take in the pretty vineyards and the towering mountains. She was about to meet the father of the bean growing inside her, the baby she was still wrapping her head around.

Somehow, she needed to find the words to tell him she was pregnant, that the pill had failed and that one of the condoms he'd used had been faulty. How, in the twenty-first century, did that happen? Weren't they supposed to be foolproof these days?

There was little point in trying to figure out the *how*; she had to deal with what *was*. However it had happened, she was now carrying a mixture of his and her genes and she had no idea what she was going to do. Frankly, a baby was the last thing she needed in her life right now. Her job with Thorpe Industries was coming to an end, and there was no guarantee that the new owner, whether that was Jude or anyone else, would take her on. The law said that employers couldn't discriminate against employing pregnant women, but the law wasn't always applied in the real world.

She needed money to pay for the lawyers she'd undoubtedly need and to keep her family's heads above water. But, whenever she thought about making her baby problem go away, she couldn't finish the thought. She was embarrassed that she'd accidentally fallen pregnant and she couldn't afford a baby. She didn't have the time, finances or energy.

But she was keeping it. She couldn't *not*. And that meant telling Jude. And that was a conversation she really didn't want to have.

Turning off onto a country road, she meandered down a narrow road bisecting two vineyards, the ragged, tooth-like mountains now directly in front of her. Winter was just arriving in this pretty valley and the vines looked denuded, like tiny, old hunched men. Addi turned into an oak-tree-lined driveway—the trees would look magnificent in summer—and her eyebrows lifted as Jude's house came into view.

Instead of the Cape Dutch house she'd expected—the old, gracious houses that were dotted around the countryside like grand old dames—Jude's house was a modern, sprawling one-storey creation of glass, wood and steel. But somehow, despite being ruthlessly modern, it looked warm and welcoming and suited its surroundings. He must have had an incredibly talented architect as it was...dared she say it?...perfect. She adored the house and loved the big trees and wild garden running up to the edges of the vineyards.

She parked her car next to a brand-new SUV—top of the line, she noted, with all the bells and whistles—and wondered how Jude could reconcile his save-the-planet views with his gas-guzzling car. Tipping the rear-view mirror so she could see her reflection, she grimaced at her red eyes and sallow skin. Using her finger, she rubbed away dots of mascara and dug in her bag for some lipstick, hoping it would give her a bit of a lift. She stroked the bold red colour over her lips and winced. All it did was highlight her bloodshot eyes and gaunt face. Addi cursed and reached for a tissue to wipe it off but, before she could, she heard a knock on her window.

Jumping, she spun around to see a broad chest and mint-coloured jersey plastered against a flat stomach, a stomach she knew was ridged with hard muscle. As she'd discovered weeks ago, his body was phenomenal and his muscles had muscles of their own. He was sexy, powerful and masculine...

Okay, enough of that now. Addi gave herself a mental slap and Jude yanked open her car door.

'Are you coming in or what?' he demanded, sounding impatient.

'Hello to you too,' she muttered, reaching for her tote bag that held her laptop and a thick stack of reports she'd had Greg print off. She hadn't had time to do a presentation; she'd just have to wing it. Addi exited her car and tugged down her fitted jacket, shivering in the cool wind rolling down the mountain and across the vineyards. Clouds were building up in the distance, gathering cold raindrops.

Addi looked at the house and wished it was hers. She wished she was walking into it after a hard day, with Jude looking welcoming instead of threatening, ready with a hug or a cup of tea. She wished he was the man she could turn to, someone who'd help her make sense of the crazy, chaotic meeting at the lawyer's office, someone utterly and for ever on her side. For some reason, she could imagine Jude in that role, could almost feel those big arms wrapping her up, being the barrier between her and the world, his deep voice encouraging her, soothing her anxiety...

You might be attracted to Fisher, Addi, but you are not looking for anything more! You don't believe in more!

Wow, she was either more upset or more tired than she'd thought, as she'd given up on fairy tales a long time ago. Prince Charming didn't exist, she didn't need anyone to rescue her; she'd sort herself out, thank you very much. People always disappointed her and there were no happy-ever-afters to be had. The best she could hope for was a 'happy for now', or for the immediate future.

Irritated with herself, she followed Jude to the enormous front door, impressed when he stepped back to let her enter the house in front of him. She turned around slowly, taking in the steel beams, the ultra-high ceilings and the slate floor. On the wall were bright abstract paintings in bold colours that were warm, interesting and, strangely, comforting.

She looked to her left, where the hallway flowed into a large open-plan kitchen, dining and living room. A large wooden table with bench seats separated the chef's kitchen from the living room, and comfortable-looking couches sat around a free-standing fireplace. But it was the view that caught and held her attention. Huge floor-to-ceiling windows ran from the kitchen area to the end of the lounge, allowing a one-eighty-degree view of the vineyards and the jagged mountain range beyond. The house was built on the edge of a slope and one level down was an impressive outdoor entertainment area and a huge pool, complete with Jacuzzi, at one end.

It was an impressive house, and it suited him, Addi thought.

'Coffee?' he asked, gesturing to the kitchen.

Ugh, no. She couldn't think of anything she wanted less. 'Water, please.'

He nodded, walked into the kitchen area and went to a brushed-steel fridge. He filled a glass before turning to his state-of-the-art coffee machine.

'Nice place,' Addi said, hanging onto her tote bag with a one-handed grip. 'I presume you are off the grid?'

He nodded. 'Totally.'

She couldn't help it, she needed to needle him, just a little. It was either that or step into his arms for a hug, and she couldn't do that. If he showed her any sympathy right now, she'd dissolve into a puddle. 'How do you reconcile your "environment first" views and your gas-guzzling car?'

He shoved a cup under the nozzle of the coffee machine and used the side of his hand to hit the start button, dispensing espresso into the tiny cup. The smell wafted over to Addi and she had to breathe through her mouth and swallow a couple of times. 'It's a hybrid, Addi. I try, as far as I possibly can, to run off electricity but sometimes that isn't always practical.'

She nodded, feeling a little foolish. She looked around. 'Where do you want to work?' she asked, wishing they could get on with it. She'd give him a run-down on the Thorpe assets and then she'd go home and spend the rest of the night trying to figure out how to tell him he was going to be a dad, and how to tell Lex that she'd messed up contraception-wise. And, most importantly, she needed time to research lawyers who specialised in family law, and hopefully get an idea as to how much they charged.

Blasted Joelle! How *dared* she?

Addi clenched her fists and jaw, trying to push away the anger. If she let it take hold, it would overwhelm her. If she cracked open the door to her emotions, despair and fear would sneak in and she'd be lost.

No, she had to keep it together. Thanks to having plenty of practice, keeping it together was what she did.

Addi looked awful, in the way that only a spectacularly gorgeous woman could.

Despite looking nothing like the glamourous woman in the slip dress he remembered from eight weeks ago—the one with the smoky eyes, the bold lips and the very kissable mouth—Jude's heart still kicked up a pace and the fabric of his trousers tightened. Then he looked closer, and concern replaced desire. Her eyes were road-map-red and puffy, and her nose looked a little pink. And, frankly, in her loose black trousers and slouchy jacket, she looked like a slight breeze could blow her away. She looked burned out and miserable, as if she needed a hot meal and a long hug.

Was she upset? Or sick?

He didn't think he was completely oblivious to the emotions of the women who briefly shared his bed, but neither had he dwelled on them the way he was now doing with Addi. He wanted to know why she was upset, whether she was okay and, terrifyingly, how he could fix whatever was worrying her. He wasn't a fix-it type of guy; he always kept his distance. So, what was it about this woman who tugged at the heartstrings he hadn't thought he had?

Walking over to her, he took her bag off her shoulder, surprised at the weight of it. Taking her cold hand, he led her over to the fireplace and dumped her bag on the closest chair. 'Take off your jacket and sit down before you collapse, Addi,' he told her, his tone suggesting she not argue. 'When last did you eat?'

She sank onto the couch but managed to glare at him. She opened her mouth, no doubt to ask him what business it was of his, but he lifted a hand to stop her snappy retort. 'I have chicken soup that's ready to be heated, as well as sourdough bread. You're going to have a bowl, and when you have some colour back in your cheeks we might, or might not, discuss business.'

She lifted her stubborn chin. 'I'm fine, Jude. And I have minimal time, so I can't waste it eating.'

Her words lacked fire and he was getting more worried by the second. What was wrong with her? He intended to find out. But, first, she needed food.

He placed his hands on his hips and cocked his head. 'Did that sound like a suggestion?' he asked. 'Because it wasn't. You will eat. We'll see where we go from there.'

When Addi didn't reply, he knew that he'd won this round. He didn't presume he'd win the next. Swallowing his frustrated sigh, he left her by the fire and walked back into the kitchen area. He pulled soup out of the fridge—his housekeeper was an amazing cook—and reached into a cupboard for a bowl. Looking back, he saw Addi scrabbling in her tote bag and shook his head when she pulled out her phone.

She started scrolling, her back hunched and her head drooping. It was so obvious she needed a break and looking at her phone wasn't going to allow her to de-stress.

'Addi.'

She didn't hear him, so he raised his voice and called her name again. She didn't acknowledge him; she was miles away, immersed in something on her phone. He walked into the utility room off the kitchen and cut the Internet connection. Thanks to being deep in a valley, all electronic contact came through a high-speed fibre connection, and he'd just killed the power to the modem.

Smiling to himself, he walked back into the kitchen, just in time to see Addi spinning around to glare at him. 'I've lost signal.'

Yep.

'I need to be connected,' she told him, sounding frantic.

No, she didn't. The world wouldn't stop turning if she wasn't plugged in for a couple of hours. He shrugged. 'The signal out here is iffy; it might come back on, or it might not.'

If she gave it any thought, she'd realise that he ran a multi-billion-dollar operation and needed to be constantly connected. He was banking on the fact she was too tired and too stressed to work that out. As he expected, her shoulders slumped and she tossed her phone onto the couch next to her.

'Lean back, kick off your shoes and stare at the mountain,' he told her. 'Breathe.'

Addi handed him another glare and turned her back on

him. He put the bowl of soup into the microwave to heat up and, when he turned back to look at her, she'd done as he'd suggested—her feet were tucked under her bottom, and she had a cushion behind her head. She was also looking at the awesome view, watching the clouds skim over the mountain, blocking out the sun. It was going to storm later, and the temperature would drop. Winter was starting to come in the Cape, and the first of a series of cold fronts was rolling in.

'How long have you owned this property?' Addi asked, her voice drifting over to him.

He sliced the sourdough bread. 'I bought the land about ten years ago and the house was completed about three years ago.'

'Do you make wine?' she asked.

He smiled. No; he didn't have the patience or the knowledge. 'I lease the vines to a neighbour and he takes the harvest. He makes a rather good Shiraz.' 'Rather good', as in one of the best in the world. He considered offering Addi a glass and then remembered she had to drive home. Besides, wine on an empty stomach—a stomach he suspected hadn't seen a decent meal for a while—was never a good idea.

The microwave dinged and he pulled out her soup. 'Come on over here,' he told her, sliding the bowl onto a place mat on the other side of the island. Addi stood up and, without bothering to put her heels on, padded over to the island, the hems of her now too-long trousers dragging against his slate floors. She climbed up onto a stool and bent down to smell the soup, her eyes closing.

'It smells good,' she told him. 'It smells like Aunt Kate's soup.'

He pushed the wooden board holding the bread over to her. 'Who is Aunt Kate?' he asked, keeping his voice neutral. He knew that if he got too demanding her shield would go back up.

'Uh…she was a great-aunt. My sister Lex and I lived with her from the time I turned seventeen,' Addi explained, dipping her spoon into the soup.

She took a deep breath and lifted the spoon to her mouth as if she wasn't sure how she'd react. She swallowed, sighed and then dug in, rapidly lifting spoonful after spoonful to her mouth and taking greedy bites out of the bread.

Jude watched her eat, fascinated. It was almost as if he'd faded away and all she could focus on was the meal. His housekeeper Greta was a good cook, sure, and the soup was nice, but it wasn't worthy of her constant murmurs of appreciation.

When Addi scraped the last of the soup from the bowl and ate the last bite of bread, she looked up at him. Her cheeks were red. She looked embarrassed at diving in but at least she had some colour. Her eyes were a little brighter and some of the tension in her shoulders had eased.

She patted her stomach and sent him a shy smile. 'You have no idea how much I needed that,' she told him.

Oh, he did. He rested his forearms on the counter and frowned at her. 'Why haven't you been eating, Addi? What's Addi short for, by the way?' He'd been wondering about that, mostly late at night when X-rated memories of the way they'd loved each other bombarded him.

'Addison.'

He tasted her full name on his tongue and found he liked it. 'So, what gives? And don't tell me "nothing".'

She stared down at the empty soup bowl and lifted a hand to her hair to run her fingers through the bright blonde. They were trembling, and it annoyed him. What was she scared of?

'Talk to me, Addison,' he commanded. She had the weight of the world on her shoulders, and he suspected that if she didn't talk to someone soon that weight might just flatten her. He'd tried to push away his need to help her, to get involved, but every time he did it came roaring back, stronger than before. This woman could turn him inside out and he wasn't enjoying the very alien sensation.

Addi cocked her head and tried to smile but it hardly lifted the corners of her lips and didn't reach her eyes. 'Are you sure you want to know, Jude?'

He wouldn't have asked if he didn't, as he told her.

'People say that, but when they hear the unexpected they tend to shoot the messenger,' Addi murmured.

'I've been around for a long time, Addi, and I'm not easily shocked,' Jude assured her. 'And sometimes it's helpful to get another person's input.'

Addi didn't look convinced. She picked up her spoon and tapped it against the rim of the bowl, obviously agonising over her decision to speak or not. He wanted her to, he realised. There was something about this prickly woman that made him want to pull her in, hold her close and be the barrier between the world and her. He felt protective of her, and he couldn't understand why. The women he normally dated—or slept with; calling what they did together 'dating' was a stretch—were independent and successful, women who neither needed nor wanted his protection and would laugh if he suggested it. But Addi, stubborn and guarded, looked as if she needed it.

He removed the spoon from her hand and stopped the annoying *ting-ting-ting* of her spoon hitting the bowl. Addi looked surprised and he realised that she hadn't even noticed the noise. She'd been too busy deciding whether to talk or how to frame her words.

Cold fear ran up and down his spine. Was she ill? Had she done something illegal? Was she in trouble? Seriously, if she didn't start to speak in the next five minutes, he might just shake it out of her.

'Where do I start?' she asked, her words a rhetorical question. She looked away from him and out of the window, her eyes focused on the vines outside. 'I'm worried about not having a job when Cole sells up Thorpe Industries. The new owners of the hospitality division might not want to take me on and a severance package only goes so far.'

He'd looked her up online. She had an excellent degree and great experience; he doubted she'd battle to find another job. 'I need my job. I've got expenses and people relying on me,' she added.

'Who?' he asked. He knew she was single, so who was she supporting?

'I live with three half-sisters,' she told him. 'Lex is a year younger than me, and she looks after our two younger sisters. Lex is also studying towards her degree. Our youngest half-sisters are six and eight. Mine is the salary that keeps us afloat.'

Jude rubbed his jaw, taking in her words. He had so many questions and didn't know where to start. Where were her parents, all their parents? Why was she looking after her half-sisters? 'Wait, let me get this right—you have three sisters?'

This time her smile reached her eyes. 'I have four, actually. Storm is our middle sister, but she doesn't live with us. She's twenty-four and has a job as an au pair. She, thank God, is financially independent.'

Right. She had *four* sisters. Wow.

He pulled his thoughts back to her initial statement. 'You should be able to pick up another job, Addi. I can't see why you wouldn't.'

She closed her eyes briefly. 'Do you remember that I told you that I couldn't be here at two o'clock because I had an appointment with a lawyer?'

Since the conversation had only been this morning, of course he remembered. She'd said it was a personal issue. 'Yes.'

'The appointment was regarding custody of my younger sisters. I was informed earlier that my flaky mother wants Snow and Nixi back. After four years away, she wants to take them to live with her in India. She's been living in Thailand for the past fifteen years. I have to think that there's a man involved…there's always a man involved whenever Joelle makes a life-changing decision.'

Right; that was unexpected.

'I need to find a family lawyer who can help me sue for custody of my sisters. I will not let them be uprooted again and I will not put them through the unstable life Lex and I endured. But to gain custody of them I'd need both a lawyer and a job—a guaranteed source of income to pay for said lawyer.'

'As I said, you shouldn't have a problem picking up a good job.' What was he missing here?

'I presume you've heard about pregnancy discrimination?'

Of course he had. Along with believing in equal pay for women doing the same work as men, he didn't believe in treating a pregnant employee unfavourably. But why were they talking about pregnancy discrimination?

'By the time I get round to looking for a new job, when I'm ready to attend interviews, I will be showing. While it's against the law for my pregnancy to be used as a reason not to hire me, we all know it happens and it's incredibly difficult to prove, especially if several decent candidates apply for the job.'

But what did that have to do with…? Oh. *Right.* 'You're pregnant?' he asked, rubbing his chin.

She tipped her head to one side and nodded, her eyebrows raised. 'I found out this morning.'

He was finding it difficult to connect the dots, to work out why her eyebrows were still raised, why she was looking at him with that 'come on, catch up' expression on her face.

Addi looked him in the eye and sucked in a deep breath. 'I don't know how it happened, Jude, but you're the father of my baby.'

CHAPTER FOUR

IT WAS DONE. There was no going back now.

Addi slid off her seat, walked over to the floor-to-ceiling window and placed her hand on the glass, staring past her reflection to look out onto the almost dark garden. The occasional raindrop splattered against the door and the temperature outside had plummeted.

It didn't feel too toasty in here either.

She'd dumped a lot of information on Jude, and he needed time to think about what she'd said, time to work through the bombshell she'd dropped. She normally never allowed her mouth to run away with her, she always considered her words, but something about Jude Fisher had made her throw caution to the wind and she'd spilt all her drama. She didn't like it.

Obtaining custody of Nixi and Snow wasn't his problem, and she'd sort herself out work-wise. All he had to wrap his head around was the fact that he was going to be a father. Whether he played a role in the baby's life was up to him. She wouldn't force him to. She'd grown up with a father who'd only contacted her on high days and holidays—and sometimes didn't even bother to do that—so she knew her baby would be fine with not having a father in her, or his, life. She'd turned out okay, hadn't she? Kids were resilient, far more so than people imagined.

Behind her, Jude cleared his throat, and Addi turned to look at him, resting her palms flat on the glass behind her. The windows, as she discovered, were actually doors and could slide into one another, opening up the entire house to the elements. Right now, she wished they'd open up so she could fall into the night. She really didn't want to continue this conversation. She'd eaten, was feeling washed out and she could sleep for a week.

She genuinely didn't know how she was going to find the energy to drive home.

'You're pregnant?'

She nodded.

'And it's mine?'

She lifted her chin at the note of disbelief she heard in his voice. 'Well, since I haven't slept with anyone else but you for years, I'd say the chances were high.' She winced, wishing she didn't default to sarcasm when she felt off balance.

Jude didn't look as though he appreciated her attitude either. 'We used *condoms*, Addison. Every time.'

Addi pushed a hand into her hair and tugged at the short strands. 'I don't know how to explain it, Jude, but one of them must've had a tear or a hole or something.'

'I've been using condoms for too many years to count and I've never had so much as a scare,' Jude told her, folding his arms across his chest.

She saw something flash in his eyes and frowned. Why did she think that something about his statement wasn't true? It didn't matter; they were dealing with the here and now, not the past.

'I don't know what to say, or how to explain how it happened,' Addi replied, her voice creeping up in volume.

'Are you sure you are…?'

'Of course I'm sure! I've missed my period and I did

three tests, Jude! I'm not making this up, I haven't made a mistake and I wish I wasn't!

'I don't want to be pregnant, Jude, I wish I was anything but pregnant because it complicates my life exponentially. It complicates my job situation; it might complicate getting custody of my half-sisters. It will definitely put a strain on what is already a difficult family set-up. I do *not* want to be pregnant but I am. And I have to deal with it.'

Jude walked over to the lounge area and dropped to sit on the closest couch. He rested his forearms on his knees and lowered his head, looking as though she'd sideswiped him with a baseball bat.

She walked over to him and sat down next to him, keeping a foot between him. 'I thought you should know, that's all.'

He took a while to respond and when he lifted his head his eyes were granite-hard and a flat, dark green. The man who'd looked so concerned earlier had morphed into a ruthless businessman.

'Okay, so what do you want, Addison?' he demanded, leaning back and placing an ankle on the opposite knee. It was a casual stance, but she knew that he was a harnessed tornado, ready to touch down and create havoc. 'A job? A cash pay-out? *What?*'

Addi stared at him, not knowing where his fierce words were coming from. She didn't want money and hadn't asked for a job. She'd just thought he needed to know, that he had the right to know. She wouldn't even expect him to pay child support, because if a flake like Joelle could raise her two oldest daughters without receiving a bean from either of their two fathers, she could too. She was smart and resourceful and she'd do it on her own, without input from anyone.

She relied on herself. Always. And she was tired of this

conversation, exhausted by the events of the day. She wanted to go home, have a warm bath and climb into bed with a cup of hot chocolate. But first she had to make the drive home.

And, the sooner she got started on that, the better.

Addi stood up, slipped her feet back into her heels and picked up her jacket from where she'd draped it over the back of the chair earlier. She removed the thick print-out from her tote bag and slammed it onto the wooden coffee table. Jude could whistle if she thought she'd spend another minute in his company discussing hotels. In a couple of days, she'd have to face him again—she still had a job to do—but for now she needed time and space. They both did.

After digging her car keys out of the side pocket of her tote bag, she pulled her bag over her shoulder and walked to the front door, leaving Jude where he was. He didn't deserve a goodbye, he'd chosen to believe the worst of her. Making a buck and working an angle was something Joelle did, not her. She might look like her mother, but she tried to be as little like her personality-wise as possible.

She'd sort this out herself, forge her own path and plough through it. She was better off on her own. She always had been.

It took Jude ten minutes to make sense of what Addi had been trying to say, another five to realise she'd left his house.

He couldn't believe that this was happening to him. This was his worst nightmare. Apart from the fact that he was freaked out that his mum had died because of a pregnancy—what if that happened to Addi?—he was once again, after sixteen years, talking to a woman about her being pregnant, trying to make sense of her words.

Jude placed his elbows on his knees and his head in his hands, memory after sour memory rolling in. He'd met Marina at university a few weeks into his second year, and she'd been the first woman to capture his heart. He'd been ridiculously, crazily in love with her, and he'd danced to her tune. Marina's friends had become his, he'd neglected his studies and he'd pulled away from his friends. She'd been all that was important, all he'd been able to think about.

She'd also single-handedly caused him more problems than anyone before or since. Admittedly, he'd been a spoiled student, one of the wealthiest at the upmarket university, and had had unlimited spending power thanks to the credit card his grandfather had handed him. He'd driven a soft top, been good-looking and, yeah, he'd been the big man on campus. Perfect bait for the money-and-status-hungry Marina.

She'd looked like a doll, dark-haired and dark-eyed, and had barely weighed a hundred pounds. But she was possibly the smartest woman he'd ever encountered—street-smart, not book-smart—and she'd seen him coming. Used to girls falling over him, it had taken him six weeks to get her to notice him and another month to get her to agree to a date. The adage 'treat 'em mean and keep 'em keen' had worked on him, and he'd revelled in the chase, thinking he would win the biggest prize.

Soon after they'd started sleeping together, he'd decided she was the woman he'd marry, the future mother of his kids, his for-ever life partner. His parents had died when he'd been a kid and his grandfather, Bartholomew Fisher, had obtained custody of him. With Bart being a workaholic, he'd had a lonely and isolated upbringing. Boarding school had been a life saver, and when he'd gone to his school friends' homes for the weekends and holidays he'd discovered real families, noise and laughter, teasing and the affection. He'd wanted that, with all the desperation of a lonely kid, lost and lacking in affection, could.

His grandfather had been a hard, impatient man, one who hadn't accepted foibles and failures. They were Fishers, and they had higher standards than most, and Jude was expected to exceed those standards. He'd had to be academically successful, a good sportsman—luckily for him, he was better than average—and socially charming. Fishers were gentlemen—they said and did the right thing. Or, more importantly, were *seen* to do the right thing. Bart had blithely told him he had mistresses, he occasionally cut legal and financial corners and he didn't shy away from a dodgy deal—the trick was not to get caught. And Fishers never aired their dirty linen in public.

Like Jude, Marina didn't have a family—she'd been raised by an elderly aunt and she'd attended university on a scholarship. He'd been a rich kid, she'd been a poor girl, but they had been what the other needed. Or so he'd thought.

While he'd been planning their life together, she'd been planning something totally different. Unknown to Jude, Marina had contacted Bartholomew and demanded a substantial amount of money for her to disappear from his life. If he didn't pay up, she would accuse Jude of coercing her into a relationship and claim she was pregnant.

Bart had rolled into the university town on a cloud of black smoke and brimstone and accused him of being the stupidest creature in the history of the world. Reeling at the barrage of information, Jude had listened, stunned, as he was told of the blackmail attempt. Bart had had his 'people'—private investigators, Jude assumed—do some digging and it had turned out that wasn't the first time Marina had put her hooks into a wealthy student—she'd done it at the University of Johannesburg and at the University of Cape Town. Bart had told him that she wasn't nineteen, like Jude, but twenty-five and was an old hand at scams.

Rocked to his core, but in love, he'd defended Marina and had told his grandfather he was wrong, that he was mistaken. Being young, dumb and far too proud, he'd chosen to stick by Marina. In retaliation, Bartholomew had cut off his allowance. Too proud to go and ask for money from his cold, unfeeling and harsh relative, he'd found a job as a bar tender at a popular club to meet Marina's and his bills.

He'd been confident and desperately naive: they loved each other and they could make this work if they pulled together—if Marina got a job. But working for a living was not what she'd wanted, and it became clear if Jude couldn't get his grandfather to reinstate his allowance she'd be out of there. He'd refused—the very first time he'd refused her anything—and had left for his bar-tending shift.

He'd returned home around one-thirty that same night to find her awake, sitting cross-legged on the bed. She'd told him she was pregnant and had opened her hand, revealing a pill. She'd told him she would abort his baby unless he arranged for her to receive a substantial pay-out. She'd said, if he couldn't give her the life she wanted, then she wasn't going to give birth and raise a child she didn't want—there were other guys out there who could give her what she wanted and deserved.

Two things happened that night, almost instantaneously. The scales fell from Jude's eyes and Jude realised she'd never loved him and he'd been just another mark. He knew instinctively that she wasn't pregnant and, when he called her bluff, she shrugged and told him the lie was worth the shot.

After kicking her out of his flat—at that point he didn't care where she went or what she did—he sat on his shower floor. He'd had a couple of moments of sheer terror before his brain had kicked in, and he vowed that he would never again allow a woman to put him in that untenable position. He would be ultra-careful about protecting against unwanted pregnancy and he'd never allow a woman to trap him again.

It took another eighteen months, and a stint at the London School of Economics, for him to mend fences with his grandfather. But there was always a barrier between them— a lack of communication, and on Bart's part a distinct lack of trust. Jude took his place at Fisher International, but Bart made a habit of looking over his shoulder and double-checking his every move.

Jude put up with it, knowing that dealing with his irascible grandfather was a small price to pay to inherit the company he truly loved. As the years passed, the sting and embarrassment of Marina's treachery passed too and he started dating again, and even flirted with the idea of living with, and perhaps eventually marrying, a British banker called Jane. That idea was kiboshed when he discovered she had flexible views on fidelity, and he called it quits.

What he didn't expect was for her to spill his story about being scammed by Marina—told to her under the influence of too many whiskies—to one of her friends working on Fleet Street. Thank God he hadn't told her about the fake pregnancy threat because that would've made the papers too.

Was it any wonder he had difficulty trusting anyone?

Bartholomew abhorred the negative publicity and raked him over the coals for being an idiot, embarrassing him and revealing family secrets. He died about three months after the tabloid article was first published and Jude discovered he'd amended his will the day after the story broke. Fisher International would still be his but, because Bart couldn't trust his judgement, all major Fisher International decisions had to be approved by a board of trustees for ten years. But Bart hadn't stopped there: if Jude fathered a child out of wedlock, or was involved in any more scandals that might tarnish the Fisher name, the trustees would remain in place for another ten years.

He was so close to being free, to being able to run his company the way he wanted to. But if Addi gave birth to his child, and the trustees were presented with that information, he would be constrained and hamstrung for another ten years. He couldn't do it; he couldn't allow the Council of Three to have the final say for another decade.

There was only one thing he could do.

Addi pulled into her space under the steel car-port adjacent to her house and sat in her car, watching the rain fall in a steady sheet. It was bucketing down now, and the storm had followed her all the way home. She shuddered as a bolt of lightning lit up the sky, quickly followed by deep, rolling thunder. It would storm and then it would drizzle for days.

Winter was well and truly on the way.

Addi looked at the house and knew she should go inside, listen to Nixi and Snow ramble about their day and be a good sister. But, after the day she'd had, she felt depleted. She didn't even have the energy to feel guilty about not wanting to be with them right now. If she knew she wouldn't freeze, she'd curl up in her car seat and go to sleep.

She was tired on a whole new level.

Addi heard a knock on her window and jumped, whipping her head round to see her sister's freckled face on the other side of the window. Lex wrapped her arms around her slim torso and bounced up and down, raindrops glistening on her red curls.

As soon as the window dropped, Lex spoke. 'What on earth are you doing, Ads? You've been out here for ages!'

Had she? She hadn't realised. 'Hey, Lex.'

Lex frowned at her. 'Are you okay? You look terrible.'

Fantastic. Addi nodded, sighed and wondered whether she should invite Lex into the car and tell her the entire story. Lex was not only her sister but also her best friend and they'd been a team all of their lives. They were in this together. But telling Lex that she was pregnant was so much harder than she thought it would be. They'd promised each other that they'd be radically over-cautious about protection, that they'd never bring an unwanted child into the world.

That they wouldn't, in any way, follow in Joelle's footsteps.

But here she was...

And by falling pregnant she'd jeopardised her job, their income and perhaps their continued, albeit casual, custody of the girls. If Joelle's lawyer used the argument that Addi had her own child to look after and raise, and that she couldn't give the girls all the financial and emotional support they needed, a judge might think they'd be better off with their mum.

And, while she really wanted to share her burdens with Lex, she couldn't—not just yet. She needed to have a plan first, to know where she was going, before she told her sister the trio of bad news. If she had a plan, she could cope. Without one, she'd flounder.

'Am I coming in there or are you coming into the house?' Lex demanded.

'I'll be there in a sec, Lex, let me grab my stuff.'

Lex nodded. Addi reached for the tote bag and her phone fell to the floor. She picked it up and saw that she had a dozen missed calls and text messages. Strange, because she hadn't heard any of them come through.

She fiddled with her settings and realised that she'd somehow put her phone on silent. Scrolling through the messages, she saw that they were all from Jude...

We need to talk.

The storm is really bad. Are you okay?

Dammit, Addi, I know you were upset when you left but can you please let me know if you are okay? There's flooding on the road you're on...

Right, that's it. I'm coming to look for you.

Addi widened her eyes at his increasingly irate and worried texts. She was a big girl, had been looking after herself and Lex since her teens, and didn't need any man checking up on her.

Will you please call me?

But the last thing she needed was another dust-up with Jude; she couldn't handle any more tonight. Pulling up his contact number, she told Lex she was just going to make a quick call, when headlights swung into their driveway. Addi turned around in her seat and immediately recognised the huge car sitting on the other side of the gate. She released a loud groan.

'Ads, there's a strange car in our driveway,' Lex stated.

Addi scrambled out of the car and placed a reassuring hand on her shoulder. 'It's fine, Lex, I know who it is.' Addi hit the button on her remote control, the gate slid open and Jude drove onto their property.

Lex turned to look at her, her red eyebrows lifting. 'And who might that be?'

'Jude Fisher. He's a...' How did she explain him? The man who'd rocked her world? The guy with whom she'd created a baby? The star of all her sexy dreams? 'He's someone I'm working with.'

'And why is he at our house at eight on a Wednesday night?' Lex asked, her eyebrows lifting even further as Jude parked behind Addi's car.

'Good question,' Addi murmured as Jude left his car and half-walked, half-ran through the driving rain to join them under the car port.

He stared at her, his eyes running over her body, and she saw him release a sigh. 'You're okay.'

Addi nodded. 'I am.' She saw his expression harden and anger flash in his eyes, but before he could blast her—because she knew he wanted to—she turned to Lex. 'Lex, this is Jude Fisher. Jude, my sister, Lex.'

Jude nodded at Lex, and her sister's eyes bounced between the big man who'd unexpectedly rocked up at their house and Addi.

'I need to talk to Jude, Lex,' Addi told her. 'I'll come in soon.'

Lex looked as if she was about to invite Jude inside, but Addi shook her head and Lex caught the tiny gesture. Her sister, no wallflower, just folded her arms. 'Will you be okay with him out here on your own?'

Addi nodded. She wasn't scared of Jude; she knew he would never harm her. They might yell and shout—and that was why she wasn't going to invite him into the house—but he'd never use his strength or power to physically hurt her. 'I'm fine, Lex, I won't be long.'

Lex stared at Jude, her eyes narrowing, and finally

walked away. Addi knew that she'd stand just inside the back door, just far enough away to give them privacy. The sisters looked out for one another.

Addi turned back to Jude, who'd pulled on a black cashmere jersey over his open-neck shirt. 'What are you doing here, Fisher?' she asked.

He put his hands on his hips and glared down at her. 'When I came out of my "I'm having a baby" shock, you were gone, and about five minutes later there was a cloudburst. I couldn't get hold of you and I went online to see social media blowing up with posts about flooding on the road you were driving on. Gale-force winds also pushed cars off the road. There were multiple accidents and, when you didn't reply, I thought you were in one.'

He looked genuinely frightened. 'I was ahead of the storm, just,' she told him.

'Look, I know that my response wasn't ideal—'

'You accused me of trying to scam you!' Addi replied, her tone turning hot.

He dragged his hand through his damp hair. 'But when you didn't reply I thought something had happened to you.'

She lifted her shoulders and looked away. 'That would be convenient, right?'

His big hands grabbed her shoulders and he bent his knees so that their eyes were level. His sparked with angry green fire. 'Don't ever say that to me again, okay?'

Addi frowned, confused, because he not only sounded angry but also genuinely upset. She wasn't sure what was happening here, and she felt as though she was holding a script but couldn't read the words. Looking down, she pulled her bottom lip between her teeth before speaking again.

'I'm sorry I didn't answer, my phone was on silent, and

I didn't hear any of your calls or messages. I was about to call you when I saw your headlights lighting up my house.'

He looked as though he wanted to argue but, instead of doing that, he dragged in another long breath and yanked her to him, holding her against his hard body. Despite not wanting to, despite telling herself that she had to be strong and keep her spine straight, she sagged against him, resting her temple against his collar bone and letting his heat envelop her. He was so warm and so solid, so damn capable. He felt like a barrier between the world and her, a place she could rest, where she could *be*. Silly, but for a moment, just one or two, she wanted to lean in, to soak in his strength—something she never did.

It wasn't her way, but how wonderful it would be to be looked after, not to feel so alone, so responsible, to be the one everyone relied on for everything. To be in a partnership, a give-and-take. But dreams were for fools, and she'd never been offered the time, space or opportunity to be foolish.

His hand held the back of her head, his fingers massaging her scalp. 'You've had a bit of a day, haven't you?'

'Yes,' she agreed. She pulled back to look up at him. 'So, to be fair, did you.'

He almost smiled.

'The soup was good,' she told him, wanting to lighten the atmosphere between them. She knew she should pull away and put some distance between them. But, before she could find the will to do that, he lifted his hand to touch her cheek, his thumb gliding over her cheekbone and then over her bottom lip.

Addi held her breath, knowing that sharing a kiss would be stupid—she was working for him, with him, they were going to have a child together and they had things to dis-

cuss—but she didn't care. His kisses and touch had the ability to take her away, to make her forget that it was a cold,
rainy night and that her life was currently the emotional
equivalent of a storm surge.

His mouth met hers and, like before, heat skittered
through her, desire on its heels. Jude nibbled at her mouth,
his soft touch more erotic than she remembered, and she
couldn't help closing the gap between them, pushing her
breasts into his chest and trying to hold as much of his broad
back as possible. She felt the dip of his spine beneath his
clothes and told herself that she couldn't, shouldn't, slide
her hand up and under, looking for bare skin.

But her body decided to ignore her brain and she sighed
when she felt his warm, bare skin under her cool hands. Her
mouth opened, Jude's tongue slid inside, and stress faded
away. There was only his warm mouth, his minty but masculine taste, and his bare hand sliding up her ribcage and
over her lace-covered breast to find her nipple. He tipped
her head to the side, seeking deeper access to her mouth,
his tongue twisting around hers. Addi slipped her thigh between his, needing to get closer, wanting her feminine core
against his hard erection. Nobody had ever made her feel
so out of control...

She was just a few feet from her back door, and a few
doors down was her bedroom...

Jude pulled away, released a curse and moved his hands
back to her shoulders, putting a few feet between them. The
sound of his ragged breathing filled the space between them
and she felt adrift, as if she'd been wrenched from a lovely,
sexy dream and drop-kicked back into reality.

She didn't like it.

Jude dropped his hands and took another step back, creating more distance between them. From inside the house,

she could hear Lex talking to the girls and the sound of their ancient washing machine. The next-door neighbour's dog released a series of yippy barks. Addi didn't know how life could carry on like normal around them. When Jude had kissed her, she'd felt something move in the universe, as though there was a crack in the night sky, that a black hole had formed and sucked her into it.

But wasn't that all airy-fairy and terribly woo-woo for a practical, down-to-earth girl like herself? She needed to stop thinking and feeling like that—immediately.

She rubbed her hand over her face and fought the urge to ask what that kiss had meant, where they went from here to put plans in place. She felt uneasy and turned on, a completely horrible combination.

Jude ran his hand over his jaw. 'I'm glad you're safely home, Addison.'

Addi looked at him, waiting for more. That was it? That was all he was going to say?

He nodded at his car. 'I'm going to go.'

He was going? But they had things to discuss and plans to make. He couldn't just walk away.

Before she could say anything, he held up his hand. 'Addi, I can see the words on your tongue—a million questions, even more ideas. Let's park it for now, okay? I need to think; you do too. We've argued, we've kissed, we've had life-changing news. I think we need to let it settle before we go into the ifs, whys and hows.'

That sounded sensible, but Addi didn't want to be sensible, she wanted a plan. Now. Tonight. She felt in control when she had a plan and liked knowing where she was going and what her next steps needed to be.

'But…'

He shook his head. 'Have a bath, get an early night. Try to chill. We'll talk soon.'

Chill—he thought she could *chill*? Had that kiss scrambled his brains? 'I'm not a *chilled* type of person.'

A smile hit his mouth, then his eyes. 'I gathered that. But nothing will change overnight, nothing *can*. So, maybe just give yourself a break and allow me time to catch up.'

He was right—spending the night worrying and running scenarios wouldn't change anything between now and tomorrow. She'd try to relax, but she doubted she could, as she told Jude.

'I'll talk to you soon, Addison,' he told her, moving closer to her to drop a kiss on her temple. 'We'll work something out.'

His reassurance was just four words—we'll work something out—but it made her feel as though she wasn't alone, as though she had someone standing by her side. Maybe she was being overly optimistic, because his kiss had scrambled her brain, but she felt calmer, less panicky and able to get a bit more air into her lungs.

But, as Jude walked to his car, she told herself to stop conning herself. People routinely let her down, and she must have rocks in her head if she thought that Jude Fisher would be any different.

Around the corner, Jude wrenched his steering wheel to the left, stopped his car, rested his thumping head on the steering wheel and tried to regulate his breathing.

He'd had a completely horrendous ninety minutes, every moment of which had been filled with visions of Addi's car being swept off the road, of her being hurt or possibly dead. When he hadn't been able to reach her, he hadn't stopped to think—he'd simply run out of his house, thrown himself into his car and belted down the slippery dirt road to the motorway. He'd kept his eyes peeled for a white hatchback, his heart in his mouth whenever he saw the flashing blue lights of an emergency vehicle. He'd never felt so helpless in his entire life—not a fun experience.

Jude pulled in his first proper breath, one that actually sent air to his lungs and oxygen to his brain. He'd been operating on fear and adrenalin for the last little while and he felt utterly wrecked.

He was a fit guy, but he felt as if he'd just completed the Comrades Marathon, and as out of breath and exhausted as when he'd run over that finish line five years ago. He felt shattered.

Jude lifted his head and released the tight grip on the steering wheel. He flexed his fingers and rolled his head, trying to loosen some of the knots in his neck.

Addi was fine, she was safe. He could just sit here and breathe. Her pregnancy news had shocked him, of course it had, but he'd been off-balance since she had stepped out of her car and onto his property. She was a potent mixture of spiky and vulnerable, and there was something about her that made him want to protect her, to pull her into his arms and be the barrier between the world and her.

He didn't know why, because she'd made it very clear that she didn't need him in any way, shape or form. With any other woman, that would have been a relief, but with Addi? Well, the craziness, of what she made him feel, was that he wanted her to turn to him, to lean on him a little, to allow him to carry some of the load she lugged around. He felt superfluous and deeply frustrated.

She still desired him—her hot, responsive kiss had made that very clear—but she wouldn't let herself need him. She was an independent woman, courageous, and, while he cursed her stubbornness, he appreciated her determination. She was tough, mentally and emotionally.

He admired that.

He respected her gutsiness. And he wanted her more now than ever.

Yep, he was lusting over the mother of his unborn child. Could he have made the situation more complicated if he'd tried? He didn't think so.

CHAPTER FIVE

ADDI SMOOTHED DOWN her cranberry-coloured swing dress and checked her thigh-high suede boots for watermarks. She wore solid black tights and a cream-coloured coat, accessorising with a green, scarlet-and-cream scarf.

For this meeting with Jude, she wanted to look something other than the pale, haggard creature he'd encountered at his house, so she'd taken a lot of care with her make-up, making her now thankfully clear blue eyes bigger and her mouth softer. She wanted to look successful, someone who had her life together, who had a plan…

She didn't have a plan.

Addi walked into the lobby of Fisher International's new headquarters and inhaled the smell of varnish and fresh paint. Jude had been caught up in the move for the past few days and she hadn't seen or spoken to him since they'd kissed four days ago.

But this morning she'd got a text message from him, asking her to meet him at ten. Assuming it was a business meeting, she'd packed her laptop, run off another set of spreadsheets and made her way to the Waterfront.

The receptionist, big, buff and with flashing white teeth, handed her a security pass and gestured her to the bank of lifts on the other side of the lobby. 'The far lift door will open—that's Mr Fisher's private lift. It'll take you straight up to him.'

Addi tried to look as though she wasn't impressed by the private lift, but she was. Normally she ran up and down the steps of Thorpe Industries, partly to get some exercise but mostly because there were too few lifts to service the building, and she hated feeling like a trapped sardine.

Addi waited in front of the lift, removed her floppy black felt hat and ran her hand over her hair. It lay flat against her head today; she was channelling Audrey Hepburn and she knocked the hat against her thigh. She was nervous and she didn't like feeling that way.

She was only going to see the father of her burgeoning baby, the man who was going to buy the Thorpe assets and put her out of a job. What was there to be nervous about?

The lift doors opened and Addi stepped inside. There were no buttons and within seconds the lift door closed and she was shooting up. Her phone chimed with a message and she glanced down at the screen. It was a text message from her mother's lawyer, requesting a follow-up meeting.

She really needed to find a lawyer—one she could afford.

'One of these days, you're going to greet me with a smile, not a frown.'

Addi's head shot up. Jude stood on the other side of the lift door, looking suave in a very pale pink shirt, grey, metallic-silver tie and dark-grey trousers. He hadn't shaved and his stubble was a little heavy, a bit disreputable, and she liked the look.

Addi tucked her phone away and walked into his chaotic office. A plastic-covered couch sat in the corner, behind a stack of boxes and to the side of a massive desk. What she recognised as a brutally expensive leather chair sat on the other side of the desk. She realised Jude's back would be to the incredible view of the Waterfront Harbour and Signal Hill while he was working.

'Why did you put your desk there?' she demanded.

'I tried to work facing the view, but I was constantly distracted,' Jude replied. He gestured to the stack of boxes. 'Sorry it's a mess, we're still trying to get set up.'

Addi took a seat in the visitor's chair he offered and crossed one leg over the other, a little pleased when Jude's eyes lingered on the gap of her thigh between her boot and the hem of her short dress. A sexy memory from the night they spent together flashed and made her squirm and burn. His eyes collided with hers and she knew he was thinking of that night too. Was he remembering the way she'd straddled him, leaning down to kiss his mouth as she'd sheathed him? Or was he thinking about how he'd dropped to his knees in the shower and kissed her between her legs?

Whoa, boy.

Addi lifted her chin and told herself to get a grip. They were here to talk business…why else would he have asked her to meet at his office in the city?

Addi heard the door open behind her and she turned to see a handsome man enter, a tiny espresso cup in one hand and a clear mug holding what she thought might be tea.

The man flashed a grin at her and placed the mug in front of her. 'It's ginger-flavoured tea—I hope that's okay?'

'That's great, thank you,' she said, returning his smile. 'I'm Addi, by the way.'

'Thabo,' the man replied, handing Jude his cup. 'I'm Jude's right hand. And his left. He pretty much can't function without me.'

Jude rolled his eyes. 'That's pretty accurate, actually. But don't be fooled—I make his coffee more often than he makes mine and, having a doctorate in business science, he's the guy I listen to. He's more a partner than an employee, and my closest confidant,' he told Addi. He leaned back, picked up his cup and sipped before looking at Thabo again. 'All organised?'

'Pretty much. I just need your go-ahead,' Thabo answered, sounding enigmatic. 'While you're away, our assistants can sort out your office and mine.'

Was Jude going away? When? Where to? And why did the thought of him leaving make her feel as though she had a boulder in her stomach and it was about to crash to the floor?

Thabo picked up a folder from Jude's desk and tapped it to his forehead in a salute. 'I'll leave you two to talk.'

Addi waited for him to leave the room before asking Jude whether Thabo knew she was pregnant. 'No, not yet. I'm still coming to terms with it myself.'

She gestured to the mug of hot tea.

'Uh, no. I saw your reaction to the smell of coffee when I made myself a cup the other day, and I assumed you might be feeling a bit off-colour with morning sickness. According to Dr Internet, ginger tea helps, supposedly, so I asked my assistant to get some in. Thabo probably just picked up the cups I asked her to make to save her a trip.'

He was not only observant but thoughtful. Addi felt his eyes on her, a little quizzical, a lot hot, and dragged her eyes off his gorgeous face to look past his shoulder to the wet and wild day happening outside. Storms were battering the Cape and nobody, least of all the meteorologists, knew when they'd see the sun again. It was predicted that the Cape would soon experience the wettest and coldest winter in decades, and she was not looking forward to it. She hated winter.

Addi picked up her mug, sipped and knew she was delaying the inevitable. She needed to know why Jude had asked her for this meeting.

'Am I here to talk you through Thorpe assets or are we going to talk about the baby?' she asked, thinking that being forthright was the best way to go. There was no point in tiptoeing around the subject; they needed to pull it out into the light.

And then pull it apart.

Jude nodded and linked his hands across his flat stomach. 'Either…both.'

Okay, then. 'Where do you want to start?' she asked.

'When are you due?' he asked, picking up a fountain pen and twisting it between his fingers.

'I've worked it out to be the end of the year,' she replied. 'They'll be able to give me more accurate due dates when I go for my first scan.'

'And when is that?' Jude asked.

Ah, she hadn't thought that far. She supposed she should, as soon as possible. 'I don't know. I need to find a doctor and make an appointment.'

'Do that,' Jude told her, and she felt steel slide into her spine. But she wouldn't call him out on his bossiness; she didn't want to start fighting with him ten minutes into their meeting.

'Yes, sir,' she muttered, unable to keep the sarcastic comment behind her teeth.

Jude smiled. 'You don't like being told what to do, do you?'

'Not even a little bit,' she admitted. 'Old Man Thorpe hired me out of university, I reported to him and he left me to my own devices. I only checked in with him when I had a problem. And, at home, in most ways I've been in charge for most of my life and I'm the one who gets things done, who paves the way, who makes the calls. I'm the oldest, so I took responsibility.'

'How old were you when you first started feeling like that?' Jude asked, looking interested.

Addi had to think back. 'Seven? Eight? I remember taking Joelle's bank card out of her purse and going to the cash machine. I went straight to the store and bought food—hot dogs, I think it was.'

'And what did your mother say about that?' Jude demanded, looking shocked.

'Joelle has a very fluid grasp on money, even less of what went into and out of her account,' she told him, before waving her hand. 'Why are we discussing my spacy mother?'

'I find you, your past and your family, interesting,' Jude told her. *Did he? Really? Why?* She supposed it was because she was totally different from the women he normally dated or was seen with. Unlike them, she didn't come from a 'good' family, and she wasn't rich, sophisticated, elegant or into art, poetry and opera.

'I think we should get married.'

Addi looked at him over the rim of her tea cup and, conscious of her shaking hand, slowly lowered the cup to the desk, trying not to spill her tea on his brand-new, expensive-looking carpet.

No, he couldn't possibly have said that, could he?

'I'm sorry, I thought you said that we should get married.'

Leaning back in his chair, with an ankle on the opposite knee, he looked relaxed, but Addi could tell he wasn't, not really. His green eyes were wary, and a muscle jumped in his rigid jaw. His shoulders were tight with tension, and he played with the laces of his shoes.

Addi tried to think of a response, and eventually settled on, 'Why would you think that us marrying would be a good idea? It's the twenty-first century, Jude, people don't get married because of babies any more.'

He nodded and rubbed the back of his neck, but didn't drop his eyes. 'I have reasons why I think it's a viable option.'

A viable option. *Good grief.* As a little girl and teenager, even as a young adult, she'd imagined a proposal that had the love of her life down on one knee, preferably holding a huge diamond ring that could be seen from space.

She'd grown up and realised that life didn't work that way, but she'd never thought both her marriage proposals would be so lacking in romance. Dean had suggested they marry over a bowl of popcorn while they'd watch an action movie, and two weeks later had tossed a ring box at her, telling her to let him know if it didn't fit. Now Jude's proposal—or was it a suggestion?—contained the words 'viable' and 'option'.

'Would you like to hear them?'

She might as well. And afterwards she'd say no, they could move on and, maybe, discuss something familiar, such as Thorpe's hospitality division.

'When I say married, I am talking of a marriage of convenience—it wouldn't last more than a year, maybe eighteen months. And nobody would need to know that.'

Well, wasn't this just sounding better and better?

Jude frowned and tipped his head back to look at the ceiling. When his eyes met hers again, he leaned forward and placed his forearms on the desk, looking deadly serious. 'Look, I know you are worried about your job with Thorpe, but if you marry me I'll pull you over into a position at Fisher International. Whether you accept my job offer or not, I will pay all your medical bills and hefty monthly maintenance, starting this month.'

She wished she could say that she would dismiss his offer, that it wasn't attractive, but to someone who had mastered the art of stretching her budget it was. How could it not be? 'Go on.'

'I will also pay the fees of the best family law practitioner in the country so that you can keep your sisters with you.'

That alone was a huge incentive to tie herself to this man for eighteen months. Addi placed her hand on her heart, scared it would jump right out of her rib cage. He was making a good case for marriage, for explaining what she would get out of it. But so far it was all very one-sided. And she didn't, for a moment, believe that Jude Fisher would give up his single status just to help her out.

He might occasionally be nice, occasionally thoughtful, always hot and sexy. But he wasn't a saint, and he wouldn't sacrifice himself on the altar of matrimony unless there was something in it for him.

She switched legs, half-turned, draped her arm across the back of the chair and nailed him with a look that said 'don't you dare lie to me'.

'Well, you seem to have the answers to my problems,' she commented, sounding a great deal more casual than she felt. 'So, what's in it for you?'

Jude drained his coffee cup and considered her question. Now came the tricky bit. How did he explain to her that, business-wise, having an illegitimate child was the worst thing that could happen to him? How did he explain that he was still being punished for a youthful mistake, for messing up? How could he even start to explain that his errors of judgement had caused Bart to lose all faith in him, so much so that he'd rewritten his will just a day after the story of Jude being conned by Marina hit the headlines?

Fishers didn't air their dirty linen in public, it simply wasn't done, and it would always be Jude's fault for letting that happen. He now had a minor paranoia about his privacy, and the thought of the contents of his grandfather's will, the fact that all his decisions had to be approved by a board of trustees and that he'd have to marry to keep his company under his control, made him want to break out in hives.

This situation was fraught with peril, and he had to be very careful about what he said.

'I don't know if you know that I was raised by my grand-father—he died about nine years ago,' he began, tapping the end of his pen against the surface of the sleek, designer desk.

Sympathy flashed across her face. 'I think I remember reading something in the press,' she replied quietly. 'I'm so sorry, Jude. Was he your only family?'

'He was, from the time I was a young kid.' When he caught her wince, he thought he should explain. 'Briefly— my mum died unexpectedly and my father checked out in every way a father could. When he died, Bartholomew took me in, but he wasn't a warm and fuzzy guy. Honestly, he was more of a headmaster or a bank manager than a father figure.

'We weren't close, and Bartholomew had very definite ideas on how I should live my life and what was expected of me. Unfortunately for him, I didn't always live up to those expectations,' he continued.

Addi linked her hands around her knees, looking intrigued. 'Well, if it's any consolation, Joelle didn't have *any* expectations of us, except that we did not inconvenience her any more than what was strictly necessary.' She waved her words away. 'Sorry, this is about you, not me. How do your grandfather's wishes connect to us getting married?'

He drummed his fingers against the surface of the desk.

'My grandfather and I had a falling out when I was nineteen. I got caught up in something I shouldn't have and it damaged our relationship.' Jude pushed fingers into his right temple to push away his headache. 'Then another lack of judgement on my part led to that incident being revisited, and my grandfather's blood pressure went through the roof. He died about three months later but not before he'd made certain amendments to his will.'

He was grateful she didn't prod and pry. He'd never told anyone about Marina, how naive he'd been. Correction: he'd never told anyone since Jane had broken his confidence by spilling his story to a tabloid to exact revenge.

Addi's dark eyebrows shot up. 'I presume those amendments are why you want us to marry?'

She was so very smart and quick on the uptake. He liked the fact that she could keep up with him and that she could look at a situation with pragmatism.

'My grandfather would never leave his company, the company his own grandfather started, to anyone outside of the family. But he had major doubts about my suitability to run his empire. He had questions about my judgement.'

Addi leaned forward, a small frown appearing between her eyebrows. 'I don't understand why, because you're one of the most respected people in the industry. You've grown Fisher International, consolidated and increased your market share. You run a good company.'

He couldn't help feeling pleased, and a little proud, hearing her words. 'My lack of judgement was in my personal life, not my business life, but Bartholomew couldn't differentiate between the two.'

'Ah.' She leaned back and wrinkled her nose. 'So tell me what was in his will.'

He couldn't tell her that—not yet. No, not *ever*. No one

knew, except for Thabo, Cole Thorpe, Bart's lawyer and the Council of Three. And the trustees wouldn't say anything because Bart had made them sign a non-disclosure agreement. To reinforce their silence, Jude also paid them a substantial yearly allowance. 'That's not pertinent to our discussion. What is relevant is that I cannot have an illegitimate child.'

Strangely, the desire to tell her more, to share his past, bubbled under his skin. There was a chance that Addi, with her unconventional mother, might just be the one person who would understand how difficult it was to have been raised by an unconventional parental figure, someone you were at complete odds with.

But he wouldn't tell her. He'd told Jane about Marina and look how that had turned out. But he'd never told Jane how sick, sad and miserable he'd felt after he'd finally accepted the truth about Marina. How he'd felt like an idiot for being conned, a fool for still loving her, weeks and months after kicking her out of his life. How he'd felt the burn of humiliation, the acidity of stupidity. Jane had reopened those wounds when she'd blabbed his story to the tabloids and they'd never quite closed again. He hated the press, but he hated the fact that he'd been so naive to trust Marina with his heart, and even more stupid to trust Jane with his past.

The caveats in his grandfather's will, the implication that he couldn't be trusted to make good decisions, was acid in an open-to-the-bone wound.

'You're not giving me very much to work with here, Fisher,' Addi complained.

He met her eyes and shrugged. 'Is it necessary for you to know my reasoning? I don't think so. I'm offering you a very good deal, Addi. Financial security, money to pay the best lawyers to keep custody of your sisters, a job if you want it. All I'm asking for is a short-term, completely secret, marriage.'

She narrowed her eyes. 'Why does it need to be kept secret?'

Ah, he'd wondered when she'd ask that. 'If the press hears about it, they'll wonder about the length of our relationship, why we didn't have a big wedding; there would be a lot of interest.'

There would be references to Marina and his idiocy and they would openly speculate about whether he was making another mistake. And he didn't trust that one intrepid journalist wouldn't dig a little deeper and somehow, somewhere, find a copy of the trust document that implemented his grandfather's wishes. He didn't want the world, his colleagues and employees to see how little Bart had trusted and respected his heir. It wasn't likely to happen, but he couldn't take that chance.

Making headlines was a nightmare, having his past replayed was a night terror and having the contents of the trust revealed—it was confidential, but he didn't trust anyone—would be the worst indignity and seventh-circle-of-hell stuff.

No, it was better to keep it secret.

'What will happen if you *do* have an illegitimate child?' Addi asked.

He pulled a face. 'My business, and my reputation, would be seriously compromised.' And the Council of Three would stay on for another ten years and they would hamper his plans to expand Fisher International. And his frustration levels would hit the roof. He was so close, just a year away from complete freedom, and he would do anything—well, nearly anything—to have his financial and business freedom.

Even marry.

Addi picked up on his reluctance and didn't push, instead choosing to stand up and walk over to the floor-to-ceiling window, looking out onto the grey, cold ocean and the yachts in the harbour.

'What if I left your name off the birth certificate?'

That was an option but not a good one. He was a Fisher, his child would be a Fisher, and keeping his or her name off the birth certificate would be denying the child knowledge of where it came from. No, marriage was the best option for them both.

'Look, I didn't think I was going to have the opportunity to be a father—that normally comes with a relationship with someone—but, now that it's going to be a reality, I want my child to have my name, Addison. I want to be a part of its life, to be a father.'

He'd never trust anyone again with his heart. After his grandfather, Marina and Jane, he'd never allow anyone to have any say over what he did and how he did it. He'd tried love but it hadn't taken. Why go back for more?

'I might not want a day-to-day wife, someone in my space, but I do want to protect my company, so I think that we can come to an arrangement.'

'An arrangement,' she murmured, her voice low and cool. He'd never met anyone who hid her feelings as well as Addi, who could take anything thrown at her and remain calm. It made him want to prick that bubble of self-assurance, to pull away her layers to see who she really was beneath that layer of calm. It felt as though the only time he'd got to the core of her was when they'd made love. Within a few seconds of kissing him, she'd started to melt, and he'd tasted heat, demand and more than a little wild.

'So how would this work?' she asked, placing a palm on the window, her eyes fixed on the horizon. He followed her gaze and, there in the distance, a container ship skimmed along the horizon, barely discernible in the mist and rain.

He saw a stab of longing in her eyes and wondered if she was wishing she could run away from her life and her responsibilities, from the daily grind. He had only himself to worry about and he did what he wanted, when he wanted, but Addi had responsibilities he hadn't. She juggled a family, a demanding job and handled the financial demands of a young family, mostly on her own. And, on top of what had to be a normally stressful life, she was worried about her job, was facing her sisters being taken from her and was pregnant.

How was she still standing?

And when had she last had a break, some time out? He suspected it was never. A holiday would be way down on her list of priorities, if it featured at all. It was obvious, even to a Neanderthal like him, that she could do with some down time.

'Still waiting, Jude.'

Right, she'd asked him how he thought their fake marriage would work. 'After the prenuptial agreement is signed, we marry quietly without fuss or fanfare. I'll take care of the paperwork.

'Once we marry—preferably as soon as possible—we carry on as normal, with you in your house, me in mine. You hire a law firm to fight for custody, I'll pay those costs and I'll guarantee you a job within the hospitality division of Fisher International, at a higher salary than you are getting now. I will also pay you maintenance and child support, starting immediately. Money will never be a problem for you again, Addison.' Her breath seemed to hitch, and Jude couldn't decide whether that was a sigh of relief or a hint that she was scared. Both, maybe?

'How long do you want us to stay married?' Addi asked him, turning around to look at him.

'At least six months after the birth of the baby, more if we can manage it.' By the end of the following year, he'd have the company, be rid of the trustees and would be free to do what he wanted.

She held his eyes for the longest time, hers bright-blue but dancing with fear, anxiety and more than a little hope. Having her money issue solved was a big deal but he knew that him funding the lawyer's fees for her upcoming custody battle meant more to her. She just wanted stability, a little room to breathe. He could give that to her and wouldn't break a sweat—the amount they were talking of was petty change to him. All he required was for her to be legally tied to him for a year, maybe eighteen months.

'What's the process?' she asked. 'What do we need to get married?'

'All I'll require from you is a signature on some documents and then I'll arrange for someone to marry us. I thought that as soon we are—' he hesitated and decided to choose different words. 'As soon as that's done, we could get back to business and start with the inspection of the Thorpe hotels. I'd like to start with the lodge in Mozambique...uh... Something Bay?'

He wasn't sure how he was going to cope with the object of all his sexual desires dressed in a bikini, but he'd cross that bridge when he came to it. All he knew for certain was that they should leave the country as soon as possible, and that in Mozambique he could arrange for her to have a little down time. She definitely needed it.

'Turtle Bay,' she corrected him. 'What about the prenup? How complicated is that going to be?'

He thought about his too-picky lawyer, who was going

to have a thousand questions and who'd want to prepare for five thousand possible eventualities. By the time Kara was done, they'd have a fifty-page agreement that would take six years to read through and digest. This was a good arrangement for Addi; she was getting a lot out of this, and she wouldn't screw him over. It didn't mean he trusted her—he didn't trust a woman with anything more than ordering her own meal at a restaurant—but he did understand that she had a lot to lose by not agreeing to his terms.

Kara would scalp him for this…but that didn't stop Jude from digging out a legal pad from his desk drawer and writing his name, then Addison's, across the top of the page with the words 'Prenuptial agreement' below. Keeping it simple, he wrote a few paragraphs, detailing their agreement and his requirement for secrecy. His sentences didn't fill up more than half a page. He drew a line for them each to sign, scribbled his name and the date and handed her the paper to sign.

Addison lifted her eyebrows and shook her head. For a minute, he thought she'd crumple it up in her fist, but then she surprised him by shrugging, placing the paper on the edge of his desk and asking for his pen.

She signed her name in a neat script and handed the paper back to him. 'I'd like a copy of that, please,' she told him, her tone crisp. Then he caught the amusement in her eyes, and he grinned. They were going to do this. They were going to get hitched.

If someone had asked him a week ago to write a list of the top one hundred things he might be doing the following Monday, signing a handwritten pre-nup would not have featured on his list.

CHAPTER SIX

ADDI STOOD IN front of the robed priest in a tiny chapel, the midday sun illuminating the stained-glass window above the altar. She shuffled her feet and, feeling Jude's eyes on her, lifted her head to meet his eyes. He gave her a reassuring smile and turned his attention back to the tiny priest, who'd insisted on giving them a homily on marriage.

She'd been unsure of what to wear to her wedding that wasn't really a wedding, so she'd chosen to wear a navy coat-dress with sheer stockings and her highest black heels. She was glad she'd made an effort because Jude looked smart and sombre in his dark-grey suit, white shirt and mint-green tie.

She was about to be married—if she wasn't already, given the sheaf of documents she'd signed in the chapel's anteroom. Addi swallowed down a surge of panic. How had it come to this?

Addi felt Jude's hand surround hers and he lifted it to tuck it under his arm. Thankful for the support, she shuffled closer to him and gripped the crook of his elbow, breathing deeply.

It would be okay…it *had* to be okay.

But, damn, she wouldn't have been human if she hadn't thought of how different her wedding day could've been. And she couldn't help comparing it to the excitement she'd felt preparing for her wedding with Dean, before the girls had dropped into her life.

She'd been so in love, looking forward to the future, ecstatic about sharing her life with a man whom she'd thought adored her. With Jude, it felt as if all her emotions were super-charged and she knew that, if this had been a proper wedding, something they'd both wanted and looked forward to, she would be the human equivalent of a Catherine wheel. Buzzing, spinning, glowing and glinting...

Would she ever experience that? Probably not. Devastation pierced her pragmatism and for a moment, a step out of time, she wanted it all. Standing there, her arm in his, Addi craved love, security and the stability of being loved by, and committed to, a strong, smart, decent man.

Someone like Jude.

Think about work, Addison. Think about anything else until you can face the thought that you are someone's—no, Jude's—wife. With more willpower than she'd thought she possessed, Addi forced herself to turn her thoughts from the priest's long-winded sermon to work and remembered that she'd received correspondence from Thorpe Industries, London, yesterday.

The memo had stated that Cole Thorpe was in the process of selling the assets he'd inherited from his brother and that, while he would issue severance packages, he suggested his staff consider other employment options.

That meant that Lex, who worked as a part-time driver for Thorpe, would need to look for alternative work. While she didn't bring in a lot of money, driving for the company did pay for her university modules and exam fees. As his driver, Lex had been spending a lot of time with Cole but, given the craziness of her life lately, Addi hadn't had much time to connect with her sister. She had asked what Lex thought about Cole but her normally garrulous sister had avoided the question. And blushed. Was something happening between the billionaire and her sister?

Maybe. Lex deserved to have some fun. Or maybe Lex was simply worried about her job. Addi wished she could reassure her and tell her that Jude was going to pay her maintenance and that she had a job waiting for her at Fisher International when it was time to move on from Thorpe.

But, if she explained that much, then she'd have to explain how it all came about. None of her explanations would make sense without telling Lex why she needed money so quickly and explaining her decision to marry Jude. She'd promised Jude their marriage would remain a secret and, because Joelle was the master of broken promises, she took any vows she made super-seriously.

She hated lying, even if it was by omission. But the simplest solution, the one that would allow her to keep her vow to Jude, would be to wait until she started at Fisher International, tell Lex she'd received a massive increase and that their money troubles were a thing of the past.

It was the truth, sort of. If she massaged it really, really hard.

Addi bit the inside of her cheek as she tried to convince herself that she was shutting her sister out for everyone's greater good. That Lex would understand that she was taking such a drastic step for her, Nixi and Snow.

Lex also had the right to know that Joelle was suing for custody, but if she told her Lex would lose it. She would start to worry, to fret, and her stress would affect the girls. Lex couldn't afford to be distracted right now; she had an exam coming up, exams she couldn't afford to fail. No, she'd tell Lex after she got some feedback from the family lawyers she'd hired yesterday, when she knew what were their chances of keeping custody of Nixi and Snow. Hopefully, this custody battle would be all a storm in a teacup, and she could avoid worrying Lex at all.

Addi wanted to spare Lex any worry she could. She also wanted to tell her about the baby, but she was embarrassed to have made such a mistake when she was supposed to be so super-smart. She felt as if she'd let Lex down, and that she wasn't providing a good example to her sisters by doing what their mother had done…five times! How did she tell them to be careful, to take precautions, to be sensible, when she'd messed up so badly? She felt like an utter fool.

She knew what she *should* do but she wasn't ready to tell Lex, she wasn't ready to tell *anyone*, her life-changing news. She was still wrapping her head around the events of the past days, coming to terms with everything that had happened. When she felt stronger, when she was in a stronger position mentally and financially, she'd tell her sisters she was pregnant, that they were financially secure and that everything would be fine.

She'd leave out that she was married. Besides, this wasn't a proper wedding anyway. If it had been, she'd have had Lex as her maid of honour, Storm as her bridesmaid and Nixi and Snow as flower girls. She would have worn a white dress with a veil, and she would have fizzed with happiness instead of carrying around a heavy boulder in her stomach. Jude would have looked at her with love in his eyes instead of wariness and, after they exchanged rings, they'd have shared their first kiss as man and wife.

Yes, it was sad that her first wedding, probably her only wedding, wasn't the fairy-tale day Addi had expected and dreamed of, but this was real life, and, as Lex would say, she had to suck it up. Real life demanded practicality and pragmatism: happy-ever-afters were a myth, and love and commitment frequently ran when adversity knocked on the door.

This was a business arrangement, a legal arrangement. Despite them being in a chapel, nobody could call this a wedding ceremony.

Business. Arrangement.

And, since that was *all* it was, she could hold off telling Lex. But, man, she still felt guilty.

The priest cleared his throat and Jude covered his hand with hers, his gentle squeeze bringing her out of her thoughts. 'I understand there are no rings to be exchanged?' the priest asked, managing to look disapproving.

'Unfortunately, they are getting resized and weren't ready in time,' Jude replied, his lie sliding smoothly off his lips. They couldn't wear rings, of course, because no one could know they were married.

The priest sniffed his disapproval. It was obvious that he thought that something was off but, judging by the faded furniture and the cracks in the walls, Jude had chosen this church so that he could make an enormous donation in exchange for the priest's silence.

Addi couldn't judge him; she was getting married because she needed Jude's money too.

The priest looked at Jude. 'Do you promise to love, honour, cherish and protect her, forsaking all others and holding only unto her for evermore?'

Addi gulped. Those were terribly serious, portentous words.

Jude didn't hesitate. 'I do.'

My turn.

Addi forced down a hysterical giggle. This couldn't possibly be her life. Addi Fields, control freak, didn't enter marriages of convenience.

'Do you promise to love, honour, cherish and protect him, forsaking all others and holding only unto him for evermore?'

Um...uh...

Could she do this? Should she do this? Addi didn't know if she could say the words and commit herself to this extraordinary course of action. But then she recalled the photograph hanging in the hallway of her home. It was a candid shot of the five sisters, arms around each other, laughing.

Yes, she could do this. She *would* do this. It was her job to look after them, to protect and nurture them, and this was the only solution available to her.

Addi lifted her chin and looked from the priest to Jude and back again. 'I do,' she said, her voice strong and clear.

'By the power vested in me, I now pronounce you man and wife.'

Well, there was definitely no going back now.

Addi stepped inside the *casinha*, a 'small house' down the beach from the dining area of Turtle Bay, and looked around at the wood, thatch and canvas structure. A huge double bed was covered in white linen and a filmy mosquito net was wrapped around the makeshift tree-trunk four-poster bed. She knew, because it was her job to know, that there was a slipper bath and an open-air shower—also with amazing views.

Hers was the smaller of the two cabins, and Jude was occupying the much larger one next door. He had a larger deck and a hammock strung between two trees. Their front garden was the white beach and gorgeous sea, and their back garden was a wild coastal forest.

Addi kicked off her shoes and half-pulled her shirt out of her skirt, thinking the band in her pencil skirt was a bit tight. She'd started to put on a bit of weight, not surprisingly, since she was feeding and growing a little human.

Addi placed her hand on her stomach, the thought punching her in her gut. Up until now, and apart from her not being able to drink coffee, the baby had been more of an intellectual exercise, a thought rather than reality. But with her stomach expanding, and with her feeling very tired, she was starting to feel the physical changes.

'Are you okay?'

She jerked her head up and saw Jude standing on the deck of her cabin. He'd changed into a pair of swimming shorts and a loose, half-buttoned cotton shirt, sleeves haphazardly rolled up to reveal his tanned and muscular forearms.

'Fine,' Addi said, managing a quick smile. Last night he'd surprised her by whisking her from the church and treating her to an evening at Snell's, Cape Town's most exclusive restaurant. Thanks to knowing the owner, Patrick Snell, Jude had managed to snag an ultra-secluded table in the private dining room, the one with the best view of the city's waterfront. The food had been exceptional, the service flawless and he'd made an effort to put her at ease.

After their meal, he'd driven her back to her house in Green Point and left her with a kiss on the cheek and a soft smile. It had been an exceptionally weird, and ridiculously chaste, wedding night.

When she'd met Jude at the airport earlier, she'd been quickly reminded that theirs hadn't been a real wedding because Jude had treated her like a colleague and not the woman he'd married the day before. Despite Addi knowing that they were heading for a tropical island, Jude's business-like approach was the bump back to earth she'd desperately needed. This was a business deal, they hadn't made a life-long commitment and, despite the white beaches and turquoise sea, this was most definitely *not* their honeymoon.

Until she'd seen the beach and the romantic cabin, she hadn't realised how much she wanted to step out of time and revel in being the sole focus of a sexy man's attention.

It was just one more thing that wasn't meant to be.

She gestured to her laptop bag. 'So, if you give me a moment to set up, we can get to work. I meant to do some work on the plane, but I couldn't keep my eyes open. Sorry about that.'

His lips firmed and she knew he was unhappy about her lack of professionalism. Despite the craziness of the past week, she would not let her standards slip.

Jude looked to the Indian Ocean, a lovely, sleepy blue, and looked at her. 'Addi, it's three-thirty in the afternoon. It's already been a long day and there is no way I am going to look at spreadsheets and figures now. And neither are you.'

That sounded like heaven. Addi rubbed her foot on the back of her calf. 'Jude, we need to work. This isn't a holiday, at least it's not for me.'

'Actually, it is,' Jude told her. He walked into the bedroom area, picked up her laptop bag and tucked it under his arm. 'I'm confiscating this.'

'You can't do that!' she cried, lunging for it, but because Jude was so much taller he simply lifted the bag up and out of her reach.

'Want to bet?' he grinned. Seeing her consternation, his smile faded. 'Addi, it's Thursday afternoon—we're staying here until Monday afternoon. It's been a long, rocky, tense ten days for both of us, for you more than me. You are mentally, physically and emotionally exhausted.'

Well, yes, maybe a little more than normal.

'For the next four days, you are not going to work, or even think about work. You're not going to do anything but eat, sleep and relax,' Jude added.

Oh, God, that sounded like heaven. Her eyes filled with tears at the thought of doing nothing. 'But—'

'Work will still be there on Monday afternoon,' Jude assured her, tucking her beloved laptop under his arm. 'And, because I don't trust you to not sneak in some hours, I'm going to take this.'

Addi bit her lip, tempted, but unsure whether this was a wise course of action. She could deal with terseness, with work demands and requests for figures and facts, but tenderness and thoughtfulness disarmed her. She genuinely had no idea how to deal with it and, worst of all, it made her realise what she'd missed out on.

She'd had so little kindness and thoughtfulness directed at her from men—Dean had been quite self-absorbed, her biological dad couldn't have been bothered and, while her ex-stepdad Tom had been great, his kids had come first and rightly so. She wasn't sure how to respond to Jude's kindness.

And, without work as a barrier between them, what would they talk about and how would they interact? Apart from that hot, wild night when they'd slept together, and the dinner they'd shared last night, she and Jude hadn't spent any quality time together. Last night they'd discussed the food and the hotels in Thorpe Industries' portfolio, nothing more personal than that.

And what about sex? If they took work away, would all those inconvenient wants and needs come rolling back in? Would they find each other hard to resist? Would they end up in bed again? This was a business arrangement, but she still had the hots for Jude, and frequently spent her nights reliving the way he'd touched her, trying to remember exactly how he tasted, the feel of his hot skin under her hands.

'I have never heard anyone who thinks as loudly as you do,' Jude complained.

Addi rocked from foot to foot and shrugged.

Jude leaned his shoulder into one of the tree trunks that served as a pillar of the four-poster bed. 'Are you worried that if we don't have work to fall back on, your precious figures and spreadsheets, we won't have anything to talk about? Are you concerned that our time together will be awkward? Or are you worried that we might lose our heads and fall into bed again?'

How did he read her mind? *How?*

Jude smiled at her shock. 'I'm not expecting you to entertain me and I'm very comfortable with silence,' he told her, reaching out to touch her hair. 'And, if we do end up in bed again, that's fine too.'

'We're working together. And we're married!' Addi told him, sounding and feeling flustered.

'Should I point out that married people often have sex?' His mouth quirked up at the corners before his expression turned serious when she didn't smile. 'If we end up sleeping together, Addi—and that will be your choice—it will be absolutely and utterly separate from work and our agreement, our marriage of convenience. It'll be because you want me and I want you.

'Clear?' he asked when she didn't reply.

She nodded, feeling as though he'd pulled all the wind out of her sails. She didn't have a comeback, didn't have an argument. Neither was she looking for one. All she wanted to do was to pull on her swimsuit and immerse herself in that luscious-looking sea, dig her bare toes into the warm sand and tip her face to the sun.

Jude sent her an understanding smile. 'Get changed, Addison, and let's hit the beach.'

Now, there was one order she was happy to obey.

After just one day of lying in the sun and bobbing in the waves, Addi looked as though she'd been here for a week, Jude decided. They sat at the intimate outdoor restaurant situated in the centre of the beach, the *casinhas* spread out to either side of the casual but luxurious dining and lounge area. Behind the tables was an open-air kitchen where the chef conjured up stunning meals that ranked up there with the best he'd eaten in his life.

Together with the luxury décor, the superbly kitted out *casinhas* and the amazing beverage section, he understood why this fifteen-bed resort commanded such high prices. The beach was why people came to Turtle Bay but there was more to do than just sun tanning and swimming. Earlier, he and Addi had taken a walk on a trail in the coastal forest behind them, and he could easily arrange to go on a game drive, as there was a private game reserve just a short drive away.

Tomorrow, they were taking a boat ride to snorkel over a reef far out to sea. He couldn't wait.

Jude picked up his beer and took a long sip, his eyes dancing between the lovely view in front of him—the sunset was a riot of pinks and purples—and the equally lovely woman beside him. Addi was a little flushed, her nose even pinker than her face, and she wasn't wearing any make-up. Her hair was more messy than usual, but in her acid-green bikini, a brightly coloured sarong knotted on her right hip, she looked stunning. A beautiful beach babe with bright hair and blue, blue eyes.

But beyond her looks was a woman who intrigued him,

someone strong, capable and so damn brave. Whenever he looked at her, he experienced a strange jumble of emotions: lust and need, and behind those a need to protect and understand. He wanted to dig, to discover, something he didn't usually spend his energy on. Lust was normally enough but Addi made him feel as though he were standing in an emotional tornado, being battered from all sides.

He was also, strangely, very unsatisfied with how they'd got married. He'd chosen that out-of-the-way church because it would afford them maximum privacy but, standing in front of that gnome-like priest, he'd wanted more. For a moment—okay, a couple of moments—he'd let his imagination run away with him and he'd imagined Addi in a stunning dress, her face alight with joy, surrounded by their friends and family, eager to walk up the aisle to him. Excited about sharing a life with him…

Wow. What had happened to the self-reliant, independent, emotionally distant man he'd been before he'd met her? He'd like him back, please.

'This is such a stunning place,' Addi said, turning those magnificent eyes on his. Her chin rested in the palm of her hand and her lovely mouth curved up in delight. 'Thank you for giving me the time off.'

'You needed it,' Jude told her. He gestured to her empty glass. 'Would you like another lime and soda?'

She wrinkled her sunburned nose. 'What I would like is a mojito,' she told him. 'But I can't drink alcohol so, yep, another lime and soda would be great.'

Jude looked around and within a couple of seconds he'd placed her order. 'How many of the Thorpe properties have you visited?' he asked, curious.

She shook her head. 'Maybe two…both of them in the Western Cape. I've never stayed at a resort before.' She lifted her shoulder and her cheeks turned pink. 'This is only the second time I've stayed at a hotel.'

He frowned. 'But didn't you take holidays as a kid?'

'You're mistaking my mother for someone who'd consider spoiling us that way. And you're assuming we had money to go on holiday. She didn't and we didn't. Surviving was sometimes a challenge.'

'Tell me,' he said softly. He wanted to know her history, what made her tick, the forces that had shaped her. He knew he was playing with fire—he should be putting some distance between them—but he couldn't help wanting to know more. Everything. He was in so much trouble here.

She stared at the sunset and when the waiter, Miguel, arrived with her drink, she thanked him and lifted the straw to her mouth.

'Joelle had us young—she was just eighteen when she had me, nineteen when Lex was born. She dragged us from house to house, living with anyone—and by anyone, I mean a man—who'd give her free board and lodging.'

He didn't know how to ask but he had to. 'And were they...okay, these guys?'

Addi nodded and he swallowed his sigh of relief. 'One or two were dodgy but nothing happened.'

Despite his parents' death—his mum's had been particularly traumatic—he'd still lived a privileged life. He'd grown up in a mansion, attended the best boys' school in the country, had every toy and piece of branded clothing a kid could want and he'd enjoyed overseas beach, snow and cultural holidays. His school tours hadn't been to the local museum but to places like Russia and the Caribbean. He thought about telling her that he was spoiled and lucky, but figured she knew that already.

'Our best times were when Joelle met and married Tom,

Storm's dad. That was our longest stretch of stability, about three years.'

He frowned, confused. 'Who is Storm again?'

'My middle sister. She's twenty-four, six years younger than me. Technically, you have four sisters-in-law,' she quipped. Then she grimaced. 'Sorry, maybe I shouldn't have said that.'

He smiled, wanting to put her at ease. 'Why not? It's temporarily true.'

'You should thank God this isn't Regency England and that you don't have to provide dowries for all of them.'

'In the African culture, I'd have to pay lobola to your sisters for allowing me to marry you,' Jude pointed out. 'Cattle are damn expensive.'

'I'm probably only worth about two chickens and a goat,' Addi quipped.

He laughed. 'If that.'

She nudged him with her shoulder, but he was happy to see she could take a joke. 'You mentioned an Aunt Kate before…tell me about her.'

'By the time we hit our teens, Joelle was finding it very difficult to persuade her lovers to let her, and her two stroppy teenagers, move in. We really bounced around for a few years; it was incredibly stressful. Then Joelle reconnected with her mum's sister; they'd fallen out years before. We went to stay with her for what was supposed to be a few weeks during the long summer holidays, and Joelle said that she was going out to look for a stable job. We didn't mind; Aunt Kate was old and strict, but we had three meals a day.'

Addi ran an elegant finger up and down her glass. 'Joelle didn't come back. When she finally showed up, two months later, Aunt Kate wouldn't let us leave. We stayed and have been in her house ever since.'

'And she paid for you to go to uni?'

Addi nodded. 'Well, her insurance policy did. After she died, we rented out rooms in the house to other students to help fund our living expenses and Lex picked up a job. The plan was for me to get my degree as quickly as I could, and then I'd help Lex pay for her to go to uni. But then Joelle dropped back into our lives, surprising us with two half-sisters we didn't know about.'

'She never told you about them?'

'Nope. She rocked up with them. She'd been living in Thailand. She asked us to take them for the weekend...'

He connected the dots immediately. 'And she did a runner.'

'We couldn't believe she'd suckered us like she did our aunt Kate. And, like Kate, we took them in. I mean, what else could we do?'

Jude tipped his beer bottle to his mouth. 'And she's still in Thailand, right?

'Mmm...'

'Why do you think she wants them back? Why now?' he asked. 'Do you think she's had a come-to-the-light, repent-of-her-sins moment?'

'Joelle?' Addi's eyebrows shot up. 'No way. No, I'm thinking that she's got a guy on the line, someone who is either very family oriented or someone who thinks that kids belong with their mum. Someone fairly rich, because she wouldn't be hiring a lawyer unless he was paying.'

Man, her mother sounded like a piece of work.

'Well, your lawyer will mop the floor with her lawyer,' Jude told her, covering her hand with his and squeezing it. As she'd told him earlier, she'd engaged a lawyer he'd recommended from a practice that had an excellent reputation in family law, and she'd forwarded all the correspondence from her mother's lawyers to hers. They'd acknowledged her email and asked for a retainer...

Damn, he'd forgotten to pay them, as per their agreement. This week hadn't only been difficult for Addi, but he was also slipping up. The hard part was over, he told himself, and they'd soon get used to their new set of circumstances. Within a week or two, they'd go back to normal. Whatever normal was.

Making a mental note to make the payment for the lawyers, Jude looked at Addi and fought the urge to take the fear out of her eyes and promise her that everything would be okay. From the moment he'd met her he hadn't been able to put her in a box, hadn't been able to stop himself from feeling more than he should. She'd burrowed under his skin, and he suspected that was where she'd stay. He desperately wanted to reassure her, promise her that everything would work out. The thing was, it frequently didn't. His mum's death from an undiagnosed ectopic pregnancy, his father's depression, Marina... Life had taught him that was a promise he couldn't make.

Some things, unfortunately, even money and power couldn't change.

Addi looked a little sick. 'I couldn't bear it if we lost them, Jude. I grew up with Joelle, and I know how unsettled life is with her, but they'd also be in a foreign country. Can you imagine how scary that would be for them? And Lex would be devastated. She's been their rock for the last four years. She adores them.'

He stroked her hair and ran his fingers over the bare, hot skin at the back of her neck. 'And you, Addi. How would you feel?'

'I'd miss them intensely and I'd feel gutted. And for the rest of my life I'd have to live with the fact that I failed those kids. That they looked to me to help them, and I couldn't, that I didn't.'

He pulled back from her and waited for her to look at him, for their eyes to connect. 'Addi, that's a big burden to place on your shoulders, a harsh way of looking at this. You took in those girls, you've paid for everything they need, have given them a bed and clothes and stability. You've loved them. And—and I'm pretty sure this won't happen—even if they do go back to their mum, you would've done everything possible to keep them here. How would that be a failure?'

Her eyes filled with tears. 'It just would be.'

He ran his knuckle down her cheek. 'You are very hard on yourself, sweetheart.' Because he was so close to kissing her, needing to chase her tears and sadness away with heat and passion, he leaned away from her and changed the subject. It was so easy to get sucked in by passion, to fall into the heat of the moment, and he had to keep his head. If he didn't, he'd end up dinged and dented again. Life with Addi was turning out to be a constant tug of war, between what he wanted and what he knew he couldn't have.

'How do your sisters feel about becoming an aunt?'

Embarrassment flashed in her eyes and she jerked back and folded her arms across her chest, looking a little belligerent. She didn't answer him and, when he cleared his throat, she lifted her eyebrows at him. 'What?'

'You haven't told them, have you?'

She pulled a face. 'No.'

'Why not?' he asked, interested. He thought she and Lex were close, that she would've told her everything—including that they'd had a one-night stand. He wondered if she knew that Lex and Cole were having a hot fling. It wasn't his place to tell her.

'Does she know that that we slept together? That we are married?'

'You asked me not to tell her about our marriage, and I promised I wouldn't, so I haven't,' she replied, sounding a little snippy. 'I didn't tell her about what happened at the Vane either.'

'Why not?' Jude didn't know why her answer was important, just that it was.

Addi took a large sip of her drink and he knew that she was trying to find a way to avoid answering. But when he kept his eyes on her face she sighed loudly. 'I wanted it to be just *my* memory...' She waved her hands in the air. 'I don't expect you to understand that.'

He did, actually. Those hours spent with her were some of the best of his life, and telling someone else, explaining, would dilute some of the magic.

'You're going to have to tell her about the baby at some point, Addi. I don't think that's something you can hide for ever.'

'I know, Jude!'

Addi lifted her thumb to her mouth and started biting at her cuticle, something he'd noticed she did when she was on edge. He pulled her thumb away and shook it gently. 'Spill it, Ads.'

She looked as though her gut was in a twist. 'I'm embarrassed to tell her!'

Okay, that wasn't what he'd expected. 'Why?'

'When we were sixteen, I sat Lex down and made her promise, swear on her life, that she wouldn't fall pregnant accidentally. I promised her the same. We vowed that having a baby would be a deliberate choice, made when the circumstances were right.' She made a sound that was a cross between a hiccup and a sob. 'It wasn't supposed to happen this way, Jude, especially given our history.'

He put his arm around her, grateful that his broad back hid her distress from the other guests who'd gathered in the restaurant bar. He rubbed his hand up and down her back, trying to give her what comfort he could. 'Your sister will understand, Addi.'

'I hope so,' she muttered, brushing her cheeks with the tips of her fingers. 'I don't want her to be disappointed in me, that's all.'

'I think you are being hard on yourself, Addi. We're allowed to make mistakes, to be human.'

Addi sniffed. 'God, how am I going to have the "you've got to be careful and use protection" speech with the girls when they are older? They'll laugh their socks off.'

'You'll tell them that mistakes happen and that, no matter what, you'll stand in their corner. That there's always a plan to be made.'

'Hopefully their plans won't be as drastic as ours,' she muttered.

'A perfect storm,' he agreed. If his grandfather hadn't been so damn unforgiving and so very controlling, his life and Addi's would be a lot easier. But there wasn't anything they could do about it. They were married. He had a wife. In a year, he'd have full control of his company.

A *temporary* wife, he corrected. In name only.

Addi pulled back from him and sent him a teary smile. 'Crazy set-up, huh?'

'Crazy.'

He looked into her eyes and saw the flash of interest, the heat burning in all that blue. She looked down at her hand, which lay on his forearm but, interestingly, she didn't break their connection.

'We had fun that night, didn't we?' she asked softly.

Fun? That was a tame word for the hottest, sexiest night of his life. He'd loved every second of their love-making and would love to do it again…and again.

He lifted her hand and placed an open-mouth kiss on her palm, wanting and needing to gauge her reaction. Pink infused her cheeks. The tip of her tongue peeked out to lick her bottom lip and her eyes ducked to his mouth. Yeah, she wanted to be kissed. Hopefully wanted a lot more.

'I loved making love with you, Addison,' he told her, keeping his tone low. 'And I'd love to do it again.'

'For how long?' she asked.

'For now, let's say that for as long as we are out of the country, visiting Thorpe hotels,' he replied. 'Back home we'd have to be super-careful so that we don't grab any press attention.'

She frowned at that, then a cheeky smile pulled her lovely mouth upward. 'Well, on the plus side, at least I won't fall pregnant,' she quipped.

He smiled at her attempt at humour and then wondered if she was saying yes, if she was giving him the green light. Needing to know, he traced his thumb over her bottom lip. 'So, will you let me make love to you again, sweetheart?'

She stared at him and he held his breath. Eventually, what seemed like years later, she nodded. 'Yeah, I think I will.'

Not wanting to wait, or give her time to change her mind, and needing her, he stood up and tugged her to her feet. Addi looked from him to her half-empty drink to the still intensifying sunset. 'Now?' she demanded. 'Can we not eat something first?'

No. He wasn't going to wait—not for her. 'They have this amazing thing called room service,' he told her, wrapping his hand around hers and pulling her behind him as he weaved his way between the tables filled with amused guests. They knew exactly where they were heading but he didn't care.

This wasn't a honeymoon, but he was going to take any chance he could to have this wonderful, lovely woman naked. And what would be better than rolling around a big bed, with the sunset tossing reds and oranges onto her soft, smooth skin and the sea providing the background music?

CHAPTER SEVEN

JUDE LED HER across the sand and up onto his wooden deck. Addi caught a glimpse of a comfortable sitting area to the right, but he angled left and led her to the bedroom, which looked straight onto the sea and the setting sun. Stopping next to the bed, he held her face in his hands and looked down at her, his expression intense.

'Are you sure you want to do this, Addi?'

Yes, absolutely. She couldn't wait to undo the buttons of his shirt and spread the fabric apart, to run her hands across his wide chest, to lay her mouth on his hot skin. To kiss his mouth and get lost in his arms. She placed her hand on his shoulder and met his eyes, gazing at that intense shade of green she'd come to associate with passion and need and want. 'I want this, Jude. I want *you.*'

He lowered his head to kiss her, but she pulled back just a little. She just needed to check one little thing. 'This has nothing to do with our deal or my job or anything else, right?'

'This is only about the fact that I can't wait to kiss your lips, to run my hands down your naked body, to touch, taste and caress you. I've thought about little else for the last two months, trying to remember your smell, the softness of your hair, that sexy sound you make when you're turned on.'

He radiated sincerity, and she knew that, at this moment,

they were a couple who simply wanted each other. This had nothing to do with the marriage certificate tucked into her bag or the agreement they'd made. Right now, he wasn't the rich billionaire, her sort-of boss, and she wasn't the mother of his unborn baby.

They were just a man and a woman who were extremely, maddeningly, attracted to each other.

'Addi, you're killing me here,' Jude muttered, his hand coming up to cover hers and squeezing. It was such a boost to her ego to have a man like Jude look at her as though she were all the Christmas presents he'd ever wanted.

She could no more resist him any more than she could stop time.

'Take me to bed, Jude,' Addi told him, her voice strong and sure. She craved him and needed to experience the orgasms that only he'd managed to pull effortlessly from her.

As soon as the words were out of her mouth, Jude covered her mouth with his, not hesitating to slide his tongue between her teeth to tangle with hers. He bent his knees just a little, and boosted her up his body, and Addi wrapped her legs around his hips, her core settling on the hard ridge of his erection.

Yes, please.

This was exactly where she wanted to be.

Jude kissed her deeply and voraciously, demanding she meet his pace, and she was happy to. She tugged his shirt up his back to glide her hands over the bare skin of his back, loving the taut muscles and his harnessed strength. He held her so easily, with one arm beneath her butt, while his other hand covered her breast. He ducked his head to pull her nipple into his mouth, enjoying the friction created by her bikini top on her hard nipple. But that wasn't enough

for Jude, and he tugged the strings holding the triangles together and pulled her bikini top from her body.

Allowing her to slide to her feet, he put one hand behind
his head to grip the collar of his shirt and pulled it over his
head in that sexy move only men managed to pull off. Addi
reached forward to place her open mouth on his muscled
chest but, before she could, he tugged off her sarong, leaving her to stand in just a pair of brief bikini-bottoms.

Jude pushed her bikini bottoms down her hips and her
clothes lay in a colourful heap on the floor. He batted her
hands away and made short work of removing his swimming shorts. She couldn't help herself, she needed to touch
him, so she ran the side of her thumb up his shaft, unable to
believe that a man could be so soft but so hard at the same
time. She loved touching him, and wanted to inhale him,
taste him, hear him moan her name as he struggled to control his reaction to her...

'If you keep looking at me like that, I'm going to lose it,
sweetheart,' Jude warned her, his hand covering her breasts
and his thumb dragging over her hard nipples.

Addi arched her back as she looked up at him. 'How am
I looking at you?' she asked.

'Like I am a cupcake and you haven't eaten for days.'
Accurate.

Jude placed both his hands on her hips, lifted her and
gently tossed her onto the enormous bed behind them. For
a moment he stood next to the bed and looked at her, her
legs slightly spread. She resisted the urge to place her hand
on her mound, to cover her breasts with her arm. It was obvious that Jude very much liked what he saw and there was
no reason to feel ashamed of being naked.

Jude placed his hands on either side of her head. Her

eyes met his and she was unable to look away. He'd barely touched her, but she could feel his mouth on her breasts, his lips on her hip bone, between her legs.

As he started to turn the images in her head into reality, she wondered what it was about him that made her feel this way, why he was the only one who could make her feel out of control and how he could make her always active brain shut down. When he kissed or touched her she was able to disassociate herself from her life. She moaned as he switched his attention to her other breast, gently sucking her nipple so that it touched the roof of his mouth. He, and the way he made her feel, was all that was important.

Addi rested her weight on her elbows as she watched Jude's progress down her body, loving the way his lips skimmed across her rib cage and how he dipped his tongue into her belly button. He gently nipped at her hipbone with his teeth and that tiny hint of pain ratcheted up her pleasure, lifting her to another level.

If he didn't touch her soon she'd lose her mind—she desperately needed him to focus on her feminine secret places, where pleasures started and ended.

But Jude continued to tease her, kissing the inside of her thigh, inspecting a scar on her knee, running his tongue down her shin bone and sucking the soft spot on the inside of her ankle.

He'd done nothing more than kiss her, and stroke his long fingers over her super-sensitive skin, but she felt as though she was a bubbling cauldron about to overflow. But, as much as she wished to let loose, she wanted to give him some of the pleasure he'd given her, make him yearn, squirm and hopefully burn.

Wiggling away from him, she pushed his shoulders to

get him to lie down and, when he rested on his back, she kneeled beside him, just taking her time to look, to pull in the details. His nipples were flat discs and the layer of hair on his chest was just enough to be sexy. It veered down into a thin trail across his hard, muscled stomach, and she traced the tan line across his lower stomach. His skin had tanned easily, turning the deep brown of surfers and sailors. He had the long legs of a runner and big, but surprisingly elegant, feet.

She ran her finger from the back of his broad hand and traced an upraised vein, stopping to inspect a scar just below his elbow. He lifted his other hand to put his hand behind his head, his biceps bunching, comfortable in his nudity. He had another scar just below his collarbone, the thin line suggesting he'd had surgery. She wanted to know what had happened and when, desperate to know everything about this man.

That was foolish, she thought as she dropped her head to place a kiss on his sternum, to drag her tongue down. They had a deal and, while they might be off-the-charts attracted to each other, they couldn't go tiptoeing around in each other's psyches. They had to keep their thoughts—and especially their feelings—out of this deal. If they didn't—and by 'they' she meant herself—life would become very complicated indeed.

Business deal, with some fun thrown in on the side.

No harm, no foul.

Taking her cue from him, Addi nipped his hipbone with her teeth and an instant later found herself on her back with Jude looming over her, his knee nudging her legs apart.

'I need you, Addison. *Now.*'

His voice was growly with need and desire, and Addi nodded, sighing when his erection probed her entrance.

Instead of pushing inside her, Jude pushed his hand between her legs, and she released a low groan when his thumb brushed her bundle of nerves. He dragged his fingers through her warmth and wetness and his eyes glinted when they met hers.

'You're so damn sexy, sweetheart.'

She didn't need words, she needed him inside her, so she lifted her hips and pushed, sighing when he entered her. But it wasn't enough; she needed him inside her, as deep as he could go. Touching her soul, if possible.

'You feel like heaven,' Jude muttered as he rocked into her. 'Hook your legs around me.'

She obeyed his rough command and he slid a hand up her lower back, angling her up, and moved further inside her, as deep as he could go. This was what she needed, what she'd dreamed what sex should be.

Heat, passion, an intense build-up, rocketing hard and fast and detonating when she hit the edge of space, exploding into colour and sensation, into shards of nothing and everything.

Addi dug her nails into Jude's backside, dimly aware of his harsh breathing, his tensed body. She felt his release deep inside her and thought that making love with him without a condom felt more intimate, more intense. As she gathered her thoughts and her shattered pieces back together, she ran her hands up and down his broad back, over his firm buttocks. She loved his body. Loved the way he made her feel.

And she was terrified that, if she wasn't very, very careful—if she didn't keep a sharp eye on her rebellious emotions—she could love him.

That would be a disaster of magnificent proportions.

* * *

Jude looked at Addi lying face-down in his bed, fast asleep. She had a white line across the middle of her back from her bikini strings, and he winced at her otherwise red skin.

He hadn't thought of her sunburn when he'd taken her, hadn't thought that the linen might aggravate her tender skin. Hell, he hadn't thought at *all*. He'd just wanted her and, as soon as she'd given him the green light, nothing but being inside her had entered his head. She'd chased every thought but being inside her out of his head.

She was so slim, Jude thought; nobody would think she was pregnant. Maybe she was one of those women who wouldn't look pregnant until she was way down the process, the ones who looked like they carried little balls under their shirts. He didn't mind what she looked like when she was pregnant—tiny or big and bold—as long as she and the baby came through the experience healthy.

He ran his finger down her spine, feeling each bump and admiring the delicious curve of her butt. He could stare at her for hours but, unfortunately, his rumbling stomach was demanding food. The moon was up and he lifted his left hand to look at his watch—it was nearly eight. If he wanted sustenance, he'd better order food soon.

Rolling off the bed, he pulled down the mosquito net and left Addi to sleep. Pulling on his swimming shorts, and a T-shirt, he decided to amble to the dining room, place an order and take a quick swim while he waited for their food to be delivered. Moving a screen in place so that the waiting staff wouldn't see Addi if they arrived at the cabin while he was swimming, he hit the beach, the light of the moon guiding his way.

He'd ordered line-caught fish for them both—he vaguely

remembered something about pregnant women needing to avoid shellfish—and, after thanking Miguel, started the walk back to the *casinha*. He pulled off his T-shirt and ran into the sea, ducking under an incoming wave.

Jude bobbed in the waves, enjoying the moonlight dancing on the sea. The water was stunningly warm and it was a perfect night, with a slight breeze settling on his skin. He'd just had amazing sex, and was about to have a wonderful meal, but there was a little part of him that worried that this had all been too easy, that something was bound to go wrong.

At his next meeting with the Council of Three, he'd inform them of his marriage, that Addi was pregnant and assure them that the baby would be born legitimate. He'd remind them that his personal life fell under the NDA and that he'd sue if news of his marriage reached the papers. But, because he believed in sticks *and* carrots, he'd also send them an additional, unexpected, bonus.

He wasn't worried about the trustees ratting him out to the papers—money was an excellent motivator and he had lots of it. Unless a reporter got suspicious and went looking, they wouldn't unearth their quickie marriage, and Addi and him could quietly divorce after the baby was born.

But, because he considered all angles, good and bad, he considered the question of what he would do if the press found out that he was married. While he did not doubt that Addi would *try to* keep their wedding secret from her sisters, she might slip up and, if it got out, what then? He stared up at the moon, thinking about how he'd deal with that scenario.

They'd have to pretend that they were in love, and that getting married had been an impromptu decision. That they'd wanted to be married and take their time planning their church ceremony and the big reception everyone expected from one of the most eligible bachelors in the country. With some luck and some charm, nobody would ever find out that they'd married to get rid of his board of trustees. It would all be fine.

Nothing could go wrong.

Could it?

The next morning, Jude helped Addi climb down from the diving boat. They'd encountered wild dolphins and seen a manta ray and a huge turtle while they'd been snorkelling but, instead of seeing the same joy on her face as he did on the other guests', Addi's face looked a little pinched. He gathered her close and bent his head to speak in her ear. 'Are you okay?' he asked.

She nodded, tipping her head back to look at him. 'I think so.'

That wasn't a yes. He stepped back to look at her, glad to see that everyone else was walking up the beach and away from the speedboat. 'What's wrong?' he demanded.

Addi wrinkled her nose and placed her hand low on her abdomen. 'I've just got a little pain. It's not something I've had before.'

Every hair on his arms lifted as his skin cooled. Thoughts of what had happened to his mum battered him. 'How bad is the pain? Are you cramping?'

She looked at him as though he was losing his mind. 'It's just a dull pain, Jude. It's nothing.'

'How do you know it's nothing? Maybe there's something wrong,' he said, admittedly sounding a little unhinged.

Addi sent him an 'are you mad?' look. 'Will you please relax? Geez, it's nothing serious.'

'How do you know?' he demanded, slapping his hands on his hips. 'You've never been pregnant before.'

Addi rolled her eyes so hard that he was sure she'd give herself a headache. 'I'm *fine*, Fisher.'

'When are you going to see a doctor? Have you made an appointment to get a scan?' He planted his feet in the sand as Addi wrapped her sarong around her hips. 'Maybe I should call my pilot up and get him to arrange for the Cessna to pick us up so that we can fly to Maputo.' He looked at his watch. It was eleven now; if they could leave by twelve, they could be in Maputo by half-one, meet his private jet and be in Johannesburg by three. His assistant would find a gynaecologist who could see her shortly after she landed. By the end of the day, she'd be getting treatment.

But, if she miscarried, where would that leave them? Divorced, he supposed. And the thought left him with such a bitter taste in his mouth that he felt slightly sick. He couldn't imagine her not being married to him, not carrying his child. But neither could he imagine a committed, day-to-day situation, living life with her. Or maybe he didn't want to imagine it because it scared him to the souls of his feet. If he lost his ability to be completely self-reliant, how would he scrape himself off the floor when it all went pear-shaped? And, nine out of ten times, it went pear-shaped.

Addi placed a hand on his bare chest and stared up at him, confused and a little irritated. 'Will you please calm down? I said that I'm a bit sore, not that there is anything wrong.'

'But don't you think we should get it checked out?'

Addi shook her head, her bright hair glinting in the sunlight. 'The pain is receding, it's almost gone. I think we should grab a drink, and you should take a breath. Or five.'

'Are you suggesting that I'm overreacting?'

She shook her head, her mouth curving up in a smile. 'No, I'm *telling* you you are overreacting. Just relax, Fisher. I'm not the first woman to fall pregnant, and I'm perfectly healthy.'

She was right, she wasn't the first, but what if the boat ride had been too bumpy, if she'd overdone it this morning? She was under his care and protection, and he didn't know enough about pregnancy to know what could cause a miscarriage or not. And, yeah, maybe there was a bit of fear that what had happened to his mum would happen to her.

Scrap that, maybe there was a *lot* of fear...

CHAPTER EIGHT

AN HOUR LATER, they sat in the corner of the restaurant at their favourite table, one that was slightly isolated from the rest of the dining area. Jude had an icy beer in front of him and Addi wished she could order one herself; there was nothing better than a cold beer or cider after a morning spent on the beach or in the sea.

She'd had an amazing morning, one that she'd remember for the rest of her life. She, Jude and another couple had hopped aboard the dive boat and, within minutes, they'd been speeding north, the boat following the line of the coast. After ten miles, they'd came across a pod of dolphins which had been just as interested in them.

Within minutes, she'd pulled on a snorkel and dived off the boat, going as deep as she could and hoping that the dolphins wouldn't bolt at the sight of these strange white blobs in the water with them. As she'd come up for air, one dolphin had positioned itself next to her and mirrored her vertical ascent, its stunningly intelligent eyes on her face. When she'd broken the surface and laughed, she'd seen it streaking away, and she'd felt a surge of disappointment.

Ducking back under the surface of the mirror-flat sea, she'd seen her new friend turn and speed back toward her, circling her. She'd wanted to reach out and touch the dolphin but figured that, since she wasn't a fan of strangers touching her, she'd give the mammal the same courtesy and keep her hands to herself. She'd dived down, the dolphin had followed, she'd come up and it had mimicked her actions. As a test, Addi had spun around in the water and had nearly gulped water when the dolphin did the same.

When the dolphin had swum next to her and nudged her stomach with its nose, Addi had sensed that the creature knew she was carrying a baby, another cog in the wheel of life. It had been a deeply profound, amazing and emotional experience and, when the dolphins had finally left them, her dolphin being the last to leave, she'd blamed her red eyes on the salt water, her tears now part of the ocean.

They'd climbed back into the boat. The skipper and other guests had wanted to discuss the experience to death, but Addi had been desperate for quiet, for some time to take in the almost spiritual experience. Then Jude had gripped her chin, placed a tender kiss on her lips and rested his forehead against hers, and she'd known he understood.

Some things didn't need discussion, and knowing that he didn't need explanations made her feel warm, a little gooey and, scarily, hopeful.

Be careful, Addison.

Addi took a long sip of lime and soda and looked out onto the bright-blue and green ocean. They would be leaving tomorrow, heading for Tanzania and another Thorpe hotel, but she didn't want to leave this spot and had no interest in returning to work. She wanted to stay here, in Jude's bed and arms, enjoying the trifecta of sun, sea and sex.

For the rest of her life, these few days would be the measure she judged her other holidays by. She'd also measure any other relationship she had in the future with the way Jude, her temporary fling, made her feel—wanted, sexy and seen.

The waiter deposited a plate of fried fish and salad in front of her, and a lobster roll in front of Jude, and she snagged a perfectly fried chip off his plate. She bit down and sighed. 'Those are absolutely divine.'

'Order yourself a plate,' Jude suggested.

She would have but she didn't want to turn into a blimp. Joelle had remained reed-thin during her pregnancy with Storm—Addi's only memories of Joelle being pregnant—but that didn't mean she would too.

'Have you had any morning sickness?' Jude asked her, before lifting his beer bottle to his mouth.

'Nope. Except for my reaction to coffee, I've been fine,' Addi replied. 'It might still kick in but I'm hoping it won't. Throwing up isn't my idea of fun.'

She forked up some lettuce and a chunk of fish, and chewed. After swallowing, she decided to ask him about his over-the-top and uncharacteristically panicky reaction when she'd climbed off the boat. 'Why did you go into a meltdown when I said I had pain in my stomach?' she asked.

'I think calling my concern a meltdown is exaggerating,' Jude told her as he tucked into his lobster roll.

She nudged him with her elbow. 'You were all "let me call a plane", "let's get you to a doctor",' she told her. 'Are you normally such a worrywart?'

When he kept his eyes on his plate, and when his jaw tensed, she realised she'd hit a very big button. She didn't know how or why, but she intended to find out.

'What happened, Jude?' she quietly asked, and put her hand on his, squeezing gently.

He shrugged and took a bite of his roll, but Addi knew he wasn't tasting any of its delicate flavours. He could pretend to be insouciant, but she saw the pain in his flat green eyes and tension in every muscle in his body.

'You are, possibly, the most level-headed person I've met, so your reaction tells me that something very personal, and painful, happened to you. I'd love it if you shared that with me.'

He might or might not, but she could only ask. She could play the 'we're going to be parents' card, but she didn't want to force him to tell her, not that she really thought she could. She wanted him to tell her because he liked her, because he felt close to her, and because she thought they were friends as well as lovers.

When Jude finally spoke, his voice was pitched just loud enough for her to make out his words. 'My mum died from an undiagnosed ectopic pregnancy when I was eight. I was young when it happened, but I clearly remember her complaining of stomach pains. I suppose that memory kicked in when you said you were sore, and my brain jumped to the worst-case scenario.'

Understandable. 'Is me having a miscarriage something that worries you?' Addi asked him.

He lifted one big shoulder. 'To be honest, it's been such a crazy time that I haven't given it that much thought. Or allowed myself to think about it.' He looked out to sea, his expression troubled. 'But maybe we shouldn't have married so quickly. There are sound reasons why most couples wait to announce that they are pregnant. It's because they don't want to get anyone's hopes up until the chance of miscarriage has passed.'

'If that happened, I wouldn't hold you to anything, Jude,' she assured him. 'I'm perfectly fine, and so is our baby.'

'How do you know?'

She had no idea. 'I just do.'

When Jude didn't respond, she thought it best that they

move on to another subject. 'Tell me about your parents,' she suggested.

He took some time to reply. 'After my mum died, my dad withered away emotionally. Three years later, he was diagnosed with cancer. He tried chemo and radiation, but nothing took. He died about a year after being diagnosed. I think he died because he didn't want to live without her, and I wasn't enough.'

Addi felt her throat close, tears lodging there. 'I'm so sorry, Jude.'

'Love can be a pretty destructive force,' he told her. 'He only loved her; there was none left over for me.'

Oh, that was just awful, and he'd been so young. 'Who raised you?'

'My grandfather. He was an austere, introverted man who had no idea how to handle a lost, grieving boy with too much energy.' Jude drained his bottle of beer and signalled for another.

'I was sent away to boarding school when I was thirteen and didn't see much of him. I spent most of my school holidays at friends' houses. But I did get monthly letters from my grandfather, which I called "the Sermons". They were a detailed road map of what was expected of me as a Fisher. Essentially, he plotted and planned my entire life—he selected my degree, when I would join the family business, what university I would attend and how I would conduct myself. Basically, no wine, woman or song.'

She couldn't see Jude spending his university years as a studious monk and told him so. He smiled. 'The first year I went wild, I partied long and hard and had far too many one-night stands with women I barely remember. Grandfather, who kept tabs on me, was horrified. By the time Marina came along, he and I were barely speaking, and he was threatening to cut off my funding unless I returned to the straight and narrow.'

Marina? Who was she?

Jude thanked the waiter for his beer and picked off half the label before answering her unvoiced question. 'She was this girl I met in a pub one night. Funny, gorgeous, intelligent. I fell—hard.'

She heard his voice crack and knew that, whoever this Marina person was, she'd hurt Jude badly. 'How long were you together?' Addi asked, trying to sound casual. She knew that if she threw a barrage of questions his way he'd shut down.

'Nine months, maybe a little more,' Jude replied. 'I was so in love with her. I thought she loved me, but I was very, very wrong about that.'

This hadn't been an ordinary youthful break-up, Addi realised. This hadn't been a burn bright, fade quickly situation. No, something had happened that had caused scars on Jude's psyche. Whatever had happened back then was still affecting the way he lived his life today. 'Will you tell me, Jude?'

'It's a long, ugly story.'

She'd grown up with Joelle—ugly didn't scare her. 'Tell me anyway.'

'My grandfather was already unhappy with me, furious that I'd spent my first year partying and that I'd barely scraped through. He didn't like my friends, the way I dressed, my lack of seriousness.'

'Did he keep that close an eye on you?'

'He did,' Jude confirmed. 'I'm not sure whether he hired a private investigator, or paid my friends for information, but he knew what I was up to all the time.'

Addi grimaced. Jude must've felt so betrayed by his

grandfather's lack of trust. 'I started pulling back from my friend group,' Jude admitted. 'I didn't know who was feeding him information, so I cut everyone off. It was…hard.'

Of course it had been; at that age, friends were the lifeblood.

'In hindsight, I was the perfect mark for someone like Marina: a lonely, rich kid.

'I fell for her—hard,' Jude admitted. 'And we got serious fast. I saw myself being with her for ever. I thought that we'd finish our degrees, become independent and be stunningly successful together.'

'But?'

'But, as my grandfather took great pleasure in telling me, Marina tried to blackmail him. She said she'd break up with me and drop out of my life if he paid her off. If he didn't, she'd tell everyone she was pregnant and that I wouldn't let her leave. What she didn't realise is that old Bartholomew would've rather cut off his hand than give into extortion. He, via private investigators he'd hired, started digging into her life. It turned out that I wasn't the first, or the fifth, guy she'd pulled this stunt on. She was older—twenty-five—and mooching off rich boys was what she did.

'I didn't believe him, I believed her. I cut off ties with grandfather and refused to have anything to do with him,' he continued.

Addi saw the pain and anger in his eyes and knew there was more. 'Carry on, Jude.'

'I wasn't hopeful that Bartholomew and I would mend fences, so I picked up a job as a bar tender. I was working and studying and trying to keep it all together, to look after her and myself. I came home after a shift and she had a pill in her hand. She calmly told me that I either had to get my grandfather to pay up or she'd abort the baby she was carrying. It was the first I'd heard mention of a baby.'

Addi's mouth dropped open. 'She was *pregnant*?'

'That's what she said,' Jude muttered, bold and bright fury in his eyes. 'I looked at her and knew, just knew, that she wasn't. I knew she was lying, and I'd had enough. I was done being played. I tossed her, and her imaginary baby, out.'

Addi wrinkled her nose. 'And you are *sure* she wasn't pregnant?'

He sent her a *'really?'* look. 'She admitted it and told me playing the pregnancy card was worth a shot. Also, I saw her about five months later and she was as skinny as a rake. Nope, she wanted money and was prepared to do, or say, anything to get it.'

Addi wanted to go back in time and slap the woman. How dared she have played with Jude's emotions like that? And why was she feeling protective over this man? She only did that with people she loved…

She did *not* love him. That was too much, too soon…

You're overreacting, Addi. Rein it in.

'I'm sorry you went through that,' she told him. She pushed her half-eaten plate of salad away and reached for her drink. 'I know what being so disappointed by someone you love to distraction feels like.'

His head snapped up. 'Your mum?'

'Well, her too. No, I was engaged to a guy I met at university. I was due to marry him three months after the girls dropped into our lives. He decided they were more baggage than he could handle and he broke it off.'

She looked away and shook her head. 'That's not completely fair. He didn't sign up for a ready-made family and he did try, sort of, but they frustrated him. He *"tried"* for about three weeks—he kept telling me he'd do better—but then decided he couldn't.'

'I'm sorry,' he said, resting his forearms on the table and shaking his head. 'It's a never-ending source of amazement to me that we are constantly bombarded with the news of relationships breaking up—this person had an affair, and that person wants out. Two out of three marriages end in divorce but, like lemmings, humans still keep stepping into the quagmire of marriage and are surprised when it doesn't work out. I don't get it.'

His words reminded her of a literary quote. 'Didn't Oscar Wilde say something about marriage being a dull meal with dessert served at the beginning?' She pulled a face. 'This is a pretty cynical conversation for two people who've just tied the knot.'

The corners of his mouth lifted in a smile. 'Ah, but the difference with us is that we have clearly defined expectations of what we want to achieve from our union and a time frame. A fling, with an option to carry on sleeping together when we get back to Cape Town. At most, eighteen months married. We're doing it right, Addi.'

Maybe, Addi thought as she raised her glass to clink it against his beer bottle in a silent toast. But there was still the niggling thought that they could do it better. But life, as she knew, often threw curve balls when you least expected it to.

Jude lay beside Addi, watching her sleep. Beyond her, he could see the dark sea lit by the beam of light coming from a moon mostly hidden behind a thin layer of cloud. The sound of the sea drowned out Addi's soft breaths. He placed a hand on her hip, marvelling at how big his hand looked on her slight body.

It had been a very strange day, and one he was still coming to terms with. While he'd never expected to tell Addi about Marina, he was glad he had. And relieved that she hadn't been anything but empathetic and supportive and hadn't questioned why he'd taken so long to come to the same conclusion about his ex that his grandfather had.

He hadn't explained his need to believe in what he'd assumed he and Marina had had—a connection, a bond, trust—but knew she'd got it. His belief in, and loyalty to, Marina had been the catalyst for so much mistrust and grief in his life. His grandfather had thought him a fool for falling under the spell of a woman, an emotional idiot for not believing his PI's evidence and he'd never let him forget it.

Bartholomew, not a fan of emotion, had second-guessed every decision Jude had made from then on and had never forgiven him for being human. And the story about how Jude had been conned hitting the papers via Jane had been confirmation that his mistrust had been warranted. Jude could, so many years later, still recall Bart's disparaging comments shortly after he'd read the exposé, his mouth lifted in a sneer.

'You're emotional, and you will believe any pretty face with a sob story. Emotion is a weakness, son.

'I don't feel I can trust you with anything more than petty cash,' Bartholomew went on to say. 'You've made some stupid mistakes, ones I can't look past or forgive. And now the whole world knows how stupid you were.'

His grandfather's words, and his disdain, were still burned into Jude's brain and made him writhe with embarrassment and want to run screaming down the beach.

It hadn't occurred to Bart that Jude had been young when he'd fallen for Marina; that hadn't counted. It hadn't mattered that he'd gone on to graduate with a top-class degree or that he'd established a successful side business. Bartholomew had defined him by his mistakes, not his successes. He hadn't wanted to appoint him CEO, but there'd been a Fisher at the helm for over eighty years and he wouldn't let that tradition lapse. But, because he'd considered Jude to be a renegade—an outlier, hot-blooded and impulsive—he'd put those clauses in his will outlining the terms of his inheritance.

His grandfather had been determined not to trust him, to punish him for being less than perfect. But in a year, he'd finally be able to step out of his grandfather's shadow and shed his influence once and for all. He'd gain full control of Fisher International, rid himself of the trustees and make the company his.

One year—all he had to do was to keep the news of his marriage, and the pregnancy, under wraps. He did not want to end up rehashing his past and risking another media embarrassment and a PR headache. In twelve months, he could look forward to a less complicated life.

Most importantly, he would finally be free to make his own decisions, free of Bart's ghost. Free to be who and what he was.

He felt Addi roll over and he looked down into her lovely, sleepy eyes. She lifted her hand to touch his face. 'Are you okay?' she asked, her voice a little groggy. 'It's late. Why aren't you asleep?'

He'd oh-so-casually suggested they have a fling, but it was feeling anything but casual now. And that was dangerous. He lifted his shoulder in a shrug. 'Too much on my mind?'

She tucked her hands under the side of her face. 'Thinking about Marina?'

He hadn't been, actually—or not too much. 'Not really.'

'Good; she's not worth your time.'

Jude stroked his hand over her hair and cupped his hand around her elegant neck. 'Are we still good, Addi? Still on track?'

A small frown pulled her eyebrows together. 'What do you mean?'

'You won't tell anyone, not even your sister, that we're married, right?'

Irritation and hurt flickered in her eyes. 'I said that I wouldn't, Jude,' she snapped.

He thought about explaining that he had a right to be mistrustful of people—Marina, Jane and his grandfather had screwed him over—but knew she wouldn't appreciate the reminder. He just had to pray she'd stick to her word. The stakes were too high for either of them to mess up now. They just had to keep their mouths shut and all would be well.

Addi rolled over and put a healthy amount of distance between them. He could tell she was angry, that she hated his lack of faith in her—it vibrated off her in waves so strong he could almost see the shimmer in the air. He didn't want to fight with her, not tonight. So he leaned over and placed a kiss on the spot where her neck met her shoulder, loving her scent.

'Sorry,' he murmured.

She didn't turn over. 'You need to trust someone at some point, Jude.'

She didn't understand. And she wouldn't unless he explained that she was asking for the impossible. He rested his forearm over his eyes and wondered where to start. His relationship with Jane was actually harder to talk about than Marina, possibly because he'd been older when it happened, and he should have known better.

'After the Marina incident, I left South Africa, went to

the UK and enrolled in the London School of Economics. That's where I met Cole. I thought it would be a fresh start, that no one would be interested in me. Unfortunately, my grandfather was an internationally famous businessman and people paid interest.'

'By "people", you mean the press?' Addi said, turning to face him.

'Yes. Because he was so vociferous in his views, so uncompromising about his values and had a habit of lecturing anybody and everybody he met, many people, especially journalists, wanted to see his feet of clay. But, as hard as they looked, they couldn't find any dirt on him.'

'So they turned their attention to you.'

'I think they sussed, somehow, that my failures would be a thorn in his side. But I'd realised that already.' He dropped his arm and tucked his hand behind his head. 'I kept a very low profile. I had few friends and Cole was one of my best. After six months, the press realised that I was boring and moved on. I graduated, joined Fisher International and ran the company's international interests from London for five years. My grandfather and I worked better together when we lived a continent apart.'

Addi sat up and crossed her legs, her elbows on her knees, her eyes steady on his face. 'I started seeing someone—Jane—after uni, and we were together for a couple of years. I thought that I could put Marina behind me, that it was a youthful misjudgement. I was older, better and wiser. Jane moved in with me and we lived together for a year, maybe a bit more. She worked in finance in the city, and was hugely ambitious, but she had no sense of fair play. Her actions started to worry me. I wasn't comfortable with how she conducted business, and there seemed to be no lines she wouldn't cross.'

Addi pulled a face and a wave of embarrassment swept through him. 'I know how to pick them, right?' he asked, trying to sound upbeat but missing by a mile.

Addi didn't comment, and he didn't see any judgement on her face. 'I found out that she'd slept with her boss for a promotion. Fidelity was, is, important to me, so I told her it was over. She told me that I was overreacting, that it wasn't a big deal.'

'But it was to you.'

She got it. Jude nodded.

'I asked her to move out and she wasn't happy being downgraded from a penthouse apartment to what she called "a poky flat at the end of the world". It wasn't—she rented a flat on Canal Walk, one of the most expensive areas in the city—but it wasn't Knightsbridge. She begged to come back, said she was sorry, but I was done, you know?'

'Mmm...' Addi nodded. 'What did she do then?'

Sometimes he forgot how smart she was, how she could connect dots at the speed of light. Jude dropped his eyes and looked past her. 'One night, a while before we broke up, after a party and having far too much to drink, I'd told her about Marina and explained how I was played. Jane later sold the story to the press, telling them that I was a terrible partner and that I was cold and unfeeling. She also said that I had a terrible relationship with my grandfather. That, admittedly, was true. She also pointed out that my grandfather didn't trust me and was unhappy about passing the company on to me. Cue share prices dropping, shareholder uneasiness.'

Addi lifted her hand to her mouth, obviously horrified. 'What a horrible woman!' she snapped, her voice hot with anger.

'A few months later my grandfather died, and I discovered he'd added some codicils to his will, hoops I had to jump through, the biggest of which was that a board of three trustees had to approve all my Fisher Holding decisions for ten years. There were also clauses in the will about my behaviour and what he expected from me.'

'Well, obviously I know about the fact that you can't have an illegitimate child, but what else?'

Jude rubbed the back of his head, mentally translating the legalese into everyday language. 'No drugs, gambling, illegitimate kids. I'll only gain full control of the business next year, shortly after you give birth.' He pushed his fingers through his hair, feeling on edge, as if he was walking a tightrope over a thousand-foot canyon.

'I'm surprised nobody knows about the board of trustees,' Addi commented. 'How have you managed to keep them a secret?'

'My grandfather insisted they sign a non-disclosure agreement, which I tightened up after I took over. I also pay them a huge yearly stipend as an added inducement to keep quiet. And we've fallen into a pattern over the years: I only ever consult them when there are massive decisions to be made. They couldn't be bothered with approving the day-to-day decisions; it would adversely affect their golf game.'

Addi flicked her thumbnail against her bottom lip. 'I now understand your reluctance to trust anyone a little better—it's because you've been badly burnt twice.'

'Three times, if you include my grandfather, who couldn't forgive me for misjudging Marina.'

'Your hatred of the press and your wanting to keep a low profile now makes sense. You don't want to rake up old stories.'

He also didn't want Addi to be tainted by the shouted questions, their demands for information, their nosiness and by the press putting their spin on a situation they didn't understand. This was between them; nobody else had a right to comment on what they had.

Whatever it was...

A repeat of being hounded by the press would be a nightmare scenario. He'd spent the past nine-and-a-half years keeping his head down, avoiding anything and everyone that would make headlines, and he had no intention of reliving that awful experience. He didn't want Addi to experience it either.

Neither did he want to be conned again, be betrayed, be screwed over.

Life had been so much easier when he'd lived it solo. But now he had a baby on the way, so that was impossible.

Maybe. Yes, Addi was the one person he trusted more than anyone else. Not fully, not yet—he didn't know if he could ever get there with anyone—but more than he had with anyone for a long, long time. It was a strange, weird, exciting thought. And one he shouldn't be having.

'I still think you should trust more, Jude.'

'Trust me'—that was what she'd meant but hadn't said. 'I know,' he murmured. 'I'm trying, Ads.'

I'm trying to trust you.

He felt the tension leaving her body, flowing out of her muscles. Scooting closer to her, he tucked his knees behind hers and placed his hand on her breast. He felt his eyes closing—he was emotionally wiped—but then her nipple spiked in his palm. When she wiggled her butt into his groin, he dragged his thumb across her nipple and felt her breath hitch. She wanted him...

And, man, it felt so incredibly good to be wanted by *her*.

Not only was she lovely, with a body that he wanted to worship on a daily, *hourly* basis, but she was fresh, kind and, well, *good*. She was like a gust of fresh air blowing through his life, dispersing the secrets and the machinations, scattering the shadows.

Addi lifted her arm to grip the back of his neck and he lifted himself so that his mouth could touch hers. It was an awkward position, so he rolled her onto her back and covered her lips with his, sinking into the spiciness of her mouth.

Making love to her was such a revelation, every single time. Sometimes it was hot and fast, filled with laughter, sometimes it was slow and languorous, almost dream-like. He pulled back and pushed her hair back, their eyes connecting and holding.

This woman was magic; she was safety, grace and freedom.

Disconcerted by his wayward thoughts—she was a fling, and it would be over in a few weeks—Jude ducked his head to kiss her again. When his lips connected with hers, he dived into her mouth, wanting the flash and heat of passion to burn away his dreamy thoughts. He didn't want to feel emotional, he wanted to ride the wave of passion and be immolated by their desire. This was about the pleasure they could give each other, not the succour their soul—*his soul*—needed.

Disconcerted, Jude wrenched his mouth off hers and ducked his head to drag his mouth down her neck. He sucked her nipple into his mouth with more desperation than finesse. He needed to stoke the fire, to make them yearn and burn, to be consumed by what their bodies wanted. Sliding his hands between her legs, he slid one finger into her, then another, looking up to see her eyes close and her mouth fall open.

Yeah, she was with him, carried away by the passion. He placed his thumb on her bundle of nerves, loving the sound of her harsh pant, and her 'take me now' moans. She was so close, and so was he. His erection rested next to her hip, hot, hard and demanding, but he needed to watch Addi fall apart first, riding the pleasure he could give her.

Sitting back, he used his other hand to play with her nipple and watched her blue eyes fog over. She was so close. He debated whether to kiss her nipples, but he wanted to watch her come, wanted to watch her body flush as the moment hit her.

He heard her beg him to come inside her, and although he wanted to, desperately, he swiped his thumb across her, her hips lifted off the bed and her pants grew harsher. She was so close...

And so was he. If he didn't find himself inside her, he might just make a mess of the sheets. 'Addi!'

Her eyes flew open at his harsh command, and he loved the way she found it difficult to focus. He'd done that. He'd made this amazing woman cross-eyed with pleasure and it was one of the greatest achievements of his life.

'Addi, I'm going to touch you again and you're going to let go, okay?'

'Need you...' she muttered, her eyes closing.

'Look at me, Addi!'

When her eyes slammed into his, he touched her again, working her sensitive nerves, and curled his fingers inside her. Heat, heart and pleasure slammed into her and, as she released a keening sound, he pulled out of her and slid inside her, moaning when he felt her warm channel grip him. He didn't need to move, to do anything, he just took a breath and let go, riding away on the force of her orgasm.

It was the hottest, most intense sexual experience of his life and Jude didn't know how to deal with it. All he could do was bury his face in her neck and hold on.

CHAPTER NINE

AFTER VISITING FOUR countries in two weeks, Addi was back in Cape Town. She'd been on so many flights lately that she was now a dab hand at moving from Jude's private plane to his waiting car, sliding into the back seat and greeting Jude's driver by name.

Going back to the real world after being spoiled by private-plane travel, five-star hotels and excellent food was going to be a big culture shock.

Addi looked around the swish reception area of Mazibuko, Cowell and Sithole, and shuffled in the leather club chair. She and Jude had flown in yesterday afternoon so that Jude could attend a meeting in Cape Town. Thankfully, she'd also managed to secure an appointment to see her lawyer to discuss the process and the progress, of getting custody of the girls. She also needed to see a doctor for an antenatal check, but wasn't sure she had time to do that on this trip.

Addi heard a door open behind her and turned to see a gorgeous woman step into the reception area. She wore sky-high heels and a stunning lemon-coloured suit.

'Ms Fields? I'm Thandi Ndaba-Green.'

She was the junior partner Addi had been corresponding with. She stood up and shook her hand. 'Hi, it's nice to meet you. I'm looking forward to hearing where we are and what progress you've made.'

Thandi grimaced and Addi frowned. 'Is there a problem?' she asked.

Thandi gestured to the small conference room off the reception area, with its glass walls and door. Addi followed her inside and turned when the door snicked behind them.

'I tried to call you this morning but I couldn't reach you,' Thandi said, crossing her arms across her chest.

Addi winced. 'Sorry, I was in the air. I saw your message but, since I was coming straight here from the airport, I thought returning your call could wait.'

'That was unfortunate because I could've saved you the trip to our offices.'

Addi looked at the conference table and wondered why she hadn't been offered a seat or something to drink. The appointment was scheduled to last for two hours so she'd expected more than to be kept on her feet and spoken to in a tiny office.

'Is there something wrong? Are you not able to meet with me?' she asked, frowning.

'I'm afraid not,' Thandi told her.

'Why?' When Thandi didn't reply, Addi's heart plummeted to her feet. 'Look, if you can't take my case, then I'll take anyone else in the firm. I just need some help.'

'I'd be happy to help you, Ms Fields, I *want* to help you, but I can't do any more work until we receive your retainer.'

Addi tried to make sense of her words because Jude had paid them over two weeks ago. 'The deposit was made into your bank account a while back,' Addi told her, utterly confused.

Thandi shook her head. 'It hasn't been, I'm afraid. Because of the urgency of the situation, I did start work on your case, hoping to see the money come in. When my bosses realised I was working on your case without payment, they were *not* happy.'

'I'm so sorry,' Addi murmured, humiliation coursing through her body. This conversation reminded her of too many from her childhood, of Joelle sweet-talking her way out of the rent being late, or trying to persuade a lover to let them stay at his place a little longer, despite knowing they weren't wanted.

'You now owe the firm a few thousand in fees. And we can't go any further until we receive payment for that work *and* the retainer,' Thandi told her.

'But…but…' Addi felt her stomach clench, wondering how much damage her lawyer's lack of action and response had caused her. She lifted her hand to her mouth and closed her eyes, trying to push down the rising tide of blood-red anger. The main reason she'd married Jude was to fund the cost of the lawyers so that she could keep custody of the girls.

'You have a hearing tomorrow, and you need representation at that hearing. If you don't, you will put your chances for custody in severe jeopardy,' Thandi told her. 'If we do not get the payment in our account, by the close of the day, I cannot represent you.'

It could take time for money to appear in an account so, even if Jude did do a transfer, they might not see it. She racked her brain, feeling like she couldn't breathe.

'To be clear, if I manage to pay you today, someone will be able to represent me tomorrow?' Addi demanded, feeling hot and cold, then *very* cold at the thought of Thandi saying no.

She nodded and Addi's stomach released one of its many knots. She was supposed to fly out to Namibia tomorrow to view three hotels owned by Thorpe Industries. 'Do I need to be at the hearing?'

Thandi shook her head. 'No, actually, it's better if you stayed away. The lawyers will meet with the judge, and we'll be arguing case law and procedure, so you don't need to be there.'

Okay. Addi flicked her thumb nail against her front tooth and tried to figure out a solution. She needed hard cash and the banks would be closing soon. There was only one other option.

'Do you take credit cards?' she asked.

Thandi nodded. 'Sure. We can go through to the finance officer and I'll swipe your card.'

Ha ha, funny.

She didn't have enough credit on any of her cards, or all of them together, to pay the retainer. And, since Jude's promised maintenance hadn't come through—she'd presumed he'd pay her at the end of the month—she had very little in her current account.

He'd promised to pay the lawyers! How could he let her down like this? She'd been so caught up in him, in the sex and being spoiled, that she'd forgotten to follow up on his promises. How stupid was she? People had always let her down and disappointed her but, because she'd been entranced by Jude's kisses, loved being loved by him, she hadn't checked and double-checked as she usually would.

And that it was Jude who'd disappointed her thoroughly was a shock she'd never expected. Somehow she'd thought that he wouldn't, or couldn't. Yet he had, and she was both angry at him and incandescently angry at herself for assuming he would be different. Angry that she felt enough for him to let this get to her on such a visceral level.

Stupid! Stupid! Stupid!

She forced herself to look at Thandi and caught the sympathy in her eyes. She wanted to help, but Addi understood that her hands were tied.

'What time do you close?' she asked.

Thandi looked at her watch. 'Two hours, but our financial lady leaves in an hour.'

She had an hour to get this sorted. An hour to save the girls from going back to Joelle. She was going to kill Jude for this. Hauling in a deep breath, she forced her mouth into something she hoped was a smile. 'Can you give me a few minutes to make some calls?'

Thandi nodded. 'Sure. I'll find you here in fifteen.' Thandi walked away and, when she reached the door, she turned back. 'Can I get you a cup of tea? Coffee?'

She was grateful for the offer, but she knew that nothing would make it down her super-tight throat. 'Thank you but I'm fine.'

Thandi nodded and walked out, closing the door behind her.

As soon as she was out of hearing, Addi yanked her mobile out of her bag and dialled Jude's number. It rang for an interminably long time before going to voice mail. Swallowing down a growl of fury, she dialled the number again, and this time it cut off immediately, suggesting that Jude had killed her call. She knew he was in an important meeting at Fisher International, but her issue was more crucial than *anything* he was dealing with.

After looking up Fisher International's number, she dialled and asked to be put through to Thabo. Jude's right-hand guy immediately picked up his phone. 'Addi, how are you? How was Zanzibar...?'

She cut him off. 'I can't talk, Thabo. I need to speak to Jude.'

'Not possible, Addi. He's in an important meeting and can't be interrupted.'

Addi ground her teeth together. 'You get in there and tell him to take my call. Right damn now.'

'Addi—'

'Thabo, *do it*! This is crucially important, okay?' Addi shouted.

She heard Thabo's assent and gripped the bridge of her nose as she waited to be connected. If Jude chose to ignore her, she didn't know what she'd do. She didn't have the time to go to Fisher International herself and get back to this office by the time they closed. If Jude didn't take her call, she might lose custody of the girls before they even started the process.

'Addi, what is the problem?' Jude's voice was sharp and irritated in her ear. 'When I ask not to be disturbed it's for a damn good reason! I have the chairman of—'

'I don't care!' Addi interrupted him, her voice rising. 'What I do care about is that I am at my lawyer's offices. There's a hearing they need to attend tomorrow morning on my behalf, but because you haven't paid them their retainer nobody will attend and I might lose custody of the girls on a technicality.'

'Jeez, slow down, I didn't get most of that.'

Addi ground her teeth together. 'Simply, you didn't pay my lawyers and the custody of the girls is at risk.'

Silence greeted her and it took a while for Jude to speak. 'But I did pay...'

His words drifted away and then she heard his low curse.

'I *meant* to pay them and it slipped my mind,' he admitted. He cursed again. 'I can't believe I did that.'

Addi felt tears gathering in her throat and she swallowed them down. Then she swallowed again.

'I'm so sorry, Ads,' Jude told her. 'Look, I'll do a transfer right now,'

She forced the words up her throat. 'A deposit might only take a day or two to appear in their account, which will be too late. I need cash or a credit card. And I need it here in an hour.'

She heard the breath Jude released. 'Okay. Wait there. I'll send Thabo with the company credit card.'

Thabo with the company credit card. *Right.* After messing up, and putting her sisters in jeopardy, Jude couldn't even make the effort to leave his office and his meeting to come here himself, to rectify his mistake. He'd told her how important his business was but, up until this point, it'd never quite sank in. Fisher International was far more important than her, than her family.

He'd married her for his business, so why was that a surprise? But somehow she'd thought that maybe, just maybe, she'd come to mean more to him—silly her.

She was racking up the stupidity points, wasn't she?

'Ads…are you there?' he asked.

'Sure,' she replied in a cold monotone. 'Thabo and the company credit card.'

'He'll leave now and will be with you in forty-five minutes.' Addi heard his instructions to Thabo and could easily imagine Jude handing over the credit card, hearing him saying something about Thabo taking his SUV and that he'd pay any speeding fines Thabo racked up.

'He's left the office, Addi,' Jude told her.

'Okay.'

She heard his sigh. 'Look, I am sorry. I messed up.'

'Yes, you did,' Addi told him before disconnecting the call.

Yep, he'd screwed up.

Badly.

Jude sat in his car outside Addi's house and lowered his window so that he could push the button on her free-standing intercom system. He was going to have to do some serious grovelling and issue a raft of apologies.

His actions could've caused her lasting harm and he owned that. He wasn't used to thinking of other people and, when he did, he did it on his time scale, not theirs. He'd told her he was going to pay the lawyers and he should've done it immediately. By not doing so, it had slipped his mind. Addi had the right to be angry. In fact, if she was anything less than boil-his-head furious, he'd be surprised. All he could do was apologise and do better...

Be less selfish and more thoughtful.

This was one of the problems with being relentlessly single. He'd forgotten how to be part of a team, to consider other people, that his wasn't the only schedule that mattered and that other people's priorities were different. He'd become intensely self-absorbed, and he didn't like it. When he was like this, he reminded himself too much of his grandfather: someone who lived in his own world, whose thoughts, desires and wants were all that mattered.

It wasn't good enough.

'It's not a good time, Jude.'

At the tinny sound of Addi's voice, Jude jolted in his

seat and looked through the slats of the gate to the house beyond. There were lights on in the bottom rooms, but the upstairs rooms were dark. He glanced at his watch and saw that it was past nine. He grimaced. The meeting with his investor had only finished an hour ago and, as soon as he'd ushered her out of his office, he'd jumped into his car and headed here.

'We need to talk, Addison,' he told her.

'We can talk in the morning,' Addi told him.

'I'm going to sit here until you let me in, Addi,' he told her.

She mumbled something, a curse or an oath, but the gate did slide open and he parked his car behind Addi's. There was an old hatchback in the other parking space, and he hoped that he wouldn't have to apologise in front of Addi's three sisters. He would, but he'd prefer to avoid that embarrassment if he could.

Jude left his car and walked up to the front door, the legs of his trousers brushing a pot plant that released a lovely smell of lemon. He looked for a doorbell but then the door opened and Addi stood there, dressed in yoga pants, thick socks and a thigh-length jersey, her face pale and her eyes tired.

He'd been pushing her, pushing *them*, hard lately, flying her from hotel to hotel, country to country, and expecting her to hit the ground running when they got there. Their nights had been spent in bed exploring each other's bodies, and some nights they'd only got a few hours' sleep.

Yes, he'd known that he only had a limited amount of time with her, and that when they returned to South Africa they'd have to be a lot more circumspect if they wanted to keep seeing each other—they couldn't spend every night together. But, because she was so very healthy, he tended to forget she was pregnant and needed rest. She could also do without feeling stressed. He'd failed to look after her.

Yes, she was working with him, but she was first and foremost the mother of his child, and his temporary wife. He should be making life easier for her, not harder. As he'd decided earlier, he had to do better, be better.

'Come in,' Addi told him, and he followed her into a small living room dominated by a cream couch covered in a bright-orange throw. Two old wingback chairs were crammed into the corner and an old TV sat on a credenza. Her laptop sat on the couch and he could see, even from a distance, that she'd been working on a spreadsheet, possibly the master spreadsheet he'd demanded, the one that needed constant updating as new data about Thorpe hotels came in.

She was trying to catch up on the work time she'd lost this afternoon by going to her lawyer.

'Are your sisters around?' he asked, wanting to know how circumspect he had to be.

Addi shook her head. 'No, the girls are with Storm in Durban, and Lex is snowed in with Cole at the ski lodge in the Eastern Cape,' Addi, told him, crossing her arms over her chest. Right…and he was sure his friend wasn't complaining about being snowbound with the woman he found endlessly fascinating.

He was allowing himself to be distracted. An empty house—good. Not hesitating, he walked over to her, placed his hands on either side of her face and rested his forehead against hers. 'I am so, so sorry. I messed up and I've been kicking myself all afternoon. Forgive me?'

She pulled back to put some distance between them 'Do you realise that, if I hadn't had a meeting this afternoon, nobody would've attended the hearing tomorrow and I could've lost the girls before we even started to fight for them?'

Shame ran through him, hot and sour. 'I'm sorry, Addi. So, so sorry. Look, I meant to pay them...'

Addi sat down on the edge of a closet chair. 'But you didn't because you had something better, or more important, to do,' she said in a voice that held no emotion. 'Your work is all that matters, Jude. Everything else comes way down the list.'

He couldn't argue with that; Fisher International had been his entire focus for years, so he said nothing. But, in his defence, he'd had a lot more on his plate than usual—a massive business deal, a temporary wife, a stunning lover and a baby on the way.

'The thing is you could've lost me the most important people in my life. But for the grace of God today, two little girls might've gone back to Joelle, who has the attention span of a flea. They could've been facing the childhood Lex and I did, but in a foreign country. Your selfishness and your lack of focus on anything but Fisher International nearly cost me *everything*.'

He'd far prefer it if she yelled at him, or threw things, but her cold, low, unemotional voice slashed him in two. He'd known humiliation and regret but that was due to things that had been done *to* him.

He'd done this, it was his actions that could've led to huge, terrible ramifications. In his effort to live his life solo, not to allow anyone into his personal, emotional space and to protect himself from being hurt again, he hadn't made time for other people, and didn't consider what they wanted or needed to be important. His 'I'll get to it when I want to' attitude had severely backfired. He'd hurt Addi and his actions had nearly cost her her sisters.

This time, he couldn't blame his grandfather, Marina or Jane...this was on *him*.

He rubbed the back of his neck. 'I am sorry,' he said again, not knowing what else to say.

And he was—desperately so. He'd let her down, disappointed her. He was just another in a long line of people who'd done that to her, and he hated the thought. He'd never meant to, obviously, but he could kick himself for being just another in the long line of people who'd let her down. It wasn't his finest hour. 'I let you down, failed you. I promise I won't do that again.'

She looked up at him and raised her eyebrows. 'That's a huge promise to make, Jude.'

He dropped to his haunches in front of her and lifted his hand to touch her face. 'I admit I am selfish, that I don't think of much beyond Fisher International, but that will change, Addi. Today was a huge wake-up call.'

He dragged his thumb over her cheekbone, her blue eyes meeting his. 'Will you forgive me? Please?'

Addi closed her eyes but she did push her face into his hand. When she opened her eyes again, he saw resignation in those blue depths, and extreme exhaustion.

Her words confirmed his suspicions. 'I'm too tired to argue with you, Fisher,' she told him. 'Just...don't, okay? Just don't do it again, alright?' she continued.

Let her down? No, he wouldn't. At least, he'd try his very best not to.

Jude stood up and bent down to scoop her into his arms. He sat down on the couch and held her against his chest, his arms wrapped around her. Addi rested her cheek against his chest and, after a few minutes, he heard her sigh and felt her body relax. She yawned and wiggled closer to him, and he suspected her eyes were closing.

He placed a kiss on her hair, wondering why he instantly relaxed when she did, why holding her in his arms was his form of meditation, his way of feeling zen. After what he'd put her through, he didn't deserve to feel this comfortable. At some point, he'd have to stop kidding himself that she was another fling, someone he could easily walk away from. He'd have to face that something was bubbling between them, something potent.

Just not today. He wasn't ready.

'Have you eaten, Ads?' he asked. He'd noticed that her tummy was a little rounder, her breasts a smidgen bigger, but her arms felt scrawnier, her legs thinner.

She shook her head. 'No energy.'

He'd thought as much. While he was tempted to walk her up the stairs, find her bedroom and put her to bed, he knew that she needed sustenance, and that not eating wasn't good for her or the baby. He needed to keep her awake while he made her something. And he hoped there were eggs in her fridge—his culinary repertoire only extended as far as making scrambled eggs on toast.

She'd fall asleep in a hot bath, and if he told her to watch some TV she'd probably do the same.

The only thing that would hold her energy for a decent time, just fifteen minutes, would be to get her to work. He looked at the open laptop.

'I was looking at the spreadsheet earlier and I think there's a formula error on sheet eight,' he lied.

As he expected, Addi sat up, leaned back and frowned at him. 'I don't make formula errors,' she told him firmly.

'Sure looks like you did,' Jude quietly replied. As he'd expected, she scrambled off his lap and sat on the edge of the couch, her back ramrod-straight as she pulled her laptop onto her knees. She muttered something indecipherable, and Jude took the opportunity to walk into her kitchen and inspect the contents of her fridge. There was eggs, cheese, some salsa and rye bread.

He could work with this.

Digging around, he found a pan, oil, a bowl and a whisk. Within ten minutes he managed to pile a plate high with reasonably fluffy scrambled eggs. He buttered some toast, found a fork and walked back into the lounge, to find her sitting cross-legged on the couch and cursing her laptop.

'I can't find an error,' she told him, sounding grumpy.

He shrugged, whipped the laptop away from her and handed her the plate. She took the eggs and looked up at him. 'What's this?'

'If you don't recognise scrambled eggs then I'm far worse at cooking than I thought I was,' he told her. He sat down next to her and nodded at the plate. 'Eat.'

'I'm not that hungry—'

'Addi, eat the eggs,' he told her, his voice hardening.

Addi glared at him but lifted a forkful of eggs to her mouth and chewed. Her eyebrows raised and she dug in for some more, alternating between eating the eggs and munching on the bread. Within minutes she'd polished off all the food on her plate. She leaned back and placed a hand on her stomach. 'Feeding me is becoming a habit, Fisher.'

If that was what it took… He pulled the plate out of her hands, put it on the coffee table and stood up, bending down to lift her into his arms. For a tallish woman, she weighed next to nothing.

'Have you been to see the doctor yet?' he demanded, walking her out of the room.

Her eyes met his. 'We've been in and out of the country for the past two weeks, Jude. When would I have had the time?'

'Tomorrow,' he told her. 'We're going to get you to a doctor before we leave for Namibia. Or do you need to be there for the hearing? If you do, we can push the trip back.'

'No, the lawyer doesn't want me there. Not this time,' she replied. She pushed her hair back to squint at him. 'And may I point out that, for millions of years, a woman didn't rush off to see a doctor just because of a pregnancy? They just carried on with their lives and got on with it.'

Sure, but those millions of women weren't under his care and protection—she was. And so far, he'd been doing a really bad job at looking after her. That would change—right now.

'I'm putting you to bed, you're going to get a decent night's sleep and tomorrow I'll find you a doctor,' he told her, his voice suggesting that she not argue.

Her eyes fluttered closed and he saw she was fighting sleep. 'Are you going to stay the night with me?' she asked as they started climbing the stairs.

After everything that had happened today, did she still want him to stay with her? She was so very generous. 'If you want me to, I will,' he said. 'Which bedroom is yours?'

'First on the right,' Addi told him. He kicked the door open to her room, walked her over to the bed and sat her on the edge of it. 'What do you normally sleep in?' he asked. They usually fell asleep naked but tonight wasn't about sex. Or him.

She waved a listless hand at a chair in the corner. 'T-shirt,' she told him.

He reached for a T-shirt and quickly undressed her, ignoring his erection and fighting the temptation to slide his lips over hers. Even though she was exhausted and irritable—admittedly, all his fault—he wanted her and, judging by the desire in her eyes, she wanted him too.

But want would have to take a back seat; tonight was all about what she needed. And that was sleep. He pulled back her duvet and gestured for her to slide under. When her head hit the pillow, he bent down to place his lips on her temple. 'Good night, Ads.'

'You're not going, are you?' she asked.

He shook his head. 'I'll be up later,' he told her. 'Sleep now.'

He was at the door when he heard her speak again. 'There wasn't an error in the spreadsheet, was there? You just did that to keep me awake.'

Instead of answering her, he just smiled and forced himself to walk downstairs.

CHAPTER TEN

NAMIBIA, THE LAST STOP on their tour of Thorpe establishments, was different from what they'd seen before. After the white sands and heat of the coast of east Africa, and the wild animals in Tanzania, the Skeleton Coast of northern Namibia was wild and desolate and had a beauty unlike any Addi had ever seen, or imagined, before. The area consisted of dunes, desert and the sea and, from just looking at the landscape, Addi understood why it was a place to be feared. The beaches were often shrouded with fog and scattered with the remains of countless shipwrecks and whale skeletons. It exuded a sense of danger, but Addi loved it.

It was also freezing.

A massive cold front had moved in from the Antarctic and a low, dense cloud hung out to sea while an icy wind created white horses on a sullen, gunmetal-grey sea. Addi stood on the veranda of their private room in the tiny boutique hotel and looked at the dunes rolling down to the sea.

Africa was such a land of contrasts, she thought. It could be pretty and calm, wild and dangerous, sleepy and exciting.

But Namibia had captured her soul. She'd met Himba women in the north of the country, enjoyed a game-viewing experience in a private game reserve adjacent to the amazing Etosha Game Reserve and they'd even flown into Botswana to a camp on the Chobe River.

But this place, wild and desolate, held her heart in the palm of her hands. Maybe it was because it was at the tail end of their trip, maybe because it was the last place she would be truly alone with Jude, but she felt a soul-deep connection to the Dune House. The thought of leaving it, and going back to her normal life, made her feel a little ill.

Addi felt her phone vibrate and, seeing it was from her lawyer Thandi, pounced on the message.

Hearing done. It went well. No problems, and nothing for you to worry about. Our case is strong. Just waiting for a date for the final hearing in front of the judge.

She heard the sliding door open behind her and turned to look at Jude, who carried two mugs in his big hands. His would be filled with two shots of espresso, hers would be ginger tea, something she'd taken to drinking to ward off the occasional bouts of nausea she experienced throughout the day.

She waved her phone. 'The custody hearing went well. Thandi's waiting for a date for the final hearing,' she told him.

His smile flashed. 'That's really good news, Ads.' He handed her a cup and Addi wrapped her hands around it, enjoying the warmth. She watched the wind lift his hair and when he sucked in a breath she smiled. 'It's freezing, isn't it?'

'It's snowing in numerous places in South Africa. Including at the ski resort where Lex and Cole are holed up,' Jude replied.

Addi nodded. 'I've been getting updates. The girls are furious they aren't anywhere near the snow.' Storm, their middle sister, had scooped up the girls and taken them on holiday to the much warmer east coast of South Africa. 'Storm thought about driving them to where the snow is, but the roads are closed and it's too dangerous.'

She was glad that Lex was having a break from the girls, and she hoped that she was enjoying a rip-roaring affair with Cole Thorpe, their joint boss. She'd sensed the attraction sizzling between them whenever they were together, and Lex deserved some fun.

Thank God for Storm scooping up the younger girls…

'And why are we out here when there's a toasty fire inside?' Jude asked.

Addi gestured to the view. 'Because it's beautiful,' she replied.

This was the last of Cole Thorpe's hotels and they'd be leaving tomorrow. Jude had all the information he needed to decide which properties he wanted and her involvement was no longer necessary.

When they returned to South Africa, they would be forced to act like colleagues, because no one could suspect that they'd been carrying on a rip-roaring, hot-as-Hades affair. They would have to act, look and be professional and she would be going home to her house, he to his.

Where did they go from here? The question was at the front of her mind, and had been since they'd left Cape Town ten days ago, the day after their fight and just a few hours after she'd had her first doctor's visit. The intense feeling that they were on borrowed time was something she couldn't rid herself of.

It was hard to accept that she was in too deep, but the reality was that she'd allowed her feelings to run away from her. If she wasn't already in love with Jude, then she was damn close, and she knew she needed to shore up her defences. She couldn't stop herself from sleeping with him—

she was a woman, not a saint—but she needed to protect her heart.

But how? And was it too late?

And why did she feel as if she was on a countdown, as if there was a timer somewhere ready to detonate a bomb in their lives? It had to be because she was worried about the girls and the custody case; it had nothing to do with Jude and their 'out of Africa', oh-so-temporary fling.

She didn't think.

'What do you think of this place?' Jude asked, putting his back to the view. 'It's really small.'

The boutique hotel only had five rooms, was incredibly isolated and required a helicopter flight to reach the hotel. But the building was stunning: a modern, steel-and-wood, open-plan lower floor with glass walls on three sides enabling the guests to have a one-eighty-degree view of the dunes and endless sea. It reminded her of Jude's house in Franschhoek.

The five double rooms were massive and each had private balconies and hot tubs, fireplaces and enormous beds. Of all the places they'd visited, this was the most stunning.

'Are you asking me to answer professionally or personally?'

'Both. Professionally, first.'

'Well, like the ski lodge Cole and Lex are stuck at, I think this was another passion project by Cole's father. It's booked solid in spring and summer but the place empties in autumn and winter. It's covering its costs, just, but you are never going to make money from it.'

Jude's eyes slammed into hers. 'And personally?'

'It's…' She hesitated, unsure about how to explain. She didn't have the words to tell him that, from the moment she'd left the helicopter and looked through the dunes to the sea, she'd felt captivated. That she could walk the desolate beach for hours at a time and feel rejuvenated, that it was an almost spiritual experience to be here.

She chewed on her bottom lip. 'I think this is the place where my soul feels most at home,' she quietly admitted.

He didn't respond to her comment, and after twenty seconds she risked looking at him to see his eyes on her face. 'That sounds, weird, right?' she lifted her shoulders to her ears. 'I don't know how else to explain it but, every time I look out to sea, when I walk that wooden slatted path to the beach, I feel like I am home.'

Jude lowered his eyebrows and nodded. 'It's a pretty special place but I did not expect you to feel so strongly about it.'

She didn't understand it either. She loved her home, but it was noisy and chaotic, filled with girls fighting, laughing or yelling. This place was pure serenity.

She shook her head and lifted her mug to her lips again. She was being silly, that was all. This wasn't where she belonged; she'd never return to this place again.

Real life wasn't isolated houses on a desolate beach, days and nights spent with the sexiest, smartest man she'd ever known. It wasn't flitting about in private planes and having five-star experiences at some of the best places on the continent. It wasn't making love outdoors on blankets in front of fires while the cold wind roared outside, or in hot tubs while elephants strolled past a private chalet. It wasn't running into the warm Indian ocean late at night or early in the morning, swimming with wild dolphins or sleeping in treehouses.

Real life was in Cape Town, behind her desk at Thorpe Industries—or at another corporation, maybe Fisher International. It was growing and birthing this baby. It was telling

Lex and the girls that she was going to be a mother—God, she hated keeping secrets from them—and figuring out how to let Jude be a part of their baby's life.

'Are you okay?' Jude asked, placing his hand on her arm. 'You look a little pale.'

'Just cold,' Addi told him. 'There's a fire inside, why are we standing out here?'

'I said that ten minutes ago,' Jude pointed out as he followed her inside. Addi walked up to the freestanding fireplace and held her freezing hands out to the flames. She sighed when Jude wrapped his arms around her waist and rested his chin on her hair.

'Are you sure you're okay, Ads?'

No.

But she nodded, glad he couldn't see the tears welling in her eyes. Yes, of course she was. She had no choice *but* to be okay. She was responsible for herself and for three other people—and a half—and nobody was going to ride to her rescue and patch her up, prop her up.

No, she was used to being alone, doing alone. And when they returned to Cape Town tomorrow that was exactly what she'd do.

This was it; they were home.

Their out-and-about-in-Africa fling was over.

Jude's jet rolled to a stop and Addi pulled her seat belt apart, grimacing at the wet and windy weather outside the plane's small, oval window. She wished she was back in Zanzibar or Turtle Bay, swimming in the lukewarm sea and wearing flip-flops. She far preferred summer to winter, though to be honest making love in front of a fire yesterday, while the wind had wailed and roared around Dune House, hadn't been a problem.

Jude leaned forward, looked past her and grimaced. 'They say that this has been the wettest and coldest winter in decades.'

Yep, let's talk about the weather, because that's what's important, Addi thought.

'At least there isn't as much snow with this system,' Addi replied, pulling her bag off the seat in front of her. Her floppy felt hat lay on top of it and she pulled it on, as well as a voluminous scarf. The weather was easy to discuss, and far less explosive than asking what their relationship would look like going forward from this point on. A bunch of other questions hovered on her tongue.

When would she see him again, make love to him again? Was this *it*? They'd inspected all the properties; they'd had their affair. Now that they were back in Cape Town, they were going to have to be a lot more circumspect, act as if they barely knew each other, that they were no more than work colleagues. And that was going to be hard. She was so used to taking his hand, snuggling into his side when he put his arm around her, sharing her bed and her body.

She didn't know how to act, or what to say.

'All you need is big sunglasses and you'll look like an A-list celebrity who's trying to look like she doesn't want the attention but secretly does,' Jude commented.

Addi poked her tongue out at him, then wrinkled her nose, thinking she was no more mature than Nixi or Snow.

'What are your plans today?' Jude asked, standing up as the engines faded away. He lifted his arms to stretch, his cashmere jersey pulling flat against his wide chest.

'Well, I want to spend some time with Lex, to reconnect with her. I have to tell her about the baby, obviously, and about Joelle seeking custody of the girls.' His mouth opened and she knew he was going to remind her not to say anything about their marriage. *Really? Again? 'Don't*, Jude.'

He nodded, looking resigned. 'Are you happy about her and Cole?'

'How can I not be?' she asked him. Lex being Cole's chauffeur and then being snowbound in a ski lodge he owned had led them to fall in love. She'd been the first person Lex had called when Cole had proposed, and they'd spent hours on video call catching up. That Cole loved Lex was indisputable and Addi was so happy for, and maybe a little jealous of, her younger sister. Lex was incandescently happy. And that was all that mattered.

'She wants to show me the new house Cole has bought. She's also asking if I'm interested in moving into their guest house.'

Cole had bought Lex a massive property that would house all the sisters in individual houses, allowing Nixi and Snow to run from the main house where they'd live to her cottage and the above-garage apartment they'd allocated to Storm.

Jude's gaze pinned her feet to the floor of the plane. 'Are you? Interested, that is?'

She shrugged. 'I haven't even seen the place, Jude! And I love my house, it's home. And I'm not sure I want to live on my soon-to-be brother-in-law's property. I'm far too independent for that.

'Lex and I have so much to talk about! She's going to rip my head off for keeping so many secrets,' Addi continued.

Jude pushed his hands into the pockets of his grey trousers. 'Lex marrying Cole will be a big boost to your custody suit. His name is as big as mine. If it gets that far, I don't know if you are going to need to name me in the papers.'

Addi knew he was worried his name would be leaked if they got before the judge. Her lawyers had agreed to keep quiet the fact that they were married, and that Jude would only be brought into the conversation if all other means to obtain custody of the girls fell through. His involvement was a last resort, a nuclear option. But, now that Cole was marrying Lex, Jude's influence might not be needed, especially as the girls would be moving into his house with Lex.

Addi understood that Jude didn't want his business to be front-page news again. But a part of her—the silly, tender, romantic smidgeon of her soul—wanted him to say that he'd walk through fire for her, endure months of being fodder for gossip for her. She was falling in love with him—*was* in love with him—and a part of her wanted him to make the grand gesture, to defend her, to move mountains for her. Not to care what the world thought…

You're forgetting that this is a business arrangement, Addi, that there is nothing between you but a baby and great sex. Your fling is over.

'After I tell her about the custody battle, I'll need Lex to come with me to meet Thandi so she can get up to speed on the case,' Addi told him. 'I imagine that, as soon as Cole hears about Joelle's latest scheme, he'll offer to pay for the lawyer's costs.'

'I'm paying for it, that was part of *our* deal,' Jude snapped.

She wasn't prepared to argue with him, not right now. 'Lex will be furious with Joelle, but she'll probably be a lot less worried about winning custody than I am. Lex is far more optimistic than I am.'

'I think the chances of a judge siding with your neglectful mother against three sisters who are raising two happy and healthy little girls is minimal. I don't think there's much to worry about,' Jude told her.

But it was her job to worry, her job to ensure that their

family was safe and protected. 'I'll relax when I see the court order, when Lex and I are named their guardians.'

'You have to have a little faith, Addi.'

He was saying *that* to her? This was the person who'd reminded her, twice yesterday and three times today, that they couldn't be linked together, that she couldn't say anything about them being married, variations on the 'this can't hit the papers' spiel. If he mentioned the words 'press' and 'secret' one more time, she might brain him.

He had no concept of faith or trust. He'd made up his mind that no one could be trusted and that included her. And that made her eyes well up and her heart sink to the floor because, without trust, there couldn't be love.

And, because she was intensely stupid when it came to matters of the heart, she'd fallen in love with him.

Stupid, stupid girl.

Addi turned away and scrabbled in her bag, using it as an excuse not to look at Jude. If he saw her eyes, he'd see the longing, the love, her hopes and dreams about their future on her face and blazing in her eyes. A house of their own, two little girls running in and out, a baby to raise and a man in whose arms she could rest at night, whose face she wanted to kiss for the rest of her life... A friend to talk to, a steady partner willing to share the responsibilities life continuously shoved her way, someone steady and reliable.

And hot.

There was something to be said for sharing her life with someone who could make her insides quiver, her knees melt and her breath hitch.

Except that she wouldn't.

There was no chance of living her life with him, raising a baby and sharing the ups and down. They would stay secretly married for another year and a bit, then they'd quietly divorce, hopefully without anyone being any the wiser. Their baby would be raised in separate houses and they'd share custody. Their sole link would be through their child…

She was weaving dreams from fairy dust, and that wasn't like her. She didn't dream or hope, she faced life as it was; living with Joelle had taught her to do that. She had to look at life the way it was, not how she wanted it to be.

Jude would never love her. She had to accept and deal with that. And soon.

'I wonder what's causing the delay,' Jude said. Addi turned to look at him and saw his frown. He bent down to push the intercom to talk to his pilot. 'Siya, what's the problem?'

'Sorry, boss, there's been a breach in security, someone tried to sneak through onto the taxiway. He's been arrested but they aren't allowing private cars up to the planes.'

Jude pulled a face. 'Does that mean we have to go through arrivals?'

'Yes, sorry, sir. An Airports Company representative will be with us shortly and he'll escort you to the terminal.'

'I know where to go, Siya,' Jude told him.

'Airport rules, sir. Joe is going to open up and drop the stairs. He'll follow with your luggage.'

'Okay, thanks, Siya.' Jude reached for his black leather jacket and pulled it on. When he looked at Addi, his expression was impenetrable. 'Okay, so we're going to have to walk through the terminal. Remember, we are—'

'Work colleagues, people who barely know each other. We can't give anyone the impression that we are married or lovers or even friends!' Addi snapped. 'I have a degree in business management, Jude, you don't need to keep reminding me or treating me like an idiot.'

'I'm not, I'm just reminding you…'

Addi saw the cockpit door open and held up her hand, cutting off Jude's words. It took all her energy to smile at Joe. 'Thanks for ferrying us around safely these past few weeks, Joe. Will you thank Siya for me too?'

'Certainly,' Joe replied, before turning his attention to the door. He opened it and cold air drifted into the plane as Addi pulled her bag over her shoulder and picked up her laptop case.

Jude gestured for her to precede him, and she realised that the temperature between them had plummeted. And not only because of the cold front currently battering the city.

Okay, maybe he'd been a bit heavy-handed earlier. He hadn't needed to keep reminding Addi about their agreement, that their arrangement couldn't become public knowledge.

Maybe he was just reminding her to remind himself, to convince himself that there was nothing between them but great sex and a baby on the way.

He wasn't making any progress on that front.

The thing was…he liked her. He *like* liked her.

Jude jammed his hands into the pockets of his jacket and rolled his eyes, irritated with his juvenile assessment of the situation. How old was he—fifteen?

He loved making love to Addi, it had quickly become his favourite thing to do. But he also enjoyed her sharp mind, and understood her sometimes prickly attitude—she was her family's protector and life had taught her to fight. And he enjoyed seeing the softer side to her, the Addi behind the shields. That woman was lovely and warm, funny and fantastic, and he didn't know how he was going to live his life without her constant presence.

Jude felt the cold wind slide down his back as they hurried across the apron, and he yanked his hand from his pocket to rest it on Addi's back but pulled back at the last minute. He couldn't touch her; he couldn't act or be solicitous. At the remote locations they'd recently visited, privacy and isolation had been high on the list of the hotels' offerings, so he hadn't been worried about their connection being revealed.

But here in Cape Town, where everyone had a mobile phone and could snap a photo, they had to be extremely careful.

Understanding that, how were they going to carry on seeing each other? They had maybe another two weeks of using the guise of working together to hide behind but, after that, once he put in an offer to buy Cole's properties, that excuse would disappear, along with her job. Once she moved across to Fisher International, it would be even harder. Along with coffee, gossip was the lifeblood of his company.

And gossiping about him was his employees' favourite sport. Jude made a mental note to contact his Human Resources director about Addi's appointment, something he had yet to take care of.

He shook his head at his lack of efficiency, shocked that, like paying the lawyers, it had slipped his mind. He rarely forgot to complete items on his to-do list, and the few things he did forget were ridiculously unimportant. Nothing had dropped through the cracks before Addi had entered his life—he hadn't even *had* cracks. But, since she'd fallen into his life the second time, he'd felt consistently off-balance and discombobulated. She turned him inside out and upside down in a way he'd never experienced before.

His mind was a mess, he thought, as he gestured for Addi to precede him into the airport terminal. They followed an

airport staff member to a passport control desk with no
queue, and an officer who stamped their passports, barely
taking the time to check their photos against their faces.
Normally, the customs official would come to the plane but,
judging by the fact that every security officer he could see
looked to be on high alert, their heads swivelling back and
forth, the security breach had been bigger than expected.

The customs official touched his hat and gave Jude a
sympathetic smile.

What was that for?

Jude started to weave his way between the other passen-
gers, making sure Addi stayed by his side. They bypassed
the conveyor belts spitting out luggage and headed toward
International Arrivals. It was then that Jude realised that
he'd lost his escort. Shrugging it off, because he knew the
way, he kept walking, wondering why the hair on the back
of his head was lifting.

What was he missing here?

The automatic doors opened and as they stepped over the
threshold into the terminal what seemed a million cameras
exploded simultaneously. Out of the corner of his eye, he
saw Addi raise her hand, and he moved to stand closer to
her, his body half-shielding her from the crowd gathered
behind the cordon.

'Why did you get married, Jude?'

'Why her?'

'Who is she?'

*'Any thoughts on what your grandfather would think
about who you married?'*

'Would he approve this time?'

How? What? How had they found out?

Knowing that he had to keep his head, Jude sent the

crowd a blistering glare and placed his hand low on Addi's back, edging her towards the exit. In six feet, maybe a little more, they would be surrounded, and he'd have to push his way through the crowd, somehow keeping his grip on Addi.

How had this happened? How had they found out? And how was he going to get them out of here? At that moment, Jude felt as he had ten years ago, intensely betrayed and awash with humiliation. He didn't feel like the man who owned and operated a highly successful company, didn't see himself as the powerful hotel whizz-kid everyone regarded him to be. No, he was ten years younger again, withering as his grandfather had ridiculed his actions.

He could hear Bart's voice mocking him, his voice more derisive than ever before.

You thought you had it together, didn't you? Not so smart, are you? Another scandal, another embarrassment. Yet another misjudgement. Are you ever going to learn, son?

Knowing he couldn't keep looking like a deer caught in the headlights—not a look he wanted to be splashed across papers and on news websites—he gripped Addi's hand tightly and steered her left. He could beat himself up later for failing to anticipate this, for making the mistake of trusting Addi. Right now, they had no choice. They had to go forward.

And suddenly, without fuss, six men dressed in black suits, and looking as though they shouldn't be messed with, stepped in front of the journalists and flanked them, creating a barrier between them and the screeching journalists.

Grateful for their presence, Jude caught the eye of the guy to his left as they forged a path to the airport. 'Who sent you?' he asked. He had his suspicions, but he wanted to have them confirmed.

'Cole Thorpe.'

As he thought. Thado was overseas and Cole was the only person who knew what time they were landing and had been around when the stories about him being conned by Marina had made headlines. He needed to send him a case of his shockingly expensive favourite whiskey for sending in the cavalry.

'Am I right in presuming that this story broke within the last couple of hours?'

The bodyguard nodded. 'There's a car in the pick-up zone, waiting to take you wherever you want to go.'

A reporter managed to jump between one of the body-guards to take an up-close photograph of Addi, with her wide eyes and panicked face. He was tossed back into the crowd by one of their bodyguards and Addi looked at him, her face pale with apprehension. 'What's happening, Jude?'

'We've been ambushed by the press, Addison,' he quietly replied in his coldest voice. 'That's what happens when you can't keep a secret. Did you do it as pay-back because I forgot to pay the lawyers?'

She braked and, oblivious to the interest from everyone around them, placed a hand on his arm to halt his fast progress across the terminal. '*What?* Do you think *I* did this? That I broke my promise to you?'

'Well, *I* didn't,' Jude snapped back.

'Not now,' the senior bodyguard snapped, and Jude cursed himself for losing his cool and control. He placed his hand on her back and propelled her forward. He turned to look at her face, grimacing when despair shot across her face and anguish settled in her eyes. They could discuss the hows and whys later; right now they had to get out of there.

They hit the outside doors and Jude let out a sigh of relief when he saw the two black SUVs parked in the pick-up zone. *Excellent.* He ducked into the SUV first, climbing across the bench seat to make space for Addi, and when she failed to climb in after him he whipped around to see her veering left and sliding into the second SUV.

And, since the press corps had followed them out of the terminal onto the pick-up zone, his only choice was to let Cole's private security drive them away in separate cars.

CHAPTER ELEVEN

ADDI BEGGED THE bodyguards to drop her at her cottage and, when they told her they had orders to take her to Jude's Franschhoek residence, she pitched a fit. She didn't want to go there with him, and if they took her anywhere against her will it would be kidnapping.

After some quiet, undiscernible conversations, Addi noticed the change of direction of the car and within forty minutes she was in her house, pacing the space next to her kitchen table. It was mid-morning, the girls were at school and she assumed Lex was with Cole. She had the house to herself, and she desperately needed the quiet and the space.

She needed time to think, to plan, to pick her shattered heart off the floor and reinsert it into her chest. She knew Jude had trust issues, and understood why he couldn't open up and trust anybody, but his first instinct when he'd seen the press had been to blame her for the news about their secret marriage getting out.

He hadn't been prepared to consider other options, nor consider alternatives to how the news of their marriage could've been leaked. His first instinct had been to assume she was to blame.

But what hurt even more, what had her wanting to curl up in a ball and howl, was that he considered her to be as vengeful and vicious as Marina and Jane, that she was vindicative enough to seek pay-back for a mistake he'd made and apologised for. That he didn't rate her higher than the two women who'd betrayed him cut her to every bone.

Standing in her kitchen, Addi finally accepted that he would never trust her, and without trust he could never love her. Not the way she needed him to.

They'd spent so much time together, weeks of laughing, loving and confiding, but their supposed closeness meant nothing to him, it didn't make a jot of difference. She'd been hurt before, by Joelle and Dean, but nothing hurt as much as Jude's instinctive, absolute distrust.

Addi pulled out a chair from under the dining table and dropped into it, resting her throbbing head in her hands. What were they going to do now? How was she going to handle this?

And, she thought, picking up her head, where was her luggage? A bodyguard had taken her laptop and handbag from her when they'd surrounded her at the airport and he'd slid into the same vehicle as Jude, assuming that was where she'd go. As a result, she didn't have her phone or her laptop and had no means of communication. Thank goodness they had a code system on the front door and their gate, as well as being able to open it with a remote, or else she wouldn't have been able to get into the house.

Addi stood up and walked around the table to switch on the kettle. She needed a cup of tea and to think, and it would help if she could stop crying. Yes, a little part of that was shock. Being half-blinded by camera flashes and deafened by shouted questions had not been a fun experience. And that guy popping up in front of her had scared her, so she had a right to feel shaky. She would be fine after a cup of tea and a few deep breaths.

Getting over the fact that Jude didn't trust her, not even

a little bit, that he thought her treacherous, would take a lot longer.

Addi poured water over a teabag and frowned when she heard her front door open and close. She hastily rubbed her fingers over her eyes, picking up tears and wiping them on her dark-green skinny jeans. Lex was back and, while she was looking forward to reconnecting with her sister, she'd wanted a little more time to compose herself before they spoke. Lex would've seen the papers and would have questions about her marriage. She also needed to tell her about the baby and the custody battle, and she wanted to be calm and in control when she did so.

Addi waited to hear her footsteps coming into the kitchen, for her to call out, but when neither happened she frowned and, picking up her cup, walked into the hallway…to see Jude standing there, her suitcase at his feet. He held her laptop bag and tote bag in a tight grip.

She most certainly wasn't ready to deal with Jude Fisher. 'What are you doing here and how did you get in?' she demanded.

He kicked her suitcase with the side of his foot. 'Delivering your stuff. If you'd got into the same car as me, I wouldn't have had to follow you here,' he shot back, looking angrier than she'd ever seen him.

'I *never* asked you to do that. And you didn't answer my question about how you got into my house.'

'I called Lex. She gave me the code. She also bombarded me with questions about our marriage and what we thought we were doing.'

'Well, I wasn't the one who asked for secrecy, was I?' Addi retorted.

Jude grimaced as he placed her laptop bag on top of her suitcase and hung her tote bag up on a hook behind her door. Addi heard the strident ring of her phone coming from the handbag.

'That's probably her now,' Jude told her, removing his leather jacket.

'What did you tell her?' Addi demanded. She'd lose it if he'd told her about the baby. He knew how important it was for her to tell Lex that news herself.

Jude gave her a sour look. 'Nothing. I told her you would answer all her questions.' Jude placed his hands on his hips and looked around. 'Are we going to fight in your hallway?'

Addi narrowed her eyes. 'We might as well,' she told him.

'Why are you so mad at *me*?' Jude demanded. 'And why did you get into another car?'

Seriously? Had he really asked her that? 'You accused me of leaking the story!' she yelled. 'You said that I revealed our secret!'

'Well, I didn't, so how else did they get to hear about it?' Jude yelled back. He shrugged and spread out his hands. 'Look, I know how close you and Lex are, I know that you don't keep secrets from each other, so I understand why you told her. She probably let it slip that we were married to someone—'

'I didn't tell anyone!' Addi screamed, hoping that a little volume would get her message across. 'And don't you think that Lex asking you all those questions about our getting married is a clue that she *didn't* know?'

He frowned, started to speak and shook his head, his frown deepening. She saw a bank-load of pennies drop and Jude ran his hands over his face. 'Right, well… I didn't think that through. Sorry.'

Addi threw up her hands, frustrated beyond belief. One sorry—was that it? Oh, he had to be joking. She slapped her hands on her hips. '*No!* No, you don't get to come in here after slinging such a nasty accusation and, on realising you were wrong, fob me off with a simple "sorry". I'm *not* accepting that.

'And, even if I could get past that—and I can't—how dare you accuse me of leaking the news of our marriage as pay-back for a mistake you made and apologised for? I am not that vindicative or nasty!'

He shoved an agitated hand through his hair. 'I didn't mean—'

'Don't tell me that it was the heat of the moment, that you weren't thinking—and don't you *dare* tell me you didn't mean it. The thing is, Jude, when the chips are down, when a stressful situation happens, people *do* say what they mean—they tend to tell the truth because they don't have time to parse their words through a filter. You meant every word you said at that moment, because you believe instinctively that I would screw you over. That I am just another woman out to hurt you.'

He didn't reply and she was glad: she would've lost respect for him if he'd tried to talk his way out of what they both knew was the truth. He just looked at her, misery and a touch of defiance in his eyes.

'Despite spending these past few weeks with me, despite our conversations and our confessions, you don't trust me any more than when I first walked into your house and told you about the baby.'

He folded his arms across his chest and rocked from foot to foot. 'I've been trying, Addi.'

'But you can't get there.' Cold sadness rolled over her and it took everything she had not to drop to her knees and rest her forehead on the floor. There was no hope for them as a couple, not even a smidgeon.

She loved him, and he felt something for her, but it wasn't

enough to overcome her fear that he'd keep disappointing her in big ways and small. Jude had let her down twice now, and she did not doubt that, unless he fundamentally changed his thinking, he'd do it again.

Love couldn't flourish where there was doubt. The two were mutually exclusive.

Jude rubbed his hand up and down his jaw. 'We've only known each other a short time, Addi. I'm not used to you, not used to this. I've been on my own for a long time and I'll do better.'

I'll do better.

How many times had she heard that from Joelle, and how many times had she disappointed her? Dean had said something similar after their fights about how he couldn't connect with the girls. Neither of them had *done better*.

After not paying her lawyers, Jude had promised not to let her down again, yet here he was. Was she really going to allow the people she loved to keep disappointing her, to allow history to repeat itself?

Didn't she deserve more? Hadn't she promised herself that she would never put herself in this position again?

'The man who wanted to marry me tried to love me enough, but he couldn't get there. I grew up with a woman who promised me more than she could deliver, and who never gave me what I needed and wanted. I kept waiting, kept hoping, and every time she made me a promise and didn't deliver I lost a piece of my soul. I won't do that again.'

Every time Joelle let her down, she lost another chunk of respect and liking for her mother.

She didn't want that to happen with Jude. He was going to be in her life for a long time, they were going to have a child together. She had to stop wanting, stop dreaming, and she definitely had to stop expecting him to be better.

It was the only way she could see them having any type of relationship going forward.

She sucked in some air and forced down her tears. She could, and most definitely would, cry later.

'We were going to re-evaluate our relationship anyway, so let's just call us done, Jude,' she told him, forcing the words over her suddenly thick tongue. 'Let's just live our separate lives, you in your house, me in mine. After the baby is born, we can get a divorce. All I need you to do is pay for the lawyer's fees, as per our initial arrangement.'

'But—what about us?' Jude asked.

'There is no *us*, Jude! There can't be an *us* because you can't give me what I need.'

'And what is that, Addi, exactly?' Jude asked, his voice low and growly with suppressed emotion. Anger or despair? She couldn't tell. 'Spell it out for me.'

'I need you to love me! I need you to be part of my life, and our baby's life, on a daily basis. I want to grow old with you and love you every minute between now and then. Because—and I hate this—I love you, Jude.'

He started to reach for her, but Addi knew that, if he touched her, her resolve would melt like sugar strands on a hot stove plate.

'But me loving you isn't enough for me. I did that with my mother, and it nearly killed me.'

'I *could* love you, Addi.'

She looked into his confused eyes and shook her head. 'I don't think you can, Jude, because you can't trust me. And because you can't put me first, ahead of Fisher International. I refuse to be the little girl I was, trailing behind the shooting star, praying that now and again you'll look back and remember that I'm there. I've done that, it's not fun. I'd rather live without you—and I *can* live without you—than be anything less than your everything.'

'You're asking for a lot, Addi,' Jude said, his eyes narrowing.

She lifted one shoulder in a desperate shrug. She wished he would leave. She desperately wanted to cry, but she wouldn't, not when he was there. 'Maybe. Maybe I should be grateful to get whatever you decide to give, but I'm not that type of girl. Like my sisters, I deserve a guy who will make me his entire world. And, if you can't be that man, then I would rather be alone.'

Jude dropped his head to look at the floor and Addi brushed past him to pull open her front door. 'Please go, Jude. If you love me a little, if you just harbour a little affection for me, go. Go before I stop being brave.'

Jude turned round, walked towards the door and stopped next to her. He leaned down and Addi tensed, hoping he wouldn't kiss her. He hesitated but pulled back. 'I'm so sorry I can't give you what you need, Addi. The level of trust you require is impossible for me.'

'I know,' Addi whispered.

As she watched him walk to his car, tears rolled down her face and dripped off her chin. Yep, watching someone she loved walk away wasn't getting any easier.

Lex sat cross-legged on the couch next to Addi, horror and sympathy in her eyes. She held a large glass of wine in her hands and Addi was tempted to wrench it out of her grasp and knock it back. She needed the soothing properties of the fermented grape.

'How far along are you?' Lex asked.

'Eleven, twelve weeks?' Addi replied, wrinkling her nose. It was difficult to think. Her head felt like it was stuffed with cotton wool and her heart was anvil-heavy in her rib-cage. On the big screen in her mind, she kept watching Jude walk away, devastation in his eyes.

Had she been too tough on him? Had she acted too hastily? Had she not given him enough time to learn to trust her—had she expected too much?

She missed him. She missed him so much that even her hair was hurting...

'When are you going to have your first scan?' Lex asked.

'I don't know,' she admitted. She waved a listless hand. 'Some time.'

'Ads, you are the most together person I know, and the fact that you don't know, to the hour, how far along you are or when your next appointment is concerns me. I'd expected you to have made six lists, booked Lamaze classes and started investigating schools.'

She'd get back to being her organised self soon. Right now, she was just trying to keep her heart and soul together, and she didn't have the energy to be a control freak. 'I'm sorry I fell pregnant, Lex. I'm sorry I messed up.'

Lex pulled back to look at her, her lovely face shocked. 'Why are you apologising to me?'

'We made an oath. We said that we wouldn't follow in Joelle's footsteps.'

'Oh, Ads, you are so hard on yourself.' Lex put her wine glass on the coffee table and lifted her hand to stroke her hair. 'I know that you were on the pill and that Jude probably used a condom. This little munchkin—' Lex pushed the tip of her finger into Addi's stomach —'obviously wanted to be here. She fought past two contraceptives to be here. God, she's a warrior.'

'She could be a boy,' Addi murmured.

Lex grinned. 'No, she's a girl. We only make girls, Ads.'

She rubbed her hand over Addi's belly. 'I'm so excited to meet the newest member of our clan, Ads. You are going to be such a great mum.'

Addi shook her head. 'I'm not so good with Nixi and Snow, not as good as you.'

Lex shook her head. 'Addi, you were working, trying to make money to keep us fed and clothed and safe. You were exhausted. You don't have to be *everything* to everybody.'

Jude had said the same. And maybe it was time to give herself a break, to accept that she'd done the best she could with the resources she had, mental, physical and financial, and move on. Everyone was fine...

Well, she wasn't, but her sisters were.

'I'm still mad you didn't tell me about the baby and the legal battle earlier, Addison.'

Addi winced. 'I was trying to spare you the stress.'

'Ads, I'm not a little girl any more and you don't need to protect me,' Lex told her. 'I'm your sister, an adult, and I deserve to be treated as one.'

Addi scrunched up her face, knowing she was right. It wasn't her job to protect Lex any more, to look after her. She was perfectly capable of looking after herself and it was time she backed down and away. 'I know. And I'm sorry.'

Luckily, Lex didn't hold grudges. 'Cole told me that it was the priest who leaked the news of your marriage to the press, by the way. He sold the story, but only after Jude's fat donation hit his bank account.'

Addi's mouth fell open. Well, that was one mystery solved. 'The greedy pig!'

Lex nodded her agreement. 'So, we have a custody hearing the day after tomorrow, and Joelle will be there. Cole and Storm will join us and, if we show a united front, Thandi doesn't think the judge will give Joelle custody.'

A united front...not quite. Jude wouldn't be there. She hadn't seen or spoken to him in more than a week, and instead of coming to terms with losing him each day seemed bleaker than the one before. A cold front kept rolling through her soul.

She felt her throat clog with tears and swallowed them down. She'd cried enough but, despite telling herself she was done, more tears rose to the surface.

'Oh, Ads,' Lex murmured, wiping away Addi's tears with the tips of her fingers and pulling her into her arms. 'It'll get better, babe, I promise.'

The thing was, Addi thought as she sobbed into Lex's neck, she really didn't think it would.

Day nine, still no improvement. He still felt utterly miserable, completely shell-shocked.

Jude stood in his living room at his house in Franschhoek—he hadn't left his house since driving from Addi's house—and rested his forearm above his head, the glass cold beneath the fabric of his sweatshirt.

Night had rolled into the valley hours before and, by the light of the weak moon, he could see the outline of the jagged mountains just a few kilometres away. His heart felt equally jagged. It was almost as if it was struggling to pump blood around his body.

He'd thought he understood what heartbreak was, and had assumed he'd experienced all the lows a person could sink to. It was mortifying to realise he hadn't been even close to complete devastation.

He was now.

Back then, his heart had been dinged, but it had been his ego that had taken the biggest beating with Marina, and it had been smacked around again when Jane had sold him out. But he'd never once felt as though he was scrambling to find his feet in the seventeenth level of hell.

He missed Addi. No, saying that he simply missed her was like calling a nuclear missile a BB gun. This went beyond 'missing'...

Jude picked up his wine glass, sat on the edge of the leather couch and stared into his unlit fireplace. The truth was staring him in the face, demanding his attention, and he had to face it at some point. He couldn't possibly feel any worse than he did.

He'd messed up at various times, and with different results, but he'd kept blundering in, not thinking about what he was doing, saying or thinking, and hoping he'd emerge with nothing more than a slap on the wrist. That ended, right now.

He needed to up his game, and there was no option but for him to become a better man. A man worthy of someone as strong and special as Addi.

He rested his wine glass against his forehead. He'd had all the advantages of money and power, and had been spoiled rotten from the day he'd been born—yes, sure, he'd lost his parents, but he'd had the opportunity to attend an amazing school and get a stellar education. He'd had a ton of friends and girls had loved him. He'd led a very privileged life.

Sure, Marina had scammed him, but he'd been young and in love. Sure, she'd made a fool of him, but so what? And had she, *really*? Even at nineteen, he'd stuck by her, showing her far more loyalty than she'd deserved. He'd believed in her, believed what she told him. Surely he deserved praise for his loyalty?

And maybe it was time to put Marina, and that incident, in perspective. He'd been young, idealistic and she'd been older and skilled at the con. But nobody had died, and it had only been his and his grandfather's pride and ego—and a small portion of his heart—that had been hurt.

Instead of looking at the situation and brushing it off, he'd spent too many years nurturing the pain, giving it and his grandfather's mockery far more power than they deserved. He'd given that year of his life far too much importance, and too much mental energy. And, as a result, he'd started to believe that love was dangerous, that women couldn't be trusted.

Jane, and the humiliation of having his story appear in the papers, had reinforced that notion and scoured his soul even further, allowing cynicism and distrust to settle in, to flourish. Instead of responding to the newspaper articles with a laugh and shrugging his shoulders, telling the press that he'd been young and an idiot, his horrified and embarrassed response had made it a far juicier story than it had ever needed to be.

He, and old Bartholomew, had been the kings of the overreaction.

Marina had been a con artist, and Jane had been nasty, but that didn't follow that every woman was.

Addi certainly wasn't. She was a straight shooter, brave beyond belief, independent and feisty. She'd taken the knocks life had handed her without letting herself be knocked out. She'd simply stood up and kept fighting.

She was the bravest woman he knew.

From the moment she'd been small, she'd stepped up to the plate to look after her sister, to try and keep their ragtag family together. She'd worked her tail off to get her degree and, when she'd had the world at her feet, she'd sacrificed her freedom—financial and social—to take in her sisters.

Whether it was hard or not, Addi did what was right. She

had more character and integrity than anyone he'd encountered before. She was the best person he knew...

And, for some reason, she loved him. And that was the biggest miracle of all.

She deserved far more from him than to keep their marriage secret and their affair under wraps. Far, far more. Miracles, love and second chances at happiness didn't come around all that often and he was pretty sure that he was running out of opportunities and second, or third, chances.

Maybe it was time he stopped moping and started *doing*.

This could backfire spectacularly, Jude thought as his driver dropped him off outside the courthouse where Addi and Lex were due to appear for the custody hearing. The girls, as Cole had told him, were in school and were being spared the ordeal of hearing a bunch of strangers argue about their future. Cole was accompanying Lex, but Addi would be by herself.

That wasn't, in any way, acceptable.

Dressed in a sharp grey suit, a white shirt and a patterned tie, Jude ran up the courthouse steps, imagining Addi sitting next to her lawyer, dressed in a severe suit, her show-no-fear mask on her face. He knew her—she would be quaking inside, but nobody would see her sweat.

Man, he hoped he made it into the courtroom on time... room seven, on the third floor, Judge Nkosi. He glanced at his watch and ran up the steps. The proceedings were about to start, and he didn't want to annoy the judge by walking in late. Jude found the right door, pulled it open and winced at its loud squeak. The room was silent, everyone was on their feet and they all turned to look at him.

Including Addi, her mouth dropping open in a perfect 'o'. He really hoped to kiss that mouth later. It had been too long since he'd held her, loved her. He needed to tell her that she was his, and vice versa, and that...

'Are you just going to stand there?'

The sharp voice intruded into his musings and Jude pulled his eyes off his wife to look at the judge. Her black hair was peppered with grey, bi-focal glasses rested on her nose and her bright-red lipstick complemented her deep-brown skin.

Her eyes were sharper than a Katana sword.

'Who are you?' she demanded. 'And why are you late?'

Jude swallowed his grimace and out of the corner of his eye caught Cole's smirk. Jude used one hand to button his suit jacket as he approached the row of people standing behind the tables in front of the judge's dais. He looked to his left and caught a glimpse of Joelle, her long blonde hair hitting her waist. She looked like Addi's older sister.

'Again, who are you?'

Right. He really should start concentrating. Jude sent Addi a small smile and looked at the judge. 'My name is Jude Fisher—'

'Of Fisher International.'

'That's my company,' Jude confirmed. He loved it but it wasn't his life any more. He had a very different list of priorities now.

'And what relevance do you bring to this hearing, Mr Fisher?' Judge Nkosi asked, sounding impatient.

'Your Honour, I'm just here to support my *wife*,' Jude said as he stepped up to stand behind Addi, his hand on her waist.

'Mmm...' The judge grumbled and looked down. Feeling eyes on him, Jude looked down into Addi's lovely, up-turned face—the face he wanted to spend the rest of his life looking into—and watched as shock skittered across it.

'I—what?' she snapped.

He shook his head, placed his hand on his back and bent down to whisper in her ear. 'Not now, sweetheart.'

As he straightened, Judge Nkosi looked up and lifted her eyebrows. 'Right, people, let's hear your arguments on who should get care of Miss Nixi and Miss Snow, and why. And please remember that the only side I am on is theirs...'

'My ruling is that the primary residence of the young ladies will be jointly shared by their eldest sisters. Their mother will be entitled to contact but, judging by her lack of interest in her youngest children,' Judge Nkosi stated, her disdain for Joelle clear, 'I doubt that she will use them. I am also ordering that Ms Cannon pay child maintenance of an amount to be decided, but I doubt that will happen either. Will it, Ms Cannon?'

'Probably not,' Joelle replied blithely.

Addi wondered why she wanted the girls back and then decided that she didn't much care. What Joelle did or didn't do had no bearing on her life any more. Her sisters and this baby were important, but her mother wasn't. Addi crossed her arms across her stomach, promising her baby that she'd be the amazing mother she'd never had. Loving, supporting and raising her child would be, for ever, her most important job.

Addi watched as Joelle dragged her eyes over Cole, then Jude. 'Sexy and rich. I taught you well,' she drawled. She raised an eyebrow at Storm. 'And what's your excuse?'

Addi heard Storm's growl and she grabbed the back of her shirt to keep her from confronting their mother. Luckily for all of them, Judge Nkosi banged her gavel and dismissed the court, suggesting that Joelle leave the premises ahead of her daughters.

Addi thought that was an excellent idea.

Feeling lightheaded, she sat down on the nearest hard-back chair, rested her arms on her thighs and dropped her head. She didn't know what to focus on first.

The girls were safe. Her family was intact. Jude was here.

He'd appeared when she'd most needed him and had stood behind her, his hand on her back, silently inviting her to lean on him.

From a place far, far away, she heard the sound of laughter, Storm's excited chatter and saw Lex hug Thandi. She heard Storm telling Jude to expect a lecture from Nixi and Snow because they'd missed out on the chance to be flower girls. Why wasn't Jude trying to hide their marriage any more? Instead of down-playing it, he'd announced it to everyone in the courtroom.

She heard Cole say something unintelligible and heard Thandi's equally indistinguishable reply.

The girls were safe. Her family was intact. Jude was here.

Addi felt a warm hand on her back and opened her eyes to see Jude on his haunches in front of her and then the world started to shrink. As she looked into his fantastic green eyes, she started to topple sideways...

And then...nothing.

Addi wrapped her head around a plush pillow and slowly opened her eyes. She was in her room at home and she could simply sleep for days.

She was about to slide back into sleep when she noticed there was sunlight on her bed. Sunlight meant that she'd taken a nap and she never took naps...ever.

Addi bolted upright, whipping her head round. The last thing she remembered was sitting down in the courthouse, feeling lightheaded because she and Lex had been granted custody of the girls.

Jude had been there. He'd confirmed the press reports that they were married.

Their secret was no longer a secret.

Addi pushed her fingers through her hair and looked down at the T-shirt she wore. It was one of Jude's. She'd taken to using it because it was soft and, no matter how many times it was washed, she could still smell his cologne on the fabric.

'Why are you sniffing that shirt?'

Lex looked up at Nixi's question and placed her hand on her chest as Nixi carefully, very carefully, carried a cup of tea into the room, followed by Snow carrying a plate of misshapen crumpets.

'We made you a snack,' Snow told her, thrusting the plate at her. Addi took the plate and kissed her bright-red head, doing the same to Nixi.

'Are you sick, Addi?' Nixi demanded, far too seriously for an eight-year-old. She looked worried but stoic, and Addi realised she was in protective mode. This was how she would've looked at eight, she realised.

Addi gripped her chin in her hand and looked into her brown eyes. 'I'm not sick, baby girl, but if I was it's not your job to fix me. It's not your job to look after me, or Lex, or Storm, and it's definitely *not* your job to look after Snow. It's *our* job to look after you. Your job is to be a kid.'

'But—' Nixi said, looking mutinous.

Addi didn't give her a chance to speak. 'No buts, Nixi. We're the adults, you're the kid. Lex and I get to make the hard decisions, helped by Storm and—' she tossed a smile at Lex '—Cole. *We* look after *you*.'

'But who will look after you?' Snow asked, picking up on Nixi's anxiety.

'Well, that's *my* job.'

Addi looked past Lex and Storm, whose arms were around each other, tears rolling down their faces, to see Jude standing in the doorway to her bedroom, tie gone and sleeves rolled up. He brushed past her sisters and came to stand on the same side of the bed as Snow. He placed his hands on the bed and lowered his face so that it was inches from her own.

'Are you okay?' he asked.

She nodded, biting down on her bottom lip. 'I guess I was a little overwhelmed.'

A small smile kicked up the side of his mouth. 'I never thought anything could drop you to your knees, Fields.'

You do, she wanted to tell him.

Instead of throwing her arms around him as she desperately wanted to do, begging him to love her, she narrowed her eyes. 'Don't expect it to happen again, Fisher.'

'Who…are…you?'

They both turned to look at Nixi, her warrior princess looking as though she was about to defend her kingdom. Right; Addi would have to have a few more conversations about her role in their family. 'This is Jude and he is…'

She didn't know how to explain him. What was he? Legally, he was her husband, but he wasn't, not emotionally.

'I am the guy who is going to look after Addi so that she can look after you,' Jude told her, not moving an inch.

Nixi didn't look as if she was buying what he was selling. Addi, needing to know what he meant by that statement, leaned sideways and sent a pleading look at Lex and Storm who, bless them, immediately sprang into action. In what looked to be a choreographed move, they each wound an arm around a small waist, lifted the girls off their feet and marched them to the door. The door shut behind them and cut off their loud and vociferous complaints.

Lex told them that if they didn't stop shouting immediately they wouldn't be allowed to be her flower girls, and silence descended.

Addi couldn't help but notice Jude didn't take his eyes off her face.

'Hey,' he said, sitting down beside her.

She cocked her head and folded her arms across her chest. 'I don't remember making my way home.'

'You came to quite quickly after fainting, but as soon as I picked you up to carry you to my car you fell asleep. You've been sleeping for the past five hours.'

Wow. 'That long?'

'I called your gynaecologist and she said that it's probably a stress reaction. The body has a way of shutting down eventually.'

'I guess it knew I could stop fighting and let go,' Addi agreed.

She folded the material of the duvet between her fingers and tried to work out how to ask him why he'd announced to the courthouse, and her family, that they were married. All it would do was reignite the press's curiosity. 'Why did you come to the courthouse and why did you...?'

'Tell everyone we were married?' He lifted her hand and placed his mouth on her knuckles, his eyes on hers. 'Because wherever you are is where I should be. And because I want the world to know how lucky I am to call you my wife.'

'I don't understand, Jude.'

He dropped her hand, placed it on his thigh and held down her hand. 'I've made a couple of mistakes when it comes to trusting women, Ads, trusting people, but the mistakes weren't half as bad as I thought they were. Yes, I was conned by Marina, but I was a kid. I trusted Jane, I thought she had more integrity than she did. Yes, I failed, but we are allowed to fail, that's how we learn. But my stupidest, most thoughtless, asinine and dumb-ass decision was to lose you.'

He closed his eyes and gripped the bridge of his nose, looking as if he was in physical pain. 'These past ten days have been awful without you. I have missed you in every conceivable way. My comment in the airport was the biggest error I have ever made and one I've regretted every day, in every way, since. My only excuse is that I was scared.'

'Of?'

His eyes traced her face and, within them, she saw love, fear and, maybe, a little hope. 'Loving you, losing you, messing this up, taking a chance. From the moment I saw you at the Vane, you scrambled my brains. I'm still trying to work out which way is up.'

Jude leaned forward and placed his forehead against hers. 'I love you so much, Ads. I love the baby growing inside you but you, *you*, are my compass point. Nothing, *nothing*, is more important than you.'

Addi felt a fresh batch of tears roll down her face, but she felt lighter and brighter, as if her body was expelling the last of its angst and letting sunlight in. She lifted her arms to drape them around his neck. 'I love you too, Jude.' Her mouth drifted across his and, when their kiss deepened, she stepped into a band of pure, bright light, both calm and wonderfully exciting.

She was about to climb into his lap to get closer when Jude pulled back and the sound of childish giggles drifted over to her. Without missing a beat, she picked up a pillow and hurled it at the door with pinpoint accuracy. The door slammed shut again and they heard the sound of small feet scampering away.

'Sorry,' she whispered. 'They can be rather full-on.'

He grinned. 'I'll get used to it,' he told her. 'But we'll need to start locking the door.'

Jude moved to sit beside her on the bed and slung his arm around her, pulling her to his side. This was where she belonged, she thought. Right here. Wherever he was.

'What now?' she asked, resting her hand on his flat stomach.

He placed a kiss on her head. 'Well, you have a few options. After talking to Cole, it looks like Storm is going to use the apartment above the garage on his mini-estate and he's employing an au pair for the girls so Lex can finish her degree. You can move into his cottage, stay here or...'

None of those options appealed. 'Or...?'

'Or we live together here, or at my flat, and spend the weekends with or without the girls at my place in Franschhoek. Or we can go house-shopping and try and find something new, close to Cole and Lex's house, a place big enough for the girls to stay over when Lex and Cole need a break.'

She was about to tell him that she was keen on that option when he held up his hand. 'I need to say something else...'

She pulled back, a little concerned, and waited anxiously while he found his words. 'I know how independent you are, and I know I promised you a job at Fisher—and it's there, any time you want it.'

'But?'

'But I'd like you to take a break. I'd like you to let me take care of you. You've had the incredible responsibility of making all the decisions all the time, the stress of making money stretch and keeping this family together, and I would like you to take a few months off. I can't see you not working—you need the stimulation. I'm thinking that maybe, when you are ready to jump back in, you could act as a trouble-shooter for Fisher, or maybe manage your own group of hotels.'

Huh. 'I don't have a group of hotels, Jude.'

He mock-grimaced. 'Well, you kind of do. I've signed all of my eco-hotels and lodges, the ones I bought in my personal capacity, over to you. Oh, and I also bought the boutique hotel on the Skeleton Coast for you, but I suspect we'll keep that as our bolthole.'

She now owned the Dune House? And she had a small hotel chain? 'You…? What…? But *why*?'

'Call it a wedding gift. Call it a thank you for my baby, my gratitude for you loving me. It's also a promise that, whatever we do and wherever we go, we do it together. Deal?'

Her head was spinning. 'Um…you could've just bought me a ring, Fisher,' she said, sounding breathless.

He leaned to the side and pulled a box out of his trouser pocket. He flipped it open with his thumb and Addi gulped at the magnificent ring comprising three huge stones—an emerald, a deep-blue sapphire and what she thought was a pink diamond. 'I figured we're going to have a girl,' he told her, laughing.

Yep, probably. He slid it onto the ring finger of her left hand and lifted her hand to his lips. 'So, shall we get married, Ads?'

'We *are* married,' she told him, laughing.

'Let's do it properly this time…'

* * * * *

COMING SOON!

We really hope you enjoyed reading this book. If you're looking for more romance be sure to head to the shops when new books are available on

Thursday 8th June

MILLS & BOON®

Coming next month

PENNILESS CINDERELLA FOR THE GREEK
Chantelle Shaw

'I had the impression on the beach a week ago that you want us to be work colleagues and nothing more.'

His dark blue eyes were unfathomable, but she noticed a nerve flicker in his cheek. He sipped his wine before he said softly, 'Is that what you want, Savannah?'

She was about to assure him that of course it was. Anything other than a strictly work based relationship with Dimitris would be dangerous. But she was transfixed by his masculine beauty, and when he smiled she felt more alive than she'd done in ten years. 'I don't know,' she admitted huskily.

The band had been playing smooth jazz tunes during dinner, but now the guests had finished eating and the tempo of the music increased as people stepped onto the dance floor.

Dimitris pushed back his chair and stood up. He offered his hand to Savannah. 'Would you like to dance?'

Continue reading
PENNILESS CINDERELLA FOR THE GREEK
Chantelle Shaw

Available next month
www.millsandboon.co.uk

LET'S TALK
Romance

For exclusive extracts, competitions and special offers, find us online:

f MillsandBoon

🐦 @MillsandBoon

📷 @MillsandBoonUK

♪ @MillsandBoonUK

Get in touch on 01413 063 232

MILLS & BOON

THE HEART OF ROMANCE

A ROMANCE FOR EVERY READER

MODERN
Prepare to be swept off your feet by sophisticated, sexy and seductive heroes, in some of the world's most glamourous and romantic locations, where power and passion collide.

HISTORICAL
Escape with historical heroes from time gone by. Whether your passion is for wicked Regency Rakes, muscled Vikings or rugged Highlanders, awaken the romance of the past.

MEDICAL
Set your pulse racing with dedicated, delectable doctors in the high-pressure world of medicine, where emotions run high and passion, comfort and love are the best medicine.

True Love
Celebrate true love with tender stories of heartfelt romance, from the rush of falling in love to the joy a new baby can bring, and a focus on the emotional heart of a relationship.

Desire
Indulge in secrets and scandal, intense drama and sizzling hot action with heroes who have it all: wealth, status, good looks…everything but the right woman.

HEROES
The excitement of a gripping thriller, with intense romance at its heart. Resourceful, true-to-life women and strong, fearless men face danger and desire - a killer combination!

To see which titles are coming soon, please visit

millsandboon.co.uk/nextmonth

MILLS & BOON

Desire

Indulge in secrets and scandal, intense drama and plenty of sizzling hot action with powerful and passionate heroes who have it all: wealth, status, good looks…everything but the right woman.